What are people saying about The Nick West Series?

Buckle up. The whirlwind is about to begin ... a blockbuster thriller in the likes of Tom Clancy and Robert Ludlum.
Jeff "Dog" Dawson, author of Love's True Second Chance

Burkett's extensive knowledge of computers and electronic surveillance and security augments the book's air of authenticity. Move over Clancy.
Bruce Hunt, author of Visiting Small Towns of Florida

This book will capture your attention from the first page! It is an intelligent suspenseful story that will want to keep you reading front to back.
Amanda G. McGraw, Amazon customer

I would unabashedly agree that Mr. Burkett could put this book up against Clancy, Cussler and Rollins...Burkett is certainly another diamond in amongst first time authors. What a great gift to all of us readers.
DC from WA USA, Amazon customer

...intriguing and unexpected twists.
L. Fajardo, Amazon customer

Pure Entertainment...The characters are so realistic it's hard to remember that this is fiction.
Arthur Levine, author of Johnny Oops

The Nick West Trilogy

Declaration of Surrender

American Sanction

Reprisal

By

Jim Burkett

Published by Inknbeans Press

Cover: Jim Burket
The Nick West Trilogy © December 2012
Jim Burkett
and Inknbeans Press

ISBN-13: 978-0615747194 (Inknbeans Press)
ISBN-10: 0615747191
Declaration of Surrender © 2010 Jim Burkett

and Inknbeans Press
Front cover: Dan Garcia
Back cover: Evonne

American Sanction © 2011 Jim Burkett
and Inknbeans Press
Front cover: Evonne, photo by Jim Burkett
Back cover: Inknbeans Press

Reprisal © 2012 Jim Burkett
and Inknbeans Press
Front and back cover: Jim Burkett

Table of Contents

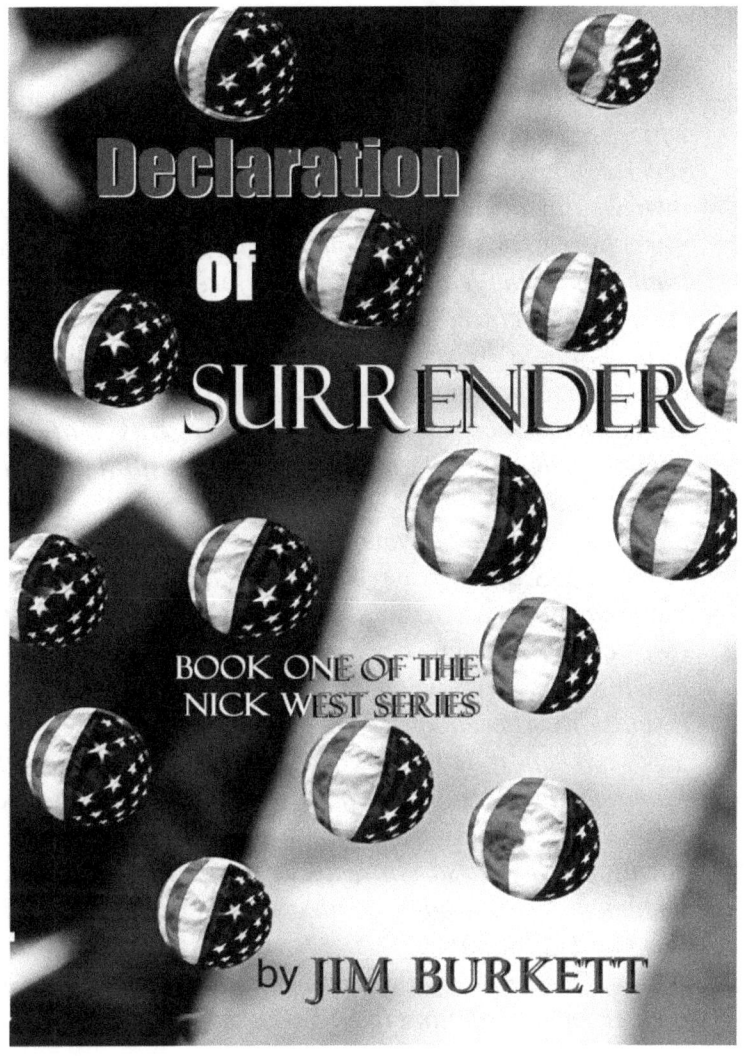

Declaration of Surrender

Believing either Germany or Japan are about to win the war against the United States in early 1945, several members of Congress conspire to protect their own wealth by secretly creating a document that would give the rights of ownership of all U.S. properties and land over to the leading country before the end of the war is actually declared.

Signed by the President, the document is passed along underground to the Germans but is eventually confiscated back by U.S. Treasury agents along with account ledgers worth millions of dollars sitting in hidden Swiss bank accounts. Days later the agents are found murdered and the documents gone.

DHS agent Nick West is thrust into the world of government assassins and sought after for treason by his own country when he discovers the location of the missing sixty-five year old document but refuses to disclose its whereabouts in order to protect his own men.

When a leading government systems analyst is found tortured and beaten to death and Nick's wife is taken hostage, he must form an alliance with an injured enemy Russian assassin in order to find and protect the document from 'what's coming' before time runs out for them and his country.

Declaration of Surrender is an edge of your seat thriller from beginning to end.

This book is dedicated to the brave men and women of the Department of Homeland Security and the United States Armed Forces, prepared to give the ultimate sacrifice in defending our great country against all threats in the fight against terrorism worldwide.

Declaration of Surrender
Book One of
The Nick West Trilogy

Jim Burkett

PUBLISHED BY:
Inknbeans Press

To my wife Cathy, who makes my life more wonderful and full of purpose every day. Her love and support are immeasurable.

To my sons Brien and Michael - no father could be more proud of the men you have become.

And last to Eric, a good friend and the inspiration behind my story.

We need the courage to start and continue what we
should do, and the courage to stop what we shouldn't do.
- Richard L. Evans

Chapter 1

Nick West down shifted the 911 into third gear, eased off the clutch and accelerated through a hard right turn. In the distance, the sun was setting behind a row of thunderclouds, flashes of lightning illuminating the hillside. After the events of that morning, he had been ordered to vacate the Department of Homeland Security premises, cool off, but above all else keep a low profile until the facts of the assault could be reviewed. The road ahead straightened and he red lined the Porsche through its gears.

There had been a last minute override made on his already approved transfer, which would now send him to a different location other than where he had requested with no explanation as to why. Having been guaranteed placement to wherever he wanted to go after this assignment was up, he had put in for Atlanta to be with his wife. He had heard that the Agency had no qualms about keeping families apart if the job called for it, but his current assignment was almost over and he had anticipated a smooth exit.

Over the last few years, he had uprooted Laura and her veterinary practice twice before, he didn't want to do it again. They had been apart for six months and with what little time he could get away, he always drove the five or six hours it took to get to her. As he drove now, he was thinking of that morning and the possibility of submitting his resignation. He loved his job but nothing was more important to him than family.

Having just taken his first sip of coffee after sitting down to begin personnel reviews, he was called into his boss's office and given the news he was to report to Washington in one week. The new transfer would mean he would be even further away from her and the only way to get to her now would be to fly.

After a lengthy dispute, the conversation escalated into a shouting match. Finally, he was told, "You put in for a transfer, you got it, now get the hell out!" Paul Brewster and Nick had always had a good relationship, but for now he just wanted out of the old man's sight.

By the time he made it back to his office, his anger had subsided some and his only thoughts were of how to break the news. The IA (Internal Affairs) agent was sitting in his desk chair as he entered. Jack Peterson was hated by almost everyone in the agency, not for his position but rather his arrogance. Once he decided he didn't like you, he was relentless in either getting that person reassigned, fired or - his favorite - beating down an agent with a constant assortment of unnecessary paperwork or depositions until they quit entirely. As a result, the department had suffered a six percent turnover rate in the past year.

Nick stopped short of his desk, standing with his arms folded, letting Peterson enjoy the moment. "You're in my chair, mind getting up?"

"Not yours for long, I hear, heading to DC where the big boys shit. I was just checking to see if I liked yours better than mine." When Peterson didn't get the reaction he was hoping for, he continued on.

"I know you wanted to go elsewhere, be with your wife and all, almost got it too, but I thought we needed you more in DC. You know, with your brains and your skills, well, let's just say they're very hard to come by, Nick. I really hated making those phone calls to get the necessary people involved in changing your transfer, but I felt it was more important to have you where it would do the most good for everyone in the department."

Nick knew Peterson was connected or had the 'juice', as it was called in the department, but not enough to pull strings that would get an agent reassigned to wherever 'he' wanted them to go. Messing with him would only make the current situation worse.

"Tell you what. If you like the chair, take it, take whatever you like, I'll even sign all the release forms for you."

"Does that include the picture of this little honey?" Nick's eyes followed Peterson's finger and saw he was pointing at Laura. When Nick took a step toward the desk, Peterson mistook his intent, jumped to his feet, catching one foot under the chair rollers. At the same time, he curled a fist and threw all of his weight into a punch hoping to catch Nick as square as possible. Off balance, he missed but the momentum carried him forward and down. Not able to bring his hands up in time, he slammed face first into the edge of the desk.

As if in slow motion, Nick saw the wood splinter on impact as it crushed the bone right above Jack's upper lip. The front row of teeth cracked at their roots and blood shot out, covering his desk. Several splatters caught across Nick's palm and fingers as he tried to reach out and grab Jack before he went all the way down.

Nick ran around to the back yelling for someone to get a doctor. The injuries were worse than he first thought. Grabbing the back of Peterson's head, he turned it slowly sideways, allowing the blood to pool onto the carpet so he would not choke as it continued to flow. He also worried about a possible neck injury. As he reached across to grab his gym bag for a towel, he also noted the right nasal cavity had been ripped open, exposing the cartilage.

Nick's boss appeared in the doorway, saw Peterson down and ran over to assist. "What the hell happened here, Nick?" For a moment Brewster wasn't sure he really wanted to help, seeing who was laid out on the floor.

"He threw a punch at me and missed, fell against the desk on his way down."

"Bull thit!" They both looked down as Jack was becoming semi-conscious. "I was trying to con-da-chu-ate the thon-of-a-bitch and all of the thudden out of nowhere, he slams me into the dethsk!" With his front teeth missing, Jack was unable to pronounce his words properly. Nick couldn't believe what he was hearing, realizing he had no proof to dispute what was being said.

"You need to leave so we can get this straightened out. Did anyone else see this happen?" Nick shook his head. By this time the medical staff had arrived and Brewster pulled him aside.

"Look, I believe what you're saying, but of all the people for you tangle with, this is the last guy you or we need crawling around in our business. They don't have a full understanding of what we do here." Brewster was trying to gather his thoughts, then said, "I'll tell them I had to send you on special assignment unexpectedly, but you need to go now before the rest of IA shows up. Stay out of town for a couple of days or a week if you need. I'll delay the transfer. If you need anything, call Baker, he'll get through to me. Go!"

Just then Brewster had a second thought. "No wait, follow me." Nick picked up his gym bag and trailed him back to his office. Reaching into a top drawer, Brewster pulled out a small white tab and handed it to Nick. He already knew what it was, but waited for an explanation from Brewster.

"That's a CS (continuous scan) SIM card. Take out your phone and replace your SIM with this one when you get a chance. Every 5 seconds the number will change on your phone, but it's synched to our database so we always know what the number is, always. Once that number is locked and dialed, you have to answer by the second ring, preferably right after the first one before it rings a second time. Two seconds after the second ring, the phone will go dead and we have to clear and recycle a new number which takes about seven seconds. That's how we will call you if we need to get in touch. Under no circumstances do you call anyone using this phone once you have changed cards, and I mean none."

"Why is it so important that I don't use it for myself?"

"Because when we call from our side, it falsifies your GPS coordinates when the connection is made. Where it says you are, you aren't. You dial and it will transmit your true location, makes it real easy for someone to find you, which we don't want anyone doing right now. I don't know how serious this is going to get, so for the time being, let's keep you hidden until we can get some answers. Now get going."

Grabbing both his gym and an instructor bag, Nick stripped off his BDU top (black dress uniform) throwing it into an open compartment and headed for the elevators and out of town.

Up ahead he could see the black sheets of rain crossing to his left, getting closer. Flipping on the built-in GPS, he selected 'Points of Interest', then punched in a request for hotels. After a few seconds, the display flickered, showing a list of seven in the area, the closest twenty-nine miles away. Without warning, the right front tire struck a small rock and lost traction. Gripping the road again, the back end jerked to the left and he cursed himself for taking so long looking at the screen. He turned into the spin and hit the gas pedal, the car realigned and he continued on.

Within half a mile, the steering wheel began to vibrate and he knew he had punctured the tire, at this rate of pressure loss, a small leak. Seeing the rain a short distance away, he calculated he had 10 minutes at most to stop, get out and change the tire before being engulfed in the storm. He would need to find a safe place to pull off, something that would provide a bit of shelter. Turning his head from side to side as he drove, he spotted a flat open patch of ground and pulled the car onto it. He needed to hurry.

After maneuvering the car onto a level spot, he reached down inside and popped the hood latch. Walking to the front of the car, he placed his hand against the metal and began fingering underneath. Just as he found the release lever there was a flash of light. Standing upright, he looked around but it was gone and he dismissed it as lightning. Bending, he felt around once more, found it, pulled and raised the hood. The light appeared again, but this time stayed on. Pushing the hood partially down, he peered over the top, blinking his eyes to keep the rain out, trying to focus in the dark. There was a silhouette of a small farmhouse three hundred yards away.

By the time he bounded past the front gate, the rain had already formed large pools of mud in the yard. He tried stepping around as many as he could, but gave up after sinking to his ankles with each step. Reaching the front porch, he sat down under the cover and began pulling off his shoes and socks, rolling his pant legs up in case he needed to leave if he found himself not welcome.

He had just laid the back of his head against the wall when a woman appeared in front of him, having come around the side porch. She placed one foot on the first step and stopped. "Can I help you, are you lost, hurt?" Nick guessed the woman to be no more than an inch short of six feet, with squared shoulders which the parka did not hide. She had high cheekbones and dark eyes. The shotgun was held firmly to her side. "You really need to answer me now."

"I'm sorry, I was just catching my breath. I'm fine, but I had a flat and needed to get under some shelter." He pointed toward his car, but the woman never took her eyes off of him. "If I could just sit here until the rain stops, I'll change the flat and be on my way."

"Where were you headed?" asked the woman.

"Atlanta. My wife has a practice there and I've got a couple days off from work, it looks like. Our different professions separate us for months at a time and right now I would just like to get there as quickly as possible and spend alone time with her."

After a short few moments, the woman stepped forward onto the porch, repositioned the shotgun for the ready and invited him in. She pushed the front door open and stood back for him to go through first. He hadn't realized how cold he had become and the fire in the back center wall of the moderate sized living room felt great. As he passed through the door, the woman said, "My name's Manny."

"Hello Manny, I'm Nick. Thanks for letting me come in." It was genuine and Manny gave him a smile.

"I've got some old clothes that might fit you while we dry yours. You go over by the fire and I'll be back in a minute. The storm's going to last all night, if you're comfortable doing so, you're welcome to stay. There's a bedroom in the back, you take that and I'll make do here."

He started to protest, but Manny cut him off. "There's a board in the floor just off the kitchen that squeaks real loud. I hear you step on it in the middle of the night and you'll be looking down the wrong end of Betsy." She motioned towards the shotgun two feet away.

With that, Manny left the room but returned shortly afterwards with a large flannel shirt, some socks and an old pair of jeans. He held them out in front and saw that he would need his belt. "Just toss the wet clothes out the door and I'll take care of them. There's some coffee on if you want any. Take it with you when you go, if you like."

Nick grabbed the clothes, turned and headed towards the back room. He could hear Manny saying something else to him as he walked, but by this time he was tired and it all sounded muffled.

Chapter 2

At 5 am the smell of frying ham, eggs and the baking of fresh biscuits started to drift through the house. The brewing of very strong coffee finally brought Nick awake and he rolled to his left with the intent of planting both feet on the floor. Stubbing his toes on the log wall, he let out a curse and reached down to grab his foot. He cursed even more as he felt the split down the center of his large toenail.

Rolling right this time, he slipped out of bed, trying to orient himself, and hobbled towards what he thought might be a bathroom. Finding the switch, he flipped it on and looked down. His leg hurt worse than it looked and he began to think that he might have broken it. Pulling out cabinet drawers, he finally found a pair of nail clippers and clipped off the broken ends. The skin underneath had already turned purplish-blue. He tried wiggling the toe and although it moved, the pain was still strong and he gritted his teeth.

Manny appeared in the doorway, took one look and said "Rolled left instead of right like I told you not to do, huh?"

"Who the hell puts a bed into a corner of a wall? You pull that ton of iron out every time you make it?"

"Yep", replied Manny. "Look around. The rooms aren't that big, so I have to use all the space best I can. Anyway, breakfast is on, mister tough guy. I laid out a clean shirt for you on the 'iron maiden', so clean up and come on."

Nick slipped the clippers back in the drawer, fingered some toothpaste around his teeth, ran his hand through his hair a couple of times, flipped off the switch and began a slow foot shuffle back to the bedroom. On the bed was the clean shirt along with his bags. He tried recalling bringing them in but gave up when he heard Manny calling. Slipping on the shirt, he followed the smells down the hallway as he fumbled with the buttons on the sleeves.

"Are you always this cheerful in the morning?" Nick asked. He looked at the table and saw several napkin-covered baskets filled with biscuits and ham. A large spoon poked out from underneath a covered dish containing an immense helping of scrambled eggs.

"Just my nature, been this way all of my life. Now get a move on. I've got the girls coming and if they get sight of you, I'm going to have a lot of questions that I don't have answers for. Besides, you're pretty good looking, so I'm sure I'm going to take a month's worth of ribbing if they do see you." Manny couldn't help but chuckle at that thought.

"I've got a flat, remember, and I can't fix it until daylight, which won't be for another twenty minutes or so. I'll explain the situation to your girls, might even tell them you're the one that hurt me while we rolled around in the sack. That ought to shut their mouths for a bit." They both let out a good laugh and Manny popped a towel at him.

Nick had liked her immediately. She was tough, straight to the point, with a hardened edge to her. Even without makeup, though, she had a natural beauty that was wholesome. In her prime, he imagined that she could have had her pick of any man. Had it not been for the small wrinkles around her eyes and mouth, with a few gray strands in her hair, he would have guessed by, the shape she was in, to be in her mid to late forties, but knew she was closer to sixty.

"Took care of your car already, it's parked just inside the barn ready to go. You had a lot of dried mud under your tire wells, cleaned that out too." She pointed out a rear window of the kitchen and Nick turned to look just as the sun was beginning to rise.

As he turned back to face her, he asked, "When?"

The gun was pointed non-threateningly at his right knee, but by her look he knew that could change quickly. "What's the P250 for? Not too many public people I know carry one of these. I'm guessing Special Forces, government agent of some kind. Would you like to tell me what you do, maybe what your history is?" Manny kept her eyes on his.

Nick had been caught off guard for one of the few times in his life. He decided there was no reason to withhold the basics of his background. "Six years SEALs, which I can't tell you about. NYPD once, Secret Service and now with DHS, at least up until recently. How do you know so much about guns?"

Manny held her gaze. "Start with NYPD."

"Four years SWAT. Mostly bank robberies, some crazies here and there, protecting visiting heads of state and other high profiles. Drug busts, those types of things."

"So you go from SWAT to Secret Service, big jump and fast. How did that happen?" She was leaning with her back to the sink, having laid the gun on the counter.

"One day we received a call that a female student had been taken hostage from her university dorm room. We get to ground zero and it all looks normal except there are no police and what we think are only a few students roaming the immediate area. It turns out the student is a senator's niece that's been taken. The senator is a longtime close friend of the President, which explains to us why no one had alerted the media and why the public had been cleared by Security, or the Secret Service."

"Fortunately, she was smart enough to turn off and drop her cell phone down the front of her pants when they grabbed her, then turned it back on and stuffed it between some towels when they gave her a bathroom break. We triangulated on the signal and were there in less than ten minutes. Since I was lead, I took command

and began to set up from my best vantage point about three hundred meters away. I spread the other team members out across three other rooftops. Car plates in front of the building showed the vehicle belonged to a new boyfriend of the nieces' roommate."

"I thought you guys did background checks on all those boyfriends and girlfriends?" said Manny.

"Brand new boyfriend, so no one knew about him. We ran an infrared scan that showed two subs and the girl on the third floor, two feet inside to the right of the window. The building was made of old cinder block, practically falling down around them. Without warning and before my team was fully in place, some rookie negotiator jumps on a bullhorn and scares everyone in the building."

"I'm watching through my scope when I saw both subs pull their weapons and point them at the girls' head along with one of the subs moving along side of his buddy, extending his right arm, getting ready to shoot the girl. There's no more time, so I pulled the trigger and the round passes through the brick wall and the heads of both subs. One shot, two kills."

Nick was hoping he had impressed Manny, but if he had, it wasn't showing on her face. "That's a heck of a shot at three hundred meters without seeing who you're shooting at."

Nick could see that Manny wasn't questioning why he took the shot, it was more of why he would put the girl at such risk. "Actually, we are qualified at one thousand meters, so it wasn't that difficult. Remember I had infrared goggles and scope, I knew where they were standing and what I was shooting at."

"Ok, so I'm guessing because you saved the senator's niece, you get offered any dream job you want and now you're buds with the President?"

Nick could sense some sarcasm but didn't understand why. "I'm not a blue suit, if that's what you're thinking. I instruct the different agencies coming through DHS in counterattack and counterterrorism. I spend my time in surveillance, planning, briefing to and on intelligence, training and running background checks so we can get the bad guys. Do you understand any of this, and what is your problem all of the sudden?"

Manny reached down, took hold of the barrel, turned the butt towards Nick and placed it down next to his cup of coffee. She hesitated for a moment, then said, "Like you say, it's my problem."

A hard knock at the door startled both of them as they heard it open, along with the voices of several women laughing and hollering. "Oh shit," said Manny, "you've got to get out of here, now!" But it was too late. Nick shoved the pistol in his back waistband and pulled the shirt corners around, having forgotten to button up the front. He had just started to stand when three new faces appeared in the kitchen doorway, all talk suddenly stopping, mouths falling agape. The three stood staring at Nick for a few moments, then Manny, then back again.

Nick recognized the one in front immediately, not knowing why. After a moment, he realized she was an identical twin to Manny. He could see the only difference was the color of their eyes. Manny's were a dark green emerald and the other women's light green with a few small specks. He could not make out any other differing characteristics.

"I guess I didn't leave quick enough, huh?" Nick could not help himself and wondered if he could keep a straight face. He walked closer to Manny, looked at her affectionately and said "Last night was great. I'm sorry I have to run, but maybe we can do this again really soon, ok?" With that, he placed both hands on her shoulders, leaned across and kissed her lightly on the cheek. She shot him a look of hate and he knew it was time to leave. The girls backed up without taking their eyes off of him as he walked past.

"Ladies," said Nick as he passed through the door.

Chapter 3

He finished dressing, grabbed his bags, placing the gun in one, and headed towards the front door. From the kitchen, he could hear Manny trying her best to settle the girls down. Most of the rainwater had rescinded, but the mud was still everywhere and very loose. Grabbing a hold of whatever would keep him stable he made his way back to the barn.

The car was clean and the tire had been fixed. He lifted the hood and threw in his belongings. As he walked around to the driver's side, the rays of the sun began to filter through the open slats. Around him lay old furniture, tires, bales of hay, some farm tools and a tractor parked towards the rear. A large old tarp covered what appeared to be a car and he narrowed his eyes to try and squint through the blinding streaks of light. This time he saw the whitewalls.

Pulling the tarp off, the '39 Packard looked as though it had been kept in good condition. There was some paint fade and a few scratches, but no rust. He ran his hand down the side across the company emblem. Opening the hood, he grabbed the latch and hooked it underneath to secure it from falling. The engine showed no signs of heavy use in a while. Some oil had collected around the head gaskets, but they were not dry or rubbery. He closed the hood and walked around to the trunk.

Pushing in the release, the trunk lid did not budge. Pressing in the release again, he began to work the lid by placing a hand on top and applying pressure as he rocked it up and down. After several tries, the trunk finally gave way. Inside to the left lay a suitcase, several small metal bins containing old Treasury documents and a typewriter. On the other side was a tire iron. Just visible, sticking up through the backseat cover and the flooring was a leather loop that appeared to be a small thin belt. He reached across, pinched the loop and pulled at it slowly until he thought it was almost out, but then stuck. After several pulls the floorboard sprang open and the camera fell onto the carpet bed.

It was a Rolleiflex 75mm model with a crank and knobs on both sides and a flip top lens cover. He pushed a button and the lens cover sprang open. Peering through the opening, he panned the camera and turned the round focus control. Next he reached and turned the film crank. To his surprise, there was resistance and he knew from the older 35 mm cameras he had used in the past, there was still film inside.

Holding the camera, he closed the trunk and walked back towards the farmhouse. Peeking in, he called for Manny but got no response so he stepped inside, making his way towards the kitchen. As he was passing through the door, Manny came walking out, running into him and knocking the camera from his hands. He had just enough time to grab the strap before it hit the floor and turn his face as the fleshy part of her palm came straight towards the base of his nose. He tensed, waiting for the blow to land, but it didn't.

"Jesus, Nick, you trying to get yourself hurt?"

Nick stared at her, knowing that this was not how a normal civilian would have reacted. She had been trained to throw that punch as a defensive tactic or on purpose with the intent to kill.

"OK, I told you about myself, you tell me about you! You stopped that punch from landing, not an easy thing to do. I asked you how you knew about my Sig, but you didn't answer. What gives?" Nick's emotions were running high, as he knew how close he had come to receiving a deadly strike.

"You don't need to know about me. I offered you a place to stay last night, fed you breakfast, and your car is ready to go. Besides that, you've got my friends thinking I'm having some kind of affair, which is not funny. I don't think there is much more to say."

He saw that she was not about to go any further with it so he refocused his attention on the camera. "I was in the barn getting ready to leave when I saw the old car. Is it yours?"

"It is now, but it belonged to my father. We had no use for it, so Mom parked it in the back of the barn."

"I apologize for rummaging around, but I forced the trunk open and found a few things. This camera still has film in it, did you know that?"

"That's his camera. It was his hobby when he wasn't working. All of his other photo stuff is still in the basement. You think the film is any good. He's been gone since 1957?" Manny reached out and wrapped her hands around the base of the camera.

"If he had an enlarger and it still works, we'll just need to get some fresh chemicals and paper, won't hurt to look."

They headed down into the basement and found the equipment under a sink cabinet. After plugging it in, Nick flipped the switch and the bulb came on, then blew out. Searching underneath again, he found a replacement and several trays. Changing the bulb, he tried again. This time it stayed lit. Next he adjusted the focus knob and saw it too was working properly. Although he would need to clean the parts, it looked like it would work fine.

Asking Manny where the nearest Target store would be, he jumped in his car, drove slowly across the mud and headed into town. An hour and forty minutes later he was back in the basement having purchased the chemicals, paper, some essentials and several throwaway or 'burner' phones he felt he might need later.

By the time he had prepared the chemicals and cleaned the equipment, she had fixed lunch for them both. Heading down the stairs, she saw the red light come on and decided he could wait. She would eat alone. Before long, she heard the door open and Nick calling her down. The red light was still on as she descended the stairs.

Reaching the basement floor, she saw, hanging across several strung-up lines, the drying photos. She let her eyes adjust, then began to take in the images.

"Did your dad photograph weddings, because that's what all of these photos are of."

"No, I don't know why he would be taking pictures like these, it's not what he did. He liked nature." She continued down the line, looking at each photo.

"Maybe a family member you don't know about, maybe he thought he would photograph it for fun?" Nick was hoping she would see someone she might recognize from when she was a little girl, but she just shook her head.

Suddenly she stopped and moved closer to one photo. Nick walked over to look for himself and saw that it was an image of several men standing next to a car with the driver getting out. The car appeared to be a sedan of some type and the men were looking around as if they were trying to find someone desperately.

Manny looked as though she were about to lose her balance, but quickly reached up, grabbed the photo off the line and headed back up the stairs. Nick followed behind, taking two steps at a time just to keep up. When he reached the top, she was standing there, staring, looking at a man she thought was dead long ago. "My father tracked this man for almost ten years. He must have finally found him and that's why he was photographing the wedding, because he knew he was there and needed a cover."

"Why would your father be tracking someone for ten years? Was he some kind of bounty hunter or something?"

Manny took another long look and started towards the den. Nick went back downstairs to gather the other photos off the lines, pour out the chemicals and switch off the lights. Having reached the dry sink, he gathered the negatives, slipped them into several sleeves, then into his shirt pocket. He dumped out the trays, ran the water to clean the contents, dried them, than packed everything back under the sink.

By the time he returned, Manny was in the kitchen, having retrieved an old photo album, and was turning the pages slowly back and forth, trying to match the image in the new photo with someone in the album. He pulled up a chair and waited.

After several minutes, she finally spoke. "My father was an agent for the U.S. Treasury Department. He disappeared back in 1957. Emily and I were only seven years old then. He was thirty-nine at the time. My grandmother and my mom raised us and they made sure we knew all about Dad, what he did and what he was like. My mom worshipped that man, never remarried even in the bad times." Nick thought of the documents and suitcase he found in the trunk of the car.

"One morning we woke up and his car was parked next to the barn, we never knew how it got there or heard from him again. Everyone looked for Dad, even the FBI, but no one ever turned up anything. About two years later a Treasury agent knocked on the door, handed my Mom the deed to the ranch and told her everything has been paid off, including the back taxes. He told her to keep her mouth shut, then pointed to his gun and said, 'Please don't make me have to come back.' "

"Do you know who the guy was your dad was trying to find, do you know his name?"

Manny turned her face towards Nick. "His name was Albert Traugott, also an agent for the Treasury. Dad and he worked together for a year or two early in his career. That's why they picked him to hunt the bastard down, because he knew him better than anyone else at the time."

"Wait a minute. You were only seven when your dad disappeared. How would you remember all of this?"

She continued to flip through the pages, finally saying, "My mom kept everything, including newspapers, photos, and news articles, anything that had any information on or about the Treasury when she was trying to find my dad. Like I said, she told us all about him, lots of stories, some of the arrests he had made, even about a few of the other agents he worked with. One of them told her why he was trying to find Traugott and..."

She stopped mid-sentence, having found the page she was looking for. Turning the album around, she pushed it towards Nick and pointed to Traugott, then her father. There were four men in the photograph sitting on the edge of a desk, all smiling, holding Tommy guns and pointing towards a newspaper being held by the third man from the right. Her father was on the far left and Traugott on the far right.

The paper was dated May 7, 1945 with the headlines showing the surrender of Germany. Further down were photos of Adolf Hitler, but he could not make out the caption. Nick pulled the photograph out and flipped it over. Handwritten on the back was the date May 11, 1945, just days after Hitler committed suicide in his private underground bunker.

"My mother told us that right after that photo was taken, the men were heading downstairs for lunch and some kid was playing marbles at the bottom. When Traugott stepped on the landing, he slipped on one of them and fell back onto the stairs. Suffered a fractured skull and broke his clavicle, along with his right arm in three places. His injuries wouldn't allow him to return to the field, so he was put behind a desk. He absolutely hated it."

Nick asked, "Did your dad and he stay friends after that?"

"No, it was just the opposite. Dad was moving up and Traugott was stuck investigating bank record titles on properties that had been bought with counterfeit money. Counterfeiting was really bad back then. A lot of states had been issuing their own forms of currency and it was difficult to tell if what was being used was legit or not, so it made it real easy to purchase just about anything with bad cash."

"So why did your dad end up chasing him?"

"Right after the war was over, many of the Germans who were able to hold onto their properties and assets, moved to the United States and opened legitimate businesses. Some of them were later identified as SS officers who had stolen land documents and personal IDs, as well as gold certificates and money. They passed themselves off as the real owners." Manny closed her eyes for a moment to remember other details her mother had told her, and then continued.

"A rumor started that there was an anti-American underground movement being funded by several of these officers, who by now were very wealthy, having provided America with ways to upgrade their weaponry and machinery. The plan was for the men to sell off a large portion of their holdings and demand payment from the buyers in gold. They were then going to take the gold back to Germany in hopes of regaining a financial power hold over the US since we were already strapped, having been at war in Europe and with the Japanese. America was trying to mend itself from the wars."

"That makes sense," said Nick. "If the U.S. banks are paying out everything in gold and it is depleted because of the commercial demands, then the nation falls back into a depression like it did in the late twenties, probably even worse. Since it's the only type of currency other countries will accept at the time, we can't purchase anything outside of the U.S. because we no longer have enough gold. If we can't purchase foreign materials, then any kind of commodity we can't produce from our own resources, it will cause a majority of factories to shut down within weeks, leaving thousands unemployed."

Manny was shaking her head yes. "We didn't have the technology then like we have today, so if they spread out the sales of different companies around the United States, no one would be the wiser for weeks since we couldn't communicate as quickly, by then it will be too late, there will be very little real gold left." Nick understood how this idea could have worked, but was skeptical that many large sales could be pulled off together without someone alerting the government.

"Anyway, paranoid by this actually happening, the U.S. decides to seize all the wealth of these families and freeze it with the exception of only allowing payment on legitimate purchases, which the Treasury had to approve. The German men found out before we could do this and dumped their personal assets into Swiss accounts. Since these banks are under no jurisdiction, there is nothing the U.S. can do except confiscate all of the bank accounts, titles and documents from the families in order to control all activity."

"Wasn't that illegal, as well?'

Manny let out a small laugh, "This is the U.S. government, remember? Anyway, they send out Traugott's team and he tells the German families they will go to jail if they don't turn over the accounts and will lose all of their money for good if they don't cooperate. He collects all the account codes and documents from almost all of the families and brings everything back to the Treasury. Except, before he has the chance to turn it over, his small headquarters is burned down with his agents inside, all shot in the head. All documents are gone or burned up as first expected."

Manny continued. "After they sorted through the burned remains, there were only two bodies found. There should have been three. A couple of days later, several of the family members completely disappeared, no trace of them ever again. The Treasury figures that Traugott went rogue and conspired with these families, collected a portion of the money for his part and left the country. That, or Traugott kept the accounts himself and fled with those families going after him. Because my dad worked so closely with him and knew him best, they sent him after Traugott."

"So after searching for ten years, Traugott just shows up again and your dad finds him." Nick tried imagining the dedication her father would have had to his job.

"Right." says Manny. "All this time Traugott's alive and well, showing up at a wedding, but why?"

"Do you have any idea what kind of money we are talking about?"

"Maybe fifty to eighty million combined. I'm just guessing, but these were very rich people and that was a lot of money at that time."

Nick gathered up the photos and asked if he could borrow them for a while. He then reached into his coat pocket, pulled a card and scribbled down a private number, address of the clinic and the home number of Laura, telling Manny to call him if she needed anything.

"Where are you taking the photos?"

"I think it's time the government gave you some answers, don't you? I'll see what I can find out. Don't forget to call me if you find something else and I'll get back with you soon." With that, Nick headed out the door.

Chapter 4

He had driven for nearly an hour when he flipped open his cell, punched in the number and waited. Listening to a series of squeals and beeps, the phone went dead, than reactivated. Typing in a pass code, the call was finally answered. The party already knew who was calling.

"Man, when you bust someone, you do a number." Baker tried to stifle the laugh.

"I wish I really had busted that ass. He had it coming from all of us." Nick didn't wait for an answer. "I need for you to run a plate to get the name and address of the registered owner."

"Nick, are you serious? I haven't done that since I was in the sixth grade. Can't you just call records?"

"This can't go through records, just you. Can you run a bounce, so no one knows where it came from?"

Baker thought for a moment. "Yeah, no problem. I'll run it through Johnson's IP, bounce it, than run an intercept. Any questions, they'll drill him but he won't have any idea and they will probably just drop it so they don't have to hassle with him. If that doesn't hap…"

Before he could finish, Nick cut in. "This is an old plate from New York, dated 1957. The plate number is 3X77-AT. Get as much information as you can. If the registration rolled over, I need to know all other names, dates and addresses, as well. If there are any other names that pop up during the search, I want a cross-reference made against our records. Got it?"

"What's this about and why would you be running a trace on such an old tag?"

"Baker, please just do it, I don't really want to go into an explanation. Call you back in an hour." With that, Nick hung up and dialed a second number.

Stu Johnson was one of the best analyst in the world. Many agencies had tried to recruit him but he would not leave. From time to time, he was loaned to the CIA and FBI teams to help track down a serial killer or terrorist cell, but he felt a passion for what he was doing and never considered a jump. However, he often took advantage of his intelligence status and would pull practical jokes on other staff members whenever he felt some relief was needed and the pressure of the job was getting to everyone. Every staff member was an open target and most took his shenanigans in stride, but sometimes Johnson went too far.

As much as he was a joker, he was also a professional and often reminded everyone of the importance of their jobs and just how important they were to the job and the agency. He had no tolerance for anyone goofing off or not doing their jobs to their full capability. Any time another analyst looked as though they were bending the rules, Johnson fired off an email to the station chief and that person's system was locked down until the complaint was reviewed, resolved, than unlocked. The review was mostly unwarranted, but it got several of the analysts angry enough to retaliate against Johnson whenever they could.

Johnson lived alone with his sick father, taking care of him in the evenings after the nurse left. He spent his nights playing games on his Wii and hacking his way into any company mainframe he felt like cracking. His favorites were insurance companies where he would leave a 'bomb' on the mail server waiting for any employee to logon to their email in the morning. Once they did, the file would lock their keyboard, then start screaming obscenities through the system speaker at full volume. If the system had external speakers hooked up, the sounds would easily travel through several departments.

In the last year, he had done this to over a dozen companies, hoping his antics would be in the papers. Checking the morning after for a small mention, he was always disappointed it was never reported. Although there was never a mention, he took great delight in visualizing dozens of people scrambling to turn off their machines any way they could, pulling cables, throwing them on the floor, slamming the keyboard down on the CPU, anything to stop the annoying sounds and embarrassment.

Baker logged-in after resetting the system IP address to mimic Johnson's and began the search. Bouncing the signal off of several towers simultaneously, the request fragmented and began filtering through Canada, Alaska, Russia, Netherlands and started a back track before hitting the NY City License and Registration department. From there, the data was rerouted through several towers worldwide before his self-developed intercept program grabbed, restructured and encrypted the information, sending it on to Baker's system with the initial request showing up entirely under Johnson's machine. The digital signals would then continue through several other towers until they became useless.

Once the data finished downloading to his system, Baker slipped a thumb drive into the USB port and transferred the file onto it, then deleted it from his own system, leaving no footprint of it ever existing. Just as he was pocketing the thumb drive, he heard the first perimeter door open, then the second. Bursting through the second door before it fully opened, two armed guards and an agent went running towards Johnson's cubicle. Everyone froze as they watched Johnson pulled from his chair, thrown to the floor, handcuffed with his hands behind his back, picked up and led out by both guards. The agent yanked out the network cable and quickly began unplugging his workstation, snatching everything up and following the guards out. Johnson was crying hysterically.

His cell phone rang and Baker jumped. Grabbing it, he pressed the volume slide downwards to silence the tone, saw that it was Nick and hit a key that transmitted a pre-recorded signal. The signal was a series of musical notes that each agent had memorized, knowing which ones to eliminate and which ones were important to remember. He then pressed the off key before waiting to see if the message was completely sent.

Nick listened to the notes. He played them back again to make sure he had understood them correctly, hitting the end key once he was finished. Flipping the phone over, he slipped off the back cover and replaced his SIM card with the one Brewster gave him. It was time to go silent.

Chapter 5

Sydney, Australia - On the second ring, the phone was answered by an automated system which scrambled the dialed number, then reconnected the party to a private line.

"Sir, a request for the tag has been issued from the United States, making a connection to the New York City License and Registration office about 20 minutes ago."

"Do we know who specifically requested the information, do they have the car?"

"At this time, we only have a name and it appears the request was processed from within the Department of Homeland Security. Whoever put through the request, they did not follow standard procedure."

"What do you mean?"

"DHS has their own dedicated satellites for processing inquiries around the world. There's no reason why they wouldn't have put through a normal request using them. Whoever put through this search, bounced it around a number of cell towers to hide their tracks, then passed the data through an encryption program before snatching it. The algorithm in the program is the most advanced any of our guys have ever seen, way beyond 128 bit."

"Can any of them tell what information was in the transfer?"

"Not a chance. They don't even know where to begin to break down the algorithm without the key. It could take weeks, months, if at all."

There was a long pause. "Contact the team and put them on alert. I want to know what DHS has and run a complete background check on the person who put through that inquiry. Tell Simon I don't care what he has to do, whatever force is necessary, I want everything that person knows." Traugott hung up the phone and the automated system once again processed a series of beeps, this time erasing the call from the phone company computer banks.

Simon Marks read the decoded instructions on his Blackberry. He and his team were to leave immediately. His concern was not with obtaining the information being requested, but that he had never been given the green light to use whatever *force was necessary*. The answers would need to be obtained quickly. Scrolling down the message, he memorized the addresses and names of persons of interest, erased the message and checked his bag to make sure he had everything needed.

On his way down to the garage, he placed calls to the other team members, giving them the meet times and a rendezvous point. Reaching the garage floor, he waited for the doors to completely open, then stepped through. Looking around, he walked past several rows of cars, turned right, pulled out his keys and pressed the trunk release. Without a sound, the trunk lid on the black Jaguar opened and he placed the bag inside. As he started to lower the lid, he heard the muffled cry of a woman and stopped.

Listening for a few moments longer, he recognized the sounds of a woman pleading for help, coming somewhere at ground level. Bending down to peer underneath his car, he saw a woman with her mouth covered by a man on top of her. Her face was swollen from where she had been struck, blood running out between the attackers' fingers. The man was not aware of anything else except satisfying his current need. Simon's movements caught the woman's attention and he put a finger to his lips hoping she would understand to be quiet.

Slipping out of his loafers, he moved as quickly as he could between the cars, coming up behind the rapist, delivering a punch at the base of the skull. Knowing it would only stun the man, he repositioned his stance and brought his knee up, striking this time against the temple. The man dropped and rolled partially off of the woman.

Kneeling, he grabbed the man's shirt and pulled him onto his back, at the same time telling the woman to stay quiet and not scream. She shook her head and began slowly getting to her feet. Several shopping bags were strewn onto the ground along with her purse and keys. As she began pulling up her panties and straightening her clothes, she said she wanted to call the police.

"I would rather you didn't." said Simon, knowing that if the police happened to want to search his car and saw the contents of his bag or the concealed compartment, he too would be arrested. He had to think fast.

"I've seen what happens in cases like this before. If you go to trial, the defense will ask you a lot of very personal questions, trying to make it look like this was your fault. They will do their best to embarrass you in front of your family and friends, even the people you work with. In the end, if you're lucky, this guy will get aggravated assault and will be back on the streets in a few months looking for someone else."

The woman stared at her assailant, knowing what Simon was saying was probably true. She had heard the stories, as well. One of her girlfriends had also been raped and they never caught the man. She had seen how the woman had become a recluse over the past year, never wanting to go out in fear the man would find her again. Her life had spiraled downhill with alcohol and drugs becoming her escape.

"Look, if I can guarantee you this guy will never rape another woman, will you let me handle it and not call the police? It's not going to be pleasant for this man."

"What are you going to do?" asked the woman.

"You don't need to know, I just need for you to say yes, then walk away and promise you won't call the police. In fact, I trust you will not remember me or my face at all." Simon looked down to make sure the man was still unconscious.

Sensing what was about to happen, the woman replied, "I will remember you for the rest of my life, but I promise I will never tell anyone about this. I will get myself checked out and that will be the end of it. If you are about to do what I think you are, I'm staying to watch justice done not only for me, but my girlfriend and every other woman this has ever happened to. Screw the law."

"Dump out what's in that plastic bag and hang on to it for me, I'll be back in a second." Simon went to his car, reached into the leather bag and extracted the utility knife. Returning, he told the woman to gather her belongings and put them in her car, they would need to leave as soon as he was done.

He then reached into the plastic bag and pulled the sides down over his arm to make a sleeve. "Are you sure you want to watch this?" She nodded her head. Grasping the man's penis, he pulled it straight out and pressed the blade of the utility knife flat against the man's scrotum. Applying pressure to the back of the blade with his finger, he cut upwards then nicked the remaining skin to severe the member completely. The man groaned but remained unconscious. Simon stood quickly, pulling the sides of the bag up, letting the contents drop to the bottom, then tied and pulled the loops together to close it.

With a soft smile, the woman whispered "Thank you", got into her car and drove away.

Dropping the bag into the front passenger seat of his car as he hurried by, he reached into his pocket, pulled a lighter and began to burn away any traces of blood from the blade as he stood at the rear of the car wiggling his feet back into his loafers. With the blade sanitized, he slid it back into the holder, tossed the knife into the open bag and closed the trunk. Following the woman out, he heard the agonized and frightened screams of a man echoing off the walls of the garage, as he turned right onto Biscayne Street.

Straight ahead, facing in the same direction, a garbage truck was blocking traffic. Putting on his blinker, he pulled into the right lane, at the same time reaching across for the bag. As he passed by, he tossed it up into the bay of truck, watching it bounce off the edge, down into the rest of the garbage just as the compactor blade was lowering. With a three-hour drive ahead of him, he reclined the driver seat a couple of inches, slipped on his sunglasses, thumbed the CD changer lever on his steering wheel and settled back.

Chapter 6

Brewster was furious. One of his top analysts had been under interrogation by a senior IA agent and the CIA for the last two hours without his presence. Exiting onto the 27th floor, he headed straight for the central conference room. Without knocking, he entered as Johnson was hurling a slew of profanities at one of the agents and he felt obligated to join in.

Stepping in between the two, Brewster shouted into the agent's face. "Back off, asshole! Who the hell do you think you are, interrogating one of my men without having me here, as well? Do you have any idea how many laws you have broken, and don't throw that 'Patriot Act' shit at me?"

The agent didn't flinch. "Back out of my face, Brewster and yes, that's exactly what's at play here. Your man is dealing with classified information at the highest level. If he knows what we think he knows, he's about to put this country in a very embarrassing situation, so you back off, asshole!"

"You've got to be kidding. Classified information over a damn license plate? Hell, we're talking what, 1956, 1957, how could that possibly be important?" Brewster turned to Johnson. "What do you know about this?"

"Nothing, I swear, Paul. That's what I've been trying to tell them. I never put through any request for any information. It wasn't me!"

"Stu, it came from your system, we've already verified that. Besides, you ran a fragmented bounce, and not many people in the world know how to do that without leaving some kind of trail. If it hadn't come from one of our own systems, we wouldn't have caught it. With all of the cyber security enhancements we've developed over the years and patches we have on our systems, it's not possible anymore."

"We'd all like to believe that, but for this, I'm telling you it wasn't me."

"Well, someone put it through and every piece of evidence says you're the guy." The agent was poking Johnson in the chest as he said this.

Suddenly Johnson's expression changed and his eyes grew wider. "Wait, that's it! All of our systems are partitioned to run multiple operating systems, but the latest patches are only running against the most current OS. Some of the older platforms allowed a user to trick the network and gave them the ability to set up duplicate IPs if they connected through a different network node. There were only a limited number of IP's that could be used back then, so you had to find a way to use them over if you needed more. Its old school, that has to be it."

"You're saying one of my guys purposely went around all protocol, used some antiquated method to get data on a classified file, then tried to hide all of his or her steps so they wouldn't get caught? No way, I know everyone of my people on a personal level. No one from this group of people is a damn spy!" Even though he said this, Brewster was having some doubts, already running every member of his team through his mind, eliminating any possibilities.

"Well, I guess you don't know your team of geeks as well as you think you do." the agent said. He looked at Johnson, "Who on this team has that kind of background or experience. I don't care if you don't think any one of your guys would do this!"

Johnson thought for a few seconds. "Could be Thompson, Bernstein, maybe even Baker. Some of these new people don't talk to me much, so I really don't know their full history or level of expertise."

"How about you, Brewster, any ideas?" asked the agent.

"I'd have to agree with Stu on the experience, but I just don't see it. It would have to be someone new, those others have been here for years, extremely dedicated to us and to each other. I'll pull all the records on new staff, do a complete check of their private lives, maybe there's something we overlooked and didn't see in their psych evaluations."

"You've got twenty-four hours, no more. After that we lock up every one of your people for treason." The agent didn't wait for a response and left.

Once he was gone, Johnson turned to Brewster. "I'm getting out of here for the day and heading home. I'm going to run some of my own tests to see what I can find. I may not be able to identify who banged the towers, but I might be able to figure out who ran the intercept. I'll call you if and when I do."

"Don't call, just come in. There's no way your home phone or cell hasn't already been serviced. I want this face to face so I will have time to get some answers before those CIA spooks come crawling back up our asses with all kinds of warrants and more accusations."

Chapter 7

After listening to what was in Baker's message, Nick knew that whatever information he was after, someone else wanted it as much, if not more. He would need to wait until Baker had time to compose another message and record it to the number he had left embedded in the message. After an hour, he pulled out a back-up phone and dialed the number left within the musical tones.

He listened as the recording began. Baker was running scared after seeing Johnson taken down and hauled away in such a manner. It did not take long for one of the technicians to find out what was going on and pass the details along anonymously to the others. All of their systems were being monitored and only certain individuals were authorized necessary top level security clearance. Everyone else was being limited to running backgrounds and other requests way below their GS pay scale.

In this message, Baker had left a set of passwords, generic name IDs and a path to a hidden drive where Nick could logon and retain the information. The first set of IDs would allow him to enter through a portal, bypassing the initial log on screen. The second was for connecting directly to the hidden drive. Heading back to his car, Nick grabbed his laptop, plugged in the satellite card, entered his ID and password and waited for the link-up. The screen cleared and a list of network drives appeared along with prompts for the next set of IDs. He entered these and waited for the next display.

Instead of receiving a list of files he had expected, a video began to run showing Baker with his face blurred out, but his voice was distinct to Nick even though it had been altered. "Nick, I don't know what this is about, but every agency has been asking questions and threatening all the employees with treason if we don't comply. They have issued all of us special passwords and are ghosting our systems. I was afraid to put anything on my system so I put this message on this drive. I need to meet with you to bring you the info. I'm not doing anything technical that can possibly be traced."

He listened to the rest of the message letting Nick know how to contact him, along with setting a time and place for the exchange. When the video finished, a prompt asked if he wished to delete the file. Nick pressed 'Yes' and the file was deleted. He then watched as several other directories disappeared from the list. Baker was cleaning up after himself and Nick knew now just how scared Baker was.

He closed the laptop, pulled the card and packed everything into the computer bag. He then called the number left by Baker. Baker answered simply saying "Hello", the nervousness coming across in his voice. They spoke for less than a minute and hung up.

It would be necessary for him to head to Richmond if he was going to get whatever information Baker held. Starting the car, he reversed, spun the car 180 degrees and began the drive back. They would meet midway between, exchange the file and depart without acknowledging each other in case they were being watched. Once the files had been reviewed, Nick would call Baker and let him know if anything else was needed, but Baker had hoped he wouldn't.

They had agreed to meet at an establishment called the 'Time Out Sports Bar and Grill' around 2:00 PM. The locals and military personnel from a base close by frequented it. Being military, they usually tended to hang out with their own uniformed friends, so there would be little notice of anyone remembering Nick and Baker as they came and went.

As Nick pulled in, he saw Baker's green Volvo parked at the far end of the lot. Entering, he watched Baker get up from the bar and head toward the men's room. Waiting a few seconds, he stopped one of the waitresses and asked where the 'john' was. She pointed in the direction of the restrooms as she continued to walk trying to steady a large tray of drinks, burgers and wings. He thanked her and headed back.

As he opened the door, Baker saw him and headed out the same door, handing him the thumb drive as he passed. Nick dropped the drive into his shirt pocket, walked over to the urinal and relieved himself after having driven straight there without stopping. After washing up, he pulled the drive from his pocket, looked at it, then decided it would be safer if he slipped it into his front pants pocket that closed with a snap.

Pulling out of the parking lot, he noted that Baker had already left, heading back either home or DHS. He pulled onto the road and headed in the opposite direction.

Chapter 8

The nurse finished packing up the used medical supplies, adjusted the air supply and was taking her patient's pulse as Johnson pulled into the garage. After checking on how his father had done that day, he made small talk, paid the nurse and went into his computer room without seeing her out. After running diagnostics for signs of intrusion, he switched off all systems except one so he could concentrate and not be bothered by outside interference from other geeks trying to penetrate his network and follow his methods of hacking. Once he was set, he went into his father's room to say 'Hello', bringing him a small glass of Jack Daniel's. Had the nurse ever found out he did this on a nightly basis on his father's request, she would have yelled unmercifully and probably quit as well.

Logging into the lone system, he quickly jumped through the firewalls at DHS, having set up and deployed them himself. The harder part would be concealing his movements as his program tapped into each system, going through the transaction logs. If he could determine the exact time the intercept ran, he could search each transaction log to find a matching time, then narrow it down based upon the file size to match on both. That would tell him who ran the intercept.

After an hour and a half, the search returned the time of 15:12:123.250. All he had to do now was run it against all systems in DHS to find the matching time, narrowing his search to what he hoped would only be one or two people. After a few key strokes, his system began cycling through the DHS network looking at the logs on each system to find a match. As he watched each non-match being eliminated, he heard the glass from his father's room crash and shatter on the floor. Knowing his father was bed-ridden, he did not move for a minute, then decided he had better check just in case.

As he walked down the hallway, he saw the door partly closed and recalled having left it open all the way. Entering, he saw a man standing at the end of the bed with a gun pointed directly at his father's head and another leaning over asking questions. He pushed the door all the way open to make a run at the man when the butt of a gun cracked across the back of his left ear. He went down hard.

When he awoke, he found himself sitting, strapped to a chair with his wrists bound to the rails, his legs pulled apart and his feet tied to the back legs. His feet had been positioned so they were flat, along with each hand resting off the end of the chair arms. He could feel the blood still trickling down his neck. Trying to see who was in the room, he turned his head, but a hand reached from behind, grabbing his chin, turning it back. The pain was almost unbearable and he thought he would black out.

With the chair turned inward, positioned facing the bed, he looked down and saw his father's eyes filled with fear, blinking above the oxygen mask. The man with the gun was standing at the end of the bed, still pointing the weapon at his father. Slowly moving his eyes, he now saw the third man's reflection in the mirror.

"Mr. Johnson, I'm sorry to have to put you and your father in this predicament, but you seem to have information that we have been searching for, for some time. If you give it to us now, we will make this as painless as possible, but you must cooperate, as I do not have much time. If you do not, I will inflict an extreme amount of pain to the both of you rather quickly." The man's voice was steady and calm. Stu's father looked at him, his eyes blinking faster.

"You sent a request for a tag number belonging to a car we will assume you have found. Give us its location and we will be on our way."

Thinking the men were from the CIA, Stu yelled, "I didn't send out the request, I have told you guys this already!" The man with the gun pointed it at his left foot and fired, the three-inch suppressor eliminating all but a soft 'poofing' sound. Johnson cried out and almost fell backwards in the chair.

"I told you I don't have much time, let's try it once more. This time it will be your father's turn. Now where is the car?"

"Wait please, I didn't send the request, it was sent to appear as if it went through my system by someone else, I swear!" Tears were rolling down his eyes as he looked at his father.

"Who sent the request?"

"I don't know, I'm trying to find that out now!" The man asking the questions turned to the gunman and nodded. The man raised the gun and Johnson screamed "No, not in the head!" He lowered the angle and fired two rounds through the old man's upper chest.

"God damn you, you son of a bitch, he had nothing to do with this." He looked at his father as the tears continued to stream down his face. "Look, I'm running a script that will tell me who wanted that information, I can show you. Take me to my computer, it's probably finished by now."

The man behind the chair pulled out a knife and cut the plastic strips from around his wrist and feet. Coming around to his side he pulled Johnson up from the chair, hooked one of his arms around his neck and walked Johnson to the series of computers he had lined around the room. Johnson reached down and moved the mouse, watching as the screen came to life, showing the application still running. A side portion of the screen showed four names that matched the timestamp of when the intercept had occurred. One of the men punched a button on the printer and it began to print out a copy of the screen.

With his hands and feet untied, he knew he had to do something quickly so the men would not get the read-out and do the same to the people listed as they had done to his father. They had all become his friends, his extended family, and somehow he would have to protect them for as long as possible. He looked across his desk and saw the large glass of ice water, now with its sides covered in condensation, a small puddle of water already running onto the wood. Moving closer to the desk, telling the men he needed to run one more sequence to get the exact match, he grabbed the glass and flung the contents onto the printer, at the same time grabbing the laptop and throwing it to the floor as hard as he could.

The laptop screen shattered and bounced several times across the terracotta tile, the printer sparked and the ink on the paper began to run. Balancing on his right foot, he threw a hard punch into the face of the man holding the gun, then spun, trying to land an elbow into the side of the head of the man who had questioned him. A hand shot up and caught his elbow, blocking the strike but allowing it to continue in the direction he threw it. Before he could counter strike, a hard fist caught him in the kidneys, then another one more powerful than the first, in the exact same spot. Stu felt his eyes roll upward into their sockets and he collapsed.

"Did you get it before we lost the names?" asked Marks of his assistant.

"There's only one left that I can see. It's a Charles Bernstein."

Marks walked back into the bedroom and retrieved his bag, pulling a small instrument out of it as he returned. Bending down next to Johnson, he grabbed his right hand, slipped the bone cutter pliers around the index finger and squeezed the handles together. The index finger fell onto the floor. He then grabbed the other hand, slipping the cutters around its index finger. "Tell me the other names on that list!" applying pressure as he screamed into Johnson's ear.

Marks knew what was on the line. This was as close as his employer had ever come to getting what he had been searching years for, and knew there would be serious consequences if he failed. If that happened, he would be looking over his shoulder for the rest of his life, however short or long that might be. Traugott had a reputation for letting people live a while before he had them terminated, each person suffering mentally for prolonged years, knowing it was only a matter of time. One man had been known to take his own life.

"I didn't see the list. You were in front of the screen blocking it and I could only make out Bernstein!"

Squeezing the handles again, he clipped through the index finger, than moved to the middle finger, removing it as well. His anger was mounting and the two assistants looked at each other, both realizing at the same time that they had never seen Marks lose his professional temperament. This was out of character and they wondered where it might lead.

Johnson was sobbing now, trying to catch his breath, the pain lashing through his entire body. Choking, he began to spit blood as sweat poured down his face. He could smell the foul, salty aroma of urine as he wet himself. Finally he cried, "It was Bernstein, Thompson, Pearson and Baker. Please, no more!"

"What are their full names?"

"Charles Bernstein, Steve Thompson, Todd Pearson, Cage Baker."

"Who would be the most likely person to have done this?"

Even though he knew this would be his last few moments, he had to protect and give these people more time. Bernstein and Thompson were married, Pearson wasn't. Baker was the person, he was sure of it, but if this was that important, he had to give Baker the most time. "It would have to be Pearson, only he would bust protocol like this. He's constantly working with different people outside DHS, so maybe he's working with someone you're looking for. Our people are too protective, and they wouldn't do it without getting authorization."

"Are you positive it's Pearson?"

"Yes, it's Todd, Todd Pearson." In his mind, he begged Pearson for forgiveness.

"I need the Administrative pass codes to get me into the DHS databases."

Johnson hesitated, then felt the cutters being slipped around his thumb. He blurted out the codes as Marks recited them over, locking them into his memory.

As Marks got to his feet, he turned to one of the men. "Kill him."

The assistant waited for the others to leave, then switched all of the systems back on, hoping he could obtain additional information for Marks. Seeing none, he turned to the man on the floor.

Johnson closed his eyes.

Chapter 9

It was nearing dark when Nick pulled into the roadside motel. He parked in front of the registration desk, checked in and headed towards his room, only three doors down. As he opened the room's door, he looked around at the limited furnishings. It looked like every other motel room with beige and dark brown everywhere. The burr carpeting was used to help cover most of the coffee or liquor stains and dirt from all of the previous occupants, or worse, one night stands or quickies. Inside the bathroom were small bottles of shampoo and conditioner along with wrapped soap sitting in a dish. In a large cabinet sat a wide flat screen, the remote laying next to it. In the corner was a small desk with Wi-Fi hook-up but he already knew it would not be required for this evening's work.

After locking the deadbolt and sliding the chain bolt onto the door, he placed his gym bag and laptop on the bed, walked back to the bathroom and washed up. Deciding he probably needed to get something to eat before starting a review of the files, he called for room service, ordered a roast beef on wheat and a pitcher of ice tea.

Changing into jeans, a black t-shirt and no socks, he reached across and retrieved the laptop from its bag, placed it on the small desk and opened it. It automatically booted within three seconds, then showed the DHS logo along with a cursor that blinked non-stop in the user ID prompt along with the password prompt showing blank. Remembering the thumb drive, he walked back over to the bed, picked up his pants, snapped open the pocket latch and retrieved it.

There was a knock at the door, followed by a young girl cheerfully calling "Room Service". Opening the door, Nick looked past the girl, eyeing around her in each direction to make sure no one was approaching from behind. It had become second nature to him by now and served well as a precautionary measure. The bill was $14.27, he handed her a $20.00 and told her to keep the change. As she thanked him, he closed the door and relocked it as before.

Sitting down in front of the computer, he quickly entered the required pass codes and plugged in the thumb drive. Finding the drive listed in the menu, he double clicked the icon and watched. By the time his finger released on the second click, the drive had already opened, displaying several files. He clicked on the first file in sequential order and it opened to display a large 'Classified' label across the top of the file and a prompt for the password. Under the password was a warning advising that only two attempts would be allowed before the file would self delete.

Nick keyed in his assigned password and hit enter. A message flashed indicating the password was not correct. One more attempt would be allowed. Thinking he may have keyed the password in incorrectly, he tried again. The screen went blank, then redisplayed the file list from the thumb drive. This time the one he had previously selected was gone. Frustrated, he dialed Baker, forgetting he had already activated and used the throwaway once already. The phone rang once, changed to a slightly different tone on a second ring, then back to the original tone on the third.

His gut instinct was telling him something wasn't right when Baker answered. "Cage, it's Nick, I need the password for the files you gave me. I lost one already."

"I didn't give the correct one to you on purpose as I knew you would call once the first file disappeared. Don't worry, I duplicated it just for that reason. Look, Nick, something really big is going on with this data I pulled for you and eventually they're going to trace it down to me. When that happens, I'm going to jail and you know it. The only chance I have of trying to stop that from happening is going to Brewster and confessing. I've got no choice."

"You tell Brewster to call me on this, I'll get it straight. Now if you don't mind, I need the password so I can get started reviewing the files."

"Alright, it's 'Solomon', but you need to get…"

"How many times did your phone ring?" Nick was nearly shouting and Baker could hear the strain in his voice.

"Twice. Why?"

"Shit! Hang up, hang up now!" Nick ran to the bathroom and dropped the phone into the toilet.

He stood there regaining his composure, thinking. Who would have the capability to tap a burner phone that has no call back number? It was a throwaway that he had used cash to purchase. There was no way to trace it. They would have to have piggybacked the call by routing it through another caller's phone and waiting for the targeted person's phone to ring and pick-up or vice versa. Baker was being tapped, but who could be on to him already?

When the phone rang, he thought he was hearing it come from outside the motel room, but listened closer to make sure. The ringing was coming from the gym bag and he realized it was his personal phone. Right after the second ring it stopped. He sprinted across the floor and dove onto the bed with his hand outstretched for the bag. He would have to wait seven seconds for the call back.

Chapter 10

Picking up the morning newspaper from the front porch, the nurse inserted the key, unlocked the door and stepped inside. She walked along the outside kitchen wall to shut off the alarm and realized it had not been set. Going into the kitchen, she dumped last evening's grounds from the coffee tray, rinsed out the last of the brew and started a fresh pot. Reaching into the refrigerator, she grabbed two eggs and a container of orange juice, placing them on the counter. Dropping a slice of butter into a frying pan, she turned on the burner, placed the pan on the stove and inserted two slices of bread in the toaster. Satisfied breakfast was on, she turned towards the hallway to check on Mr. Johnson.

As she passed, she poked her head into Stu's bedroom and saw that he had not slept in his bed the night before. That or he had left early, making his bed before leaving, but she doubted it. As she passed the computer room, she heard the constant hum of the many systems Stu had running twenty-four hours a day. She knocked lightly, but there was no response. As she began to open the door, she recalled him asking her never to go in unless he asked her to, so she pulled the door shut and continued down the hall.

"How are you feeling this morning, Mr. Johnson?" as she scooted by the bed towards the window. "It's beautiful outside today. Let me open a window to get you some fresh air. Maybe you'll hear some birds that you like so well."

After opening the window, she went over to fluff the pillows and check the oxygen levels. Getting closer, she noticed he was not wearing his mask and rushed to his side. Feeling for a pulse, she found none, threw the covers back to begin CPR and saw the blood. Running towards the computer room, she flung open the door, hoping Stu was still there listening to some music with his headphones on or immersed in what he called 'code' and had simply not heard her come in. Seeing the remains of what looked like Stu, she covered her mouth and ran towards the front door. Halfway down the hallway, she vomited the breakfast she had eaten before arriving, but kept going.

Once outside, she fell to her knees and began to scream. The police arrived within minutes of a neighbor's call and entered the house with weapons drawn. A call went to dispatch that two bodies had been found, one with two gunshots to the chest, the other with one to the head, one to the left foot, along with multiple amputations of the fingers, and facial disfiguration.

The first officer on the scene was talking to the detective, who had just arrived. "The coroner hasn't shown up yet, but we believe the time of death was around 7:00 or 7:30 pm for the deceased we found in the bedroom. The other guy, possibly an hour later. The coroner will have to confirm the exact times, though. I have to tell you, he looks like he had the shit tortured out of him first before they killed him. Why, I don't know. Poor bastard had his face kicked in."

"Anything else?" asked the detective.

"Yes, his ID shows he is DHS."

The detective stood motionless for a second, then said, "Seal it up, everybody out. No one and I mean no one, goes back in. Leave everything as it is. Get on the phone and get extra men out here to cordon off the onlookers. I want only DHS looking at this. Get them out here quick. Move it."

"What about FBI?"

"My brother is DHS. They look at it first, then if they feel it's something the FBI should be involved in, let them make the call."

The cop made a notation in his log, then double-timed it up the lawn towards the house.

Twenty minutes later the house was completely sealed, with the bodies still inside, untouched, as DHS arrived on the scene. They asked for the lead detective, spoke with him for a few minutes, then advised that all information gathered to that point was now classified and should be handed over to Homeland.

Upon entering, they headed straight for the computer room, followed by two technicians carrying an assortment of equipment. They ignored the body and began connecting cable leads into the USB ports that ran from their laptops and other equipment. One of the techs picked up Johnson's shattered laptop, popped open the case, ran a new PIN ribbon to the hard drive and began tapping on the keys of his own computer.

"Can you tell anything yet?" asked the SAIC.

"Not yet, but thankfully he had the laptop interior wrapped in a separate hard case, absorbed the impact and left the hard drive intact. It's running fine. I'll have something for you shortly."

The second technician interrupted. "This is different. Looks like this guy created a special export file that captured an image of everything he printed, goes back six months. The last screen image is from one of our systems. See the logo? A couple names are printed out to the side in this last capture. The rest of the data behind the image is jumbled, looks like the application was running through a script, trying to isolate the data. The characters were changing at thousands per second, you won't get anything from that."

"Can you run the names, see if there is a pattern, maybe if and where they work within DHS?"

The first technician pointed towards Johnson. "How about him? Run his name as well?"

"Run it, but I already know who he is, well, was."

Forty-five seconds later the technician turned the laptop screen towards the SAIC, "You need to look at this. They are all together under Brewster."

The SAIC (Special Agent In Charge) took a deep breath, letting it out slowly, trying to piece together what he already knew. "His group of guys, their IQs are off the charts. They gather and analyze the top intel from around the world for most of our agencies. Whatever he had, someone else wants it enough to kill for it and not worry about covering up. We need to get those other guys on this list locked down, safe and protected."

The second technician was still running a scan of the drive when the SAIC turned to him. "Well, any other good news from you?"

"It looks like he was trying to run a match for a specific time stamp against the transaction logs of the other systems."

"Which systems?"

The technician lowered the screen and looked at the SAIC. "All of them, every system in DHS. I'm going to have to try and pick up where he left off. Could take a while."

"OK, grab whatever you need out of here without disturbing anything else. We need to let forensics in so they can do their thing. Maybe they might find another lead that can start making sense of why a genius gets his fingers cut off."

SAIC McCallister shut the driver door on his vehicle, reached into a side pocket for his phone and dialed Brewster direct.

Brewster jerked the phone from the cradle while in the process of trying to calm himself down. Baker had just confessed to running the data search and telling him of West's involvement. Knowing who was on the other line, he gave himself a few extra seconds, deciding he needed to hold onto that piece of information for a little longer.

"Dan, I told you we needed more time to search through our logs, we don't have an answer for you yet."

"Paul, that's not why I'm calling. You need to contact a couple of your guys and get them under protection now." Brewster could hear the concern in McCallister's voice. This was not the same man who had been in his office the day before threatening to charge his team with treason.

"Why? Who do I need to pull in?"

"Your man Johnson is dead, tortured before he died. My technician tells me Johnson wrote some kind of app that captured whatever was being fed to the printer and the last image on file shows a list of some of your other techs' names printed around the same time he was killed. So, we have to assume they are in danger, as well. What was Johnson trying to find?"

Brewster looked at Baker motioning him to sit down and stay put. "He was trying to find out who ran the trace on the license plate from New York. He wasn't the one who did it, Baker was."

"How would Baker know anything about this specific license plate. Does he have any idea who it belonged to or what it's about?"

Knowing he would not be able to hide anything now, he relented. "Baker says West called and asked him to run the search, asked him to keep it under the wire, that he was researching something personal for someone else."

"West? The guy who sucker punched Peterson, one of IA's guys? Isn't he an instructor of some kind?"

"First of all, we don't know what really happened in that office, and second, with West, it's a lot more complicated than him just being an instructor. He's done a lot of ops for us that I don't even have clearance to talk about." Brewster had already regretted saying it.

"What do you mean it's more complicated than that? Who the hell is he?"

"Let's just say he's off limits and you know what I mean by that! There are some people Peterson is unaware of that have West's six, otherwise he would have never even thought of screwing with him. As soon as Peterson started trying to dig up dirt on West, his career was over. He just didn't know it yet. West is not even aware of the people watching over him."

McCallister went back to the first line of questioning as he threw the car in drive and started towards DHS. "Who's he trying to find out information for?"

"Baker doesn't know and we won't know until we hear from Nick." Brewster didn't want to let McCallister know that he had given Nick a CS card and that he planned to call him as soon as he hung up from the SAIC.

"If Baker is there now, you keep him there. I'm on my way in, shouldn't be more than 30 minutes. In the meantime, you need to get your other guys in quickly." McCallister read off the names to Brewster, verified he had them right and hung up.

Brewster ran the CS card id through his system and waited for the most current number to show, hitting the 'Enter' key as it did. The phone rang twice, hanging up when it wasn't answered. He waited for the recycle, but decided he had better call the names on the list first, along with sending agents to their home addresses, as well. Before it could redial, he punched the cancel button.

Chapter 11

Todd Pearson watched as Nicole stepped from the tub, reaching for a towel while pushing the shower curtain back against the wall. She saw that he had opened the door all the way and was watching her, so she smiled and left it that way. Facing him, she began to towel off, then turned around and placed a foot up on the edge of step stool, exposing what she knew was her best asset.

They were to be married in Hawaii in three days, with their departure scheduled later that evening. Having played between the sheets all morning, she had expected him to be out of bed and selecting his clothes from the closet while she showered.

Instead, he had laid in bed thinking back to when they first met at the seminar, both linguistic experts, each capable of speaking nine different languages fluently. Initially paired together during an exercise, her job was to translate a thirty-page document from English to Arabic while he did the same using code that would display both languages side by side on a screen. The assignment was to last all day, but by early afternoon both had finished and they decided to catch a late lunch out and a movie.

Over the next two years, they continued to date when time allowed, taking every opportunity to schedule conferences and seminars together. Driven by their intellect, they spent most of their time trying to outdo the other by challenging each to learn the other's craft. Within a year, the challenges changed and became harder and harder once they could no longer out match the other at their vocation. The hard work they put into finding the selections they came up with had become as exciting as the passion they put into their lovemaking.

Having finished, she dropped the towel and walked bare across the tile to the double sink and picked up her comb. Setting the part down the middle, she began combing out each side, tilting her head back and forth as she pulled the comb through her shoulder length strawberry-blond hair. Knowing he was watching every move, she exaggerated her body movements just to tease.

Because he was making no effort to move, Nicole laid down the comb and came to the side of the bed where he was still staring. "You're not packing. You need to get up and get started. You said you would before I got in the shower."

"Tell you what. You start packing just as you are. I'll watch, and when you're finished, I promise I will pack everything I need in half an hour."

She reached up and cupped her breasts, "No, I'll tell you what! If you want to see these again before we fly out tonight, you get up now and pack! You're making me nervous that we are not going to make the flight on time."

Todd rolled his eyes and exited at the end of the bed. He opened his closet door, "See, I'm packing," as he slowly pronounced the last word.

The knock at the door, then the ringing of the doorbell, sent them scrambling to put clothes on. Todd pulled the bedroom door closed as he made his way down the hallway, stopping to punch in the code to disable the alarm. He peeked through the eyehole, unlatched the chain and opened the door a few inches. "Can I help you?'

Standing at the entrance, the man replied that he was from Internal Affairs, flashed his ID, then abruptly closed it before Todd could verify the name knowing he would at least recognize the DHS logo and leave it at that. "Are you Todd Pearson?" Acknowledging he was, the man then asked, "May I come in?"

Todd hesitated, looking at how the man was dressed. A clothes horse himself, he knew of no IA agent who could afford a two thousand dollar Armani suit, a three hundred dollar tie, nor a pair of Salvatore Ferragamo shoes. Most agents couldn't coordinate a pair of pants and sports coat. To Todd, their demeanor always carried an air of impatience, this man was relaxed and extremely confident.

"Can I ask what this is about?"

"We are checking on who might have additional information on the arrest at DHS earlier of one of your co-workers. I'm just trying to find out if there was any involvement with someone else or if they acted alone. I'll just need a few minutes of your time."

"Are you talking about Johnson and that tag search he ran? We are a little shocked that he would do that, I mean not the tag search, but the way he did it."

The man in the Armani suit nodded and said, "Yes, that's what we are investigating. Really, would you mind if I came in. I would prefer not to discuss it out in the open and it is getting a little warm."

Pearson looked back over his shoulder to make sure Nicole was not in view and opened the door for the man to enter.

Inside, the man took an empty chair, and Pearson sat across from him. Looking around, Marks made several comments on the interior style and the great choices Pearson had made in purchasing the furniture and art pieces. "You have selective taste, Mr. Pearson. Most of the younger single people I investigate bought their stuff at JC Penney's or IKEA."

"How can I help you Mr. ..., I'm sorry I didn't catch your name?" Pearson had heard it but wanted to make sure the man didn't change it.

"Special Agent Matt Rivers. Do you know Mr. Johnson outside of work, drink beer together, maybe talk about something other than shop?"

"I only know Stu from work. He and I aren't exactly friends. From what I understand he was a loner. I think he spent a lot of time at home taking care of one of his parents. Is he in a lot of trouble?"

"I really can't say. Do you have any idea why he might have put a trace on that tag. Did it mean anything to him. Was he a collector of old cars and perhaps already had the car garaged somewhere?"

Todd could hear his phone ringing from the back bedroom and heard Nicole pick it up and answer. He turned back to the man. "No I don't think he did, but if he had purchased a car like that, I think he would have stored it in the garage in back of his house."

The man looked at Todd with a bit of suspicion. "You said you weren't friends. How would you know he had a garage behind his house?"

"Stu was proud of his house. He took a picture when he bought it and put the shot up in his cubicle. In the picture, you could see the garage in the background. What's so important about the car? I would think IA would be more interested in what Stu did and how he did it, not the car. Isn't this more of the FBI's type of investigation?"

Before he could answer, Nicole stuck her head around the corner and called Todd's name. "The phone's for you honey, oh, I'm sorry, I didn't know we had company." She was trying to act innocent even though she had listened in on the full conversation.

As Todd headed back to the bedroom, Nicole played hostess, asking if the man cared for any coffee, then stated she was getting some herself.

"Pearson here."

"Todd, its Brewster. Just listen for a minute. I don't want to upset Nicole. We've had a development here and need for you to come in until we can get it straightened out. I've already sent a car to pick you up. Since Nicole is there, she'll need to come in with you, as well. I know this is sudden, but it's important."

"We are heading out to Hawaii tonight remember? Getting married, all that kind of nonsense?"

"Todd, just shut up and listen. Johnson is dead, your name was on a list found on his computer and we think whoever killed him may be after everyone included on it. Johnson was tortured. Whatever they are after, they will do the same to you and Nicole to get it." Brewster could hear Pearson's breathing quicken and asked if he was OK.

"Brewster, I've got an IA guy sitting in my living room right now asking me questions about the tag and the car. Did anyone send him?"

"The only IA agent who knows about this is McCallister. Get Nicole and try to keep the guy talking. I'll get our guys to speed it up getting there. In the meantime, don't do anything to make whoever he is, know we are on our way. Try to relax and be calm."

The last few words were lost in transit as Todd stood looking at the man standing in the bedroom doorway, with one arm wrapped around Nicole's neck and the other holding a gun pressed to her head. "Whatever you know about the car, tell me right now or you will leave me little choice. It's up to you."

Nicole spoke a few words to Todd in Chinese and Todd responded in like. Marks pressed the gun harder to her head. "You've got about ten seconds, Mr. Pearson."

"Mr. Rivers, I have told you all I know about Stu Johnson. If I knew any more I would tell you. Apparently you are after some information that relates to a specific car that none of us know anything about. Whatever it is, we don't care. Please let her go and leave."

"Who was on the phone, and don't lie. I will know."

"It was my boss. He said someone had killed Johnson, which I will have to assume was you, and he has sent a car to bring us in for protection because you have a list of names with mine on it. I'm guessing that's why you're here thinking I know something, but I don't, so please just leave." Todd didn't want to scare Nicole by telling the man named Rivers that he knew Johnson had been tortured.

At that precise moment, Nicole bit down into Marks' wrist, gnawing her teeth deep into the flesh. Marks pulled away as Nicole began running down the hallway, hoping Todd would have enough time to grab the baseball bat and strike Marks. Bringing the weapon up, Marks fired two shots, striking Nicole, watching as the impact lifted her off the floor, twisting her in mid air and dropping her on the flat of her back.

As he turned to fire at Todd, the baseball bat struck him on the forearm and hand, causing him to drop the weapon and clutch at his broken fingers and shattered wrist. When Todd swung a second time, the man reached out and grabbed the end of the bat with his opposite hand, jerking it from his hands. Todd made a dash for the open door, but the bat caught him across the ribs. He saw the next strike coming and turned his body just as it came down on the back of his shoulder blade.

As the bat was lifted a third time, Marks waited to see if Todd was going to get up. In the distance, the sound of sirens could be heard and he stopped to listen. Throwing the bat aside, he reached down, grabbed the gun and headed for the back door and his Jaguar that he had left parked at end of the block. As he passed Nicole, he realized that she was turning blue, unable to breathe and gasping for air. He bent down, placed his lips on hers and blew several breaths of air into her lungs until she began to cough.

Lowering her head back to the floor, he stood, then ran out the back door to his car, clutching his arm to his side. Once inside, he leaned over towards the passenger side, unable to use his right hand, and started the car by inserting the key with his left. Having started the car, he shifted with his left hand as well and pulled away slowly, trying to avoid being noticed. He could see the flashing lights in the distance.

Coming in a different direction, the retired veteran police officer, now working as a security guard, was making his surveillance rounds of the neighborhood. Earlier that week, the vehicle had been equipped with a new dash cam that automatically recorded any activity directly in front once a police officer opened his door and stepped out of the car. He had been manually testing the device when the Jag pulled in front of him after having stopped at the stop sign.

Chapter 12

Erik Fenstermacher sat across from James Traugott, drinking an early morning cappuccino, listening to a man whom he knew was being tormented by a decision he was about to make. Word had been received that Simon Marks was injured while interrogating a DHS agent named Todd Pearson, jeopardizing the recovery of a set of documents that, up until this point, Erik had no knowledge of. From what he had learned from this conversation already, he was to track down Marks and determine his ability to continue with the operation. If he were able, then his job would be to protect and assist in the recovery and make sure both teams returned to Australia safely.

There had been no hint as to what the documents contained, why Traugott wanted them so badly or why he had sent Marks to get them. If Marks had been activated in the United States, then they were extremely valuable, worth taking the risk on not only Marks' life but the entire organization. If Marks were to be caught or even recognized, there would be a worldwide investigation into his current assignment, history, his accomplices and every kill, which would eventually lead to him.

They had been partners once, contracted to eliminate targets throughout Europe and the Middle East, mostly. They were a perfect team, Marks preferring to extinguish at close range by the use of a pistol, knife or even hand to hand. Fenstermacher's choice was using a long-range rifle with the simple pull of a trigger, firing at a target up to a mile away. Both were experts at their acquired skills, neither caring who made the kill as long as it was completed and untraceable. Each had the equal weight of the other and no kill was sanctioned until both had evaluated the other's plan and agreed on how it was to be performed.

Only under special circumstances would they make an exception and allow a contractor to advise them on how he or she wanted the kill to be performed. Seldom did they take jobs where only a warning message needed to be sent to the other party so *they* would understand their future should they continue trespassing into that person's business. They were assassins, and their kills were not meant to be made spectacular, but rather precise and efficient. In and out. Leave no DNA, fingerprints, hair, spent shells or any other evidence that could possibly be used to identify their existence. They would only take a job where they were both in agreement that it could be performed in this regard.

But that changed twenty years earlier when Marks refused to take a sanction to kill the wife and family of a wealthy landowner who would not allow the trade of weapons to an expanding militia, using his poppy crops as payment. Although he felt protected from the warring groups by letting the crops be grown on his land and used for illegitimate purposes, he knew that an eventual overthrow of the existing government by this militia would bring more poverty and despair to the people he cared most about, a country where he was born and tried to bring economic stability by using the money he received for education, hospitals and jobs. Weapons were of no use to him and he did not believe in the killing of innocent people for the sake of getting richer.

Fenstermacher took the job alone without Marks, killing the children as they played in their yard from a distance of twelve hundred meters. He shot the eleven-year-old son first, then the daughters as they came to his aid, thinking he had tripped and fallen. As they knelt down to assist their brother, he fired two rounds in succession, hitting each girl in the upper torso. A house servant saw the children go down and walked outside to see what they were doing. When he saw the blood, he turned to run back into the house, yelling for help as he kept looking back over his shoulder. A round caught him through the neck but not before the guards heard his alerts. The remaining family was moved to a 'Panic' room within the mansion, while dozens of guards expanded out onto the property.

As they did, the father followed, crouching down behind four of the guards making their way towards the fallen children. With each few steps, a round hit a guard until only the father stood over his lifeless children screaming into the air, begging for the gunman to take his life, as well. Erik knew that eliminating the father was not part of the deal and had been forewarned that if anything happened to the owner, not only would his fee not be paid, but from that point forward his name would be added to an 'unclassified' list of international targets.

Through his scope, he watched as the father ran from one guard to another, picking up their weapons and firing them where he thought the gunman might be hiding. Then without warning, Erik lay in disbelief, unable to change the next course of his life when the man grabbed a pistol from one of the guards' holsters, put it under his chin and pulled the trigger. Regardless of the circumstances and how it could be explained, a contract would now have his name on it even though he had not made the kill. Grabbing his rifle and scope bag, he sprinted towards his vehicle parked two hundred yards away, leaving the casings where they had landed, ejected from where he had chambered each round.

When Marks found out he had taken the contract, he ostracized Fenstermacher, helping the local police in his capture and incarceration. Within seven months, Erik orchestrated his death and escape by paying off the authorities and guards. Pulling three of his own teeth without an anesthetic, the guards would later kill and let burn beyond recognition another inmate in Fenstermacher's cell, throwing in the extracted teeth at the last possible moment. They would be scorched, but there would be enough DNA left to make a positive identification. In the confusion of the smoke filled prison, Erik was led out through the wardens' entrance to a waiting car where he would be taken to a private plane and flown out of the country. Placed upon his seat beforehand were the trial transcripts listing the jury, police officers, prosecutor, judge and Marks' name.

"If Marks fails in the assignment or his efforts have the potential of being traced back to me, it will be necessary for you to eliminate him and his team. Only I, though, will make that call, understood? I will then need you to continue, find the documents and return them to me immediately. When the items have been located, you will open the satchel and verify the existence of one document and one document only. You will not review the document, only verify its existence." Traugott was staring at him directly when he looked up.

"What is its importance? How will I be able to identify only that specific document if I don't know what I am looking for?" asked Fenstermacher.

"What's in the document is not important to you, only I. When you have the satchel, before opening it, you will call me and I will instruct you on what to look for. You also may not review the other papers. Just bring them to me. I want to be perfectly clear on that, do you understand me on this point as well?"

Erik shook his head, acknowledging that he comprehended what he was being told, but was concentrating instead on plans of how to kill his old partner, regardless if Traugott would allow the termination or not. He would find a way to justify the kill with or without approval, but Traugott already seemed to be reading his mind.

"I am well aware of your history with Marks and that you would gladly welcome the opportunity to even the score, but this is not the time. It is imperative that the documents are found and secured by me as quickly as possible. When this is over, you two can kill each other however you like for all I care and, hopefully, it comes to that."

Erik resented the last remark and wanted to strike out at the man now, but remained composed.

"Everything has been arranged for your departure. You will meet the rest of your team once you set down early tomorrow evening. They will have secured your belongings and have all of the necessary items you will require for you to complete your assignment."

"I would prefer to go this alone. I do not work with a team." Erik was now insistent.

"Mr. Fenstermacher, perhaps I have not made myself clear enough. The team is not for you, it is for me. They have been given instructions to kill you immediately if you decide to leave with the documents or alter the plan in any way. You will perform your job as asked. They will only be there to provide whatever assistance you may need, but they will be there whether you like it or not. Your payment has been amended to allow for these inconveniences to you. If you do not have any other questions, I ask that you please leave immediately. It is a long flight."

Erik stood, making a mental note to deal with Traugott once he had completed the task and returned with the documents. He would try and book a different flight, arriving earlier than planned if possible. If he was to have a team, he wanted extra time to evaluate their skills and decide how best to use them.

Marks knew that Traugott would be sending in another team to assist once he had called and provided details of his injury. He had not divulged that he had left witnesses, knowing what the resulting orders to the new team would be. Todd and Nicole were under protection in a hospital recovering from their injuries. Their names would be kept confidential so there would be little possibility of Traugott's technicians making the connection to him anytime soon. By the time he had located the documents and returned them, the information would no longer be pertinent. The details on the new team members being assigned to him would be received soon and he could plan further. Until then he would relax and listen to the taped recordings from the earlier wiretaps.

Ten minutes into the recordings, his Blackberry pinged and he opened the message, letting the recordings continue to play in the background. The information on the team was now being sent and he tapped the 0 key four times in order for the decryption device to activate. The team would consist of three additional members. He recognized the first two from other dealings he had through prior contract work and was pleased by the choices. One was a former race car driver from the Formula 1 circuit, the other was a planner who could create any diversion necessary to provide for the teams' escape should it be required. Both had never hesitated to kill when they were ordered to do so.

The last was a shooter. He clicked on the folder containing their identity along with other qualifications and waited while the photo appeared on his screen. He stared, knowing it was not possible. Fenstermacher was dead, having burned to death in a prison fire twenty years earlier. His body was positively identified through DNA matching. It was first generation technology at the time, but he saw the teeth himself, recognizing the bicuspid that had a small discoloration he had seen hundreds of time before.

If Erik was alive, then Traugott had sent him for one true purpose; only if he failed. The recovery of the documents was the primary objective, but once they were found, Marks knew that Erik would have other plans in mind. He would be patient while the operation unfolded, saving Marks for last after executing all other members of both teams. Erik would choose his moment when the job was complete and Marks would need all of his skills to anticipate that exact time.

With his injuries, though, he feared he would not be able to protect himself well enough to survive. Erik would do whatever was required of him throughout the operation, but when it was over, Simon would need to take whatever action he felt necessary, including killing Erik's team immediately, before he could use them to kill his. Each team's men were the best at what they did, but they were not killers like he and Erik and that would surely play a decisive role in the eventual outcome.

Marks pressed the button on the Blackberry to acknowledge the receipt of the message and the details of their arrival. He had sixteen hours before their plane landed. He would need to update his team and plan for his and their survival. As he started towards the door, the recording began to play West and Baker's message. He recognized Baker's voice, but not West's. Listening to their exchange, he realized that Baker had only followed West's instructions. It was West who had put in the request. Baker simply ran the trace. He would need to find out more on West.

Sitting at his computer, Marks typed in the pass codes he got from Johnson and began searching through the DHS databases, hoping for a hit that would tell him why this man would have knowledge of the car. What was his job at DHS that would give him authority to access data so classified it required Congressional approval? Within minutes, he had West's employment records and began to read through the file. West was married to a doctor of veterinary medicine whose practice was in Atlanta. His current position was that of an instructor, training other agents coming through DHS in counterterrorism and counterattack techniques. Military background showed him to be a former SEAL with advanced training in intelligence gathering and infiltration. He moved further through the file and saw the NYPD initials and stopped. West was SWAT, a shooter.

Chapter 13

When the phone did not ring again, West went back to his computer and keyed in the password given to him by Baker. The same files once again displayed and he selected the duplicated one, which this time opened. He learned little from the file other than who the owner of the car was and its maintenance records. It verified the owner was Albert Traugott. It also showed the tag ID and registration information, along with the owners current address and age. Attached to the file was a scanned paper history of when the car was seen, what maintenance was performed and who the mechanic was.

The next file was on Albert Traugott. Most of it confirmed what Manny had already told him, but it gave a family history showing parents, uncles, aunts, one brother, no sisters and related relatives by name. It also listed dates of birth and deaths along with last known addresses. There was a short biography next to each member. Albert had only one brother with the records showing date of death, September 11, 1951. Although no other siblings were listed, it did show a child by his nephew with the name of James Albert Traugott II. His birth date was December 17, 1957, with no known address recorded. There was also no additional biological information.

Clicking on the third file, it brought up the name Alexander Rayfield. An employee of The United States Treasury Department, Nick realized this was information on Manny's father. As he read, he began to understand why her father was such an exceptional man and why the Treasury had selected and trusted him, not only to track Traugott, but to return all monies to the families from whom their fortunes had been taken should the ledgers be found. It listed each family name and the amounts requiring return. Manny's estimate had been way below the real sum of the accounts.

The final file detailed the last known whereabouts of Alexander Rayfield and his prior communications to the Treasury. From the dated notations and witness accounts, Traugott had called Rayfield to meet at Hampton Park, where he would turn over all documentation to him, then return to an undisclosed country where he had been living for the last ten years. Traugott's brother's son was getting married that day and it would provide the cover needed to make the quick exchange. The girl was six months pregnant and her family had threatened to abort the pregnancy if they were not wed. Traugott knew this would be his only chance to intercede with the feuding parties and relinquish the materials he had been protecting for a decade.

Unknown to Traugott and Rayfield though, the meet had been disclosed outside the families and a contracted kill had been placed on both of them. During the transfer, a bullet struck Traugott's nephew, who was standing next to Albert. Rayfield grabbed Traugott, shielding him from the shooter, and pushed him towards the car. As Traugott started the car, a second bullet hit Rayfield in the lower spine as he climbed into the drivers' side passenger seat. All of the witnesses testified that a satchel could be seen hanging from Rayfield's shoulder as he fell forward into the front dash. The tag number on the car was '3X77-AT'.

In addition, an unknown person was seen jumping into Rayfield's car, which pursued the fleeing automobile.

There was one last notation by an agent indicating the car had never been found and it was believed the documents were still with the car, stashed inside for later retrieval. The 'Declaration of Surrender' remained undiscovered.

What was the 'Declaration of Surrender'? Nick tried recalling if Manny had mentioned this document, but couldn't. He read over the files again, looking for any other references, but saw none. Not wanting to call Baker again and involve him any further, he decided he would need to contact Manny, at least letting her know what he had learned about the disappearances. Opening his bag, he retrieved the only phone left, the one Brewster told him not to call out on once he installed the SIM card.

He hesitated, knowing the call would re-establish his personal number, but decided the risk was worth it. Placing the call, he heard the phone ringing, then the answering machine pick up. Listening to Manny's voice instruct the caller to leave a message at the 'beep', he hung up and turned the phone off. Closing the computer and gathering his personal belongings, he left the hotel room and headed towards his car. He would need to drive the forty minutes back to Manny's house and talk with her personally.

As he pulled out into traffic, a black Jag slid in behind his Porsche. Up ahead a Range Rover diverted itself into the same lane and began to slow, keeping pace with the other morning drivers. They continued for the next several miles until the traffic began to thin and the exits began to spread out further and further. The Jag contacted the Range Rover that it was time. The driver of the Range Rover hit his brakes as Marks accelerated, coming up behind the Porsche and ramming it only hard enough to buckle the fender and hopefully cause the driver to pull over. The person in the Range Rover watched in the mirror as the two vehicles exited the roadway and came to a stop. He did the same and began to carefully back his way in reverse down the breakdown lane.

Nick was already out of his car, looking at the damage when Marks opened his door and got out. Pretending to be in deep shock, he approached, waving his hands and shouting that it was entirely his fault and asking Nick if he was all right. Both stood assessing the severity to their own vehicles and then one anothers'. The fender on the Porsche was bent slightly downward, but otherwise looked good. There was no damage to the lights and Nick knelt down to peer at the frame and exhaust.

Concealed with his back to oncoming traffic and the Jag blocking any view from the cars coming the other way, Marks placed the end of his gun to the base of Nick's skull and pulled back the hammer. "Mr. West, if you wish to see Laura alive again, please do not do anything other than stand and face me. I don't intend to hurt either one of you unless you give me no other option. Coming towards us is one of my associates and as soon as he stops, I will pull the gun away and you can stand, but I assure you, he will not hesitate to shoot you if you do not cooperate." Nick turned his head slightly, looking through the windshields to see the Range Rover come to a stop. Inside a man turned in his seat, aiming a pistol directly at him.

Nick could feel the gun being taken away and stood as instructed. "This apparently wasn't an accident was it? If you don't intend to hurt us, why did you threaten to kill my wife?"

"It's not me who's going to kill her, rather someone else who will be landing on American soil in less than twelve hours. You have something he is coming after and he will eliminate whoever gets in his way, using whatever method is required to collect it. If that means killing everyone who has come into contact with you or you care about, he will and he will do it swiftly."

"What does he want from me that could possibly make him want to do that?"

"The same thing that I was sent after, Mr. West, the car."

'Traugott's car?"

"Precisely," said Marks. "Now please, we need to get off the road before we bring unwanted attention to ourselves. There is a house about a mile and a half to your right off of this exit. I need your help if you want to keep your friends and wife alive. Please."

Chapter 14

Arriving at the airport, he passed through the automatic doors empty handed, went through security and headed towards the terminal shown on his boarding pass. As required, he had arrived several hours early for check-in, but was hoping he could catch an earlier flight. Scanning the flight marquee, he noted a flight with a departure time within the next 15 minutes, one gate down.

The gate attendant advised that the flight was booked and there were no additional seats available. Thanking her, he turned to the passengers waiting to board and stepped out of earshot of the attendant, asking if anyone was willing to exchange seats for his flight ticket. After getting no takers, he approached an elderly man sitting alone and offered him fifteen hundred dollars cash along with his own ticket for the exchange. The new flight schedule would get him to Richmond four hours sooner.

Fenstermacher sat in first class, his tray lowered, holding the portable iMac currently displaying a video of a recent band concert the promoter was pushing to raise funds for some third world country for which he had no interest. Through the earphones, the audio was streaming the latest data on Marks' group and updates the technicians had been able to extract from the communication satellites hovering over the United States. There had been no further information on Marks or his whereabouts. Hitting the 'Enter' key, the next audio message began to play. He listened as a trained interpreter read from a script that had been received and translated only forty-five minutes earlier.

"Five agents employed by the Department of Homeland Security were identified in a memo from DHS as candidates with knowledge of car plate number '3X77-AT'. Their names are as follows: Charles Bernstein, Steve Thompson, Todd Pearson, Cage Baker and Stu Johnson. Of these five, Stu Johnson has been erased. It is believed the internal trace by DHS was originated by Stu Johnson, but further communications identify the requester as Cage Baker."

The message abruptly stopped and he hit the 'Enter' key again to continue onto the next one. "Phone records for Cage Baker show calls placed to an unknown subject. Phone logs are untraceable. Current candidates Cage Baker, Charles Bernstein and Steve Thompson are under protection at DHS. The whereabouts of Todd Pearson is still unknown."

As he was about to select the next message, a stewardess approached, offering a glass of champagne, asking if there were anything else she could do to make his flight more comfortable. Declining the champagne as he closed the computer, he said he was fine, just needed to close his eyes for a bit and pressed a button to recline his chair. The stewardess reached into the compartment above his head and brought down a small pillow, sliding it into place as he leaned forward, then back.

Where was Todd Pearson? Surely Marks completed his business and finished off Pearson in the same manner as he had Johnson? He would not leave any chance of being identified by a witness. He would have performed a clean head shot before leaving, especially if Pearson had injured him regardless of how bad. Erik had seen Marks cut in a fight only once before. When it was over the man lay dead, having bled out from three major arteries that Marks selected and severed in less than five seconds. It had angered Simon that someone had been able to get close enough to hurt him even though the cut required only seven stitches to close. He would not have left a witness under any circumstance.

He pulled his cell phone from his pocket and contacted Traugott's lead technician to run the records on all hospitals and clinics within a two hundred mile radius to see if anyone had been admitted without a proper name, cross checking social security numbers to verify the match. They would also need to match on gender, height, weight and eye color from the DHS records. If blood was drawn, they must also match against blood type. He was to be notified immediately on any possible matches found. Closing the phone, he rested his head back on the pillow and shut his eyes.

Seven hours into the flight, Erik's phone vibrated, waking him from a light sleep. The technician responded with news of a possible match on Pearson along with information of a woman being admitted at the same time with gunshot wounds. The same doctors were attending both persons but the physicians did not hold admitting privileges. Admission records did not show any name for the man, but the woman was listed as Nicole Lane. Attached to the audio sent by the technician were the hospital admission notes.

Erik scanned through the notes and saw nothing unusual in the admission records. On a separate page were the admitting physician's initial assessment and comments with notations he had made in speaking with Lane. It outlined the meeting with a man from DHS Internal Affairs and her fiancé Todd in which the man was asking about an unknown car. It further documented the exchange and the assault. The final notation caught Erik by complete surprise and he sat up so fast that the attendant asked if he was all right. The notation read 'I couldn't catch my breath and the man bent down to perform CPR on me. If he hadn't I would have died.'

Several of the passengers turned in their seats to try and determine where the annoying laughter was coming from. Erik had tried to keep himself composed, but the admission by this woman was the answer he had hoped for, that had come out of nowhere, and his own outburst surprised even him. Without realizing it, Marks had given him all he needed to make the kill justifiable. There were two people he had left alive that could now identify him. He would report this information to

Traugott and get his permission to eliminate Marks along with his team. For the team members, he would request a small fee, but for Marks, it would be his pleasure.

Erik opened his laptop and began a Google on Nicole Lane, searching through the different Internet engines trying to get some kind of link to positively identify her relationship to Todd Pearson. After a few attempts, it returned wedding announcements, her personal blog and a link to Todd's business website. He was ecstatic. He had his proof. He wondered if Traugott would want him to track down these two individuals and silence them before he returned with the documents. If so, the risk and monetary reward would be even greater.

The fifteen hundred dollars had been well worth it, as he would have extra time to plan for taking out the first team after learning this information. Separating Marks from his assistants would be difficult because at some point, Marks would know that Erik had discovered he had left witnesses and Traugott would have given the go ahead to tie up any loose ends. Erik dialed Traugott and relayed the information he had, along with asking permission for obtaining from the technicians any electronic communications Marks had received or transmitted after arriving in the United Sates. There was a lengthy delay, then he heard the word 'Approved'.

Chapter 15

Nick drove through the gate entrance left open after Marks had keyed in the entry code and continued on. Behind him the Range Rover pulled up closer and followed at the same speed. Six hundred yards ahead, a Victorian three story mansion sat on a perfectly manicured yard, with lush greens and gardens surrounding a circular driveway. As he pulled up to the front, Marks was already standing waiting for him.

Passing through the foyer, Nick could see the home had been vacated by the owner, probably on an extended vacation in Greece or Italy or some other place he wished he were at the moment. As they entered a large living room, Nick could hear the front door open and the driver from the Range Rover entering. Marks directed Nick towards a chair, then sat opposite so he could study his body language as they spoke. From that, he would be able to tell if Nick was sincere in wanting to help or was just trying to appease him until he could devise a plan to escape or, at minimum, try to overwhelm them.

Once Nick sat, Marks decided it would be best to start filling in the gaps, as he knew there would be a lot of questions and he didn't have the luxury of being able to take his time to answer all of them.

"Mr. West, my name is Simon Marks and you're probably wondering who I am and what this is all about. I will tell you what I know and then I will ask you some questions. It is important that you answer quickly and truthfully as we don't have much time before a man will arrive in Virginia set on killing me and possibly you, if it comes to that. As I mentioned to you already, he will also kill whomever he feels may be a threat to him."

"I will be honest with you as long as you're honest with me. My only concern here is the safety of my wife. If I even think for a minute you are responsible for any harm that will come to her, I will kill you myself. Do we understand each other?" Nick said.

"That's fair enough. I am here because I was sent to pick up a very old package and return it to my employer. The package contains some extremely important documents that only he feels safe in returning to whom they belong."

"Who is your employer and why does he think I have these documents, if that's what he is thinking?"

Marks hesitated for a moment. "We know that you do not have the documents, but we are hoping you do know where they are. For the time being I would like to keep my employer's name out of the conversation."

"I thought you were going to be honest and answer my questions!"

"I plan to, but there are things we need to discuss first. Can we agree on that? Like I said, I need to know information quickly in order to determine what other questions I will ask. All of your questions will be answered."

Nick shook his head that he agreed and Marks continued.

"You requested information on a car registration through an employee of DHS, a Mr. Baker. He transmitted the request going through different channels not normally submitted by DHS. Why?"

"You mean Mr. Johnson, not Baker." Nick was wondering how the man knew it was Baker since no one outside of DHS had that information. "Before I answer that, you need to know how that transpired and who I am."

"Mr. West, I know who you are, who you work for, all of your friends, your wife's name and location, kin, what you do, your bank accounts and exact financials. I also have information on your military and NYPD history, who you dated in high school, with whom and when you had your first piece of ass, etcetera,

etcetera. Please don't think I haven't already investigated every possible shred of data on you I can find. If you would like for me to recite it to you I can, but please, the longer we take at this, the more likely we all won't be alive tomorrow. Now please, answer my questions."

Nick was annoyed that so much classified information was available on him and wondered what extent of resources the man had at his fingertips. He decided to go ahead and answer. "The tag ID was from a photograph I developed. There was an accident at work in which an IA agent and I were involved. I was asked to take a few days off until the facts of the accident could be determined and clarified. On the way out of town, I was caught in a heavy rain storm and had to pull off of the road and find shelter."

"This was two nights ago around six-thirty, is that correct?"

The question shocked Nick. "How do you know that?"

"How do I know that? Gee, let's see. Maybe it's because your car has a registered GPS system, Mr. West? By accessing the company registration records, I also know the coordinates of where you pulled off, although I didn't know the reason or what you were doing. Please go on."

"I ended up stopping next to a farmhouse. From there I was able to make it up onto the porch where the owner later allowed me to spend the night until the rain stopped and I was able to leave."

"Is the owner the one with the photograph?"

"Not like you may think, but yes. I told you I developed the film. When I was leaving the farmhouse the next morning I found an old car in the barn, but not the one you're looking for. Because I have a passion for antique cars, I started checking it out and eventually found a camera in the trunk. It turned out to have film in it, so I purchased all of the necessary chemicals and made prints from the film. The one photo with the car you are looking for was in the batch."

"Do you know who the car belonged to and why it was in the barn? How did the camera get in the trunk of the car?"

"The car belonged to the original owner of the farmhouse. The woman I spoke with said the car has been sitting there for a long time and the owners' wife refused to depart with it."

Marks stood and began to pace in front of Nick. "Did she know who the car belonged to? I mean, did she have a name?"

"Why is that important, Mr. Marks?"

"Tell me who it is if you know, please!" Marks was almost screaming, a large vein displayed in his forehead.

"Alexander Rayfield. Do you know that name?

Marks felt his knees buckle and could hardly stand. He sat and stared at Nick. His hands began to shake and his voice was trembling. "Did she tell you anything about the car or who Rayfield was?"

"She said that he and a man by the name of Albert Traugott worked together for the Treasury Department once and that Traugott stole a lot of money you are looking for. Rayfield was sent to track him down and spent years trying to find him. Traugott decided to come out of hiding because of a threat to his family and contacted Rayfield for a meet. He was about to turn over everything when Rayfield was shot in the back. Apparently Traugott and Rayfield were able to get away in the car I believe you are looking for."

Marks pounded his fist on the table. "Traugott didn't steal anything. He was protecting a secret document as was Rayfield. There were people in your Congress who were trying to get their hands on it and if they had, your country would have ceased to exist, at least as you know it."

"What are you talking about? A document? It's not over a couple of million dollars?" Nick was on his feet now, squaring off face to face with Marks.

"You really have no idea about the car or what this about, do you?"

Nick could see the anger in Marks' face and realized he needed to let him explain. "No I guess I don't. I do know that whatever you're after, it is very serious. I've told you all I know so I'm going to ask you to tell me what you know. Maybe together we can figure out where we go from here and hopefully find what you are after."

They both sat down and Marks took a few moments to figure out where he wanted to begin.

"The Swiss accounts are not the important items we need to find. They are worth millions, but they are nothing compared to the worth of one other document in the satchel. In the early forties, your country was going bankrupt from fighting in Europe and then the Japanese at the same time. The United States was very close to losing the wars. Several people in your Congress met secretly to discuss what would happen in case your country was overthrown and what their personal loss and outcome would be. In hopes of protecting only themselves, they created a document called the 'Declaration of Surrender'."

Nick interrupted. "Some of the research documents I received mentioned it, but didn't give any specifics."

"They wouldn't. It was highly classified, and for a while, those people were the only ones who knew about it. Believe it or not, you had Nazi sympathizers within your Congressional ranks. Some of them had no choice because they owed other people who put them in office. Movie stars, bankers, a lot of very rich people. Do you remember the McCarthy trials, 'McCarthyism' I think it was called?"

"I do. A lot of innocent people had their careers ended and were blackballed by their communities and by everyone who had ever been associated with them. It was our own version of the Salem witch trials. Some ended up being put in prison or killed themselves as a result."

"Well, I think it was a conspiracy to shift the suspicion elsewhere so no one would suspect them. Anyway, the document contained instructions on how the properties of the United States would be divided between those Congressional members and whatever country might be getting ready to overthrow the United States. They wanted to make sure they were protected by simply handing over your country before it was imminent the U.S. would fall to another power."

"Not possible. The other members of Congress would have vetoed it when it came to the floor and they would probably have hung those bastards for even considering such a plan." Nick was finding it hard believe that any member would even conceive of such a plan like this.

"Some things only need the signature of the President of the United States. This was not a document that needed voting on." Marks looked at Nick for his reaction.

"What, the President was in on this?"

"Your president would have shot them himself if he had any knowledge this was going on behind his back. The document was slipped into another pile requiring his signature. These were trusted men and he was in the midst of trying to win a war that many felt was going in favor of Germany. He signed the document without knowing it and by doing so, it became a legal and binding document the moment he did. He was the most powerful man in the world. No one would or possibly could dispute his intentions whether it was an error or not."

"Certainly Germany wouldn't try and use the document today if it were found?"

"The senators didn't know who would eventually come to power, either Germany, Japan or even an ally of one of these countries, so it was worded to be inclusive of any country."

"You're saying that any country who has possession of this document could claim all United States territories as theirs?"

"Yes, but I doubt the United Nations would enforce it. However, it is a legal document signed by a sitting President and any country who wants to pursue a lawsuit could do so. As slow as your court system works, imagine your country coming to a standstill for years, maybe decades, because every piece of property and every business, bank, home, community, or whatever could not be sold or titles exchanged until all disputes were settled. Your country basically shut down for only a few days after 9/11 and look at the billions it lost. All of these years later you are still feeling the effects and you're now in the middle of the greatest real estate depression this country has ever known."

"You underestimate the American people. Life would go on until the courts settled it. Nothing would change up until that point."

Marks leaned over in his chair. "I applaud your belief and trust in your countrymen, but who's going to want to pay their mortgages knowing their property can be taken away at any moment? No other country would do business with you or invest in the United States if they knew their financial gains could be lost or they themselves could be pulled into the lawsuits. It could be days or a lifetime before anyone got an answer. No one is going to risk that."

Nick was beginning to understand the magnitude now. "Any country, even knowing they would lose in court, could change the U.S. into a third world country within months as the proceedings dragged out. The entire infrastructure would collapse, land values and U.S.

currency would be worthless. It would be an incredible victory for even the smallest country."

"Now you see the importance of finding the document, and as soon as possible. As I said before, there is another team coming in this afternoon that is supposed to assist, but I doubt they have that in mind. The man leading that team will hold the document and sell it to the highest bidder once he finds out what it means, becoming a billionaire overnight. He will leave no one alive, not even his own men." As Marks said this, he was wondering what Erik had already discovered about the DHS agents he had left in the house.

"I still don't see how I can be of help. The photos are the only information I have of connecting what you have told me and what I know. I'd like to help, but, honestly, I've told you everything."

Marks jumped to his feet again. "Even if you don't know anything, I need your shooting skills to protect me and my team until we can find and secure the document. The man coming is going to know more than both of us together by the time he gets here and he is going to kill all of us, the owner of the farmhouse, anyone you or I talked to or called in the last two days and anyone connected to this search, including Mr. Traugott, once he has the satchel. I know this man better than anyone in the whole fucking world!" He dropped back down into the chair as if he was already defeated.

Neither spoke for a few minutes. Nick looked at the driver and could plainly see in his eyes he was begging Nick for his help as well. "Your employer is Albert Traugott?"

"James Traugott II, his brother's grandson", Marks said. "Albert Traugott died about ten years ago and James stepped up to take over his business. It was a natural progression. I've worked for the Traugotts for around twenty years now."

"There was a pregnant woman in one of the photographs. The baby she was carrying would be James?"

"James's mother abandoned him when he was five. Albert brought him home to live with him."

"Did Albert Traugott ever confide in you on what happened to Rayfield?"

"Regardless of what you may have heard, they were best of friends. The night Rayfield was shot, he was trying to save Albert's life. He was hit by a bullet fragment that lodged in his spine. They were running for their lives, but Albert got him to a hospital as quickly as possible. Unfortunately, the hospital did not have the proper equipment and the doctor who performed the operation had little experience. He ended up paralyzing Rayfield."

"How badly?"

"Almost completely. He could move his head to eat and chew, but that was about the extent of it. Mr. Traugott hid Alexander until he was well enough to travel, then they both flew back to Australia where Mr. Traugott thought he could get better treatment for Alexander. However, Alexander caught pneumonia during the flight and died about ten days later. Albert was devastated."

"All right, I'll do whatever you need. I have the photos in my car. Maybe if you look at them they will give you some clues. In my gear I only have a handgun, that won't help much. I'm going to need a long range sniper rifle, but that will mean I have to go back to DHS, not what I want to do right now."

"Please go with Victor and get the photos. I have the necessary equipment you will require so you will not need to travel back to your headquarters."

Nick pushed himself out of the chair and started towards the front door, but turned at the last moment when he saw the phone. "I need to make a call first if these phones are working. I want to let Manny know about her father, then we can get on with our business."

Marks put his hand on the receiver, blocking Nick from picking up. "Who is Manny?"

Nick pushed Marks' hand away as he picked up the receiver. "Manny Rayfield, the woman at the farmhouse and Rayfield's daughter."

"I told you I knew where you pulled off that night. I did a search of all the people living within three miles of the area, but didn't have time to do any title searches, which now I wished I had. The only mail registry for that farmhouse is a 'Madeline Harrison'."

"Ok, so Manny is short for Madeline, but I don't know where you got Harrison from." Nick put the phone to his ear and punched in the first three digits.

"If she is one and the same, did you know your *'Manny'* is a U.S. Marshal, actually one of your most decorated marshals?" Marks jaw tightened as he watched Nick hesitate, then return the phone to its cradle.

Chapter 16

The plane caught a tailwind and arrived sooner than scheduled by forty-five minutes. Erik was pleased that he would now have almost five extra hours that Marks had not anticipated him being there. It would allow him the time to research additional information alone before having to meet up with his assistants. He would be able to learn what Marks had already discovered and possibly more on what was so important in the satchel that warranted the extra compensation Traugott had been willing to pay without giving it much thought.

As the plane touched down, his phone vibrated once again and he flipped open the screen. There were several text messages with the subject heading 'SM Messages' that contained audio links to phone calls received and made by Simon Marks. The technicians once again had done their jobs as he expected and had compressed and digitized the recordings for transfer. He inserted his earpiece and began playing each one as the plane taxied down the runway, heading towards the inbound gate.

The final recording of Baker and West began to play as the plane rolled to a stop and the passengers stood. Sitting across from him midway through the flight was a very large man who had been moved from Coach to First Class after a scuffle. The man had failed to purchase two required seats because of his girth and started a confrontation with another man whom he was sitting near. When the large man reached over another passenger to grab the man he was arguing with, a sky marshal stepped in, placed him in handcuffs and escorted him to the front of the plane where he was told he would be questioned and possibly arrested by the airport police once the plane landed.

Erik was already standing in the aisle when the large man stood, knocking him backwards, and the phone from his grip. Erik reached out with both hands and shoved the man forward. As he reached down to retrieve the phone, the man stepped towards him and purposely tried to stomp on the phone. Erik was just able to grab it and pull his hand away as the foot came down and scraped one of his knuckles. Aware of the sky marshal sitting next to the man, Erik restrained himself from kicking out and shattering the man's kneecap. Instead, he stood and directly faced the man who was smiling back at him.

"Fuck you for pushing me. Don't ever push me," the man said. Erik continued staring at the man, capturing a mental image of the man's features, hair and eye color, complexion and facial structure. After a moment, the man turned back towards the sky marshal and Erik saw the man's plane ticket sticking out of his rear pocket. He reached down and with one swift motion slipped it out and stuck it in the side pocket of his bag. He would not forget this encounter. For the time being, however, he would have to concentrate on the name Nicolas West and what information his technicians could find before meeting up with Marks.

As he exited the aircraft, he texted his request to the lead technician as he followed the fat man and sky marshal down the ramp toward the terminal. Just ahead, Erik could see several airport police standing by the doorway, so he reached into his coat pocket and slipped a pair of aviator sunglasses out. Although he knew the glasses were out of style, the size of the rims would help conceal a larger portion of his face that the ceiling cameras would capture as he walked past.

A large black sedan was waiting for him as he left the airport terminal. Walking around to the driver's side, he looked in all directions to see if he was being followed before sliding in behind the wheel as the attendant held the door open for him. Once seated, he plugged in the cell phone and spoke the command for the directions to his hotel. The onboard GPS system quickly displayed the information and a female's voice greeted him by his alias, then began to verbalize the current road name and position. He followed her instructions and was on his way out of the airport towards his hotel within a matter of minutes.

Driving down the interstate, he was mentally replaying the Baker and West conversation as a series of questions began to form. From the conversation, West had initiated the request to track down the car registration and ownership. He had also asked Baker to keep it out of the mainstream search so no one else was aware of what was going on. Why would he do that? Did he already know the location of the car or have something that did? Who was West, anyway, and what information did he already have? Did he know what was in the satchel?

He knew Marks would have already found West and obtained whatever information he could from him. The question of whether he had left West alive afterwards was now valid since he had left two survivors already. In the distant background he heard a female voice telling him he had missed his turnoff and would need to exit at the next ramp and reverse his direction. Angry at himself for having missed the departure ramp, he re-established his thoughts, concentrating on just getting to the hotel and following up with the technicians. Having turned around, he saw the large sign ahead with the hotel's name. Pulling into the valet circle, his phone once again rang and he saw that the call was the one he had been waiting for, West's information.

After being handed a ticket from the valet, he grabbed one bag and headed into the lobby where he found a secluded area and flipped open the phone cover. Pressing the required series of buttons to retrieve his calls, he selected the last message and began reading the screen showing the first document with West's biography, family members and acquaintances along with addresses and phone numbers of all.

The second document listed West's current employment and position, contacts, make and model of the car he drove, registration and work schedule. On the second page was the recorded GPS coordinates from his car for the last 7 days, which the technicians had been able to retrieve as easily as Marks. In addition, the technicians had also included the exact road name, the time the GPS was activated and what building structures were in the immediate vicinity of those coordinates.

Looking through the list, he noted that almost all were the coordinates of either DHS or an apartment complex where he was currently living. Others were for two restaurants, a movie theater, a grocery store and gas station, all within a twenty-one mile radius of where he lived. Reading further down he saw four coordinates that caught his interest. One was for a location one hundred and twenty eight miles from DHS and the other was two hundred and forty seven. The third was seventeen miles from the most distant location and the last was one hundred and forty-two miles south of that same location.

Checking the time stamps, he could see that West had arrived outside of Richmond two nights ago and did not reactivate the GPS until the following morning, which meant he had spent the night. Early the next morning, he made an hour and forty-five minute round trip traveling north seventeen miles, then returning to the previous coordinates. At nine forty-seven AM, he left, heading south, then turned around and drove nearly one hundred and fifty miles back towards Richmond an hour later. The last coordinates were for a restaurant and bar where he stayed only seven minutes. Why would he travel that distance and stay for only seven minutes? It had to be for a meeting, but with whom?

He switched off the phone without checking the rest of the information and proceeded to the front desk to check in. Upon giving his registered name, he was told the suite was currently being cleaned and would be available within the hour. He thanked the concierge and said he would be back shortly. Heading towards the dining room, he requested a table further in the back that would allow for some privacy.

Opening his bag, he extracted the small computer and laid it in front of him. Once he had placed his order and the waiter left, he began searching on the name Nicolas West to see if he could obtain any additional information the technicians had not found yet. Returning nothing new, he typed in the different names from the contact list he had been provided. When that returned nothing useful, he decided to look at the different places West had visited in the last week, beginning with the location of where he had stayed overnight.

Opening his phone once again, he read through the message and found the listing. Reading across, it listed an address and he ran a search. Displaying the name, address and driving instructions to the address, he highlighted the name 'Madeline Harrison' and pressed 'Enter'.

Chapter 17

Nick looked at Marks in disbelief. "What do you know about her? Do you think she's legit about Rayfield being her father and not knowing anything about the car before I showed up?"

"I wasn't able to do a complete background check or family history other than a quick search on her name. All that came up under Harrison was her service in the agency and accommodations. It said she retired a couple of years ago to move back home to take care of an ailing parent. Had anything mentioned the name Rayfield, I would have dug deeper."

"We're going to need to go back and talk to her, get some answers and see if this is in any way connected to her prior job. I don't like being taken advantage of if that's how she played this once she found out I was with DHS and had resources that could possibly help her."

Marks held up a hand. "No way, at least not now. Did you forget we are about to become targets ourselves? You don't have your rifle and I am sure you are not familiar with mine. You're going to need to fire some rounds, see how she handles, the way she pulls and feels in your hands."

"If I can get within fourteen to fifteen hundred meters, I should be OK. I've been trained to use a large selection of long rifles."

"At fourteen hundred meters, Erik can decide which eyeball to place a round through. At fifteen hundred, he'll simply take off the top of your head. If you want to live, stay out of the two thousand meter range."

A shiver went up Nick's spine, one that he had not felt since the night he watched three SEALs go down in an extraction that had gone bad. They were in the process of searching a terrorist when his comrade triggered an explosive device concealed underneath his clothing. A small amount of C4 had been bubble wrapped around one of his legs and on detonation, blew thousands of small ball bearings contained within the wrapping, outward in the direction of where the SEALs were standing. Nick had just stepped behind the terrorist to frisk his backside when the blast occurred and the terrorist received the full impact of the round pellet shrapnel meant for him. His men were shredded before his eyes.

Because of the building structures around New York, Nick had not needed to practice at any range greater than twelve hundred meters from the day he joined the force, and it had been a long time since a situation required those skills. With a greater the distance, a shooter had many more difficult factors to take into consideration. Wind velocity, rotation of the Earth, angle, drop ratio, MOA, humidity, was the target stationary or moving? Very few men could guarantee a kill shot at a distance of over 2000 meters. A hit, 'yes', but a guarantee would be almost impossible.

"You said you had all the equipment I would need. What kind of rifle and ammo do you have?" Nick knew he would not have anything available to him from DHS with that kind of range. The weaponry was there, he just didn't have access without getting proper authority and giving one hell of a reason for needing it.

"It's a McMillan Tac-50, fitted with a Nightforce NXS 8–32x56 mil-dot telescopic sight, with Duplex crosshairs. It's in my car, but you will need to get acquainted, as it was custom built to my specifications and reach. It can only be used with a bipod. There's no need to change out any butt stock rubber spacers since it's got a pretty good dual chamber muzzle brake to reduce recoil. There are other modifications, but it's not necessary you know about those."

Nick had never used the rifle, but knew of several Canadian snipers who had. "What's the effective range?"

"Right at 2,000 meters, but it's made kills further than that. This estate has a meadow with a clearing that will be suitable, but you only have a range distance of about sixteen hundred meters to become acquainted. In order to give us any kind of chance, you will eventually have to shoot outside the eighteen hundred meter range, so you must become dead-on with your shot. I did not foresee this situation and only carried with me a couple five round magazines. At most, you will have to sight-in using no more than four rounds. That will leave you half a dozen rounds to take him down."

"All right," said Nick. "I'll get the photos, then we can head down to the meadow. Is there a chance anyone will be able to hear us?"

"I've been in this business a long time, Mr. West, because no one has ever seen or heard me coming or going. There is a suppressor on every weapon I use. You will not need to worry."

Nick nodded, then headed out the door towards his car. A few minutes later he returned and handed Marks a folder containing the photos. Marks opened the folder across the small table in front of him and began looking and turning over each image as he viewed them. Nick waited, watching. With three photos to go, Marks hesitated, then picked up one, turning it around for Nick to see.

Marks looked at Nick and said, "Do you know who any of these men are?"

"I only know who Traugott is because of Manny. The rest she had no idea."

Marks pointed to another man just visible standing beside a Ford car. "This man was a long time trusted friend of Mr. Rayfield and was employed by the Treasury at one time. He was in charge of running the fleet of cars used by them. The man was meticulous with those cars and thought the world of Alexander. Traugott talked a lot about him and showed me other pictures, but never told me his name."

"What are you thinking?"

"You said Mr. Rayfield's car was returned to his home or farmhouse a couple of nights after he disappeared, right? How much of the car did you check, Mr. West?"

"I told you. I only checked out the engine and trunk compartments. I looked through the windows at the front and back seats, but there was nothing visible. At the time, I didn't realize I was looking for anything important."

Nick could see Marks was getting excited. "We need to get back and check inside the wheel covers now. I think we are going to find our answer to where the satchel is!"

"What? Why?" Nick was shuffling the photos back into the folder and trailing behind Marks as they went through the foyer.

Marks stopped and spun around facing Nick. "Years ago, mechanics used to put the bill inside the hubcaps after working on a car so it wouldn't be lost transporting it for delivery. You said the car was dropped off at the farmhouse secretly during the night and Mrs. Rayfield never drove it after that."

Nick could see where Marks was heading. "That's what Manny said."

"My guess is that if the man in this photograph was able to find Rayfield after they escaped, Rayfield would have turned over the satchel to him for safekeeping because of his injury and that man used this old habit to leave a note in the hubcap as to where the satchel could be found. He probably figured Rayfield would be back later or someone from the Treasury would figure it out."

Nick recalled the files Baker had sent him and remembered them saying that someone had followed the men in their getaway, driving Rayfield's car. "There's only one way to find out. Let's go."

Chapter 18

Emily looked out the window and saw the red Mercedes approaching up the driveway followed closely by an SUV. Fifty yards from the farmhouse, they separated and she counted four men in all, two in each vehicle. The Mercedes continued towards the farmhouse, but the SUV began to slow and drive around towards the side. She had been expecting Manny's return from the grocery store before the men arrived. Now she would have to entertain them herself for the time being.

Manny had told her there would be two men arriving to begin the foreclosing procedures, so it caught her by surprise there were more. Perhaps Manny was misinformed and the extra men were required for processing the inventory of their belongings or they were simply witnesses who needed to be there, as well. She looked around the room to make sure everything looked in its place and waited for the knock at the door.

When the Mercedes came to a stop, the two men inside exchanged words for a few moments, then Erik stepped from the passenger side door. He briefly peered at the house and surroundings, giving the other men time to place themselves around the exits and to make sure there were no occupants outside the house or in the barn. He wanted to make this quick, get the information he needed and be on his way. He nodded to the driver and he pulled away to join the others out of sight.

Satisfied enough time had passed, he proceeded to the porch and front door. Finding no doorbell, he rapped, then stepped back, waiting. After a moment, the door opened and he saw the woman he had viewed in the photos from the U.S. Marshal's employment records. "Mrs. Harrison, it is a pleasure to meet you. My name is John Michaels. May I come in?"

"Manny isn't here just yet, but yes, please come in and I will get us something to drink. Will the other men be joining us soon?"

Erik stepped inside and walked with Emily towards the living room. He then stood looking at the woman in silence trying to understand what she had meant. "You aren't Madeline Harrison? I thought she lived at this address."

"I'm her sister, Emily. Manny should be here soon. She appears to be running a few minutes late. We have gone ahead and pulled all the documents you requested, signed the transfer papers and put them back in order as best as we can."

Documents? Why would they be giving them up so easily and why was a transfer needed? He would take what he wanted as he always did. There was never any other option. Erik looked at the woman and asked, "What documents are you referring to and who requested them from you that you would need to sign papers?" He wondered if Marks had already contacted the woman and she had mistaken their identities.

Emily was now beginning to feel uncomfortable as the other men had not yet joined them and she could no longer see the vehicles parked outside. "Aren't you from the bank to begin the foreclosure?"

"No, I am not. I'm here to see Mrs. Harrison, your sister, as you say." Erik knew Manny's mother had died seven months earlier of cancer, so he had not expected any other persons in the house except Manny when he had arrived, let alone another sibling who looked just like her. "When do you expect her?"

"If you're not from the bank, then I think it is best if you leave and come back when Manny is here." Emily began to stand, but the man reached out and grabbed her by the wrist, pulling her back down onto the couch.

"We are going to stay until your sister arrives, then I have some questions you two will answer. There was a man here the other night that has something I am after and I intend to get it from him. I assume that she knows where he is and what he has!"

"Are you talking about the man who developed those pictures for Manny? She tells me she never met him before that night, that she only let him stay because of the heavy rains."

"What pictures are you talking about?"

"If you will let me go into the next room, I'll get them for you. The man let us keep the ones of our father and a couple others."

Erik stood and motioned for the woman to get up. "I'll go with you."

As they entered the den, Emily stopped inside the doorway and pointed to the stack of photos on the desk. "They are right there." When the man started walking towards the desk, Emily pressed herself against the wall, lowering her hands and reaching slowly around her back, feeling for Betsy. She watched as the man picked up West's business card, glimpsed at it quickly, placed it in his top pocket, then picked up the photos.

Finally her fingers found the barrel and she wrapped one hand around it, waiting for the right moment. When Erik appeared to be immersed in the photos, she stepped to her left and yanked the shotgun upwards. Her other hand had just found the stock when her brain registered the presence of the man next to her as he pushed the silencer against her temple, freezing her actions. The man reached over and took the shotgun from her grip.

Erik turned, holding the photos in one hand and the 9mm in the other, pointing it directly at her forehead. "That was extremely stupid on your part, Mrs. Harrison and I'm tired of going along with your illusion of who you say you are." Placing the gun on the desk, he walked towards Emily throwing the photos at her one by one, than suddenly stopped. He was looking at the image of the men standing around the car. There was Traugott with the satchel in his hands. The car tag was clearly visible.

"Where did these photos come from?" Erik grabbed Emily by the hair, forcing her to look at the photo he was holding.

"They are from a camera found in my father's car in the barn. Mr. West found the camera in the trunk and developed the film that was inside. That's my father right there in the photo on the floor."

"Is this the car that's in your barn?"

"No, my father drove a different kind of car!"

Letting go of her hair, he reached down and snatched up the photo. "Who is your father?"

"Alexander Rayfield." As Emily spoke the name, out of the corner of her eye she saw a figure pass by the outside window, heading around the side of the farmhouse towards the kitchen. She suddenly remembered Manny and felt the panic rising in her chest. She wanted to scream, to tell Manny to run, but she knew Manny would do just the opposite and bolt headlong into the room.

"I know why you're here. Let my sister go and I will get it for you, please!" Emily was in tears, pointing towards the back door, pleading as Manny walked into the kitchen calling her name and apologizing for being late.

The man standing behind Emily placed his hand around her mouth and pulled her further into the room. He held the gun to her head and waited. As Manny entered the room she caught sight of Emily and the gunman, freezing in her tracks. Erik noted there was no sign of any panic in her motions and knew instantly that Emily had been telling the truth. He was now looking at the real Manny, understanding why he had mistaken her identity. They looked exactly alike.

"Mrs. Harrison, please do not make any attempt to save your sister. We aren't here to hurt you, so it would be wise of both of you to stay calm. Your sister was telling me she knew why I was here, so Emily, please go on, why am I here?" Erik stepped closer to Emily, stopping only inches away from her face.

"I lied. I don't know what you're after. I only said that so you wouldn't shoot my sister when she came in the door."

Erik stepped back, suddenly reaching back and slapping Emily so hard that her body tore loose from the man's grip and she fell to the floor unconscious.

Manny stepped in between the man and her sister, looking directly at Erik. "You're looking for a leather case with some kind of papers in it. It's very old. It was given to my mother right after my father disappeared!" She then turned and charged at the man with the gun, pushing him aside and kneeling down next to Emily. "I'll get it for you, but you let her go first, completely away from here or you might as well kill us both!"

"It's here in the house, now?" Erik couldn't believe what he was hearing and began looking around frantically hoping to see it sitting right out in front of him as if by some miracle it would be that easy.

"Yes, but you let her go first, then I'll get it for you."

"You get it for me now and I won't kill her in front of you, do you understand?" Erik turned his head towards the gunman and the man once again took aim at Emily. "I will give you two minutes, no more." Pointing to his associate, Erik told him to accompany her and make sure they came back quickly.

Manny looked down at Emily and could see she was beginning to move. The movements were slow, but they were steady and Manny knew at least she had not broken any bones. She was thankful Emily remained unconscious, though. If she did not figure out something quickly, the man would kill them, but at least Emily would never feel any pain.

"When you have what you want, you make sure we are together in our last moments, that is all I ask." Manny stood, trying to engage the man in a conversation while her eyes roamed the room looking for some answer that would allow her any chance of avoiding what she knew was coming. She had to stall these men as long as possible.

"I am glad you see the situation for what it is. I know your past experience has brought you to this conclusion. It's not part of the job that I enjoy, at least not always, but it is a necessity. Please get the bag and I'll be on my way after I have concluded my business. I promise to kill you as you have asked."

Erik actually did enjoy this part of his job. Over the years he had come to love looking into the eyes of his victim, watching the fear mount, listening to them pray to their God for forgiveness for all of the sin they had done on Earth, begging Erik that he be merciful to them and always for their family knowing they too would be included in the contract. They would willingly give all their riches to him if he would spare their life just this one time. He waited for the moment when they completely broke down, sobbing and speaking unrecognizable words, than he simply pulled the trigger and walked away. The elation he felt was immeasurable.

On the desk in the right corner she saw it, the handle pointing outward where he had laid it down. She closed her eyes, trying to visualize the distances between the desk, Erik, and the man standing behind her. Could she cross that distance, get the gun and have time to fire before either one of them shot back? The man who had held Emily already had his gun drawn, so she would have to fire at him first, then Erik.

"Get it now," said Erik, jolting her out of her thoughts. "Your time started twenty seconds ago, so stop standing there, go now!"

Manny started back through the kitchen, opened one of the drawers, extracted a small key, then walked towards her mother's bedroom. She had not been in the room since her death, but knew it was the only way she could get to the case that was locked away in a compartment of the closet. Crossing the room, she opened the closet door and inserted the key into the hidden lock. Reaching far back into the opening, she felt the leather strap of the case and pulled it out, showing the bag to the man, then headed back towards the den.

As Manny handed Erik the bag she said, "Please keep your promise and do not wake her. Shoot me first, then her. That way neither of has to see the other die."

Erik lowered his head for a moment then instructed the man to do as she asked. The man slid his weapon back into his holster to reach down, pick up Emily and carry her into the next room, not realizing his mistake. Manny saw her chance now as neither man was armed. With her weight moving forward, she struck Erik in the throat with a closed fist and bounded for the gun on the desk, praying the safety was not on. As Erik fell backwards, he twisted his body and reached for Manny's foot, catching only her toes, but it was enough.

Manny fell forward onto the coffee table, but was able to grasp the gun as she went down. Spinning with her arms out, she fired two rounds backwards catching the gunman once in the chest, before hitting the ground. Her head hit the floor and she felt the blood begin to pour from the wound. In the background, she heard Erik screaming as another man came running across the back porch, through the kitchen. Dazed, she raised the gun towards the door and fired two more rounds as she saw him enter. Getting to her knees, she swung the gun in the direction of where Erik had been standing, but he was gone.

After a moment, she heard the cars start and made her way, crawling, to the window. As the cars passed in front of her, she took aim at the rear window of the Mercedes, but at the last moment the SUV cut in behind and blocked her view. She struggled to maintain her vision and fired the remaining rounds, shattering the back window glass. As she lost consciousness, she saw the SUV swerve, crash through the fence, then pull back onto the road.

Chapter 19

Erik looked into his rearview mirror in time to see the SUV swerve and the fence posts crack and shatter as it drove over them, trying to right itself back onto the pavement. Pressing harder on the accelerator, he headed towards the highway only a hundred yards ahead, turning a hard right once the wheels connected. He had the satchel, that's all that mattered. The hell with the men he had just lost. His intentions were to rid himself of them anyway once he possessed the documents.

Traugott told him not to look inside the bag, but he never listened to anyone other than himself. He would drive back to the hotel, open the case and find out what he had been paid one million dollars to obtain. Whatever it was, he knew its value was ten-fold, maybe even a hundred. Once he located the right buyer, he could disappear forever and not worry about ever being found. The new surgery would hide his identity once again, he would be free to pursue whatever he wanted, with whomever he wanted and could erase his past without a trace. He would now be able to kill for the fun of the sport, picking and eliminating his own chosen quarry. Traugott would be the first on his list.

Manny awoke with a jolt, her muscles aching and her vision still blurred. Trying to turn her head, an incredible pain shot through her neck and she winced, only succeeding in making it worse and she groaned. Suddenly she felt a warm hand touch her forearm, then a voice she had heard before, but could not place. Her body stiffened at the thought that the men had returned to finish their assignment. Shutting her eyes, she waited for it to be done and over. The voice returned. This time she knew who it belonged to, opened her eyes and slowly moved them in the direction of the sound.

"Don't try to move, Manny, you have a concussion and possibly a ruptured vertebra." Relieved that she was now awake, Nick tried putting some humor into the situation and said, "I'm guessing this is your handiwork, it would have been nice if you had left us someone alive to question." He chuckled but could see that Manny didn't appreciate his attempt. "Emily is fine. She's resting, but her face is swollen. From the size of the mark, it looks like someone hit her pretty hard."

"He got away." Manny's eyes moved towards the window as she began to recall the events. "Emily thought it was the bank, so she let them in. If I hadn't stopped by the flower market, I would have been here on time before they arrived." Her eyes began to water and she tried blinking away the tears.

"I told you, she's fine, all she needs is some rest. It is you we have to worry about. Can you answer some questions?"

Manny started to shake her head yes, but felt the pain return. "Yes, it's OK, but why are you back here? I thought you left to spend a few days with your wife or do the research for us later."

"What, and miss this?" Nick instantly regretted the comment. "What we found in that camera has a lot of people very nervous. When I sent that request to find out more on what your father was working on, starting with the car tag, it triggered a lot of deadly responses that no one could have imagined."

"What, on a theory that there are old accounts worth millions? Those accounts have been frozen for decades and the bank won't open them without proper ID and the original documents. The people that are owed that money are probably all long gone and dead by now. Hell, even our own government can't claim ownership because they belong to foreign citizens, even though the gains were made on American soil." Manny was beginning to sit up, ignoring the pain. She had endured much worse from past experiences.

"They're not after the money. There's something else that can potentially cause a lot of problems for the United States. What do you know about a document called the 'Declaration of Surrender'?"

Manny stared at Nick for over a minute. "That document is real? It's in there with the other paper accounts? Shit, Nick!"

Nick was now convinced this woman was not who she said she was and that he had been made a fool. She had refused to tell him who she was and hid knowledge that she clearly had on a very important piece of the puzzle. "Obviously you know much more than you lead me to believe. I think you're still with the U.S. Marshal's office trying to find the satchel, hoping to avoid a catastrophe we're all heading for once and if it is found by someone else, Mrs. Harrison, not Rayfield."

"The only thing you have right is I am Mrs. Harrison. It's my married name. My husband left me two years ago while I was trying to take care of my dying mother. He had gotten to the point of where he could no longer touch me or stomach the sight of my scars from the surgery after I was shot. He couldn't take my mother's screams in the middle of the night when the morphine wasn't working. In the last month of her life, she constantly called my father's name. It was too much for him so he emptied our accounts and just left. My real name is Madeline Rayfield, my father was Alexander Rayfield!"

Simon stepped forward, looking at Nick. "I told you, her file showed she retired a few years ago and came here to take care of one of her parents."

For the first time, Manny saw the other man and let her eyes settle on his face. "Who are you? You look familiar. And what the hell business is it of yours, snooping through my file?"

"That's not important, Manny, we need to figure out what you do know and what happened here." Nick stuck out his hand and waved Simon back.

Annoyed that he was being pushed to the side, Simon turned and headed towards the barn. "I'm going to check on what we discussed earlier, I'll be back as soon as I can."

Once Simon was gone, Nick began questioning Manny again. "Why did your sister let them in? You said she thought they were from the bank. Why?"

"I told you before, it's my problem."

"Your problem?" Nick was enraged. "Three days ago I didn't know you even existed. Now I have some psycho killer on my ass thinking I have something he wants. Not only will he kill me, he's going to kill anybody even remotely associated with this mess. It's more than just your problem, lady! You know what, the hell with you, you're on your own!" Nick knew he did not mean it, but the words just came out. He stood there unable to move or know what to say next.

"Foreclosure. The bank is here to foreclose on the farmhouse. Mom didn't have much insurance. Her policy had little medical coverage. I had to put the farmhouse up as collateral to cover the doctor and hospital bills."

"How much do you owe? Won't the hospital make some other kind of arrangement with you?"

"Do you have any idea how long it would take for me to pay back eight hundred thousand dollars on my retirement income? No, this is the only way. Emily and I will figure it all out later. We've got another week or so before the final papers have to be signed and we have to leave. Today was just to start the process. So, what else do you want to know?"

"Did any of your work have anything to do with this? I want to believe everything you're saying, but you need to convince me you really are who you say you are."

"Emily and I really are his daughters. When I finally accepted he wasn't coming back, I joined the U.S. Marshals. Mom thought it would be better for me because I wouldn't be measured against him and wouldn't have to subject myself to constant questioning. Worked for them for almost 40 years until I was forced to retire for medical reasons. We didn't do the kind of work you do, but there certainly was a lot of investigative work required in order to find our person of interest. I preferred to be in the field and after a while the promotions stopped being offered because I kept turning them down."

"How did you know about the 'Declaration of Surrender'?"

"We received constant memos and notifications every day, issued by every government office there was at the time. Sometimes they came from unknown outside sources we couldn't identify. One day I got the memo about the 'Declaration' and thought it was some kind of joke. I read it a couple of times, then tossed it without showing it to anyone."

"Well, apparently the document was very real because the team who did the research for me, are being threatened, and are about to be arrested for treason by the U.S. government. Those same charges may be leveled against me. I thought it was the importance of the car, but it's not and all along I couldn't imagine it was because of a couple million dollars lying in some Swiss accounts."

"You gave that man the satchel, Manny. Why did you do that?" Emily was now standing in the doorway, bracing herself against the frame. "I looked and saw the drawer open."

Manny was shocked by her sister's appearance and could see the swelling was worse than what she thought Nick had described.

Nick turned back from Emily to Manny. "Who did you give the satchel to? You had it all this time?"

"It wasn't the satchel you think it is, it was my father's attaché case he carried when he worked for the Treasury. I was trying to save our lives. It was the only thing I could think to do until I figured something else out. I was trying to stall as long as possible."

"He asked for the satchel specifically. That's all he wanted, there wasn't anything else?"

"No, but I figured that's what he was after by the way he was looking at the photo you left and the way he was pointing at the satchel in it. I saw him screaming at Emily from outside the window before I came in. I already knew what I was walking into because I could see the other two men in the barn. It wasn't easy staying calm and not doing anything, but I was thinking of Emily."

"So you really don't know any more than what you're telling me? No idea where the case is, how your father's car got here that night, who you gave your father's case to, nothing, absolutely nothing?"

Manny started to say "No," when they heard the name 'Joe'. Emily had spoken the name 'Joe' and they both looked at her. She was lost in deep thought, searching and finding a memory from long ago that had hidden itself until now.

"It was Joe." Emily was slowly moving her head back and forwards, confirming that the memory of that night had not been a dream she had believed it to be, all along.

"What are you talking about, Emily, who's Joe, the man I gave the case to?"

"The man who brought the car home that night. I couldn't sleep because Mom was arguing with him, so I got up and watched them out my bedroom door. Mom was crying and he was trying to give her something, but she wouldn't take it. He finally left, saying he would keep it safe until Dad was better. I saw him stop by Dad's car. Right after that he was gone."

"Could you see what he was trying to give her or recognize who Joe was?"

"His back was to me and I could only see Mom. That's how I knew she was crying. I just remember calling him Mr. Joe because he was Dad's friend. There was some kind of belt hanging down from what he was trying to give Mom."

Nick could see Manny recalling the man, as well. "Yes I remember him too, his name..."

"Joe Bellows was his name." Marks was standing holding a musty sheet of paper in his hand from where he had just come in from the barn. "It was in the driver's side hub. It's not a bill, Nick, it's a note written on a receipt from a place called Bellow's Garage. Joe Bellow was the proprietor. The garage was established in 1937."

"What does it say, Marks?" Nick walked around behind Simon so he could read it himself.

"I don't know what it means, but it says, '*All will be safe in the wall. Got Everything Through Today and Yesterday*'".

A minute or two passed before Simon folded the paper, handing it to Nick, then turned to Manny and Emily. "The man that was here today, can you describe him?"

Although Manny had retired, her skills at observation were still as sharp as they had ever been. "He was six foot two, weighed about one ninety, graying but originally blond hair with hazel blue eyes that had a tint of green around the iris. Probably in his late forties, early fifties and spoke with a clipped accent. Do you know anyone like that?"

"I'm afraid I do and he's early. I thought we had more time so we're going to have to get going and find this garage before he finds out about it. At some point, the technicians at his disposal are going to turn up this information too and I'd rather we get there first."

"We'll probably have a good head start because it will take him some time to find out he has the wrong satchel."

"What satchel are you talking about, Nick?"

"The one Manny gave him. That's right, you weren't here for that part of the conversation."

Simon's expression became surreal. "Once Erik discovers he has the wrong one, he will be back. He knows Manny knows about the real one, but he doesn't have any idea yet that we have arrived, as well. Either we all have to leave now or stay and wait."

Nick looked at the girls, then back to Simon. "Emily and Manny's injuries aren't going to allow that. Manny has a concussion and Emily can hardly stand. We've got no choice but to stay and come up with a plan."

"You're the only one who can shoot, Nick. If he gets you, and the probability of that is very real, we won't stand a chance. Hell, he could torch the place and pick us off one by one as we ran out. No, we need to leave, all of us."

"You look afraid, Simon. I expected more from someone who has been in your business this long."

"Afraid? No, I'm not afraid, but I know what this man is going to do to these women and you if we can't stop him. Whatever pain you think you can imagine will be just the beginning."

Nick looked at each of the other three, than fixed his stare on Simon. "You say you know this man. Then you have a good perspective on what actions he will take, what plans he might formulate. If we can figure that out and stay one step ahead, then we should be able to stop him."

"I knew him years ago. His tactics will have changed. He will certainly be a different man. The only thing that will not have changed is his revengeful nature. If you don't kill him immediately, he will kill you and the rest of us without mercy. He may take you out quickly, but the rest of us he will toy with until he's ready."

Emily spoke up. "I've always heard a leopard can't change its spots."

Simon smiled. "No he can't, but in time, all of nature eventually changes in order to survive. He will have learned other ways of killing his prey and it does scare the hell out of me not knowing what they are."

Chapter 20

The drive back to the hotel took just over an hour. Erik pulled into the valet line but saw three cars ahead of him and decided instead to park in the first open spot. Painted in the space was a handicap emblem, but he didn't care. Exiting the car, Erik saw the attendant motioning for him to get back in the car and pull out. He ignored the request, grabbed the bag and waited for the attendant to get closer. When the attendant was only a few feet away, Erik threw him the keys, identified his room number and told him to move the car himself. The attendant stepped aside for Erik to pass, not wanting to engage in a confrontation.

Reaching his room, he slid the passkey through the slot and waited for the light to turn green. It did not respond and he thought to himself that he needed to calm down. He was almost finished with his task. A phone call to Traugott and he would be on his way back home, away from this Godforsaken land. But before he left, Marks would be his final contract, a personal vendetta for which he had waited a long time.

He would contact Marks to set up the meet and offer his assistance. Afterwards, when the operation was completed and he had him within striking distance, he would cut him over and over, letting the screams echo through his ears like the greatest concerto ever heard. A bullet was not how he wanted to end Mark's life. He desperately wanted to be looking into his eyes, feeling his body go limp as the warmth poured from it and his soul went to Hell. He had spent two years learning to wield a knife so skillfully that a man never knew what happened until the pain coursed through his body and he felt the flow of blood ebbing from the wounds. He could kill a man in a fraction of a second or let it take hours if he wanted. For Simon, he hoped it would last an eternity.

On his second try, the passkey light turned green and he quickly opened and shut the door behind him, locking each latch carefully and placing the chain in the groove and sliding it down its track. Eying the room, he walked across and placed the case on the floor next to the bed and sat down. Today's events had cost him his team, but at least he had obtained the case and the documents. Anger engulfed him and he yanked the case handle upwards and threw it onto the bed.

Traugott had told him not to open the case and look for himself. He would give the instructions on what to look for. Doing otherwise would cost him his compensation. Rage coursed through him. He let no man or woman control him, but knew he must make an exception this one time.

By the second ring, Traugott's assistant had identified the series of tones and patched the call directly. "I have the case and have not opened it, as you requested. Tell me what I am looking for and I will verify if it exists after we have renegotiated my fee."

"We have already agreed on the price and as far as I am concerned, I have been more than generous. You will honor that agreement and tell me if the document is in there. For your own good, I would not try and blackmail me, Mr. Fenstermacher. Now let's proceed."

Erik weighed his comments but decided to press on since he was the one holding the case. "All of my men died trying to recover this case. I barely made it out myself. I recovered it without any help from someone who has failed you. However, I was not able eliminate several witnesses so I will have to lie low for a year or so before I am useful to you or anyone else. I want an additional ten million. Whatever you want from this case, I am sure it will be well worth it to you."

Traugott thought about the accounts and what the document could bring on the open market if the United States was not willing to come to an agreement. With the ledgers, he could purge the accounts of all monies, easily reimbursing Erik on his new demand. "Open the case, Mr. Fenstermacher, and tell me if you find a document titled 'Declaration of Surrender'. Do not look at anything else for the time being. If it is there, read down and tell me the name to whom the second to the last signature belongs, on the last page."

"Do we have a deal or not? I can easily find a buyer, now that you have told me what I'm looking for. I think ten million is an insignificant request on my part, don't you agree?"

Traugott sighed, knowing he had been outmaneuvered by a man much more foolish than he. "We have a deal, but you have made a grave error that will cost you somewhere in the future."

Erik held the phone in place with his shoulder as he began to loosen the center strap, pulling it back from the buckle, then rolling the cover flap over. Inserting both hands, he popped the sides open so he could see inside. Fingering the pages one by one, he read through each heading until finally, there it was, the 'Declaration of Surrender'.

"I have it. Just a second and I'll read you the name." Erik flipped the last page over, then quickly turned the entire document over again and started looking through it page by page. Panicking, he reached in and pulled them all out, hoping the signature page had detached itself and was there amongst the other documents.

"Mr. Fenstermacher, what is taking so long. What signatures are on the last page? Just read them all to me."

Erik needed to buy time. "Tell me who I am looking for and I'll verify it is listed. I can't read these signatures."

"Do you really think I am that foolish? If I provide the name, all you will have to do is simply say 'Yes' and repeat it back to me. The signature is very clear, legible enough that even an eight year old could read it. If you can not read it, I suggest you get out of your business right now."

He was caught and would have to come clean. "There's no signature page. It's a document about the 'Declaration', nothing else." Erik threw the pages across the room.

"I am assuming that there are no account ledgers either?"

"No. There's just a bunch of notes and hand written pages. There are a few typed documents, but that's it."

"Your men died for a bunch of hand written notes and you positioned yourself to extort another ten million dollars from me for them. You left witnesses Mr. Fenstermacher and you have nothing useful for me. I am rescinding my original payment now, as we speak, and can assure you that in the next 48 hours, you will be of no use to anyone as well. Goodbye, Mr. Fenstermacher."

Erik let the phone drop to the floor as he stood there in silence, disbelieving how only a few short seconds could change a man's destiny. In the time it took to take a breath, he went from having all of his desires granted to counting his final hours. He would find Marks and make what was left of those hours his final act. It was time to call and let him know he had arrived. Maybe he would be lucky and everything would fall into place. Perhaps Simon already had the case and the mess could be straightened out as if nothing had happened since the moment he had touched down at the airport.

When Marks' phone rang, he did not recognize the caller ID, but knew it had to be Erik. In his business, every contact number was verified and recorded with complete accuracy, because one simple misdialed number could easily alert others of your location and could cost you your life. He turned to West and told him of his suspicion, then connected the call.

"Erik, it has been a long time. I thought you had gone to meet your maker years ago, but obviously you have a way of eluding death. I hope to change that once this is over."

"Perhaps it is I who will end your life. Because of you, I spent years underground before I could put my skills back to use. You cost me much more than that time. You cost me my reputation, and you know what that means in our work." He waited for Marks to respond.

"You alone cost yourself whatever measure of a man you were. No one shoots an innocent child, Erik. I am humiliated that Traugott would even conceive of us working together on this or any other operation. I understand his need to claim the documents, but this is unacceptable beyond reason." Hearing Erik's voice again had brought back the hurt of a betrayal of which he thought he had finally let go.

"We have no choice, Simon. We are both professionals that have been hired to do a job. It is for both our good that we set aside our differences to team and find the package Traugott sent us for. You must be willing to accept that."

"Professional? Perhaps that was a long time ago for you. I see you ran out on your men, who are dead at my feet. We found another dead one at the wheel of his SUV after he bled out from a wound to his neck, your own man that you left behind. You have no concern for those who die protecting you and you say you're a professional?"

"We all take risks. That is what we are paid for. Those men died because they were too inexperienced for this job. That is why we must meet and work together. That is what we must do!"

Marks thought for a moment then, said, "There is no need for us to meet, as I know that you arrived hours ago, with no intent of letting me know you were here. Instead, you tried to retrieve the package on your own, for your own purposes, not Traugott's. Whatever you have to say to me I do not trust and will return it to him myself, alone."

Erik pounded his fist on the table in front of him and screamed 'No" into the phone, watching the business card fall from his pocket as he bent over. "Without us working together, you will have little hope of finding it. I have received a large amount of data from our techs, who have found the location of where the case is. We only need to meet so we can recover it together and return home. I was sent to help you because you are injured, and that is what I am going to do."

"If it were true that you had the location already, you would have returned with the package and left me to my own certain death. No, Erik, you are playing your old tricks on someone who taught you everything. I already have all the help I need. It will only be a matter of a few hours before I leave you to suffer your fate. You are desperate in some way. I can hear it in your voice."

"Who do you have better than me? A couple of old women I left for dead, huh?" Erik was panicking and knew his time was running out. He had to convince Marks to at least meet. The hell with the case, it was too late for that now, but he had to find a way, any way, no matter what, to get Simon within his grasp one more time. He reached down and picked up the card, reading the name 'West' along with his title, an address, phone number and Nick's wife's name.

"It is time to say goodbye, Erik. Should we both survive this and our paths cross in the future, we can settle this once and for all, but I doubt we will." As he began to close the phone, he heard Erik say the name 'West'. He put the phone back to his ear and said, "What do you know about West?"

"That's him, that's who you have helping you?" Erik laughed. "A Russian born assassin and a U.S. law man working together. How ironic, but pathetic, at the same time. Have you told him who you really are, Simon? Does he know you're responsible for the deaths of a lot of people or does he think you're just some courier come to fetch a package?"

"He knows who I am and why I am here. The man you are describing died twenty years ago because of you. I changed my ways in order to protect families, not take from them ever again!"

"Well, well, then, he must be there with you. Please hit your speaker button, Simon, I wish to speak to both of you. You will find this quite interesting."

Simon cupped his hand around the cell's microphone and told Nick that he would need to listen as Erik was aware he was present. Nick nodded and Simon keyed the button. "We are both listening."

"Mr. West, I've read a lot about you. You are a very impressive man, at least I thought you were until you partnered with an old friend of mine. I'm certain he has told you who he is and why he is there. However, I doubt he told you that he has butchered hundreds of men including one of your co-workers named 'Johnson', cut one finger off at a time until he told Simon everything he knew".

Nick looked at Simon and Simon offered no explanation, nor did he change his expression. It was apparent to Nick that Erik was telling the truth.

Erik let the information sink in, knowing all too well that Simon had not told him, then continued. "I need for you to convince Simon to bring me the case. Because he indicated he would be leaving in the next few hours, I would have to believe he either already has it or knows where it is. Otherwise he would have accepted my help earlier, knowing the consequences of further failure."

"Why would I possibly have any reason to convince Simon to work with you, let alone bring you the case, which we may or may not have?"

Erik had had his fun but the cat and mouse charades were over. "I am one hour closer to Atlanta than you are right now, Mr. West. Time enough for me to get to Laura and carve her to pieces before you get there. I will give you until four o'clock to bring me the case or you will only need a small box to bury your wife in." With that, Erik hung up and started for the door, leaving all belongings hanging in the closet or folded neatly in the dresser drawers. He knew he would no longer need them.

Punching in a number as quickly as he could, Nick dialed Brewster direct. When Brewster picked up, he didn't give him time to respond. "Paul, it's Nick, I need you to get a team from Atlanta to Laura's place within the next hour. They need to get her out of there now!"

"First, you tell me where the hell you have been and what's going on! I've got FBI all over this place, agents down and Baker in lockup facing twenty years for treason. McCallister is so far up my ass, only his toes are sticking out. And second, I can't because I've been relieved pending an investigation for covering your ass. I'm about to loose my damn pension. You better have one hell of an explanation for what's going on." Brewster's chest began to tighten and he was suddenly short of breath and needed to sit.

"You tell McCallister I've got Traugott's satchel. He'll know what I'm talking about. If he doesn't get a team to Laura's place now, I'm handing it over to the first jihad fanatic I can contact and let him know what he has. Millions of dollars will pour into their training camps for weapons and recruits. You tell him all charges better be dropped against Baker or I will go public with what one of our distinguished Presidents and some of our current senators' family forefathers did in the past. If he wants to be the hero in all of this, that's fine. You just tell him to get on the phone to Atlanta now!"

As he hung up, he turned back to Simon. "You better pray that satchel is at that address and we can find it. You're going to answer for Johnson, but if Erik even scratches Laura, I swear I will kill your old partner first and let you rot for the rest of your life in the worst prison I can get you transferred to."

Chapter 21

After making sure Emily and Manny would be able to take care of each other, Nick and Simon headed for the car. Pressing the trunk release, Simon reached in and smacked a section in the back of the trunk liner to open a hidden panel. A long rectangular door opened and he extracted a case, handing it to Nick. "Get familiar with the feel and the bolt action, if nothing else. Once we have the documents and get to where we are heading, you won't have the convenience of a test run. The bolt mechanism has been enhanced, so whatever you are used to won't respond the same, I promise."

Nick responded, "We're going to have to take the time later if we can. Otherwise, I'm going to have to trust in my training and reflexes." Having packed the case back in its hidden compartment, Simon slid into the passenger seat while Nick took the wheel. As they pulled out onto the road, Simon punched in the address on the GPS with his good hand and waited for a match. The satellite signals required locating and Nick cursed that it was taking so long. Finally the display showed a matched address of 'seventy-eight point two' miles away and Nick gunned the accelerator.

McCallister spoke with Brewster and placed the call to Atlanta. When the Bureau Chief was finally connected, McCallister identified himself and made the request with as much urgency as possible. "You need to get agents out to an address I am sending you now. It should be popping up on your screen at any minute. There is a woman in extreme danger that needs to be protected and extracted now. Get her to a safe location. Her name is Laura West!"

He listened as the Bureau Chief made an excuse of being short handed, but McCallister persisted. "I don't care how short handed you are, get your ass up and get out there yourself if you have to! You get this woman protected now and I'll see to it that your staff is increased. Otherwise you won't have a staff to worry about."

Agents Chavez and Pennington took the call as they were sitting down to lunch. It had been the first time that week either of them had been able to take a lengthy break and they intended to enjoy it. When Chavez answered, he replied they were at lunch and to call another team, but when he heard it was a direct request from the Chief, he looked at Pennington and told him to wrap it up, they would have to grab something already prepared and eat on the way.

They selected a few sandwiches from a glassed refrigerator, threw a ten-dollar bill on the counter and made their way across two lanes of traffic to their car. Pennington began to remove the plastic wrap from around the egg sandwich as Chavez checked the rearview mirror, then looked over his left shoulder before pulling out onto Lexington. "Just our luck, as always," said Chavez. "Say, when's the baby due, got to be any day now, huh?"

"Yeah. Peggy says she's thinking of going with an epidural instead of natural as she said she has wanted to do all along. I guess she got to talking to some of her friends and they all told her to do the drugs, she'll be happier in the long run. I told you it's a boy right?"

"Only about twenty times and stop rubbing it in. You know I have twin girls. Jesus, if I ever get them through high school, the wife and I are going to throw the biggest party you ever saw. Nothing wrong with girls, but man, I can never figure them out from one minute to the next. One minute they love you, the next they're screaming they hate your guts and slamming doors in your face."

"Brings back a whole lot of memories of my sister. I know what you mean. But hey, it works for me, gives me two built-in babysitters once the kid is here. Shit! I left my cell back at the restaurant, we've got to go back." Pennington was searching through his pockets in his coat and pants, but already knew he had forgotten to pick it up.

"We can't, we go back and we'll be late. Anything happens to the woman we are picking up and your and my careers are over. I'm not taking that chance."

"We are going to maybe lose twenty or thirty minutes, right? I need that phone. If my wife goes into labor, she won't have any way of contacting me. We've both got other agents' numbers and addresses on our phones, you know that. You want to take a chance of it falling into the wrong hands?" Pennington was almost begging.

Chavez knew he was right. The information was far more important due to national security. A few minutes one way or the other probably wouldn't matter. He could make up the time by running the siren and light if he needed to, even if it was frowned upon for that purpose. "If we're late, it's my ass, not yours because I'm senior, you understand?" He caught the next open median and reversed course.

Twenty-five minutes later they were back on the interstate, exceeding the maximum speed limit by thirty miles per hour. If any cop couldn't read their DHS tag, then Chavez would flip his badge up against the window and he hoped, stop any pursuit in its tracks. He didn't want to use the siren unless it was absolutely warranted.

Almost two and a half hours had passed since they received the initial call, as they exited the interstate. It was an additional ten-minute drive off the interstate until they turned onto a long dirt road leading to the entrance. Overhead was a wrought-iron grate reading 'West Veterinary Hospital'. To the right, posted on the fence, was a smaller sign, which read 'Only four legged kind can be assured kindness'. Behind the fence lay seventy acres of the greenest pasture and grazing land either Chavez or Pennington had ever seen, completely surrounded by a forest of trees.

Continuing the drive, each man looked left and right, taking in the sights of the large variety of animals roaming free, corralled or kept in the numerous barns for their own protection while they recuperated. "This isn't a hospital, it's Noah's freakin' Ark." Pennington was laughing at his own humor as the men pulled up to the only building that looked like a structure that a human would occupy. Chavez knocked on the door and stood back, waiting.

From behind, they heard a woman asking if she could help them, then watched as Laura stepped onto the porch heading for the door. The two men displayed their credentials long enough for Laura to read over them quickly and put them back in their coats. "We are from the Department of Homeland Security. Are you Laura West?" Pennington loved saying he was from DHS and always enjoyed the responses he saw in peoples' faces when he did.

"Can I ask what this is about?" Laura was wondering why Nick had not contacted her first, then began to worry, realizing that perhaps something had happened to him. "Does this have anything to do with Nick?"

Chavez spoke up, making sure he replied first before Pennington gave her the wrong impression. "Your husband is fine. We have been asked, however, to escort you back to our office for the time being, for your own safety. We were only told…"

The projectile hit Pennington in the back of his head, spraying bone fragments, gray matter and crimson as it exited the other side. Instinctively, both Laura and Chavez bent down, with Chavez reaching out and taking Laura by the hand, trying to pull her towards the car. Opening the driver's side, Chavez instructed her to keep her head down and crawl across the driver's seat to the passenger side. Following behind her, Chavez inserted the key, started the car, dropped it into drive, and hit the accelerator, making a sharp right turn in the driveway as he tried to head back out the entrance.

They had traveled almost 200 feet when Laura heard a dull thud as a second round penetrated the exterior door and hit Chavez's exposed rib cage two inches below his left armpit. It traveled through his heart and right lung, hitting the opposite interior rib cage and ricocheting throughout, ripping apart organs and tissue, finally coming to rest on top of the large intestines. The force of the strike caused Chavez to pull the steering wheel left, catching a divot in the road and flipping the car over onto its side. Chavez's body fell across the seat onto Laura, pinning her to the opposite door.

As Laura tried to push her way out from underneath, she saw a pair of legs approaching towards the front of the car. Looking up, she watched as the man continued until he was only a few feet away, stopped and raised the gun. She crossed her hands in front of her face as he fired through the windshield.

Chapter 22

Erik's words played on Nick's mind as they drove until he couldn't ignore them any longer and decided he had to confront Simon. "He said you have butchered hundreds of men. Is it true?"

"It's an exaggeration, but I have eliminated more than my share of men who deserved it."

"I thought in your line there was no emotional involvement with who you killed. A contract was a contract, so why would you say they deserved it?"

Simon looked at Nick without expression. "There are a lot of bad people in this world, Nick, and you know it. People who shouldn't be walking the streets, let alone have any kind of social interactions with any other human."

"I agree, but that doesn't mean you alone get to become their judge and executioner."

"It's not quite like that." said Simon.

"Then explain it to me. I'd really like to know how you decide one person's fate over another's based upon what inhumane cruelties they inflicted on someone else. Where do you draw the line on what is acceptable and what's not?"

"I don't make the decision on who gets chosen, just if I want to accept the contract or not."

Nick thought for a moment on what Simon had just said. "Traugott chooses?"

"No, he has nothing to do with it."

"I'm confused. I thought you worked for him."

"Mostly. But there are other individuals that I do work for when it's necessary."

"Who?"

"Do you really want to know? It's sometimes people you would normally associate with."

Nick was stunned. "Yes I do. I'm a DHS agent who goes by the book, on a mission to find a lost item that will close an ugly chapter in American history. I'm most likely going to get myself shot or jailed by my own people because I've withheld classified information and am working with an assassin responsible for taking hundreds of lives, probably American lives at that!"

"You think who we are and what we do is so different? You think I am immoral because I take the lives of those who killed or ruined other innocent people for no other reason than they could? What the hell is it that you think you do?"

"You and I are different and I think the way you do it is wrong."

Simon shoved his finger towards Nick's face. "You and I are exactly alike. You just don't want to admit it. We fight for what's right in this world. The only difference is who we do it for. Yes I have killed people in America, but not Americans. I have to travel where they go, no matter what country they travel to."

"What type of people have you killed in America?"

Simon did not want to answer. "I've helped many countries deal with the worst-case offenses that they could not resolve or handle legally. Sometimes it's a serial killer, a rapist, possibly a supplier to a terrorist cell. Most of the time, they don't even know it's been taken care of. The incidents just stop."

"That doesn't answer my question about who you have killed in America. Anyway, we have a system of justice in place meant to prosecute people who break the law. That's why we are a civil country."

"Really? Let's look at a scenario, OK?"

"I'm listening if you've got a good one." At this point, Nick had wished he hadn't started the conversation, but had no other choice but to appease Simon.

"A man kidnaps a four year child, then *plays* with him or her for a week or so until he tires of it, cuts their throat and throws the child's body in a dumpster. He eventually gets caught after he's done this to a half a dozen or more kids, but during his lockup until the trial, someone screws up and all the evidence except maybe on one murder is lost and now that evidence becomes questionable. The judge has no choice but to consider only the one murder charge and exclude any other mention of multiple murders to the jurors."

"Loss of evidence is not new to anyone anymore. Our teams see it every time we go into a court room these days."

"Yes, it happens more than the public knows about. Now because there's only one murder to tie the guy to and his lawyer knows it's not a sound case for the state's prosecutor, he plea bargains with the other lawyer, who's merely out for political gains, and gets a five year sentence for his client. Because the jails are so overcrowded, the guy gets released after one year due to good behavior because, guess what, there are no children in jail for him to play with."

"OK, the system sometimes sucks. It's still the law, and if anyone is to blame, then it's us, and we as a society need to take a lot harder look at who we are electing and at what laws are being passed."

"Seriously? That's how you feel, that's your answer for this guy? You think he gives a fuck about the law? Let me finish my story."

"No, it's not the answer to every issue, but putting a bullet through someone's head isn't either!" Nick already knew that whatever was coming next from Simon, it was an argument he had heard already only too many times.

Simon looked exasperated but continued to speak. "So the guy gets released and after a short time he goes back to his old ways and snatches another kid, except maybe now it's some millionaire or a high-up government employee's son or daughter. Holes up somewhere while the police, FBI and every other known agency looks for him. Some reporter does a background check on the guy and discovers the multiple murders and that the guy was released just after a year. "

"I've heard it before, Simon."

"Shut up and listen. The public goes wild and the governor or another official finds him or herself facing non-reelection. Phone calls are made all the way up the ladder by unknown nameless persons until my phone rings and they want the guy dealt with. You, of course, are called in as well, because it's now a perceived national threat since it's a govern-ment employee wrapped up in this."

"Are you saying no one gave a shit earlier because the other children weren't from rich families or our government only takes care of its own?"

"Let me finish my damn point, Nick! A decision comes down that there is no other solution but to kill the guy. We both get there at the same time and are ready to take our shot. Which of the two of us is wrong versus right in what we are about to do?"

"You forget I'm the law. You're not."

"You're not seeing what I'm getting at. We are both going to kill this guy for the same reason, plain and simple. Because I'm not the law and I pull the trigger first, are you going to arrest me? If it was your kid, are you going to throw me in jail anyway? You think the public cares who takes this piece of crap out? Don't forget that perhaps I was contracted by the same government you answer to even though that will never be divulged?"

"This is a fictional scenario, right? Simon, you take money to kill someone, you don't see any wrong in that?"

"Oh, and you don't get a paycheck? Your government pays you to eliminate any threat against its country and its citizens, whether it is foreign or domestic. Other governments pay for services that do the same."

"So, you're a contracted assassin for the government, any government?"

"I told you, I get to choose my assignments. If I feel the target is a legitimate threat to that country or its people, I'll consider the contract if it is not politically motivated. You know, you don't always have to kill a man, to kill a man. I kill people only if it's just, not because of money or someone wants power or revenge. By the way, I've never taken money for my services because I believe in what I'm doing, just as you do. However, to be honest, I am compensated in other ways."

"What other ways?"

"Cars, boats, planes, food, and homes supplied wherever I travel. Everything I need is at my disposal. All of my expenses and purchases are also paid for by someone else I don't even know."

"You don't feel any remorse for what you do?"

"Remorse?" Simon looked shocked. "You've never gotten the itch when you're looking at that little red dot you've painted on a forehead, to forget your oath for just a split second, and pull the trigger on some low life you know is going to skip through the system? Some guy who maybe killed one of your men, just laughing at you the whole time he did it?"

"Sure, every team member feels that way at some point, but we can't."

"Oh that's right, all the red tape and all. Well, I don't have any red tape and I never will. You've heard the expression 'someday he'll get what's coming to him'? Well, I'm 'what's coming'. I'm a ghost and unless I want you to see me, you never will, even though I'm right over your shoulder, and I'm not friendly. My status carries worldwide immunity."

"Come on, everyone has to answer to someone! You can't be picking off bodies without someone asking questions."

"Come on?" Simon ripped off a piece of paper from a notebook in his car and wrote down a name and number, handing it to Nick.

"Olexia Syshchenko. Who is she?"

"When you get through playing games with the bureaucrats second guessing or questioning your every move, and all the bleeding hearts, you call her and give her my name. Otherwise, she doesn't exist, got it? You want to help make this world a better place for your family, for everyone, the way it should be done when all else fails, call her. I do what I do because it's right!"

Nick slipped the paper into his coat and looked down to see the gas gauge reading a quarter of a tank left and decided they had better fill up. He spotted a sign for a station up ahead and pulled into it shortly afterwards. As he pumped, his mind tried to rationalize Simon's arguments and he found himself agreeing with most of it, but his lifelong morals and ethics wouldn't allow a final persuasion.

When they pulled back onto the highway, Nick spoke first. "Look, I know there's a need for what you do, whether I feel it's right or wrong. Hell, when some agency makes the call that we're the *solution*, people like you and me, our names are probably side by side in their Rolodex. It's just a matter of the situation and the legal implications that determines which name gets selected. Let's just agree to respect each other's opinions and professions."

Simon shook his head indicating he would at least honor Nick's request.

Nick continued. "People, you said people, not men. Does that mean you've accepted a contract on a woman?"

Simon looked out the window. "Once. A woman in Paris."

"What had she done that would warrant a contract?"

A minute passed before Simon replied. "She was beautiful, highly educated and well traveled. She and an accomplice would move around the country and set up shop in very wealthy business districts, then begin passing themselves off as buyers, or investors, whatever was needed to target specific individuals. They mainly went after executive men traveling abroad and would schedule an elegant dinner at an expensive restaurant for their first meet. Over the course of several additional meetings, she would become extremely flirtatious and would finally invite the men back to her place to close a deal."

"No man ever turned her down?" asked Nick.

Simon replied, "None that were ever documented."

"What kind of place did she take them back to?"

"It was always some luxurious high-rise. Once she had the guy in the sack, her partner would burst in and start taking photos, then blackmail the guy, saying they would send the photos to his business partners or competition."

"So there's a few shots with another woman. I'm sure some of the guys had enough balls to say "No" to their scheme."

"They made it hard to say "No", even though someone finally did. At gunpoint, they would make the man dress up in different kinds of S&M outfits and pose them in very humiliating positions along with making them look as if they were enjoying it."

"So why send the photos to the partners and not the family?" Nick had heard this was the new approach being used by most corporate blackmailers.

"Think about it. If you had been caught in that situation, would you rather have to face your wife and hope for forgiveness and understanding, maybe a divorce, or your vast network of business associates, knowing your little excursion could cost them their entire livelihood from the fallout. No matter the end result, your career would be ruined, not to mention the embarrassment to family amongst yours and your children's friends. Imagine if a competitor who was already in the process of trying to 'raid' your business got hold of those photos."

"So, how did you become involved?"

Simon cleared his throat, than went on. "They hooked a CEO of a large aerospace engine manufacturer and when he refused to pay, they kept their promise and sent the photos to his biggest competitor. However, they didn't know the two businessmen had family ties and an incredible amount of respect for one another."

"The competitor agreed to pay?" asked Nick.

"Yes, but three days after the man returned home, he committed suicide. That night I was called directly by the family and asked to fly to Paris and get the money back."

"That doesn't sound like you were asked to kill her."

Simon ignored the comment. "I spent four days tracking them down before I found where they had moved on to. Once I knew that, I pitched my story one evening at a conference they were attending and they contacted me the next day. We met a couple of times and she finally made her proposal. As I mentioned, she was very beautiful, I could see how she was able to seduce so many men."

"So you went back to her place, then what?"

"Well, I played along with her game until I heard her partner, whom I had been waiting for, come through the door. When he started to put the gun in my face, I reached out, pulled him down and crushed his larynx."

Nick stared at Simon for a minute. "How did you control the woman after that?"

"I put the gun to her head and walked her over to a desk where I had her write out a confession, then persuaded her to transfer all the monies back into their victims' accounts and I had her give me all of the negatives."

"You didn't think to let her go after that?"

"Nope." said Simon quickly. "I wouldn't let myself stop thinking of all the hurt and humiliation she brought to those families, so I took her outside, picked her up and tossed her naked off the 40th floor balcony."

"She didn't put up some kind of fight or scream when you took her out there?"

"Only on the way down. I never hesitated. She had already cleared the railing by the time she realized what was happening."

Chapter 23

Precisely at noon, the Jag pulled up to the address listed on the billing receipt, but the parking lot, what was left of it, was empty. Commercial garbage dumpsters, wood crates and an assortment of fifty gallon drums littered the area. Where there were once windows, concrete blocks were used to seal up all exposed openings. Through decades of sand, rain and snow, the name 'Bellows Garage' was barely visible. Only someone who knew the building and its long forgotten prior occupants could recite the name.

"Looks like it's been converted into a small warehouse. That one door there isn't blocked, so somebody is coming and going. Let's walk around and see if there's another entrance or a window that was left open for ventilation. I'm guessing we will be out of luck, but let's look anyway." Nick shook his head that he agreed with Simon and they both began to search.

As they reached the back, they saw that all of the bay doors had also been sealed in the same manner. Along the top of the second floor near the roof was a series of windows, each shut and securely locked from the inside. A glass pane had been broken in the center window, but neither of the men wanted to be seen trying to climb and break in through that entry. They returned to the front and walked to the car. Opening the trunk, Simon reached inside his toolkit and took out a small set of bolt cutters. "Never know when you'll need these."

"Gee, are those standard issue on a Jag now?" Nick smirked as they proceeded to the front door. Taking a quick look around, Simon handed Nick the cutters and he slipped them over the tongue of the deadlock, applying pressure using his forearms. The lock gave way and Nick unlatched the flap, turned the doorknob and walked inside, followed by Simon. To the right was a light switch and he flicked it up, turning on several rows of overhead incandescent lights. Stacked in the corners were dozens of boxes, old parts and a single antique car that had rusted over the years all the way through the floorboards.

To the right was what would have once been the reception area, and two offices behind that. On the door of the larger office was the name Joe Bellows III, Proprietor. Nick and Simon walked down the hallway, glancing at the numerous awards and photos that hung on each side of the hall. Several of the photos were faded, and it was not easy to tell what the original image was. As they walked, they opened adjoining doors and peered inside. More boxes, a couple desks and chairs, along with remnants of prior staff family photos. They decided to head back to the front offices to see if they could find any files that could help them locate the current address of the owner.

They walked into Joe's office and could immediately see that it was being kept up and cleaned by whoever was taking care of the property now. Along the walls were file cabinets, a coat rack, and old signs that had been neatly screwed into the walls, appearing to have been there since the place opened in 1937. Along an adjacent wall was a series of license plates that were arranged in the year issued, showing the gradual changes in their designs that took place over several decades. Nick walked closer to the wall to get a better look when he heard the front door open.

From outside the office they heard a voice calling for them to identify themselves and could hear a large dog panting, followed by a low drawn-out growl. Nick guessed it to be a German Shepherd in the neighborhood of one hundred twenty to one hundred and thirty pounds. Without leaving the office confines, Nick spoke his name and the fact that he was from the Department of Homeland Security. In case the dog attacked, he pulled his gun and checked to make sure he was close enough to close the door in time, if needed. If he was not, they would have no place to run and he would only have time to get off one shot. Following Nick's lead, Simon called his name.

After a moment, they were relieved to hear the dog's owner tell it to heel, then asked what they were doing there. He also told them they had a lock to replace.

"We were trying to see if Joe Bellows was still around, even though he'd be in late eighties, early nineties. Any chance you might know if he still lives in the area?" Nick was certain the man didn't but gave it a try anyway.

By now the man had entered the office and was staring at the intruders. "Joe Bellows is my grandfather and he still lives nearby, but he's not available to answer any questions. What do you want with him?"

"We were hoping he could help us and answer a few questions about an event that happened back in the forties. We think he may have had some involvement and can help us find something we are looking for."

Joe's grandson looked back and forth at the men. "You need to leave. Joe is still very sharp mentally for his age and probably can answer whatever questions you have, but he had a stroke a couple years back and doesn't get around as well as he used to. The stroke causes him to slur a lot when he speaks so it's hard to understand what he says unless you've been around him for a while. I don't want him to get upset and possibly have another attack."

Simon interrupted, trying to be as sympathetic as possible. "Look, we've come a long way and have a very tight schedule we must follow to try and get this information. We will only take a few minutes and then will leave. This is a matter of national security, otherwise we wouldn't ask to see him. If you can understand his speech better than we can, perhaps you can write down what he is saying to help move it along. Please."

Joe stepped back and looked down at the dog, pausing before he replied. "If I see at all he is getting nervous or upset, you're out of the house. I have no problem using Dodger here to take some meat out of your ass if you don't leave when I say to."

"You have our promise, but please, we need to speak to him now, if at all possible." Nick was already heading towards the front door. "And yes, we will replace the lock with whatever you want."

The three men and the dog walked two blocks, made a right at Syracuse and walked three more. As they approached a row of well-kept homes, Dodger began to prance in circles, then pull at the chain. They walked to the front of the house and were told to wait while the grandson checked to make sure his grandfather was up to seeing anyone. Five minutes passed before the grandson returned and told them they would have to come back. "Granddad doesn't want to really see you at all, but I mentioned the thing about national security and he said come back at 4:00."

"We told you we were on a time line and can't do that. We need to talk to him now. We have exactly three hours to get to Atlanta and we're already late. If we don't get what we came after…"

Before Nick could finish, the owner called the dog's name and he responded by barking very loud and showing his teeth.

"Please, it's very important. If you could mention the name Rayfield to him, that's all I ask. If he still says 'No', we will leave." Nick was concerned at this point they would walk away empty handed after having made a drive that Simon had tried to talk him out of. It would be a complete waste of time that he could have used for getting to Laura, as Simon had told him. He would need to come up with another plan while he waited for the grandson to return a second time. The two men and dog moved up onto the porch as they waited.

After a few minutes, Joe returned. "I don't know what it means to him, but he said that only you can come in, your friend will have to stay outside. I'll try to help you with his speech, but if he starts choking or anything like that, the conversation is over and you're out of here. Clear?" Nick thanked him and they both went inside. Dodger stood next to Simon, watching his every move.

Both men walked into the kitchen and sat down next to the man in the wheelchair. The grandson pulled his chair in closer so he could understand the old man better but was surprised to see his grandfather look directly at Nick and ask him what he knew about Rayfield. His voice was more clear and pronounced than he had heard in years, but it was still strained.

"Mr. Bellows, I am here because you used to know Alexander Rayfield. We believe you were with him the night he was shot and escaped with Traugott. Is that correct?"

"I was, but why do you want to know that? That was a long time ago. They're both dead now."

"Yes, I know that, but we think Mr. Rayfield might have given you something that he asked you to protect. There are a lot of people looking for that item and if a foreign country finds it before we do, the United States could be in jeopardy. Did Mr. Rayfield give you anything before he died?" Nick looked at his watch, knowing they had already run out of time for getting to Laura by the hour Erik had given them.

"Nope, he didn't give me anything, I never saw him after that night, either." Bellows looked at Nick waiting for a challenge.

"Mr. Bellows, I have photographs of you that night. I have testimony from eye witnesses who knew you and said you were there and that you left with Rayfield." Nick knew he was making some of it up, but continued. "I believe Mr. Rayfield gave you something that he knew was important enough to only give to a very trusted friend and I think you tried giving it to Mrs. Rayfield a few nights later, but she wouldn't take it. Emily saw you bring the car to her mother and that she was very upset by what you were trying to give her."

"You know Emily and Manny?" Joe was trying to lean forward in his chair, his face showing a large smile with eyes widening as he spoke. The grandson was looking at his grandfather closely, getting ready to end the conversation if needed.

"That's how this whole thing started, Mr. Bellows. I'm trying to help them find out what happened to their father, and at the same time clear his and Traugott's name and get those contents back to a safe place. I told you, what he gave you is very important to this nation. We need to find it quickly. My wife's life depends upon it right now, as well."

"How's Manny doing since she was shot? I used to send her information to wherever she was stationed on any news they found out about her father. It was a terrible thing about her getting shot protecting those agents. She went into that alley firing her guns like John Wayne or something, saved five or six of her own people that night, didn't even care about her own safety!"

"She seems to be doing fine, but I didn't know how she was injured. She wouldn't tell me anything personal about herself." Nick looked at his watch again.

"If she didn't tell you anything about herself or about me, then how did you know where to come looking?"

"What? All that matters is I found you and that you can help us." Nick wanted to keep the man talking about the night Rayfield was shot.

"How did you find me? There's only one way you could have found my garage after all this time if Emily or Manny didn't tell you. If you want me to believe you know those girls, then you can answer. Those are two of the most wonderful woman who ever walked this planet, so answer my question. I won't have you tricking me!"

The grandson stood and told Nick the questioning was over. The grandfather was getting upset and Nick needed to keep his side of the bargain.

"Let him answer. If he can't, then you can kick him out." Joe's grandfather was beginning to turn red but continued to stare directly at Nick.

"Inside the drivers' hubcap on Mr. Rayfield's car, you left him a message that it was safe in the wall and you got everything through today and yesterday, whatever that means. The address of your garage was on it."

The grandfather looked at Nick, annoyed at his reply. "Whatever that means is the answer you're looking for, Mr. DHS man. You figure that out and you'll have what I was trying to give Barbara that night. Yes, Alexander did give me a case, but told me to hide it good and to never give it to anyone except his wife or someone I trusted as much as him."

Nick was getting frustrated. "There's no reason not to trust me, I'm telling you the truth. Manny and Emily are twins whom I met only three days ago. Manny is the one who told me about her father and Traugott, except she believes her father was trying to find Traugott because he stole what the case contained. Simon, the man outside, filled me in on what really happened and I believe what he is telling me. Emily recognized you that night, except she knew you as Mr. Joe. From the note and what she told us, that's how we found you."

"You say you met them both. What makes them different, Mr. West, that you would be able to tell them apart? Answer that and I'll know what you're telling me is the truth and you're not just some ass with a lot of facts."

Nick thought back to the day he saw them together in the kitchen. "Manny has dark green eyes, Emily's are light green."

"You're wrong Mr. West, Manny's are blue." The grandfather knew Nick was telling the truth, but wanted to test him to make sure he wouldn't change his answer if he really knew for sure.

"I'm not wrong and if you knew them like you say, you know it, too."

"Yes, you're right. No one would know that unless they were in their presence long enough to realize that feature. If you were there that long with them, then they trusted you and that's good enough for me. You read that note carefully and you'll know exactly where to look in the old garage."

"I don't have the time, Mr. Bellows, to try and figure this out. A man is holding my wife and will kill her if I don't bring him that case. I have no intention of turning it over, but he doesn't know that. If I can at least show him I have it, I hope he will let her go. I should have left forty minutes ago." Nick was doing his best not to rattle the old man, but he was losing his patience.

"Look at the note, Mr. West! The second part is an acronym I made up for a sign in the garage so I wouldn't forget. Tell me what it said again."

Nick pulled the note from his pocket and read the second sentence. "Got everything through today and yesterday."

"Man, I was a clever one back then. Don't you see it? The first letter of each word. 'G E T T Y'. Getty, it's behind the '*Getty Oil*' sign. Joey will help you find it. You find it and help those girls out. You tell them I've never forgotten about them!"

Nick bounded through the doorway, ignoring Simon and Dodger, leaped off of the porch and continued running in stride with the others joining the chase behind him. By the time he reached the garage, he was three hundred yards ahead of Simon and Joe, but Dodger was right beside him, having barked the entire distance. Grabbing the door handle, he flung it open and headed for the largest office, having remembered seeing the sign earlier. Ten seconds later, he stood staring at it, six feet up on the right interior wall, as it glared back at him.

Rusted screws were holding the sign in place. He ran back down the hall, opening doors, looking for a hammer and crowbar. Behind the second door, he saw the large toolbox against the back wall and began pushing boxes out of the way to get to it. Inside the third drawer was a five-pound hammer and tire jack. They would have to do.

Re-entering the office, he saw Simon and Joe standing, looking at the sign. Angling the sharp end of the tire jack against a bottom screw, he struck the opposite end, breaking off the screw's head. He repeated this action and broke off the head of the other bottom screw. Placing the tire jack under the sign, he lifted and saw the hole behind it. A small amount of air exited the opening and they could smell a scent of mildew and dried leather. With both palms on the bottom of the sign, he pushed it up until he was able to let go with one hand and reach inside.

His hand touched the back of a leather case encrusted with a thin layer of green mold. He inched it upwards until he could clasp his fingers around the top and clamped down. With a tight grip, he tugged at the satchel until it popped through the opening. Turning it around so they could all see the latch, he hesitated, then placed it under his arm.

"We'll have to look at it in the car. There's no time now!"

Chapter 24

Laura watched as the man kicked at the windshield, striking the holes made by the bullets. They had entered Chavez's body as he lay motionless, already dead, his weight pinning her to the door. Finally the window cracked all the way across and disconnected from the seal holding it in place. Cupping his hand around the edge, the man pulled it loose and threw it on the ground behind him.

Grabbing Laura by the arm, he allowed her to work her way out, holding her so her back was to him, and pulled her in closer once she was upright. Erik felt the woman tense and knew she was about to try and free herself from his grip. He let go and threw his arm around her waist, picking her up just enough so her feet were barely able to touch the ground and lose all traction. The maneuver would prove to be costly.

Laura bent and raised her leg as high as she could, than threw her full weight into a powerful kick, raking her steel-heel down the front of his shin bone starting just below the kneecap, tearing away flesh underneath his pants leg as she drove her foot downward. The pain was so intense Erik screamed, released her completely and dropped to one knee as tears filled his eyes. Realizing the woman was trying to get to the house, he ignored the pain and started running after her. With twenty feet to go, he lunged and tackled her from behind, sending them both sprawling to the ground.

Moving as quickly as he could, Erik climbed onto her back, placing his left forearm securely across the back of her neck, reached into his jacket of the right hand pocket and extracted the syringe. Laura continued to kick and flail her arms, trying to land one more punch, when she suddenly felt the sharp needle plunge into her neck. Within seconds, her movements began to slow as the muscle relaxant took effect. She could hear, smell, see and understand everything going on, but she was starting to lose all feeling, unable to move any part of her body.

The man flipped her over on her back and began searching her for any weapon she might have on her, groping as he went along, letting his hands linger and massage the various parts of her body as he searched. She could do nothing and began to worry if he would take it further. Satisfied there was nothing, Erik sat back on the ground and pulled up his pants leg, which had already begun to stick to his leg where the blood and other body fluids had begun to dry. Around the torn flesh, the skin had turned bluish black and part of the bone was visible. He was able to push some of the flesh back in place, but several large sections were missing.

Standing, he applied pressure to the leg and felt a sharp pain run down the inside quadrant into the foot. It could be a possible hairline fracture, he thought. If so it would change his plans for when Nick and Simon arrived. He looked around, surveying the property and tree line for a setup position. At best, he could only hope to travel out six to eight hundred meters for any type of clear shot. Otherwise he would have to conceal himself in the woods, thereby eliminating his ability to shoot from any angle. He looked down at his leg and knew he had no choice but to take care of it first, before an infection set in.

Laura lay on her back, staring up at the sky. She tried blinking, but her eyelids would not cooperate, staying open, fixed in their current position. She was thankful there was an overcast, hoping her eyes would not dry out by the time the drug wore off. With luck, it would rain a small amount and provide some relief, even though there was no feeling in them presently. She could hear Erik's footsteps moving away from her and she began to panic, realizing that he was leaving her paralyzed on the ground. If a predatory animal were to find her, she would be defenseless.

Erik entered through the front door and made his way back towards the surgical facility. In there would be supplies that he could use to sterilize the wound and suture the mutilated skin. Walking on the leg felt better, but it would require time, which he did not have, to mend. Opening the dispensary cabinet, he rummaged through the supplies until he found what he needed.

Sitting on the long silver surgical table with his leg propped up and knee bent, he gently swabbed the area with peroxide, then pushed as much skin back into place as possible. Picking up a small syringe filled with Novocain he injected the entire area and waited for the drug to work. Threading a number three suture, he hooked it underneath the lower layers of skin and began suturing upward, tying off and clipping the ends when he came to areas of missing derma. Finally he applied a disinfectant and wrapped the lower leg in bandage. For the time being the Novocain had relieved the pain and he was able to walk about freely. He decided he would place a few additional syringes in his pocket should he need them later.

Laura was still lying quietly when he returned, but was beginning to show signs of small amounts of movement in her fingertips and lips. He bent down and placed his arms underneath her, lifting slowly, making sure he did not put pressure on the sutures and rip them out. Carrying her into the house, he placed her limp body on the couch and closed the door. Simon and Nick were not expected for another hour, provided they were on time. If not, he was prepared to make good on his threat, knowing he would enjoy every cut on such a beautiful woman.

Satisfied she would still be under the influence of the drug for at least another forty-five to sixty minutes, he went outside and walked across a small clearing to the back of a two story barn. Parked there was the red Mercedes. Inside were his rifle and other necessities of his trade. Opening the side door, he ran an arm through one of the loops of a backpack and slung it over his shoulder, then picked up the rifle case and scope bag. He would assemble them shortly once he found a place to lay Laura's body.

When he reached the clearing again, he changed direction and walked towards the highest point of the property, hoping to find a spot where she could be laid flat and not be visible as the two men drove in. If she were to be seen as they approached, the element of surprise would be lost, even though they knew he was there. However, they would not expect to be engaged in gunfire so quickly.

He was also concerned about the steady stream of animals that roamed the acres, hoping that none would impede his view at the last instant before firing. A clear line of fire would be essential in making sure he took out Nick with the first shot, saving Marks for the knife fight he had so longed for. If he missed that first shot, his location would be given away and he would need to relocate quickly. With his injury, that would be impossible.

The flat spot was not ideal, but was the best he could find. Several stones of different sizes occupied the small area and could cut off circulation if Laura had to lay on them for any given length of time. The vegetation was also short, which would not give him the coverage he had hoped to find. He glanced towards the woods another one hundred meters away, but felt less confident that was the answer. This would have to do.

Moving further down the hill away from the house, he searched and found a covered area for himself that would allow a constant visual of both Laura and the clinic. Placing his gear on the ground first, he sat and lifted the rifle case onto his lap, unclipping the latches, extracted the weapon from the padded enclosure, then put the case back on the ground. He rotated the rifle in his hands, checked the chamber, felt along the varnished wood grain and breathed in the smell of gun oil. To him this smell was more erotic than any woman's perfume and the touch of the steel more pleasing than any female body he had ever laid with.

He guessed the distance to the clinic door was nine hundred and fifty meters, an easy shot depending upon the circumstances. After attaching the scope and making adjustments, the actual distance was nine hundred and thirty-seven meters, a shot half the distance of what he was accustomed to making. With Nick down, he would make a direct assault on Simon, knowing he would not be capable of shooting back using his gun hand with the broken fingers. The kill would be his finest. He would make it last, being sure he did not puncture any vital organs until he was ready and heard Simon begging for him to end it.

The movement in his groin brought him back to reality and he immediately thought of Laura lying on the couch. She would be starting to get feeling back and needed to be sedated once more before the scheduled arrival. If she were to regain muscle control before he could get back in time, he would have to deal with her in a different way, one that would require a permanent solution. He placed the equipment back in their protective coverings and rechecked the spot before heading down to the house. With thirty-five minutes to go, it would soon be over.

Ten minutes later he reached the clinic door, laying his bags at the entrance. Feeling for the syringe in his coat pocket with one hand and turning the doorknob with the other, he stepped inside and saw Laura still lying where he had left her. Walking to her side, he lifted her right arm, tapped a vein and inserted the needle, pressing the plunger slowly until the liquid was drained.

For the first time, he noticed how truly beautiful she was, her auburn hair stretching over the pillow and down onto the cushion of the couch. Running his eyes over her body, he could not help but notice the athletic build and wondered if it was from working out or the constant physical labor of her daily activities. Her legs and arms were muscular and the stomach flat. Lifting and placing her body on the shoulder above his good leg, he felt a small pain shoot down the opposite one and was grateful the Novocain was still working and that Laura could not move. He would need to make sure the walk back up the hill was done at a steady pace.

Chapter 25

Nick hit the interstate and began weaving in and out through the various lanes at ninety miles an hour, even though the posting was seventy. Simon leaned forward and punched a button on the dash, producing an alternating beeping sound. "At least we'll know when we hit a speed trap. Perhaps you might want to slow down when we do." Nick looked at Simon and pressed the accelerator down further.

"Mind if I look in the bag to make sure we have what we came for and don't die for nothing?" Simon watched nervously as Nick missed the car bumper in front by two inches as he switched into the right hand lane.

"Help yourself. Regardless, though, we are not stopping until we have Laura and that maniac is dead. Whatever you haven't told me about him, now would be a good time. You said it's been twenty years. Do you still think he's capable of pulling off a shot like you said?" Nick took a quick glance at Simon, then straight ahead again.

"There's no telling. If his eyesight has deteriorated due to age or something else, then I doubt it. I know that my reflexes aren't what they were once, even though I still consider myself one of the best. Put me up against a man twenty years younger with the same skills and I will make a fight of it, but I couldn't promise you the outcome like I once could. He may have changed his technique. Some men prefer to take a quick shot and get it over with, some crave the feel and rush of a human being expiring in their hands as they snap a neck or sever a man's stomach."

Satisfied he had answered the question, Simon placed the satchel on his lap, thumbed the latch and opened the cover, laying it back as far as it would go. Inside were more than a dozen ledgers neatly placed and in order. Their binders were placed facing upwards and out to protect the pages as well as possible. In the middle were several yellowed, faded pieces of paper wrapped in a wax like covering. To the very back was a large envelope tied securely by a string, the label waxed shut along the edge. "Looks like the documents."

"Close it back up and keep everything as it is. I don't want anything falling out or damaged." Nick continued looking ahead.

"Aren't you curious to know if the 'Declaration' was signed by your President?"

"My only concern is getting to Laura before time runs out. You keep it and get it back to whomever you trust to do the right thing with the money and the papers."

"Traugott was the one person I felt I could trust, but he bumped my name to the top of the contract list. Kind of puts a damper on our relationship, don't you think?" Simon meant it to be funny, but his laugh quickly vanished.

The radar detector began to beep faster and Nick decelerated to the posted speed, accelerating once again when it began to slow. "Anyone else you can think of besides him?"

"Assassins tend to be lone wolves, Mr. West. We don't keep a social calendar handy. I'd say you are about as close to someone I can trust as anybody. By the time this is over, I hope you have someone in mind to give it to, provided one of us makes it."

Nick thought about that for a few minutes before speaking to Simon again. "We will need to plan based upon what you think he will do once we are there. His techniques may have changed but I'm guessing his strategy and purpose for getting us there is something you are familiar with."

"How he plans to kill us will be limited by his surroundings and the circumstances at the time. Once we are there, I will be able to determine that better. You will be the first one he will go after. If he succeeds, he will then kill your wife as painlessly as possible, saving me for last. There is no doubt he knows I'm injured and can not fire a weapon, so he will take his time, with me as payback. I know you are worried about getting there by the hour he gave you, but I assure you he will not harm her until you are out of the way. He knows he'll have no leverage if he does it sooner."

"If he didn't take Laura by surprise and she put up a fight, would he hurt her then? What if she caught him off guard?"

Simon looked puzzled. "Nick, are you serious? People like us are schooled to the point of it being instinctive to take out an attacker as quickly as possible. We don't think about the harm we inflict, only the end result. Someone who isn't properly trained wouldn't have a chance, especially against someone with experience. God, for her sake, I hope she didn't try something that stupid!"

"Well, that's the thing, she has been trained. Laura's a fitness nut like me and to keep us in shape, I made her train with me as a sparring partner. Once she started, she really got into it, going with me to the firing range, learning and using the different weapons and quizzing me in my studies. Other than the classified intelligence training, she could slip into the role of being a federal agent very easily."

"Damn!" said Simon. "I've heard all these years that American husbands couldn't make their wives do anything. That's why real men live in Australia."

"Yeah, well, fuck you too, buddy." It was a badly needed pressure release and Nick laughed from his gut for the first time in days.

"Tell me about your wife. What made her want to become a vet?"

"She told me her father grew up on a farm and was pretty good with livestock, and animals in general. One day they were driving down the road and saw a yellow lab get clipped by a passing car, so they pulled over and took the dog to their house."

"Is that the property she is at now?"

"No, but pretty close. Anyway, her dad saw the back leg had a small fracture and showed Laura how to splint it. She cared for the dog until the leg healed and it could make it on its own. About a year later, the dog made its way back to Laura and woke her up scratching at her bedroom window late one night. Her dad and she delivered nine pups together. I guess that's how she fell in love with it."

"How many people work at the hospital or clinic where Laura is?"

"It's a recovery clinic really. Her practice is in Atlanta. On the weekends she works it by herself just making sure the animals are healing properly. There's a small operating room in the back of the main house. Other than that it's seventy acres of open land and a few barns and stables surrounded by thick oaks and shrubbery. Why?"

"Because if she's alone, there won't be the urgency of having to neutralize other targets. He can control the situation without having to watch his back. Because of that, he will be calmer, so if she attacked him, he would be more likely to knock her out and restrict her movements so he can keep an eye on her. If she hurt him, though, at the minimum he's crippled her. I wish I could tell you otherwise, Nick."

At 4:27, Nick turned off of the interstate and gunned it towards the entrance to the hospital. Passing under the sign, he saw the overturned car and a body lying on the front porch. It was a man's torso and he breathed a sign of relief. As he got closer, he saw a head protruding from the missing windshield of the car lying on its side. Without warning, Simon shoved the satchel in front of Nick's face, blocking his entire view.

"What the hell are you doing, I can't see anything!" Nick moved a hand upward to brush the satchel away, but Simon grabbed his wrist and held it firmly.

"He'll be in front of us, probably planting a crosshair on you right now. What's in this satchel is too valuable for him to chance taking a shot, so he'll wait. When I tell you to, turn left and park behind the house. Exit out my door. It will keep you closer to the house and cut down on his angle. There's a body about seven hundred meters up on the ridge to the East."

"Can you tell if it was a woman?" Nick tried turning his head in that direction as he spoke.

"I can't, the distant is too far to make out a shape. I only know that whoever it is, they aren't moving. Now turn left."

Nick made a hard left and pulled in behind the building. Exiting the car and making their way around back, both men entered through the back door into the interior of the clinic. Strewn about the floor were discarded blood stained cotton balls and swabs. On the table were small blotches of dried blood and suture line. Laura would never leave the place looking like this. She was professional in every way and would have thoroughly cleaned up after herself. There were no animal tracks or dirt on the floor, so Nick quickly ruled out it being surgery on an animal. Erik had to have performed the surgery himself, for whatever reason, and he hoped it wasn't Laura's blood.

He turned to Simon. "I think either Erik or Laura is injured. I'm sure Erik did the surgery, otherwise this place would be spotless. Are you sure you couldn't make out a shape of the person on the ridge?"

"Honestly, I couldn't. We need to get a pair of binoculars or my scope to see that far. Are there any in the house?"

Knowing the answer already, Simon started out the back door. Three minutes later, Simon returned with a gun case in hand. Laying it across the surgical table, he flipped open the latches and grabbed the scope. "We'll need to move to the front of the house, but stay low. If he's changed positions, he may be able to see us through the window."

At the window, Simon raised the scope, waiting to see if Erik might squeeze off a round, then slowly raised his head and eye up to the glass. He panned the area very carefully until he found the person, then adjusted the focus ring until he saw the body clearly. "It's a woman, Nick, and she has auburn hair. I don't see any blood on her clothing, so it's possible she is just unconscious."

Nick was surprised at the amount of rage that was beginning to well up in him. He had been in this situation hundreds of times, but had never felt this way. Never had it been on such a personal level. Trying to fight his emotions as the rage increased, the question of right or wrong no longer mattered. He would kill Erik with his bare hands. He wanted to feel it, and the thought of doing so now became instinctive.

He took the scope from Simon's hand and began to peer into the distance, hoping he would see some kind of sign of Erik lying out there waiting. He then redirected the scope to Laura lying completely still some eight hundred and fifty meters away.

"We need to get to her somehow. He's probably set her up as bait, hoping we would make a run to get her, then pick us off as we approached. Probably wait until we were right up on top of her, then take his shots.

Simon looked at Nick. "I think you're right, but I really believe he hoped you would lose it and run up to her on your own. That way he could eliminate you and leave me for whatever he has planned."

"Do you really think he wants to kill me first, because, if so, we need to plan something around that."

"What do you mean?" Simon could see that Nick was already trying to form a strategy.

"If we go in, then you lead. I'll be right behind you in your footsteps. If you don't think he will shoot at you, then your body will block me and he'll have to wait until we separate. Once we are there, we get Laura and you switch to the end position, blocking both of us so we can hightail it out."

"Then we'll need to come in right at him and we don't know exactly where his position is. If he's off to the side and we guess wrong, then you won't have a chance."

"Think back. Did he ever do this before on another contract you did together?"

"That was a long time ago. I'm not sure." Simon shut his eyes, trying to put the current situation out of mind and remember all of the times they planned hits together. Then it hit him. He had forgotten the kidnapping contract where they snatched a small boy to lure in the father for a kill. "Yes, we did, once. Erik took a position directly behind the body, 90 degrees looking straight at their back. He told me a person would approach from the front to make sure the person was alive. They would get down on their knees to roll the body over, thereby exposing their own torso and provide a perfect shot. Anywhere in that area the bullet hit would be a kill shot. We'll have to get around the front of her and come in that way."

Nick looked back through the scope and saw a line of trees approximately one hundred and twenty meters from her. "The trees. If we can make it along that inside line, then when we are in position, we can make a run for Laura. There's one other thing we need to do and I'll explain that on the way. Are you ready?"

Simon reached down and grabbed the box of ammo and rifle. "I'm ready, but are you, Nick? If Laura is dead, we're going to have to lie down beside her and wait him out. Are you going to be able to handle that?"

"If she's dead, then I'm not waiting for him to come to us. We'll back track and find him, let him become the prey this time."

"Nick, there's one other thing. If I don't make it and you do, there's something I need for you to do with my rifle. It's very important. You need to promise me that you will follow my exact instructions."

"We need to work together to make sure that doesn't happen, but if it does, then yes, I will, I promise." Nick lowered himself and headed toward the back of the clinic.

As they approached the door, Simon spoke. "All right, but no matter what, we must stay together and you will have to do whatever I tell you to do. I understand your state of mind right now and you're going to have to treat this like any other hostage situation you worked before until we know if she is alive or not. Once we know that, then we can move forward with other plans."

Nick did not respond, but instead went out the back door, looking for a clearing, and started towards the woods with Simon right behind. They made sure they kept the building at an angle behind them to obscure any visual sighting by Erik, and kept low. Fifteen minutes later they were making their way down the inside of the tree line in the shadows. The sun would be down in an hour, but for now it was playing into Erik's eyes, giving Nick and Simon an advantage.

Another fifteen minutes passed before they were lined up with Laura. Nick estimated an all out run to her would take less than two minutes carrying the weapon and trying to stay low and tight on Simon's heels. Nick gave the final instructions. Each took a deep breath and started running. Twenty steps into the run, Simon stumbled and fell, coming down on his broken wrist, trying to catch himself. Nick dropped to the ground and stayed with him until Simon recovered, both lifting their bodies at the same time and continuing the run. The meters clicked away as they began to gasp for air going uphill, now only forty-five meters away from Laura.

Twenty, fifteen, ten and then the shot rang out, followed quickly by a second round only a split second later. Simon went down, then Nick. The second round had caught Nick in the shoulder, enough to kick him sideways and down. It hurt like hell and he could feel the numbness begin to follow. He tried flexing it, but could not. There was a continuous stream of blood coming from the wound and he knew he had to stop the bleeding as quickly as possible or he would soon pass out.

Had Simon been wrong, Nick wondered, as he steadily moved his eyes towards his friend? There was no movement or sound coming from the man. He looked at his chest to see if it was rising and descending, but it remained stationary. Nick could not see any blood, and desperately wanted to pull himself over to him and verify if he was dead or not. They had agreed that if one went down, they both went down, hoping to confuse Erik. Nick turned his attention to Laura, no movement coming from her, either.

They would all have to wait now for Erik to make his next move. Had they fooled him? Would he take the bait and come out of hiding to check his kill or kills? Nick could not take his eyes off of Laura, willing her to move any part of her body so he would know she was alive. Simon had told him to keep it together, but the longer he lay there, the stronger the emotions became and he felt his chest start to heave knowing he would never hold this woman again, feel her breath on his cheek or the gentle touch of her hand. Then he saw it, a small twitch of her right foot, and his eyes began to water.

Chapter 26

Not far off, a twig broke, then another. For almost half an hour Erik had waited but could no longer contain his excitement, He had to be sure. He had not wanted to kill Simon this way. The others he did not care about. If Simon was still alive, he had already begun to think of the ways he would slice away at him, removing the skin, then muscle tissue, letting the organs go into shock until they began to shut down. He remembered all the surgical instruments he had found in the different drawers at the clinic. He would make use of them all. The other two he would leave to the buzzards or until someone stumbled across their carcasses and ruined his or her perfectly good day.

Ten feet from the bodies, he stopped and looked at each one. Laura was beginning to move, first her legs, then her arms. Lifting her head up and off the ground, she began to look around at her surroundings, still unable to get complete control of her limbs. Erik chambered a round and stepped towards her, coming up behind and lowering the barrel. Placing a finger on the trigger, he rested the steel against her head and waited for Laura's reaction to what was about to happen.

The knife drove deep into his upper thigh as Simon held it tight, trying to twist and push it into the bone. Erik rotated his body, doing his best to stay aligned with the knife, felt the blade's movement and threw the rifle to the side. Reaching down, he grabbed Simons' hand with both of his and held them as he pulled his leg away. With the knife free, he brought a knee up into Simon's face, but missed when Simon was able to pull back enough to let it pass by an inch away.

By the time Erik brought his leg back down, Simon was on his feet slashing the knife across Erik's abdomen. A four-inch gash cut across Erik's lower torso and he pressed his hand against it, looking at the blood coming from the cut. Erik spun and caught Simon in the ribs with a foot, sending Simon reeling backwards, but he remained on his feet.

Charging towards Erik, Simon held the knife low, and then at the last possible moment brought it up, hoping to catch Erik in the groin or stomach. Erik crossed his wrists, using them to block the move, clamped his hands around Simon's arm, twisted his body, and lifted Simon off his feet, throwing him over his back and onto the ground with the knife falling at his feet. He reached down, picked it up and dove at Simon as he was getting back to his feet.

As the men rolled, Erik began to stab the knife into Simon's body, trying to avoid a critical placement, hoping to slow the man down but not kill him yet. Simon blocked as many thrusts as possible, but knew he couldn't sustain his defense much longer. With his last strength, he stopped trying to deflect the knife and drove a thumb into Erik's left eye socket. Erik immediately let go and fell away, his vision temporarily blurred by the ruined eye and the tears welling up in the other. Getting to his feet after several attempts, he swung the knife from side to side, trying to keep Simon away in hopes he would regain enough sight to plunge the knife one last time.

Simon lay on the ground, his body bleeding from the multiple wounds, unable to regain enough energy to pull himself towards Erik. He could hear Erik gasping as he came towards him. Planting an elbow, he ignored the pain and rolled himself to his side, looking directly at Erik as he approached. Behind Erik, he could see Nick sprinting towards the man that he knew was about to take his life. He lifted his head as Erik dropped to his knees in front of him and watched as the knife was swung in an arc, piercing his temple and continuing into his brain. Erik held the knife until Simon's eyes closed, then let Simon fall sideways to the ground.

As Nick ran towards Erik, he saw Laura moving and changed directions, running to her side and trying to lift her to her feet. He could feel her swaying as the blood began to flow back into her muscles, slowly but surely becoming steady enough on her feet for Nick to push her forward and tell her to run. As she pulled away, a large rock caught him square between the shoulder blades, knocking the wind out of him, forcing him to the ground. Erik picked up another rock and moved towards Nick. Thirty feet away, Laura lost her balance and fell. She lifted herself up to all fours, then saw the object ahead of her and pushed herself towards it, trying to move her four limbs in unison.

Standing over Nick, Erik brought the rock down as hard as he could, but with his vision blurred, the rock missed, smashing against the ground next to Nick's head. Nick kicked out against the bleeding leg and caught it flush against the tibia bone, buckling it backwards and snapping the leg in two. Erik rolled onto the ground, his face a mask of agony. He tried looking at the new damage with his one good eye but all vision was blurred. Getting to his knees, Nick slammed a fist into Erik's ribcage, then several to his face, one catching the side of his nose. Blood was streaming out Erik's nostrils down into his mouth.

Nick tried hitting him again, but a sharp pain shot through his shoulder, knocking the last bit of breath from his lungs. He fell over forward next to Erik, rolling onto his back to try sucking in more air, each gulp more painful than the last. His head began to spin and he blacked out.

Using his elbows, Erik pulled himself back to Simon to retrieve the knife and slowly made his way back to Nick, who he could see lying still, his head turned and pressed against a rock on the ground. The crawl was slow and excruciatingly painful. At times he had to stop and let the pain pass until he could move on. Finally reaching Nick, he grabbed his jacket lapels, pulled himself onto his body, raised the knife and sent it downwards towards the center of Nick's chest.

Erik's skull shattered, ripping away all but the lower jaw and a dangling earflap as the 50 caliber projectile exploded inside. His body flew backwards and fell to the ground, his hand still clutching the knife. For the next five minutes, Nick and Laura did not move, letting life continue around them as their minds processed their current existence and their bodies dealt with the pain. Regaining full consciousness and raising his head, Nick looked around until he saw Laura lying prone, her head down, resting on the butt of the rifle, her finger still clutching the trigger, not moving, with the exception of her back raising and lowering in breath.

On his feet now, he could not feel his arm. The numbness had progressed downward to his hand, but the bleeding from the wound had slowed. He held it tight to his body as he made his way over to Laura, lying down beside her, stretching his good arm over her body. Neither said a word.

With her head down, still resting on the rifle butt, Laura finally spoke in a soft Southern voice. "We really, really need to have a serious talk about you bringing your work home." They both began to laugh, but neither moved.

Chapter 27

After two weeks of recuperating and spending some quiet time with Laura, Nick decided it was time to head back to DHS and keep his word of submitting his resignation. The satchel had made its way through all of the proper channels with the account documents and ledgers turned over to the Swiss bank and government authorities. The 'Declaration of Surrender' was now in the hands of the U.S. Government, having been thoroughly dissected and hand carried to the deepest dark corners of its archives. No current senators would learn of what evil their ancestors had committed, but those in real power would remember and see to it they lost in the next election. If not, there would simply be an accident with an ongoing investigation that lasted until no one cared any longer and would go away unnoticed.

When Nick arrived, the atmosphere was somber, everyone going about their business as professionally as possible, nothing out of place except the break rooms being empty. He had expected to see some staff standing in the aisles talking about their weekend before their shift started, but everyone was seated, working. As he walked through the department, he noticed eyes being shifted his way, then back to their monitors when he made eye contact. No one said anything to him as he proceeded towards Brewster's office. He wondered what he was walking into.

Brewster was placing a photo of his wife in a box along with his other personal items when Nick entered, shutting the door behind him. Before Nick could ask, Brewster thought he would cut through the awkwardness.

"Yes, you're seeing what you think you are. Let's say I was persuaded to take early retirement without causing any trouble. It's a better deal than twenty years in prison. I'm walking away with seventy percent of my pay and full benefits. I will probably have to do security guard work in a few years to get by, but Susan and I will be OK. Wasn't what I was hoping at the end of my career, but who gets what they want in life anymore?"

"Paul, it's not fair, you had no way of knowing what this was about. No one knew anything until it was too late to understand the implications of the contents of the satchel. If anyone should be taking the brunt, it should be McCallister and myself. We knew what the case contained, and I should not have gone above anyone's authority."

"Nick, first of all, I let it happen. I probably should have followed all the rules but it's not me when my guys are involved and they're getting shit from the upper pricks when they don't deserve it. You had no idea when this started where it would go, how important what you found would be. I wasn't about to let you or Baker take it up the ass without cracking some balls myself. I knew where this would all end way before it happened, so stop feeling bad for me." Brewster pushed the contents of the box to the side to make more room.

"What if I go to McCallister...?" Nick was trying to come up with another way to get Brewster reinstated but Brewster stopped him.

"Leave it alone. You and I aren't the type to beg. Seriously, I'm glad it came to this; I don't know how much more I could have taken of their egos and political agendas. This isn't about what we did wrong, it's about them covering their asses. Someone always has to be a scapegoat and it will never be one of them if they have any way out. They point their fingers when we fail and slap each other on the back, give themselves raises and pass around cigars when we succeed. Nothing is going to change that." Brewster dropped another photo in the box as he turned to begin emptying a shelf from the bookcase.

"I'm sorry for what's happened. It would have been better if they had allowed you to resign, but I guess this way they have taken their little victory. I swear I can already smell the cigar smoke."

Brewster looked back at Nick. "Speaking of resigning, I need for you to sign this paper and date it now. You also need to put the exact time down as well. Before you do, though, hold up a second, I've got to get Jenny in here to notarize it. There's a guy with some fancy credentials in your office waiting for you, asked me to make sure you did the paperwork before you saw him." Brewster slid the paper over to Nick, then called Jenny into his office.

"Any idea what he's here for or what department he's from?" Nick was annoyed they were pressing for him to go, too. He was leaving voluntarily; there was no need to strip him of his DHS identity without allowing him to leave on his own terms.

"Nope, but he's foreign and just said to make sure you brought this to him signed and notarized."

When they were finished Nick told Brewster he would stop back when he was done and perhaps they could talk some more about getting the agency to reconsider. "Just stop back and say goodbye, that's all you need to do."

Nick walked back through the office and could see the atmosphere had not changed. He could tell that several of the people he had considered friends wanted to talk but they remained in their chairs, trying to go about business, doing their best not to bring attention to themselves. When he reached his old office, he was shocked that the man waiting for him was sitting in a side chair, not behind his desk as the arrogant IA agent was the last time he was here.

They exchanged introductions and the man asked if he had brought the paper signed and notarized as requested. After reading down through the necessary signatures and making sure the notary stamp was embossed correctly, the man smiled and told Nick they could began. Nick walked around and sat in his chair as the man pulled up directly in front and reached into his briefcase, placing a stack of papers on the desk.

"Before we begin, on behalf of the German government and the United Banque of Genève, we wish to extend our deepest gratitude for your honesty in returning all accounts and documents. We thought for sure that only a small percentage would be received, but it appears all of the account ledgers are intact. Without the ledgers we would not have been able to close the accounts and return the monies to the remaining family members."

Nick looked down at the stack of papers. "Mr. Bordier, you're confirming then that everything that was originally taken was in that satchel and you are going to return the money to the current living family members of the original owners? You've been able to identify those persons?"

"By tracing their family trees, yes, we know who they are. There will, of course, be fees paid to the bank, some contractual obligations fulfilled and taxes that need to be set aside, but the rest will be paid to them."

Nick continued. "What about the accounts that were stolen from the families by the SS officers pretending to be the real people. Were you able to find out to whom that money belongs?"

"We have done a thorough search, Mr. West, that began a long time ago but could do nothing until the ledgers were found and returned."

"Can I ask how much the accounts are worth?" Nick knew he would not get a straight answer.

To his surprise the banker responded. "The original accounts totaled over three hundred million dollars between seventeen families. Over the years, they have grown a considerable amount."

"So each family gets around twenty million or so, is that correct?"

The banker laughed. "Mr. West, please let me explain. The money that was originally deposited was done so as investment, not into what would be known as savings accounts. The bank was given the authority to invest whatever amounts were deemed appropriate as long as the original deposits remained intact. That money has been invested and reinvested hundreds of times over the last sixty some years. Many banks and institutions in Germany and other countries were begun and have profited quite nicely as a result of those investments. Each of these institutions was required to return a portion of those profits back into those accounts. Do you understand?"

"Is there any chance of you telling me what all those accounts are worth now?"

"Only that it's in the billions, Mr. West. That's all I am allowed to say." The banker raised an eyebrow, letting him know this line of questioning could go no further.

The banker began reading off the different documents that required his signature, making sure Nick understood what each one represented. It was extremely important that each be completed correct and reviewed before the banker went to the next. For almost an hour they sat together, going page by page, then Nick waited another fifteen minutes for them to be scrutinized by the banker once again for his approval. Finally the banker opened his briefcase and filed the documents away.

"So we are through then, because I would like to get going." An hour of sitting and completing paperwork had put Nick on edge and he was anxious to get on the road.

"For the bank, the German government and the U.S., yes, we are through. However, there are papers for you personally that must be completed in order to resolve the remaining accounts. You must know that all of this is highly classified and can never be revealed to anyone.

You have signed many papers today, Mr. West, that insures you will not divulge what we have gone over. Because of this, we now need to complete a few more transactions, then we will be finished. Shall we proceed?"

Nick let out a small sigh and knew there was no way of avoiding it. When it came to paperwork, especially government paperwork, you might as well kiss your entire day goodbye. Nick shook his head and the banker extracted a small package, opened the label and laid the remaining documents on the table.

Twenty minutes later, Nick was staring blankly at the banker. "You do know that I work for the U.S. government and that I am not …"

The banker held up Nick's resignation. "Not according to this. You resigned ten minutes before we began speaking, otherwise I would not have been allowed to talk to you. For all parties involved, it was important that you were strictly a U.S. citizen without any government affiliation. By signing and time stamping to the exact minute you resigned, I have been talking to you this entire time as a U.S. citizen, not a government employee."

"This is legal, then?" Nick sat looking at the papers, wondering what he should do.

"It is all legal and actually approved by your government. If you will sign the final document, we will be done."

"I'll sign it if you will do something for me, and it has to be done today, by close of the business day!"

"Whatever you wish, Mr. West. Please tell me what we can do for you."

Another ten minutes passed and Nick signed the paper. Getting up from the table, he reminded the banker again. "Today, it has to be done today."

"I give you my word, Mr. West, and it has been a pleasure. Please make sure you file your copies of the documents in a safe place. Once again, on behalf of my superiors, thank you, and it has been an honor."

Nick walked back to Brewster's office and caught him lifting a box onto the floor. "I wanted to stop and wish you the best of luck and say goodbye one last time. I also wanted to thank you for covering my butt on the many times I messed up and I can assure you, we all feel that way."

"Well, you probably were my biggest asshole of a headache, but you're welcome. You take care of yourself as well and look me up from time to time. You know this is not over, they won't just let you walk away. They're going to need you and you won't be able to refuse your country."

"I'll do that, Paul, and who knows, maybe I have other plans. By the way, tell Baker to call me. I have a job for him. Just tell him he has to like animals because he'll be working from the ranch."

"Oh really, got one for me too? I'm not too proud to muck stalls." Brewster laughed, which actually caught Nick by surprise.

"Not what I had in mind, at all, but I've got a feeling you'll make out OK. One last thing. There's going to be a man stopping by your house this evening. Let him in."

Brewster tapped his fingers on his desk. "If he's a friend of yours, no way."

Nick said with a large grin, "Hell, Paul, can't you please grant me one last wish before I head out, you son of a bitch? I can say that to you now because I don't work for you any more. Wow, it actually feels pretty good!"

"Get your ass out of here before I have you arrested. You're a civilian without a visitor pass. Federal offense, you know."

Nick closed the door as he shot Brewster the finger.

Chapter 28

Manny and Emily sat on the couch, waiting the arrival of Mr. Douglas Irwin from the St. Clair Bank. The appointment had been scheduled for 1:30, but he was running an hour late and the girls were getting concerned. Over the many years the family had been doing business with him, they had never known the man to be late for anything. Emily began to check through the window every five minutes and Manny fussed with the belongings in the farmhouse. Finally, a car could be seen turning into the driveway.

Looking out the window one more time, Emily let Manny know Mr. Irwin had finally arrived and was getting out of his car. Manny did a quick scan of the room and was satisfied everything was in its place as best she could make it. When the knock came at the door, both girls took a deep breath and answered it together. As he entered, there was a distinct look of despair on his face and they knew that the foreclosure proceedings would not go well. Today they would learn their financial fate from the sale of the farmhouse and what amount remained after paying off the medical and hospital bills. The amount they would see afterwards would set the direction of their futures.

Mr. Irwin apologized for his tardiness and asked the girls if they were ready to get started. Neither was eager, but decided it was best to get it over with as quickly as possible and start making plans on how they would survive in the coming years. They had agreed they would stay together and continue to help one another as only sisters could. Regardless of the difficulties ahead, they would see it through as one.

Manny spoke first. "We've looked over all of the papers you left us and completed them as you asked. I'm sure you will want to review each one first, though, before we finish the rest of the signings. I hope you don't mind, but we may have some questions we will ask as you go over each one."

"I'm sure you will have some questions and I will do my best to answer them. As much information as I have on any of these matters I will tell you. Let's begin with the transfer of the property title and go from there."

Irwin laid out the forms and the girls signed as he placed each one in front of them. He explained that all of the medical and hospital bills had been paid in full and the title had been transferred as directed by the officers of the bank.

As the girls listened, Irwin continued to speak. "An account has been set up in each of your names and the deposits were split equally into the accounts. Because of the type of accounts set up, neither of you will be required to ever pay taxes from your funds or on the interest. Arrangements had been made to pay those out of a separate account operated by the bank."

With the documents signed, Mr. Irwin presented the girls with their account statements and check ledgers sealed in individual packages. They all stood and exchanged goodbyes.

"So, when do we have to be packed and out of the house? I'm sure the bank will want to take possession as quickly as possible so they can find a buyer." Emily's voice was low but stern and proud.

The question caught Irwin by surprise. "I don't understand why you're asking me that. Did no one from the bank call you before I arrived?"

"Call us about what?" said Manny.

Irwin smiled but the girls did not see the reason. "Please sit down. The transfer of title was not to the bank, but to each of you. Both of your names are on it and all of your outstanding debts have been paid off. If you didn't know this, then perhaps you may want to open your statements I just gave you."

Manny and Emily sat for a moment trying to comprehend what the banker was saying, slowly lifting the envelopes and sliding out the ledgers. On the inside cover was a deposit in the amount of one hundred million dollars each.

The girls began to scream and started firing questions at the same time towards Irwin. "Ladies, I told you there were questions I could answer, but this is one I have been sworn not to. Before you say there has been some kind of mistake, I assure you there hasn't. Now I've got to be leaving as I have one more stop to make. Would either of you know a Mr. Paul Brewster?"

Chapter 29

The flight from Richmond to Atlanta would take just enough time for Nick to read the file he had been given containing the details on the distinguished career of Madeline Harrison. Manny had served as a U.S. Marshal for almost forty years, staying in the field, as she preferred, turning down many promotions along the way. The documents on the commendation medals she had received during that time took up nearly a quarter of the file.

In her last assignment, she and nine other agents were escorting a high profile drug cartel's son back to the United States when their convoy was ambushed as it drove down a narrow street through town. The lead vehicle was blown to pieces by a hand held rocket launcher, killing two of the agents instantly. As soon as the explosion occurred, several trucks pulled in behind the convoy to block their exit and Manny jumped from her vehicle, running back to the one carrying the fugitive.

Reaching in, she grabbed and yanked him from his seat and was immediately surrounded by two other agents trying to cover both of them as she dragged the man through an open door into a building. When she began to slam the door behind them, one of the agents caught a round in the shoulder and she pulled him through to safety before closing it.

Glancing around at their surroundings, she noted that the building contained no lower windows, only the door she had entered. Towards the back she saw a staircase and ordered the other agent to cover it. The firefight continued outside for another ten minutes before shouts could be heard and the sounds of gunfire stopped. Several holes had been punched through the door and she peered through them.

In the distance, she saw the remaining agents being led towards a back alley by three men, each pointing or pressing a weapon to the agents' heads. Knowing she had no time to cuff or immobilize the fugitive, she decided to go against protocol, raised her arm and brought the butt of her pistol down across the back of his head. She saw the agent guarding the staircase nodding his disapproval, but at the moment didn't care. Slowly pulling the door open, she stepped through and headed for the alley.

Upon rounding the corner, she heard the first gunshot and stopped, checking to make sure her weapon contained a full magazine. At the wall, she tilted her head to get a better view and saw one of the agents face down in a pool of his own blood, having been shot execution style. Each of the other agents had been placed on their knees and their captors were standing behind them. A man moved down to the next agent and placed the barrel against the back of his head.

Before the man could pull the trigger, Manny charged them, firing as quickly as she could, screaming for the agents to drop down as she rushed forward. Each of her rounds found their mark, but not before one of the captors turned and squeezed the trigger on his automatic weapon. Five rounds cut across her body, catching her in the right thigh, hip, abdomen, left shoulder and wrist. As she fell, she fired one last round through the man's heart.

Over the next year she would require seven operations before finally walking out of the hospital. Unable to return to the field, she continued for the next three years training and directing teams that eventually led in the capture of over eleven hundred fugitives before retiring and returning home to take care of her mother.

Towards the back of the file were the names of the agents who had died that day and the subsequent final documentation of closure. Of the five agents killed, three of their families would eventually face foreclosure on their homes, along with four of their children having to drop out of college for financial reasons. Although the insurance settlements were standard, it would not be enough to carry the families through the next several years until they could rebuild their lives.

Nick reached out and picked up the phone on the back of seat in front of him. Sliding his credit card through, he dialed the banker's number and waited for his voice. They talked for several minutes, then hung up after verifying the details. The 'Rayfield-Traugott Foundation' paperwork had been approved and completed, with the one hundred and sixty million dollars that had been solely intended and given to him, deposited into its account. Pennington and Chavez's names would be listed as the first official recipients of a free grant to assist and continue the lifestyle of the families of those men and women who gave their lives protecting and upholding the laws of the United States of America. With Baker's help, the fund would continue to grow and stay ahead of the needs.

Placing the card back in his wallet, he saw the piece of paper Simon had handed him in the car. Taking it out and turning it over, he read the name and number again. There was a promise to keep.

End

Author's Comments

Thank you for the opportunity to have hopefully entertained you with this book of fiction. All characters contained within are fictitious and any similarity to any real person or persons, living or dead, is coincidental. For those curious to know if a United States version of the 'Declaration of Surrender' type document exists, I have no knowledge of one ever being created or signed. The idea behind this story is from the complete imagination of the author.

On a personal note, I would like to extend my greatest appreciation to all personnel who continue the fight against terrorism both off and on American soil. No words can express my deepest gratitude.

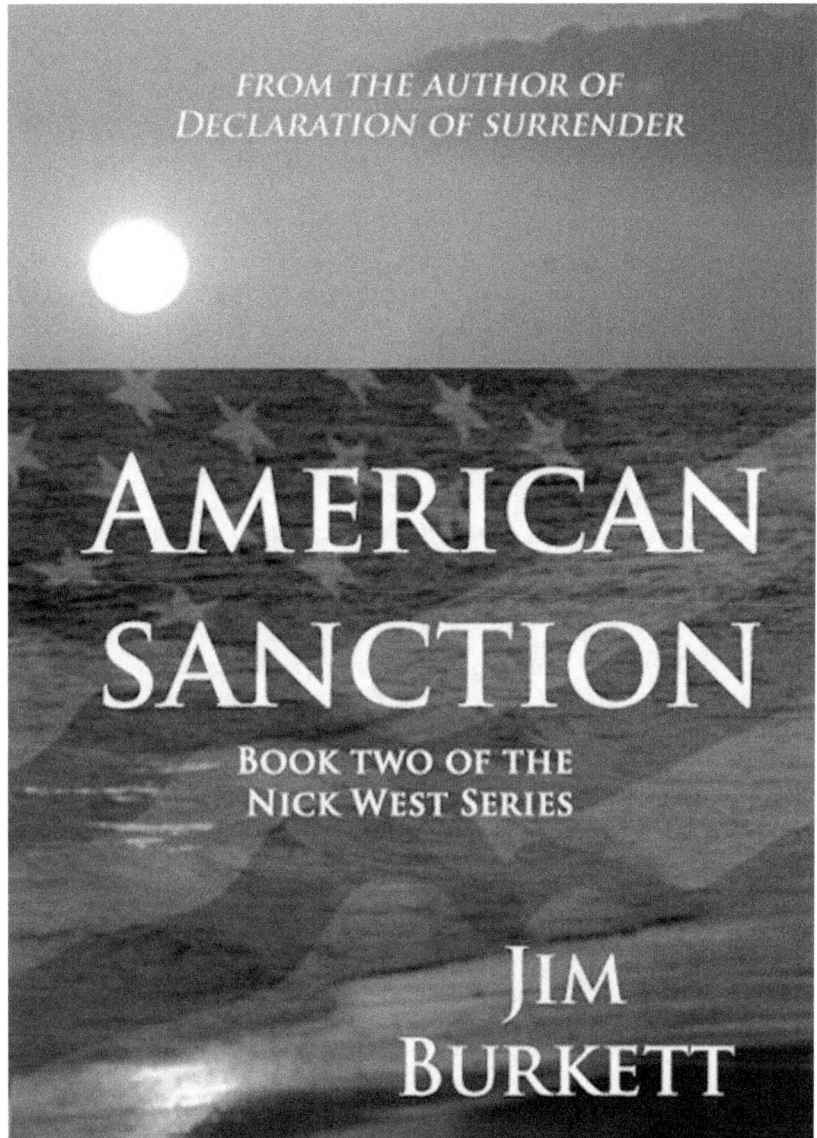

FROM THE AUTHOR OF
DECLARATION OF SURRENDER

AMERICAN SANCTION

BOOK TWO OF THE
NICK WEST SERIES

JIM
BURKETT

While keeping a promise to a friend, ex SEALs and DHS Special Agent Nicholas West is caught up in a terrorist plot to release and sell a chemical agent more deadly than any ever seen by any country, to anyone willing to pay the price. The target is the United States.

After delivering a highly classified weapon to a covert organization, the weapon itself reveals that a terrorist, thought to have been killed years earlier, is still alive and has murdered a US Senator. Discovering the terrorist has recently released a chemical toxin on the streets of California, the organization issues a sanction and limitation of only 72 hours to find and kill the terrorist before he has a chance to market the deadly chemicals to other buyers operating with their own agenda.

It is a story filled with secrets, murder, humor, friendships, betrayal, sex and horror. The twists are many and it's not over until the last page. When you think you have it all figured out, guess again!

From the author of 'Declaration of Surrender' comes a tale that you will want to read a second time and pass on to your friends. Prepare to believe in the unbelievable.

American Sanction

Jim Burkett

Published by
Inknbeans Press

This book is dedicated to the crew members of *Earthrace*, world record holder of a powerboat circumnavigating the globe, set on June 27, 2008. To my good friend Pete Bethune and his team - Adam Carlson, Mark Russell and Rob Drewett.

*Don't be afraid of death so much as an inadequate life. -
Bertolt Brecht*

Chapter 1

EuroAmerican flight 1419 began its descent into Munich as the sunlight blinded the pilot's visual sighting of the airport below. Captain Michael "Red" Ross was looking forward to the next two weeks after having scheduled and rescheduled vacation time over the past six months. The delay had been caused by a walkout of pilots who felt their six figure salary and benefits weren't enough to keep their several mistresses, in different locations around the world, happy. Those who had not walked out had been compensated very well for their loyalty, along with being given the more favorable flight routes. It had been over two years since his last leave and the upcoming time in Bermuda, and extra money, would do him and his family good.

Coming from within the interior, he could hear the sounds of the passengers' anticipation of arrival as they began to make their preparations for landing. He thought about several of the passengers he had met as they boarded the aircraft, and had extended a pleasant greeting to him. There had been the mother with her three sons, one of whom had just graduated from an Ivy League school and was on his way to Germany to begin his career. His mom teased that she would soon be able to retire and finally get that big vacation she had always wanted. The son promised he would make it happen.

Another was a couple who were on their honeymoon and seemed a bit too energetic for his liking. The new bride was having a hard time keeping her hands off her new husband, and although the man appeared to be trying to settle her down, Ross knew he was loving every minute of it.

His favorite had been the woman who had slowly made her way through the plane's entry door, with hands protectively covering her mid-section. Looking down, he guessed she was about 8 months pregnant and expecting twins.

Having remembered all of their names, he reached out

with one hand, picked up and began checking the passenger manifest to find their seat locations. The mother and her sons were in seats 14A through 14D. The expectant mother was seated in 21B and the new couple sat in first class, seats 2A and 2B. Ross made a mental note to be and sure to wish each of them the best of luck as they departed.

Approaching Düsseldorf International Airport, he could feel the crosswinds pushing the airplane gently off course and he applied several degrees right rudder to realign the plane's desired position. He listened as each aircraft ahead of his was given their call-sign and runway assignment. After finally being cleared, he switched on the Seatbelt and No Smoking signs, extracted the landing gear and relayed the departing instructions, as well as the current weather forecast, to the passengers. Touchdown was in precisely four minutes.

Applying the left rudders this time, he began a small banked arc towards runway two-four-seven, pulling back on the throttles to slow the air speed. With less than two minutes to go, he leveled the wings to *horizon* and made one final visual check to verify all of the plane's instruments were reading properly. A mile and a half away, a man peered through a field scope, following his approach, waiting for exactly the right moment. With the plane one hundred and fifty feet above the airfield, he flipped a switch on the remote he held in his hand.

Preparing to reverse engines and apply the brakes, Ross saw the small flicker on the instrument panel, coming from one of the warning lights. It was very brief and did not display again. Had he not been looking directly at the panel, he would have never seen it, nor would the logs show the blip ever being captured within the recordings of the black box.

A low voltage electrical charge flowed through a lead wire to the detonator located under the floor board of the co-pilots seat. As the current passed down the lead, it tripped and closed half of the primary circuit required to produce the spark needed for ignition. A secondary trigger sat waiting its command.

As the wheels touched the tarmac, Ross began pulling further back on the throttles and the plane eased down gently. Applying both feet firmly on the brakes, the 187 passengers could hear the engines screaming in unison as they strained against the immense gravitational pull, trying to assist in slowing down the metallic 20 ton beast hurtling down the concrete at over 300 miles per hour.

Nearing the end of the runway, the tower relayed instructions to change course and turn onto runway two-nine-zero, and approach gate seven. As he made the turn, he lifted his eyes from the flight deck; ahead was the largest commercial passenger airliner he had ever seen. He recognized it immediately. Sitting on an inside runway, the Stratobus A900 was preparing for its maiden voyage. At a cost of nearly 600 million dollars, there were only three in existence.

Across the bottom of the two wings, there were attached a total of six Rolls Royce engines, all fitted with electrically actuated thrust reversers. The avionics employed an Integrated Avionics architecture used in advance military aircraft. The seating capacity for this flight had been limited to 900 passengers, with all passengers being treated to first class, VIP luxuries. Cruising speed was Mach 0.90, nearing 600 miles per hour. On board was a small shopping center, casino and movie theater, along with a half dozen other small restaurants and gym facilities.

Reducing roll speed to twenty miles per hour and closing in on the Stratobus, he could not help but stare at its size. His own aircraft was dwarfed by the vast wingspan of the other plane. He watched as the last of the fueling trucks pulled away and the turbines began to start up as EuroAmerican flight 1419 eased even closer. Four hundred yards from the craft, Captain Ross once again heard the tower instruct him to cross over runways in front of the Stratobus and proceed towards the terminal. In the short distance, the turbines continued to increase speed.

Inside the solid glass terminal were just over one

thousand passengers who had stayed after arriving from their earlier flights. In the mix were an additional hundred or so photographers, cameramen and reporters, present to capture the takeoff of one of the most spectacular aeronautical achievements mankind had ever built. From the exterior of the terminal, it would appear as if the people inside were stacked eighty feet high, separated only by the steel skeletal framing that ran both horizontally and vertically inside the glass casing. The elevators appeared to be individual, moving human spinal columns. It all reminded him of the ant farms he had played with as a boy.

Pulling back on the throttles four degrees to decrease the speed several knots, Ross reached for the Unfasten Seatbelt switch. Flipping it, he completed the secondary circuit. The back of the plane lifted from the blast, ripping away the tail section as the fireball ran the length of fuselage, then back out the open end of the carnage, sucked towards the whirling turbines of the Stratobus.

As the plane slammed back down onto the tarmac, seats sheared from their mountings. The charred bodies of seats 14A, 14B and 21B were among those engulfed in the fireball and sent flying towards the spinning blades of the Stratobus. In less than ten seconds, the first of the flames and bodies reached engine number three. The engine coughed several times, then began to shred apart as millions of small metal fragments exploded from their encapsulated compartment and headed outwards in all directions. In contemporaneous harmony, each of the remaining five engines began to erupt.

Glass in the terminal began to splinter, then shatter, sending billions of slivers cutting through the panicked crowd. One by one, the floors began to collapse. As the Stratobus became a raging inferno, the heat began twisting the wind currents at cyclonic speeds. Small to medium size aircraft and buildings structures became airborne, quickly becoming vaporized as they passed through the fire. Those who survived the flying glass and heat began to stand. One by one, they were lifted from their shoes, vacuumed into the vortex.

In the distance, a man smiled. After several moments, he turned and walked towards the master bedroom. Inside, two adults lay tied together, their eyes and mouths covered by a thin layer of cloth. Next to them, their four month old son played in his crib. Raising the Glock 17, the man double-tapped the heads of the parents, then placed the barrel against the chest of the child. Tightening his hand around the grip of the pistol, he began to slowly pull back on the trigger.

A hand grabbed him by the shoulder and he heard a voice telling him it was time to go. As they both ran out the door, he quickly fired one round through the crib.

For the next five days, the inferno continued to burn, taking with it over two thousand lives. A total of seventeen firemen and police officers would also perish. Dozens more would have died had they not been told to stand down until it was safe to approach the remains and begin tagging the bodies that had not been completely turned to ash.

Chapter 2

Large rain droplets smashed against the office window as the swirling wind outside pounded against the building's structural frame. She stared, looking out, oblivious to the sounds and fury of another approaching seasonal storm. From her vantage point, she could see the cliffs below, the waves continuing to carve away at the granite rock as they had done for thousands of years. Lost in her thoughts, she fixated on the smooth patterns and details like a buyer examining a masterpiece of art one last time before a purchase.

Passing a hand gently over her stomach, she could remember where the baby's foot had pressed against the inside wall. It had been such a small human feature in the cup of her hand. Simon would have been proud, she thought, as the tears rolled down onto the black dress, now hanging loose from her shoulders. She had hoped to surprise him on his return from the United States, knowing she could never break silence and contact him during a mission.

The doctors had warned them both that it would be an exceptionally high risk pregnancy at her age, but given the amount of scar tissue from the past incident, going full term would be almost impossible. For a while they put the idea aside. In their business, everything was a risk, but Simon was dead set against taking on any risk that he had control over that put her life in jeopardy. They finally accepted the fact that their careers took precedence and that bringing a child into the world could carry tribulations that neither wanted to accept.

Two and a half months after Simon had left for the United States, the self-testing applicator clearly indicated she was pregnant. Almost four months into the pregnancy, the doctors advised her she would not carry the baby full term and recommended she either abort now or prepare herself. She refused to believe they were right, but they eventually would be. Two days after the loss of the baby, she was notified of Simon's death.

The funerals for both the baby and Simon were more than she could bear, having needed support reentering the car that waited to return her to headquarters. Her superiors begged her to take leave and get the much needed rest her mind and body would require, but this is where she felt most safe. Work would become the only obsession that gave her life purpose now.

Ignoring their requests would soon result in signs of fatigue and other poor decisions. Three weeks had passed and although she was handling herself professionally to all who came in contact with her, she remained devastated inside and did not know how much longer she could keep up the pretense without breaking down completely.

She never heard the phone ring on her desk and did not respond until a hand touched hers. Turning slowly to face her assistant, her mind could not register the words that were being spoken until it comprehended the name 'Nicholas West'. As she looked up, she could see the ex DHS Special Agent standing outside her office, accompanied by two large well armed guards, each holding an M4 and strapped with a 9mm sidearm. In West's hands, he held the case containing her deceased husband's material goods, a sniper rifle she had given him as a birthday present 5 years earlier.

As she stood and approached Nick, she already felt a bond with the man, a man her husband had trusted and given his life protecting, a man to whom he had passed on a final request, knowing that this man would see it through to the end, out of total respect and gratitude. Nick West was a man of honor and beyond reproach.

Extending her hand, she placed it in Nick's, then wrapped an arm around his neck, pulling herself against him warmly, lingered for a moment, then stepped back, offering a smile of welcome. For Nick, it was an unexpected greeting and he was unsure how to respond. Maybe it was how they welcomed one another in this country, he thought.

The staff was mildly shocked as well by the gesture and eyed one another for a brief moment, not having ever seen this behavior before from their superior. Whoever Nick West was, they immediately felt a guarded camaraderie with him and began to go back to their assigned responsibilities. The armed security held their positions until she nodded towards them, then took one final look and left.

Entering her office, she held the door then closed it behind him after Nick had passed. Pointing to a chair for him to sit, she began to walk around behind her desk, at which point Nick noticed how frail the woman looked. Nick waited for her to sit, then took his chair.

"Welcome to Ireland, Mr. West. I hope the flight was pleasant. Also, thank you for bringing my husband's personal belongings back. It means a great deal to both of us." She did not feel it was important to go into any further detail on her last comment.

Nick held his surprise as best he could, as it never occurred to him that the woman sitting on the other side of the desk would be Simon's wife or that he was even married. Now the quick hug made sense. The more he learned of Simon, the greater the admiration and realization of just how private the man was. He also knew it was, in most part, the need to protect his loved ones from his enemies.

"I have to confess that of the little time I spent with Simon, he did not mention to me that you were his wife. He only asked that I contact you and bring the equipment back in case he was unable to. I am very sorry for your loss."

"Simon would not have been able to reveal that to anyone, even if wanted. We have very strict disciplines not to ever let anyone know that information. I could tell you didn't know I was his wife by your reaction, and that is good. And I will trust you will not repeat that knowledge outside this office." She held her gaze on Nick for a moment, then felt slightly embarrassed that she had said it.

"There is no need for me to; I know the importance of why you are asking." He hesitated before asking the next question.

"Simon was very adamant that I bring the rifle back to you and you alone. If I felt my trip here was in any way in jeopardy, he wanted me to destroy it immediately, especially the scope. Can I ask why?"

Olexia Syshchenko looked at him in surprise. Simon would have never passed along that request had he known he was not going to return. Even so, it solidified her gut feelings that Simon had trusted this man more than she had ever known him to trust anyone before. Evading the question for the moment, she asked, "May I see the rifle?" as she placed her hand out towards the case.

Nick inserted the key Simon had given him, turned it, then flipped up the three latches. Extracting the rifle with both hands, he laid it on her outstretched hand, expecting her to half drop it onto her desk, due to the weight. Instead, she gripped it expertly and lifted it onto her lap with her one arm.

"I'm afraid I can't tell you anything about the rifle, its mechanisms or advanced design. These are all trade secrets that only a handful of technical people and I have authority to know."

Nick was not used to being denied information about anything he asked. Most questions pertained only to 'need to know' requests, so if he asked, then it was relevant. He never crossed into territory that he felt was not his business, only caring if it was critical to the mission and would keep his men or himself alive. "Alright, I can respect that. However, in all honesty, I did look over the entire weapon and saw some things that had me curious."

"Again, Mr. West, I cannot answer those types of questions. Whatever you want to know about its design, you simply do not have the authority. The only reason you are aware of some of its components, is because my husband trusted you. I would like to ask that you do not pursue your line of questions any further."

"Please accept my apologies." Nick was annoyed by being spoken to so bluntly, but understood. "Now that I've delivered the rifle, is there anything I can answer before I leave and travel back to the United States?"

"No, everything has been taken care of as far as Simon's body being returned, and you have brought us the second most important item. I want to thank you again for helping my husband. It was always very hard for him to trust anyone other than myself, so he must have felt something very strong with you. May your trip back home be a pleasant journey." With the conversation abruptly finished, she pressed a button on the underside of her desk and the two guards reappeared before Nick had fully stood and straightened his jacket.

Waiting until Nick and the guards had entered the elevator, she punched several digits on the phone and waited for the senior engineer to walk through the door of an adjoining office. As he stepped in, she immediately asked him if the scan had been processed and a positive ID had been made. The engineer assured her Nick was authenticated, however, the finger imprint on the trigger of the rifle did not match Nick's. The imprint was from his wife.

"Were there any other prints found on the rifle?" asked Olexia.

"No, it's completely clean. The only two prints were Mr. West and his wife, Laura."

"Please take the weapon to have the chip extracted and read. Let me know when you're ready and I will be there. No one other than you or I are to be present. You will process the encryption and video yourself. Absolutely no one else is to touch any part of that rifle."

The engineer took out a small card and inserted it into the butt of the rifle. The card contained a code that opened the only compartments of the two existing rifles that held the multi-million dollar chip. Upon the press of his finger, a latch holding the scope released and he gently eased the wrapped electronics from a concealed compartment, placing it in a small airtight container the size of a dime. Turning towards the door that led in the direction of the lab, he spoke over his shoulder as he hurried out. "I should be ready in fifteen minutes."

Ten minutes later, Olexia was sitting in a theater while the high definition screen played the decrypted recordings. The video had been forwarded ahead and began with the last image of the man who had killed her husband. She watched as the man's head exploded and his body fell backwards, thrown off of DHS Special Agent Nick West by the impact from the 50 caliber projectile. There was no movement for several minutes until finally she saw Nick rise from the ground and approach the position of the rifle, his body growing larger as he got closer. She saw a continuous flow of blood streaming from his shoulder as his arm dangled lifelessly by his side. In the background, she saw the lifeless image of her husband's body.

Holding back tears and trying to keep her voice steady, Olexia said, "Run the video back to the beginning and let it play forward. I want to know every last detail of my husband's life before he was killed." The engineer now understood why she had asked that no one else be present. Even he felt uncomfortable watching while his employer sat grief-stricken in the same room.

Over the next half hour, they watched several unknown faces appear and disappear from the screen. In the corner was a much smaller secondary screen that identified each person through the HDR (High Dynamic Range) facial recognition software. If there was no match, which was very seldom, a duplicate image was taken and automatically fed to an in-house database where a large team of technicians would continue the analysis. In the opposite corner, a clock showed the date and time of when the video was recorded, as well as how much time remained until all recordings ended.

With four minutes, forty-seven seconds left, the screen flickered and Olexia knew immediately that Simon had switched the recording to manual, disengaging all electronic surveillance features. It meant that he had intended for the recording to be held internally and not transmitted for elucidation. Why?

There was a small break between recordings when the screen went black, then returned to the next video. When the following video displayed, it showed the back of a man's head moving in a direction from front left to right, then back to the left again in very quick, erratic movements. He was engaged in a conversation with another man and his actions indicated he was angrily disagreeing with what was being discussed. In the next set of frames, the man reached out and grabbed the other man by the lapel of his coat, swinging him around and placing a gun to his face.

Seconds later, the man appeared to be pleading for his life before his head was thrown backwards as a plume of pink substance exited and a large piece of hair and bone tore away from his skull. She continued to watch intently as the gunman spit on the man's face, then released his hold to allow the body to collapse to the ground.

Redirecting her eyes to the person holding the gun, her body tightened and her mind froze as if gripped by a chill that pierced all the way through, down to her core. "Oh my God!" She grabbed for the phone. "Stop him! Don't let West get out of the building!"

Chapter 3

Nick slipped the electronic key into the rectangular ignition slot and pushed the start button. The Porsche 918's engine exploded with the harmonious sound of the bass exhaust and revved with the slightest touch on the gas pedal. Turning his head to check street traffic as he backed out, he caught a glimpse of the guard holding a small plug to his ear and pressing it in tighter as if to make sure he understood what was being said. Based upon the guard's reaction, Nick began to feel some uneasiness. Looking back at the guard, he saw the M4 swing up and point directly at him. To his right, another guard quickly followed suit and pointed his M4 at the engine block, causing Nick to immediately apply the brakes, shift into neutral, reach up and switch off the engine.

Outside, he could see the both men holding positions, and listened as he was ordered out of the car. Opening the door slowly, he climbed out, asking why he was being detained at gunpoint.

"Sir, we have orders to return you to headquarters. We were not given a reason, nor is one needed. You will come with us and that is not a request, sir!" The man was overreacting to the situation like a new recruit trying to impress a superior officer. It may have been in part due to his original training, but it was not impressing, nor intimidating West.

Nick stood so he could see both men at the same time. "Regardless of what this is about, I'm only going to ask you once to lower your weapons. At this moment I'm not a threat to you, but if you insist on parading me through your headquarters like this, I promise you, I will be." Nick stared straight into the eyes of the overzealous guard, awaiting his next move. He had spoken calmly and directly.

In times past, the guards' theatrics had brought a few men to tears, but both security men could see they were dealing with a seasoned professional, and brought their weapons even higher, pointing them directly at Nick's head, motioning for him to begin walking back towards the building. Nick could plainly see the apprehension on their faces.

Upon entering, the guards lowered the automatic weapons, but produced their sidearms, with one man taking the lead in front of Nick, and the other, a close but safe distance behind. When the elevator floor button was pressed, Nick saw that he was being escorted back to Olexia's office.

Stepping off the elevator, Nick followed the lead man. Instead of turning towards her office, however, they continued down a series of hallways until they came to a sealed door. To the right was a panel displaying both a fingerprint and retina scanner. "Sir, please place your palm on that screen and lean forward towards the small laser dot, keeping your right eye open and directly in front of that lens."

When Nick started to question the order, the guard took one step back, extended his arm and placed the nose of the 9mm an inch from Nick's forehead. "Sir, I will not ask you again."

Before the man could blink, Nick grabbed his wrist, pushing it upwards, at the same time taking a small step backwards and throwing an elbow hard into the other security man's throat. Having immobilized the second guard for the time being, Nick countered, throwing a hard punch into the gunman's armpit, causing the arm to become temporarily paralyzed.

Placing his forearm in the crux of the guard's elbow, Nick bent the man's arm back towards and past his shoulder. As the man's elbow joint snapped, Nick forced the man downward, bringing up a knee and catching him squarely under the chin. The man's head snapped to the left upon impact and Nick released his grip as the man fell hard on both knees.

With one last effort before blacking out, the guard reached for the dropped gun with his remaining good arm. Nick slapped both open palms against the man's ears, causing the rupture of both eardrums and total loss of equilibrium.

The man fell face forward. For the rest of his life, the guard would hear ringing in his ears and never get a full night's sleep again.

Spinning back around, Nick saw the second guard still clutching at his throat, gasping for air. His eyes widened as Nick stepped forward and shot a punch into his chest, directly at his heart. Not wanting to cause further damage to the man who looked at him with terror in his eyes, Nick let the man sink downwards until he rolled onto his side, gradually curling into a fetal position.

Stepping over the two fallen men, Nick returned his attention to the scanners. It was possible this institute had his fingerprints, but he never recalled having taken a retina scan for anyone while either employed in the military, Secret Service or DHS. He knew the match would fail and wondered what would happen next. Nick placed his open hand on the flat screen and his right eye an inch from the scanner.

A small blue laser light shone directly into his eye for a brief moment, accompanied by a tiny stinging sensation to the right of the eyeball. He blinked twice, but otherwise ignored it. Within a matter of seconds, the match was confirmed and the doors slid open revealing Olexia standing in the doorway.

Seeing her men down, she threw a cold stare at Nick, then, without saying a word, turned and began walking down a dimly lit corridor. As he stepped through the opening, he heard Olexia's voice. "In the future, I would appreciate you not causing my employees harm and the loss of their jobs." A panel of soft lights lit the floor and he could see Olexia's silhouette disappearing into a room containing a series of computer banks and a large projector screen.

Nick quickened his pace and followed. Once he had taken a seat, Olexia began adjusting several of the panel's switches. When the instruments were set to her satisfaction, she paused and looked at Nick. Her personality had taken on a different, more direct and serious tone. The change put Nick on alert, changing his manner as well.

"Did my husband confide in you anything before he was killed? Did he mention to you what he was doing prior to him meeting with you?" Olexia was trying to keep her composure steady, but Nick was able to read the strain in her voice and knew something new had developed, from the time he had left her office, until now.

"No and no. The first time I met your husband, he had a gun pointed at the back of my head. Not your normal introduction that gets things off to a good and meaningful relationship." Nick tried to read a change in the expression on Olexia's face, but there was none.

Anticipating his response, Olexia pressed a button on the console. Nick shifted in his chair as the lights dimmed further and the screen began to display a high definition video of two men arguing. The man directly in front was Senator James Brighton. Nick recalled that the man had been in the papers several weeks earlier, having committed suicide after learning he was under investigation for bribery and theft of classified governmental documents.

As Nick continued to watch, he saw the other man reach out, grab the senator and swing him in a full 180 degree turn, so the senator's back was to the screen. In the next instance, he saw the gun swing up and blow the senators brains out. So much for suicide, he thought.

In the next instance, the shooter looked up directly at the camera, holding a steady gaze as if he was looking at an object in the far distance. Nick's heart jumped. The face was older and much different, but unmistakable.

What had once served as the right side of the shooter's face, was gone, replaced by unnatural layers of skin from the multiple grafts taken from his own legs and torso. Nick glanced at Olexia, not having wanted to take his eyes off of the screen. Her expression confirmed what his mind did not want to accept or know was true. Abdul Qasim Ahmad was indeed alive. Ahmad had survived despite several intelligence report confirmations to the contrary.

Following the news of his death, Nick's own team had been dispatched to Afghanistan to eradicate several men who were in the midst of planning an attack against those who they believed had murdered their leader. Had they succeeded, the realization of a nuclear war would have been brought to America's doorstep.

Chapter 4

"When did you get this, and from whom?" Nick was trying his best to keep his emotions in check as he stood and moved closer to the screen. The clarity of the image was remarkable.

"From you, Mr. West, about 20 minutes ago."

The answer took him by surprise. Pointing back towards the screen, he turned to Olexia, no longer wishing to be polite to his hostess. "What are you talking about? I've never seen this footage before and I sure as hell would have recognized Ahmad way before I ever got here. That man was supposedly killed almost six years ago in a sniper kill by one of his own men."

"Your American intelligence is faulty. We had heard, on occasion, rumors that he was still alive, but all of our resources indicated he was either dead or left an invalid as a result of, well, we will call it an accident."

"Well then, I would say both of our teams of intelligence experts were wrong. Now answer my other questions." Nick was looking back and forth between the screen and Olexia.

"The rifle that you brought back has many additional features that we developed, mostly to protect ourselves from an unauthorized kill. One of those features allows the user to record whatever they are targeting."

"What? Through the scope, maybe some kind of optical insertion at the end of the barrel?"

Olexia stared back at Nick. "I told you. The specifics are classified."

Nick took several steps forward until he was less than six inches from her face. "That man just executed a U.S. Senator and is responsible for the deaths of over eighteen hundred people. I don't care what kind of authority I have or need. You will tell me what I want to know, now!"

"Mr. West, you hold no authority over me or my organization. You had better understand that you are a guest and have no security clearance since you left your employment at DHS. I can have you arrested right now and you wouldn't see daylight again until I alone authorize your release. Screw with me the wrong way and I'll have you buried alive in some unmarked grave or have your body dumped in a swamp somewhere. Are we clear on that?"

"Lady, you can threaten me if you like, but *you* had better understand that you have information on the death of a U.S. senator that was ruled a suicide. Now we can call it a homicide. The man that killed him was the second most wanted international terrorist ever known before Osama bin Laden was taken down. If you think I will not let it be known that he is still alive before you do whatever you plan to do with me, you are badly mistaken.

"Don't threaten me, Mr. West. I promise you, you will not like the consequences."

Nick did not back down. "My government will tear your organization apart for years to come and will arrest anyone it finds remotely associated with it, no matter who they are or mistakenly believe they are beyond our reach. Are *we* clear on that? "

Knowing what actions the United States could and would take against her and her beloved organization, she stepped back and hit the console lights to stop the video. Her threats were useless on this man and he was proving to be a worthy adversary. She knew she would have to tread very carefully and appear submissive to his demands, for the time being. It would now be a matter of survival, not just for her, but for all of them.

Olexia would need to do whatever was necessary to guarantee no one outside of her group learned Ahmad was still alive. She decided it would be beneficial if they worked not as opposition, but partners.

Clearing her throat, she began. "The scope is the heart of the rifle. Everything is calibrated and recorded digitally. The most important feature is the built-in high definition camera that records all shots and sends a data feed back to us to verify the kill. Our clients demand that we prove our work. It is also used to resolve any disingenuous disputes regarding the positive identification of the target by employing facial recognition."

Olexia stopped for a moment to gauge Nick's reaction, then continued. "When a kill is sanctioned and a member is sent to complete a mission, the identifying points of a target's facial characteristics are fed into a digital chip located at the base of the scope. When that person's face is scanned and the data feed is received, unless there is a match, the rifle will not fire. This assures us of complete target accuracy prior to our kills."

"What if the shooter has no other choice but to take a shot in a situation that requires it, whether it matches on a target or not?"

Her reply was quick. "There is an override, but every member knows that if it is used, we can no longer protect the sanction. If they disengage the mechanism and kill someone in error, they are accountable to whatever agency or country hired us."

"You said there is a data feed. I have to believe that the transmission is encrypted some way so as not to be intercepted during the transfer." Nick was thinking of the files that he had received earlier from Baker.

As if Olexia could read Nick's mind, she responded. "Your Mr. Baker has long been instrumental in helping us with that, even though he is completely unaware of his gift to our organization. Although we have not yet been able to duplicate his latest efforts, we were able to break a portion of his key last year before it became impossible for us to keep up with his skills. We would love to have him in our fold."

"So Simon took this footage while under contract for another kill and couldn't eliminate Ahmad since it wasn't sanctioned?"

"Simon had full international immunity. He could have killed anyone he needed to provided it was justifiable, but that would have meant he would no longer be able to complete his sanction. Simon never failed, or at least that's what we thought."

"Will you answer me something else?"

"Ask, but I won't guarantee I'll answer." Olexia was already worried what would happen to her should her superiors ever learn of this conversation. She had already crossed all barriers of what would be considered acceptable by them. Under Nick's threat, though, she had taken the risk.

"How do you have a retinal scan of my eye? I have never provided that to anyone."

"When you first entered the elevator, you felt a small brush of air against your face, probably thinking it was air pushed by the closing of the door. It is timed that way so no one's suspicions are aroused. The small air blast blows away any moisture or particles on your eyeball, at the same time a small scanner digitally snaps several hundred images of its entire surface. That information is then fed into our database, compared against existing patterns and tagged. We also do both 3D and 4D bio-scans of your entire body, including fingerprints, skeletal and facial structures, any possible hidden objects, and collect any hair follicles that are dispersed. Those follicles are vacuumed when the air blast is triggered. In a matter of seconds, we know more about you physically than your lover, or should I say wife, as it happens to be."

"Doesn't that fall somewhere within the realm of 'invasion of privacy'?"

"Not our concern. We do it to protect ourselves. If a positive id was not made of you before you reached the third floor, the elevator would have stopped and you would have been escorted elsewhere. Fortunately, we already had your fingerprints from your military records, otherwise our original meeting would have been delayed somewhat or would have never happened."

Nick nodded. "So by an entire body scan, you mean everything?"

A small smile appeared across her face, understanding fully what Nick was asking. "Don't worry Mr. West. I can assure you your wife is a very happy woman."

Rolling his eyes, Nick continued. "Let's get back to Ahmad. Senator Brighton was killed 17 days ago in Wyoming. Any idea why Ahmad targeted him?"

"Senator Brighton led the charge in getting U.S. Sky Marshals assigned to all commercial aircraft leaving and entering United States airspace after 9/11. One of his sub-committees was responsible for monitoring assignments on all non-military aircraft, including Secret Service aboard Air Force One."

"You think he's after the President?" Nick blurted out.

"I think he at least needs to know about your air traffic patterns." With that, Olexia began pressing a series of buttons to turn on the overhead lights.

"What else do you know about Ahmad that I should be aware of before I report this information back to my government?"

Olexia stopped pressing buttons. "You can not report any of this! You place all of us in extreme danger, including your own citizens, if Ahmad gets wind that we know he is alive. If you insist, I will not allow you to leave. Do you understand what I am saying?"

For the first time, Nick was beginning to understand the fear Olexia was now showing. Ahmad terrified her. From watching her handle Simon's weapon, he knew she was not a civilian. She had special training skills that went beyond practice at some gun range. This was a professional and she was scared.

"What do you propose, then? I have a terrorist running around the United States and you want me to keep my mouth shut. That's not the way I operate and I am sure you know it."

"Yes. I am well aware of what actions you will take once you get home. I need for you to allow me a few days to make arrangements to eliminate Ahmad on my own." She was almost imploring Nick for this one request.

"I should be making phone calls right now, lady. The last we knew of his whereabouts was seventeen days ago. My guess, since he is already in the United States, is that he has already laid out any ground work he needed to have done, months ago."

"If you make any call, I assure you, you will not make it back to the states. That is not a threat on my part, but a guarantee he will be aware of your actions very quickly and will take actions to make sure you do not return. We are standing in a sound proof room for a reason."

"Alright. So, I will ask you once again. What do you propose?"

Olexia had already thought it through. "You work for me until Ahmad is dead, then you can walk away. You have two options. Only one will keep you alive. If you leave here and decide to pursue Ahmad on your own, many of your people will die, including you and your wife. At least with me, you will have everything and anything you need to accomplish that task."

"Olexia, I appreciate what you are offering, but I will take my chances. If he is in the United States, I will find him before he has a chance to find me."

"He most likely will not fight you on your own soil. He hates America and he knows if he dies, he will be buried there. There would be no greater insult to him and he won't chance it."

Nick took in a breath and let it out slowly. "Then I propose we work together on this. You from your side and I from mine. Once he is dead, though, whatever information we share goes public, and I release it after seventy-two hours, regardless."

Olexia thought for a moment, knowing if her seventy-two hours were up and Ahmad was not dead, she would have to kill West, but she would keep that decision to herself. She knew the man was not bluffing and would contact his old friends at DHS immediately once the timeline had expired.

"You will need to be sheltered from any repercussion that may happen as a result of your actions, but we have a deal."

Nick looked at her solemnly. "There is no deal, just an understanding. I think my government will be pretty lenient with whatever actions I may take to capture a terrorist or dispose of one if needed."

Olexia laughed quietly and turned away from Nick so he could not see her sneer. "You seriously think he will allow himself to be captured? Please take my full offer, Mr. West."

When Nick did not respond, she looked back around, only to see him heading down the corridor, not waiting for any further discussion. They had seventy-two hours to hunt down Ahmad and he wasn't going to waste any more time.

She had only seconds to make a decision of how to protect herself should Nick West not keep his promise. Back in her office, she picked up a pen and signed her name on the official document.

Chapter 5

Abdul Qasim Ahmad sat quietly, relaxing outside, sitting at a small two chair café table, his espresso diluted by the heavy cream poured only moments earlier by an indifferent, unassuming waiter. As he smiled politely at the pedestrians that walked past, he stirred his coffee, flipped the pages of a local paper and watched the traffic coming and going from a men's hat shop across the street.

Inside the shop were Omar Hemed and his wife and three children, along with eight customers all glancing at an assortment of items perfectly arranged on open shelves. Through the window, Ahmad could see Omar laughing, with both his hands gesturing in several directions, appearing to try and explain the latest styles to a man who had no interest in what he was trying to sell. The man had entered the shop only to appease his wife's insistent nagging that he try and cover his bald head with something other than a forty dollar toupee.

Beads of sweat began to form on Abdul's forehead as he became mesmerized by the hand movements, unable to take his eyes off of them. They were the same gestures he had watched six years earlier, before the bullet ripped away the right side of his face.

He mind regressed to the memory of him and Omar arguing over a plan to send his men into what amounted to be a suicide mission. The frontal attack would require the majority of their men, exposing their flanks should the enemy decide to spread out and encircle the charging battalions. Disagreeing entirely, Ahmad felt his men should break into groups and charge individually from different points, causing the enemy to continually move about so his men could develop a stronghold position.

As Ahmad listened to Omar, he noticed him removing a red scarf that he always wore around his neck. Often times, he wondered if Omar continued to wear it when he made love to his many wives. As Omar began to move away slowly, taking inch long backward shuffles, Ahmad suddenly realized the reason for this unusual behavior. As his heart began to race, he turned his head slightly upwards toward the hillside and saw the flash. He had been betrayed by his closest friend and comrade. The removal of the scarf had been a signal. A split second later, the bullet ripped through his flesh, tearing away the right side of his face and cheekbone.

Now he watched as Omar rang up a sale, wishing the buyer a prosperous New Year as he said goodbye to them. Omar then turned to next customer to repeat the shameful display of disgrace to his past. He was once a man that was much-loved by those whom he commanded. They would be shamed by their sins and beg forgiveness from Ahmad if they were to ever learn of Omar's duplicity. It was time to enter the shop.

Standing, he reached down and picked up the Fedora, running a fingertip gently around the three-inch ribbon, making sure it was secure. Underneath, a small wire was attached to the underside of the ribbon, with the other end leading to a thin strand of C4 explosive and a slender packet of Musarogen, hidden by the band.

With the Fedora placed and pulled down to cover the right side of his face, Abdul Ahmad strolled to the front door, holding it aside for the woman who was holding several packages, to exit. He watched to make sure she did not take a second look at him, then entered. He could clearly hear the voice of his betrayer, causing him to recall the memory once again as the sweat began to reappear on his forehead. May you rot for eternity, he thought to himself.

Standing at the counter, he waited for the oldest son to finish the money exchange with his current customer, than stepped forward, reaching up and pulling the hat from his head. "Good morning. I would like to see if I can have a new black ribbon mounted on this hat. This one is worn. I would like to leave it and come back in about an hour, if that is convenient for you?"

"Of course. Would you want the same type ribbon or something in a different style?" The son's voice was that of his father's, causing Abdul to swallow before answering. The son was clearly trying not to stare at Abdul's scars, but Abdul had seen the looks before, and dismissed the angry thoughts in his head.

"What is on there now will work fine." Abdul kept his face turned slightly, watching to make sure they were not interrupted. As the son shook his head in agreement, Abdul began to turn towards the door, raising a finger and pointing towards a hanging clock on the wall. "Then I will return in an hour, and please tell your father, Omar, that Abdul said hello."

With that, he quickly made his way to the door, picking up his pace as he pulled the door shut behind him. Out of the corner of his eye, he could see Omar approaching his son, again gesturing as he walked to the other side of the street. When he was satisfied he was at a safe enough distance, he turned back towards the shop, with his back to the wind.

He looked on as the son spoke with his father, showing him the hat and pointing to the ribbon. Abdul could read lips very well and his pulse quickened when he saw the son speak his name. Omar's eyes searched frantically as fear gripped his body. He turned to stare into the eyes of his avenger as the son pulled at the old ribbon.

The explosion began as a small flash, like a light bulb popping, with just enough force to rip open the plastic casing holding the Musarogene. A minute spark caught the hat on fire, but not before the toxic molecules were dispersed into the air. The case held enough chemical to kill or maim any living organism within 20 feet, but if it were to escape and be carried into the winds, it would kill as far as the currents blew. Omar and his son began clawing at their face and eyes, trying to relieve the burning as their skin began to peel away at every touch. One by one, the customers began coughing, then followed in the same unsuccessful attempt to end the agonizing blistering of their flesh. With each breath, the molecules were inhaled deeper, continuing to burn and scald the interior layers. Capillaries and vessels began to burst, filling their lungs with blood.

Desperately attempting to try and help one another, they could not as their eyeballs began to discharge fluid and contract. Unable to assist his wife, a man panicked and ran towards a glass window, crashing through it in hopes of finding aid. With a forced push of air, the molecules found a new direction and quickly followed the man out the broken window, escaping their current confinements.

Inside the shop, the hat continued to burn and soon ignited a rack of ties that had been lying across the counter. The counter erupted into a massive blue, red, yellow and green flame, catching everything on fire within its reach. As the other windows burst, the flames leaped and set fire to several patrons walking by, unable to duck and escape in time, setting their clothes ablaze. Some of the crowd froze with horror as they watched others staggering, rubbing and tearing away multiple layers of epidermis, screaming and imploring for any compassion a stranger could give. Instead, the people around them began to urgently scratch their own bodies. As the chemical worked its way through the layers, muscles began to constrict and spasm so violently, arm and leg bones broke at their weakest points, ripping and protruding through the now thin layers of skin.

Next door, a small grocery store specializing in rotisserie meat items began to catch fire. Along the wall sat dozens of containers of propane the store sold for use in grilling. As the flames lapped around the containers, the owner and an employee began turning them on their sides and rolling them away. Rushing too quickly, one of the employee's hands slipped, hitting a shutoff value and opening it. One canister after another began to ignite.

Other row shops soon became a part of the expanding firestorm. Across the street, a lone man stood watching casually, smiled, then turned and walked away, his defiled face pressed against the wind.

Chapter 6

As Nick sped towards the airport, he punched the phone button on the steering wheel console and spoke the name of the only person he employed that could research what he needed.

After several long rings, the voice came on the phone. "Nick, what the hell are you doing in Ireland?" said Baker.

"Not right now, I'll explain later. I need this conversation scrambled before I continue. Let me know when you are ready."

Baker knew that Nick was aware that all incoming and outgoing calls were private, so the comment alerted him that something was not right. "Our conversations are always concealed, you know that. No one has the sophistication yet to decrypt our vocal recordings. So what's up?"

"I just needed you to be aware of the importance of this call. I need you to find any intel that anyone has on Abdul Qasim Ahmad. Search all international networks as well, going back far as the intel will take you. Pay the most attention to the last six to seven years. It has to be done without alerting anyone."

Nick took a quick glance at his speed and noted he was 38 mph over the limit. He kept having to remind himself that he no longer had privileges and eased off of the accelerator, slightly. He couldn't afford the time lost pulling over for a ticket or his name recorded on any file inside of this country. If he had to appear before a grand jury, he would have to explain why he kept secret the knowledge that a terrorist had killed a government official and he had not reported it immediately.

"Why do you need intel on a dead guy?"

"It turns out that is not the case. He survived his injuries." Nick listened to the silence on the other end and wished he was able to see Baker's face. "The guy's still alive and running around in the United States, at least he was seventeen days ago. It also appears he decided he would kill Senator Brighton as he passed through."

Baker almost stuttered as he spoke. "Brighton's death was ruled a suicide. They've already closed the case on it, as far as the public believes. You know for sure Ahmad did it?"

"Yes I am. I watched it with my own eyes."

"How is that possible, Nick? You've been nowhere near Wyoming for the last three years."

Nick ignored the question. "My plane touches down at 9:37. I need you to meet me at the hangar and have whatever data you have at that point, ready." With that, Nick pressed the phone button again to disconnect the call. He looked at his watch again and saw that he had twenty minutes to make a thirty-five minute drive. He pressed hard on the accelerator and ran through the remaining gears of the Porsche.

Two miles from the airport, he passed the police car parked behind an overhang and saw the radar gun sticking out of the window. He knew it was a speed trap set up simply to try and catch travelers running late for a flight. It was easy money for the local stations, as no one would waste the expense of flying back to Ireland to dispute the charges. They would just pay the fine on the spot and continue on their way.

Too pissed to slow down, he kept his foot pressed on the pedal and waited, peering at the rear and side mirrors. Thirty seconds later, the police car pulled in behind with lights flashing, gaining speed on his rear bumper. Just outside the airport entrance he pulled over onto the shoulder, took a glance at his watch and knew he would not make his flight. To avoid have his name being recorded, he would have to pay the fine.

Watching the officer exit the police car, Nick noticed the cop undoing the latch across the handle of his weapon, take hold of the grips and pull it roughly an inch out of the sleeve. Nick placed both hands on the steering wheel as he wanted them up and ready in case there was a problem.

Standing next to the closed window, the officer moved his hand in a circular motion for Nick to lower it. Complying, the officer asked the driver for his license and registration as he had done a hundred or more times before.

Looking over the registration certificate, the officer finally spoke. "I'm guessing you're running late for a flight, Mr. West? Doesn't matter, though, we have very strict rules on speeding in this area. Please wait in your car and I'll be back in a minute."

Nick knew the entire process was routine and he would either be handing over a small ransom of cash shortly or being hauled off to some smelly backroom in an old defunct building, miles from where he was, in order for the officers to conceal their illegal activity. Once there, he would be stood in front of someone pretending to be judge while they screamed and threatened that he either come up with the cash or else. The financial raping of foreigners was repeated in every country. This one was no different.

After only a few minutes, the officer was back at his window, except he was gasping for air, having bolted from his seat and run back to Nick's car.

"Mr. West, my sincerest apologies. I didn't know, I swear. Please, what time does your flight depart?"

Nick, even though bewildered, kept his composure. "I have eight minutes."

"Follow right behind me. I'll call ahead and get you on it."

Chapter 7

Provo Canyon, Utah - From the outside of the deserted building, no one would have guessed it to be occupied even by the rats, snakes or other numerous creatures that scurried around at ground level. Large sections of the exterior walls had crumbled years earlier, with the mortar decaying at almost all floor levels and turning back into dry sand. Entire brick walls had simply fallen off its steel skeletal framing and rained down on those walking by underneath, with no one coming to their rescue. They had either been killed instantly or suffered a long agonizing death. Unable to free or defend themselves, several had become prey to the scourging dogs. No one bothered to bury the dead for fear of becoming a victim themselves should they get too close.

Ahmad approached the guards, who at the moment were half standing, half sitting. Their bodies were propped against the wall with their heads down, transfixed on the floor, their eyes slowly blinking, trying to fight back the stinging and keep them open. Lack of sleep and food over the last week had worn them down to the point of near exhaustion. Even as he came closer, they did little to alter their stances, infuriating Ahmad that they would show such little respect. Under the circumstances, though, he allowed them this one mistake.

The third floor level had been converted into a lab, its interior sealed and closed off from anyone entering without proper authority. It was for everyone's best interest and health, including those on the outside. On occasion, a lab worker's body had been brought out on a stretcher, covered by a large white sheet. The sheet had then been covered and wrapped by several sheets of thick plastic, wound tightly around the blood soaked cloth. The smells could not be contained.

Ahmad stood in front of the men who still had not become fully conscious of his presence. Finally he reached out and shook one of the guards by his shoulder. The man opened his eyes and immediately stood at attention as he slapped the other guard across his chest to wake him up. Looking directly at the men, he started to ridicule them, but abruptly stopped. He recognized that the fear in their eyes was not due to the sight of himself, but rather what might escape when they would be required to open the door for his entrance.

Ahmad stood for a moment outside the door, speaking quietly with the guards, reassuring them they would not be harmed. Already dressed in a HAZ-MAT suit, he slipped on the helmet, secured the fastenings and pressed a small button on his belt. A small blast of air entered the air hose and he heard a small hissing of air which told him immediately there was a leak. Adjusting the helmet gear, he felt and heard the click of the locking mechanism and took in a deep breath of air. Holding it in his lungs, he listened once again for the sound. When he was satisfied the helmet was properly fitted, he nodded for the guards to open the door.

As soon as the doors were partially opened, Ahmad rushed through, turning his body sideways as the guards slammed the doors behind him. Once inside, he looked around to make sure all of the containers were either locked away or sealed and that the biochemist was not testing the pathogen on one of her few remaining human specimens.

Walking to the freezer door, he peered through a window and saw the remains of what looked to be a small dog. Its hair and flesh had been ripped to the bone by its own clawing, its face covered in frozen mucus and blood from the open blisters and skin. After several minutes had passed, he made his way over to the microscopes lined along the edge of the table. The woman, sensing his presence, stood upright and faced him.

"How are the batches coming along? Have you made any more progress on the timing release?" Ahmad asked.

"I have succeeded in encapsulating the chemical spores, but without a human to test the final results, my best estimate for release after ingestion is twenty minutes. From there, the subject will expire within a maximum of two hours, most definitely sooner, depending upon their size and health." The biochemist studied the man for his reaction.

"The dog. Was its fate by ingestion or direct contact from the chemical?"

"That was my own dog. I had him in here to keep me company and to watch my back since those imbecile guards you placed outside can't stay awake longer than 10 minutes. One of the dried capsules fell on the floor and he snapped it up before I could. It took thirty-seven minutes for him to die, for the reasons you can plainly see."

"How long have you had the dog in there?"

"It died 4 days ago. As soon as I saw that he had downed the pill and I wasn't able to make him regurgitate it, I ran him into the freezer. Within 17 minutes, he began gnawing at his undersides."

"Did you record the dog's death, as you have the humans'?" Ahmad showed no sympathy for the woman's loss.

"Record my own dog ripping out his intestines? No. I didn't think its death was important enough to your studies." She was offended by the question.

"In the future, you will record all experiments and accidents."

When she indicated she would do so, Ahmad continued with his questions.

"Have the men outside given you any problems? Have they treated you with respect?"

Irritated by the initial intrusion of her work, then by the questioning, she blurted out, "No, not really. They act as if I'm the only woman they have seen in weeks. I hear them talking outside and it frightens me." She hadn't thought of the reaction Ahmad would have to her words.

"Have you been able to fill the canisters with the contaminated spores? Are they ready for distribution as we have spoken about?"

She tilted her head in the direction of a side room and replied, "They are in there and ready. You know that the spores have not been encapsulated. If anyone breathes them in, they will die immediately. They cannot be released in their current form, it is too dangerous."

How quickly and agonizingly a person died, he already knew. When she had not been looking, he had stolen a small quantity, sealing the bag tightly and using it later in California. The results had been beyond his expectations.

Ahmad turned back towards the door, then to the woman. "Are you ready to do the final testing on a human? Is everything prepared to make a final analysis?"

"Yes," she said. "I will just need to clear a small area to sit and secure the volunteer. How soon can you have one here?"

"Twenty seconds, and prepare for two experiments. I want you to give the first subject one capsule and the other, three doses. If the speed in which the effects occur increases with a larger dosage, I am going to have you remix a single batch for me. Now please get ready and also increase the freezer's temperature to 55 degrees".

Ahmad walked towards the doors and paused to listen to the two guards. When he heard no sounds, he pushed the doors open to find them leaning against the exterior wall again, both resting their heads against it. Grabbing each man by his hair, he yanked them back through the doors and began dragging them towards the freezer windows. Slamming their faces against the three-inch glass plates, he watched them as they began to cower, staring in revulsion at the remains of the dog. Each guard began to flail their arms in an attempt to break loose, but Ahmad held tight as a few of the punches found their mark. Soon the men were too exhausted and gave up any further attempt.

Turning and pulling the men vigorously towards the empty chairs, he placed each in one and strapped a leather band around their chest and tied their hands to the spine of the chair. He was furious that one of the men had succeeded in striking him in the right side of his face and decided at that moment to alter his plans.

Next to him on the table were the capsules and water he had asked for. Looking directly at the man who had struck him, Ahmad curled his fist, twisted his body, brought his arm up and back as far as it would go, before putting his entire weight into the punch. The assault was so violent the man's head snapped backwards, nearly touching his shoulder blades. As the head returned forward, Ahmad struck him once again, this time breaking the jaw and separating it from the skull by over an inch.

Now certain the man would not be able to bite him, Ahmad picked up all four capsules, tilted the man's head backwards and dropped them into his mouth, followed by a small drink of water. Still conscious, the guard tried to push the pills out with his tongue but was seized by the throbbing from his broken jaw, the pain forcing him to swallow hard so he would not choke.

With the pills now swallowed, Ahmad quickly untied the man, stripped him of his garments, brought him to his feet and opened the freezer door, pushing the man inside. As the man staggered forward and fell onto the hard cold floor, Ahmad closed the door behind but left the latch unsecure. Taking hold of the second guard's chair, he tilted it sideways, spun it around towards the freezer door, opened it once again and pushed the chair through. This time, however, he secured the latch and pushed the bolt of the lock closed.

Standing next to the freezer windows, the woman had begun clocking the event as soon as Ahmad had given the first man the pills. They watched as the man in the chair pushed himself away from the dog and his companion, who was now just beginning to scream. The biochemist continued making notes, but became engrossed in watching her doomed subject.

Three minutes had passed before the first effects began to show, but not from the man who had been given the pills. The guard tied to the chair began to vomit, his eyes turning a milky discoloration. Unable to bend forward and spit the contents onto the floor, he began to choke on his own bile, and slowly suffocate. Large pulsating ripples of flesh began appearing around his neck, caused by the muscle spasms from the airborne chemicals that had been absorbed into his circulatory and nervous system. Soon his entire body began to spasm and twist in unnatural positions.

They continued to watch for several minutes until, suddenly, the second guard began to show signs, and Ahmad and the woman turned their attention to him. Ignoring the screaming, they watched as the man's chest and abdomen heaved in and out, turning a purplish hue underneath the skin, darkening with each passing minute. She knew immediately that the man was beginning to hemorrhage internally. With him naked, it was easy to see by the reactions, all of the parts of his body the pathogens were attacking from within. The increased dosage had not only increased the speed of the initial reactions, but it had increased the intensity of the effects.

As with the other man, the muscle spasms began rippling through his entire body, not just in specific areas. She began to tremble, thinking of the pathogen she had created. There was more severe twisting of limbs and appendages, with fingers bending backwards and sideways, breaking at the joints, followed by each wrist snapping. The man's hands dangled from the snapped wrists and forearms. Twenty-three minutes had passed. Blood and body fluids began escaping from multiple orifices as the man's body continued ripping itself apart. Forty-one minutes and forty-two seconds into the experiment, all movements stopped.

"I will need a separate batch containing the same amount of dosage in each capsule as the man I gave the four pills to. You have one week to complete the last of the spore generation, then I need them dried and ready for a secondary disbursement."

"That will not be a problem.", said the biochemist.

"Out of curiosity, why did the first guard have those reactions when I did not give him anything?" Ahmad did not quite understand.

The biochemist did not change her expression and looked directly at Ahmad. "The spores do not die, they hibernate forever until the temperatures allow them to rejuvenate. When you had me reset the freezers to a higher temperature, the spores that originally attacked my dog and escaped its body were no longer dormant. The air circulation from the freezer's fans blew the spores onto the first guard and those that came in contact with his eyes and mouth began attacking the open membranes and later his circulatory system."

"There is no way to kill the spores once they are released?" asked Ahmad.

"The chemical spores are made up of similar compounds as those found in mustard gas used by the Germans in World War 1. There have been reports of farmers and wildlife dying after coming in contact with trees that had been sprayed by the gas some 40 to 50 years after the end of the war."

"That explains the intense burning of the skin, but what about the violent muscle spasms?"

"There are additional synthetic compounds I added that resemble Sarin gas. Once they enter the blood stream, the chemicals cause an increasing imbalance of the brain's electrical charges that drive motor skills. It's much like a person who suffers from epileptic fits, except the impulses are much more severe and terrifying."

Ahmad placed a hand on the woman's shoulder. "Please have all ready by next week when I return. You have done very well, and I am very pleased. You will be rewarded more generously than we originally agreed upon."

The woman watched as Ahmad left through the lab doors. Although the money would be very generous, it is not what she had hoped for. For now, the touch on her shoulder would have to do.

She had worked hard to get the man to notice that she was, first and foremost, a woman. Over time, she believed he would understand her desires and finally act upon them. For now she would have to remain content that he knew she was loyal to him, helping his cause, and someday, this would behind them and they would be together.

Chapter 8

Baker was standing on the tarmac of the private airport as Nick's plane came to a halt after pulling into the hangar alongside a waiting car. In his hands was a small packet of data he had been able to find on Ahmad. According to the intel, the man had been terminated several years earlier in Afghanistan by a foreign government agent. Baker knew that meant a 'ghost', so he decided to start with the oldest data first, then work forward.

Ahmad was the second son of a wealthy business man, having had ties to the royal family of Iran. His father was heavily involved in the exporting of oil reserves for the royal family, which, years later, grew into a business for both exporting oil reserves and the importing of weapons. His father soon began traveling with a contingent of armed guards and Ahmad's ability to come and go as he pleased became very limited.

At first he rebelled against the new restrictions, but later decided to make the best of it. He began studying his father's works, questioned every detail of his business and learned as much as possible from not only his father, but his close associates. By the time he was 18 years of age, his intricate knowledge of the business exceeded that of all the men who ran the daily operations. But more importantly, it gave him the understanding of how to protect what would eventually be his someday.

The associates eventually began to respect his input and ideas as much as any other man legally bound to the business. On occasion, his father allowed him to address the committee when speaking at their meetings, an honor never bestowed before on any individual not an officer of the business. The board never objected to his participation.

On his parents' twentieth anniversary, the family traveled to Belize in order to vacation and take time away from the business. The constant stress had aged his father ten years in the last two, and only at the insistence of his wife did he finally give in to her demands. However, it would appear to be his decision to all of those who knew and respected him. Ahmad would make sure.

Prince Sahid offered the use of his yacht as an anniversary gift and the family traveled for almost a month before the explosion killed Ahmad's family and nearly all of the crew. The yacht had been in port refueling when the eruption occurred. His father, mother and brother had been in the dining galley having lunch when the spark ignited the fuel tanks. Ahmad had left twenty minutes earlier, wanting to visit a local dive shop, claiming he had punctured the outer lining of his buoyancy compensator and needed to purchase another. There were spares on board, but he insisted that all equipment should be in proper working order.

Since the yacht belonged to Prince Sahid, the final investigation concluded that a charge had been attached to the fuel tanks. In the most likely explanation from the inspector, it had been triggered by a timer or pressure switch and the attempt had been made on the Prince's life, believing he was aboard when the fatal accident happened. Ahmad knew better, but played the grieving son for as long as custom demanded. In the end, he controlled the company, along with an additional seventy-five million dollars he received from both Prince Sahid and the insurance settlement.

Under new leadership, the company shifted direction, both legally, and even more precisely, illegally. The vestiges of those that did not want to follow his plans and orders were found shortly afterwards throughout different parts of the city. It did not take long for competition to dry up, giving his business the opportunities to thrive even more.

Large quantities of weapons were imported, then sold to whomever would pay the highest price regardless of their reasons or needs for wanting them. Weapons were supplied to both governments and individuals, it did not matter which. Money was all that mattered. Only opium would have brought him a greater and faster return, but then there were the high risks and payouts he was not willing maintain. His partners disagreed, but Ahmad did not want to listen to their arguments.

Trading in the sale of weapons, he soon began dealing directly with al-Qaida and the Taliban, making contacts that went far beyond casual acquaintances. After many months, he had gained their trust and was asked to establish dealings with their enemies. At first he did not understand the request, but eventually learned that more important than weapons was the information he would obtain from men eager to boast of their own self-importance.

By bringing back information from the different tribes, they could determine their size, what weapons they had to fight with and how trained that were to use them. If lucky, he was told, he might also be able to recognize battle plans and where sworn enemies were hiding. With this information, al-Qaida could easily overtake the other groups at will.

Ahmad also learned that information paid well. The business continued to prosper and the earnings no longer seemed as important as before. It was what power it brought. With power, an enemy feared you. It was no longer significant that they respected you.

Ahmad had no interest in joining any of the terrorist groups, however, he would seek revenge using his own methods, on his own accord and for his own reasons. Having learned many skills from the training camps over the years, he spent weeks, sometimes months in the preparation of the smallest details, making backup plans and recruiting only a few that he trusted. If he was not sure of someone's absolute skill and loyalty, he would test them by having the person strap on a suicide vest while undergoing the maneuver. If the person demonstrated the skills needed to his satisfaction, Ahmad would disarm the device himself. Otherwise, he would dial a phone number that activated the trigger. Very few survived.

During the first months after the invasion of Iraq by the United States following 9/11, Ahmad watched as many of his business partners changed strategies and began working for the U.S. government in hopes of avoiding prison, or worse. They began providing intel of the camp positions and ranking leaders. As the camps began to fall, so did the business of supplying weapons. Ahmad did not hate the Americans for what they were doing, but rather the corruption and cowardice of his partners. He began to totally distrust and target the infrastructure of his own company officers. It would be only a matter of time before they would turn him over to the military.

Overnight, he transferred all monetary company assets to his Swiss accounts, fleeing the country using fake passports, finally arriving in Germany. For the next two years, he tracked the whereabouts of the remaining officers of his former company, and their travels. On November 22, 2005, four of those officers would be aboard EuroAmerican flight 1419, bound for Munich.

During that time, until the actual bombing of the flight, several international agencies had worked in cooperation in trying to determine Ahmad's location and interests. Several men had been sent in an attempt to infiltrate his operation, but none were successful, and all had died trying, either in a scuffle at the camp with the other men or at Ahmad's own hands. Finally, a woman was sent, having mastered all weapons training and explosives. She spent almost two years undercover, then disappeared for several months, returning just days prior to the bombing.

She had been present with Ahmad at the time the trigger was pressed and the current tripped, but was unaware of the target or that the couple in the home would be eliminated. She had successfully relayed the intel of Ahmad's next move and location of a new bombing, planned in Afghanistan, back to her agency and a sanction was issued. The kill had to be done immediately before the attack on a new target of such magnitude could be coordinated and carried out. The assassin was well thought of within the agencies and had been used on numerous occasions, having never failed a mission.

Eight days later, he lay prone on the rocks overlooking the camp, watching as the man in the red scarf began to step away from the target. As he gently pulled the trigger, there was a small burp, and through the scope, he saw fragments of bone and tissue rip away from the skull. The targeted man flipped backwards and did not move. As the assassin began to chamber a second round for the confirmatory kill shot, the man in the red scarf walked in front of his fallen leader, blocking the ability for him to center the placement of the round. The assassin quietly retreated back into dark of the night, leaving no trace he had ever existed.

Nick stopped at the open doorway of the plane and scanned the hangar interior, finally looking down at Baker. Normally, Baker issued a friendly 'hello', but his expression remained somber as he simply stood still and waited for West to exit the stairway. Upon touching the ground, Baker walked forward, handing Nick the envelope containing the information he had been able to find in such a short amount of time.

"That's all of the data I could find on your man given such short notice. As far as the world knows, he died years ago and there has never been any other activity that suggested otherwise. Now you're telling me he's alive and in the United States. Again I need to ask. Is there any possibility you could be wrong?"

Nick looked at Baker and shook his head. "I saw the man in a video kill the senator. The quality of the video was as good as if I were standing there, so, no, there's no doubt in my mind that I saw the man I say I did."

Baker cleared his throat. "Then there's a bigger problem we need to discuss on the way back to operations."

"What could be bigger than a terrorist running loose in the United States, killing senior high level government personnel?"

"Killing American civilians with chemical warfare on U.S. territory."

Nick stopped dead. "What are you talking about? Why didn't you say anything before I left Ireland?"

"Nick, it just happened eight hours ago in California. At first they thought the casualties were due to a fire, but as rescue workers approached, they became very sick and their skin started blistering almost immediately. The CDC was called in and they are having a tough time quarantining the area where the explosions occurred. So far, there have been nineteen deaths, about half of those from the explosions of propane tanks located in an adjoining business."

"Did anyone see someone release the chemicals or know how they became airborne?"

"I tapped into the cameras that run along the main entrance of the shops and ran the footage through cleanup. From what I saw, it looks like the first explosion came from a hat shop on Freemont. When I examined the footage, there are people falling down minutes after the explosion, right outside the shop. I would say that was your point of origin."

Nick stepped closer so as not to be overheard. "Is there any activity coming from any of the agencies that have any information on who the terrorist might be?"

"I can tell you who they aren't suspecting. If you hadn't told me Ahmad was still alive, I would have ruled him out as well. One other thing you need to know. When I narrowed down where the explosion occurred, I ran the footage back and saw a man leaving the store in a pretty big hurry. Once he had crossed the street, he stopped and turned around facing the store. I'm guessing that would be your man."

"Any facial footage caught on camera?"

Baker smiled. "I think it's your guy, but I only have comparative photos from six to eight years ago. You need to tell me for sure, since you have a more recent sighting. Any chance I can get the footage you saw?"

Nick thought for a moment, then nodded his head yes. "I'll need to make a call, but if I can't get approval, you're going to have to hack into one of the most sophisticated and secured system databases I've ever seen. If you're caught, we all go down and I don't mean prison, nor by our government. Do you understand what I mean?"

"Who the hell did you go see in Ireland, Nick? You're actually sweating!"

"I can only tell you that their technology directs how other countries develop. I saw some things that I did not even know existed and you are actually the reason for some of it."

"I don't follow. What would I have to do with anything regarding their technology, whoever you are talking about?"

"You apparently developed some kind of advanced algorithm that has permitted them to increase the clock speed, exponentially, on the chips they use in their mainframes without overheating the boards and components. By using your formulas, their engineers have been able to develop a liquid coolant gel that is embedded in the boards and reads heat spots. When the temperature increases in a specific spot, the coolant expands and decreases the temperature as needed."

Baker took a step back and looked at Nick. "Yes, I know exactly the algorithms you're talking about, but those are classified."

"Apparently not anymore. They have used what they have learned from your work in other applications that have allowed them to design other devices that can scan human images in 4D and interpret whatever results they are looking for, within seconds. Those body images are so detailed, they can actually splice the scans into molecular imagery."

"Shit! Damn it! I spent years developing that code and they stole it?"

Nick responded. "I'm guessing you didn't patent it?"

"Yeah, right." Baker's tone and sarcasm were not missed by Nick.

"Well, if it's any consolation, they couldn't interpret all of it. They said they would love for you to come work for them and bring in your mathematical skills, let alone your brain." Nick hoped the comment would make Baker feel a little better, but could see it didn't.

"No, I am serious, Nick. They actually told you they are using my algorithms and code? And now they have developed some futuristic technology that even our government can't come close to duplicating and I get no compensation? "

"I don't think they are the kind to send you a check and a thank you for allowing them to pilfer your work." Nick would have enjoyed watching Baker continue his ranting but the seriousness of the situation kept them both attentive.

Baker looked at Nick. "When we get back to the ranch, I need to know your exact location in Ireland and who you talked to. When you make that call, I'm going to be listening in so I can begin a trace and lift a few confidential IP addresses and passwords."

Nick's mannerisms changed completely. "Hold on, Baker! I call the shots, and these people don't play games or give second chances. If they even suspect someone is trying to penetrate their security and access their classified data, they will find and eliminate you within hours, and anyone else involved. They don't have the same rules that you and I have to follow!"

"That's why you were sweating, then?"

Nick was looking right at Baker. "Let me ask you a question. Did you alter any of my personal records to stop that cop from giving me a ticket?"

"What cop and what ticket?"

"Right outside the airport, a cop stopped me going forty-five miles per hour over the speed limit. He took my license and registration to run it and check for any outstanding tickets or warrants. In less than two minutes he was back at my car window apologizing, then ran traffic clearance for me to get on a plane they held up for over ten minutes in order for me to board. I'm in a foreign country and I didn't even have to go through any check points. Getting the picture?"

"I'm starting to, but no, not really."

Nick couldn't believe it had happened. "These people have absolute immunity from any government and law enforcement agencies in the world. Those agencies depend upon them to eliminate any threats worldwide that they can't legally take care of themselves. They have an entire organization that is made of every conceivable force necessary to carry out their assignment without risk. Their people are completely protected and apparently I am now earmarked as one of them whether I want to be or not."

Baker blinked a few times, still looking at Nick. "Am I supposed to say 'Fuckin A' or something like that, because I'm not sensing you're happy about it?"

Chapter 9

Olexia sat at her desk looking over the latest specs her IT people had been able to find on Ahmad. The facial image captured during the assassination of the senator had been run against millions of those on file in their data bank. So far there had been no matches, even with removing the right side of his heavily scarred face and replacing it with a split image of the left. There was no doubt it was him, but apparently there was no paper or electronic record of this man's life. It wasn't possible, she thought.

How could this man still be alive and no one know it until now? Simon had supposedly killed him years earlier by placing a .50 caliber round through the side of his head and watching as his skull blew apart. Even the antiquated camera used in the scope during that time had shown half the man's face disappear after the impact.

The stress of knowing Ahmad was still alive and the depression from her loss of both her husband and baby, were beginning to take its effect. Her blood pressure had risen to deadly levels twice during the day and she needed a long break, but it wasn't possible. Not now, maybe never again. Sitting back in her chair, she began taking in breaths and releasing them at a slow steady pace. Her thoughts immediately returned to Ahmad.

Accepting he was still alive, it would now be her priority to track the location of the man and complete the job without anyone else knowing he had survived. If any of the agency's clients knew a mission had failed, there would be skepticism on their part in using her organization's services again.

In addition, there was the concern of retaliation from not only the target, but the possibility of those clients turning against the board members, demanding payback and her resignation. In this job, resignation meant a contract was placed upon you that assured everyone of your silence.

She hoped Nick would keep his promise, but she needed someone else on the outside that had no association with the organization. They would need to complete the kill and ask no questions. When the job was finished, that person would need to be eradicated in order to be confident they would not talk or decide to blackmail her when their funds ran dry.

Her mind raced through a succession of men and women they had used on occasion and that she had personally approved from prior assignments. The person had to be a loner who had no friends or family that would ever miss seeing them again.

Ten minutes later, she keyed in the name Darryl Coats and waited for his dossier to display. Reading through the file, she noted that the man's last assignment was seven months earlier when he was contracted to permanently remove a female operative suspected of stealing government pass codes and supplying them to a local drug cartel. Having the codes to specific systems, the cartel was able to access and monitor weapon shipments and payroll deliveries. On three separate occasions, the shipments had been intercepted with no chance of tracing the whereabouts of the stolen goods due to the thieves leaving all potential witnesses dead.

Coats came highly recommended, as his methods of killing a person left most deaths ruled an accident or by natural causes. Once assigned a target, he became totally immersed in studying their daily life patterns and habits. Mostly he watched for routines that provided a risk factor, such as walking down long flights of stairs, driving in heavy traffic, catching trains or staying out late drinking. Taking advantage of those dangers often meant he would never become a suspect in the cause of their death.

His greatest skill was the quickness of his hands. When it became necessary to kill a person directly, he preferred to do so in a crowd, where he could sever a jugular vein as he passed or plunge a knife into the heart of a person as he walked up and pretended to be a friend from long ago.

The actions were so swift that the target seldom knew they were hit until Coats was several steps away. A quick push off of the 7:13 platform and the victim would be guillotined as the train passed.

Olexia contacted Coats, and within three hours he was sitting in the large office, facing her and listening to her request. The target was to be eliminated within forty-eight hours, once their location was established. As soon as the kill was made, he was to leave at once for a prearranged destination on which he would be given details once the death was confirmed. At no time during the operation was he to contact any other persons and he was to work alone. Intelligence and surveillance data would be sent to him via a small encrypted satellite phone that he was to keep on him at all times. It would have the appearance of a normal type phone, so no one would suspect.

"What if I am unable to kill this man or woman within the forty-eight hours you are giving me? We are talking about caves and rock formations that are almost impossible to traverse, and in some cases, even find." Coats was already uncomfortable with the sanction, as he deplored time constraints.

"You're assuming the kill will be in those surroundings? We can not be certain where he will be found, but in this case, we do not believe it will somewhere in an inhospitable terrain." Olexia was beginning to rethink her choice of selecting this man.

Coats shrugged his shoulders. "Ninety percent of my jobs have been. That's all."

Olexia continued. "The individual will be located first, at which time you will be transported to that zone and dropped within three miles of the target. You will then have forty-eight hours to complete the task. A man of your skills and capabilities should have no problem."

"How do I get out? It's not like I can call for a taxi."

She was becoming exasperated with the man and it was causing her further stress. She really wished she had made other arrangements before making this unfortunate decision. "Your progress will be monitored and you will have assistance from my people. As soon as your kill is confirmed, you will be evacuated by one of our own air team and delivered to a sector approximately five miles from the border. From there it will be up to you to get across and to safety."

"What if I am caught? I'm guessing there won't be anyone coming after me, right?"

Olexia chose her words carefully. "You are going after a man who is already listed as dead by every agency and country on Earth. No one will even imagine it is him until you are long gone. Your only concern will be if you fail."

"Why should that be a concern? If he is already dead, then a second or even a third attempt shouldn't raise any eyebrows." Coats sat up straight as he watched Olexia lean in towards him.

"Because if you fail, you won't have any chance of making it out alive. He will kill you after he has bled every ounce of information and blood from your body. You will rot from the depths of some God forsaken cavern he dumps you in. He is better at this game than anyone, so you do not want to fail!"

Coats looked at Olexia as he narrowed his eyes. "It sounds like you know this man personally. Do you?"

For a moment Olexia did not respond. "Do you accept the assignment? An amount of one million dollars has already been deposited into your account for your inconvenience today, which you may keep, regardless. Another nine million will be deposited upon completion. Please answer yes or no, Mr. Coats."

Coats ran his index finger across his lips several times, then stood. As if beginning to walk out, he turned back towards Olexia. "You better make sure your people are there once I kill this son of a bitch. I want to be gone before his body hits the ground."

"I assure you, Mr. Coats, my people will be very close by and will take care of you."

Chapter 10

Nick sat next to Baker as he scanned the digital video downloaded from a camera that was placed almost directly across from the hat shop. When the video showed a man exiting through the front door, Baker stopped the footage.

"Up until this point everything seems fine. Everyone is going about their normal lives and activities. From the video, you can see that there were no unusual suspects, no one getting out of a van or car and leaving it unattended, no deliveries, etcetera."

Nick stopped him. "How and where did you get this video so fast?"

"There are several well placed security cameras in and around the businesses that operate in the vicinity. I tapped into their feeds and downloaded the videos. I then examined each one until I saw this one."

"Have you sent your findings to the FBI? I mean, how did you find out about this before they got a chance to review the video? I haven't seen any news on this."

"If you recall, I'm not too fond of other agencies outside of DHS. Those guys were going to send me away for treason, remember? There were a few underground broadcast groups that announced the explosion before any news teams could get there. As soon as I saw a mention of the possibility of chemical warfare, I started scanning for feeds. Someone walked into that store and purposely released an agent that was meant to kill not only the occupants, but innocent people. That agent is so toxic, it continues to kill anyone not completely protected who walks within two square blocks of that area."

Nick looked back at the screen. "What else do you have?"

"Hang on. I'll bring it up."

Baker turned a small dial and slowly progressed through the video until the man he had mentioned earlier was standing across the street, looking back towards the building.

Zooming in on the right side of the man's face, he turned back to Nick and asked, "Do you recognize him?"

"It's Ahmad, no doubt. Who else do you think might have already seen this video and recognized his face? Have you heard any more newscasts going back and forth?"

"There's not going to be anyone viewing this tape unless they pulled it prior to me downloading it and viewing it within minutes after the occurrence. The application I developed erases my connection activity, including anything I have touched."

"So you think you are the only one who has this footage."

Baker thought for a moment. "Unless someone beat me to it, I'm the only one who has this particular footage. I can't guarantee there aren't other angles from other cameras, though. I wasn't able to download everything. Once I saw this, I stopped going back and pulling the remaining feeds. If there were any cameras I didn't check, I'm sure by now there are a dozen agencies scanning every frame. I can tell you this, though. This is the only one that was capturing footage directly across from the square."

"Any chance one of the other cameras you didn't check, caught a facial view of him arriving or walking down a street?"

"I can't be sure. But from this video, it looks like he never turned his face in another direction, once he walked out of the hat shop, until the very end when he turned around. Let me check those video feeds, just give me a minute."

A couple moments later, Baker looked at Nick and shook his head. "No. This looks like it's the only one."

"Does that mean there's no facial imagery, or what?"

"It means there's no other video in any of the remaining cameras that I still show as active. So either the other owners didn't have their cameras going or the video has already been downloaded and erased from their locations."

"Any chance you can determine which scenario it is?"

"Not without exposing a trace and I know that you don't want that possibly happening."

"Alright. We will just have to work with what we have. Anything more from CDC on the final death count and contaminations? Have they been able to figure out the life expectancy of this toxin?"

"Slow down, Nick. They don't even know what it is yet or how to contain it. The release of this agent just happened a few hours ago. At this point, they are still evacuating the area and testing anyone who was within blocks of ground zero when the explosion occurred."

"Yeah, I remember how long it took for them to lock down the area and investigate the anthrax scare a few years back. At least we know who the person responsible for this is, this time."

Baker corrected Nick. "We know who released the agent, but we don't know who made it. This agent is made up of very complex chemicals. It's not like anthrax where anyone can begin making it by using eggs. Look at how quickly these people's bodies begin to break down once they came in contact. They're scratching at their eyes almost immediately. It's not a gas, otherwise they would be grabbing at their throats. These people are scratching off their skin, scratching out their eyes, they are trying to spit. Those reactions are caused by spores of some kind that release their contents once they get into the wet membranes of the body."

West raised his eyebrows. "So you're a chemist in addition to being a highly paid geek?"

"I only date girls who can carry a conversation at my level. One of the brightest I ever dated was a girl who had studied chemistry and had her PhD degree by the time she turned eighteen."

"Please tell me you got lucky once in a while?"

Baker chuckled. "You would be surprised, my friend."

West relented and went back to talking about the spores. "Then it's kind of like a pill releasing medication."

"Exactly," said Baker. "Except the size of the spores are too small for any human to see. The speed in which these people react is what you would expect to happen to someone who swallowed a large dosage or was hit by millions of these spores at one time. Those people were walking outside along the street when they became exposed to maybe a few dozen spores."

Baker sat back in his chair and waited for Nick's response. He was used to Nick relentlessly firing off question after question, but was surprised that the questioning had stopped abruptly. By Nick's expressions, Baker knew his mind was elsewhere and already working on some plan. He continued to wait for whatever Nick would tell him next. Finally Nick spoke.

"Were there any survivors at all that we can talk to and see if they remember anything new, or perhaps something they might have forgot to mention?"

Baker looked back at Nick. "There was one survivor within the immediate area of the blast, but we won't be able to talk to her. It was a nine week old baby."

"Why did a baby survive when everyone else died within minutes?"

"Yeah, that is strange. Even stranger is the fact that only her nasal cavities were burned from the chemical agent, nothing else. If the chemical got into her nose, it should have traveled down into her lungs from the air passage."

"No one knows why?"

Baker leaned back across his desk, reaching for the instrument panel. "They are testing, but it's still early in the game. Best guess is it was something in the mother's breast milk. Some kind of natural antidote."

Nick stood and approached Baker from the side, making sure he had Baker's attention. "I'm going to make some calls and I need for you not to get involved for the next forty-eight hours. When I am done, I will let you know. Once that happens, you had better be ready to bring your best game."

Baker looked at Nick as if he was getting ready to square off in a fight. "I always bring my best game no matter what I do. I'll stay out of your business but I'm not about to stand here and be insulted."

"It's not an insult. If we have to hack their systems, I can guarantee you once anything pops up on what we are doing, they are going to hit back very, very hard. You're going to do nothing but play constant defense, trying to protect our whereabouts from cyber attacks. One slip-up and we lose. Permanently."

Chapter 11

The drive back to the ranch took Nick longer than he had anticipated. Having spent the early morning hours with Baker at their private headquarters, it now put him driving through downtown Atlanta during the lunch rush. Once he cleared the slow traffic, he was able to obtain interstate speed once again.

The ranch had once been his sanctuary. It had been a place to lay low and spend quiet time with Laura. They would spend his days off tending the animals, having long candlelight dinners and dancing slowly into the nights, both on a living room rug and in bed. Now, he saw Simon every time he entered through the gates.

As he pulled through, he could see Laura in the distance, walking very slowly with an injured orangutan. She had seen him enter and began to wave, then bent down and began talking to the animal. To his surprise, the orangutan began to wave as well. Pulling up to within 20 yards of them, Nick stopped the McLaren and waited for Laura to give him the signal that it was OK to approach on foot. When she did, he stepped out, closed the door gently and started walking towards her.

"So, do you speak their language or just grunt and make wild animal noises?" he asked with a big smile.

Laura shot him back a flirtatious pout. "That would more your department, if I recall last Friday night correctly."

Nick let out a laugh, throwing his head back a few inches. "Yeah, you've got me on that one. Any chance I get to go 'ape shit' again anytime soon?"

She looked down at the orangutan, noting the comical reference. "Well, Tarzan, I have finished feeding all of the other animals. Perhaps if you would walk Oscar back to his cozy pen for me, I can go in and start preparing something for you."

Nick reached over and took Oscar by his hand and began walking him back at the same pace he had observed

Laura doing earlier. Once Oscar settled in, Nick turned and began to sprint back towards the house.

A quick shower and he slid in beside Laura, pulling the covers over them. Sliding one of his hands down the crease of her back, he gently began massaging and exploring the different parts of her body with the other. She uttered a small moan and pulled him in even closer to her. For the next several hours, the outside world would simply be non-existent.

When the sun rose the next morning, Nick had already been up for two hours trying to research any additional news and information on the attack. The news anchors were currently reporting it as a chemical leak from a tanker harbored nearby. There were reports of three casualties due to explosions, with a mention that all remaining persons affected had been transported to multiple hospitals for observation and treatment.

He thought about calling Baker, but did not want to wake Laura yet, knowing the conversation could get heated if Baker took any more offense to his comments. Nick knew the man took extreme pride in his work and was the best he had ever seen at what he did, but it bothered him that Baker might push his talents and ego too far.

Olexia needed to know what they had learned, but the thought of her having control over the information he was about to give them did not play into his plans should she run out of time on their agreement. Knowing that he may have already been classified as a member of the organization, after his visit, angered him. What kind of influence and power did they have that they were able to instantly give him immunity from all prosecution, even if, for now, it had only been a speeding ticket?

He found his mind wandering for a few seconds before refocusing, and reached across to pick up his phone. Stepping further back into the house, he dialed the hangar and gave instructions for them to be on standby for a return flight to Ireland.

Hesitating, he decided it was important to find out what limitations there might be of the immunity he had. He ran his finger over the display screen of the phone and found the name and number he was looking for. Pressing the call button, he listened as the phone rang several times before an old voice from his past finally answered. "Dawson, it's West. What are your plans for the next day or two?"

"Jesus Nick! You call me before I've even had a chance to take a shit and shower and you want me to roll out of bed and come running?"

"Hey man, what about, it's great to talk to you after all these years, Nick?"

"What the fuck, West? Speaking of that, how's Laura?" Dawson knew that last line was going to cost him.

"Remind me to kick your ass once I see you. I was going to try and be pleasant this once, but you never give me the chance. You still having to jerk that two inch pecker of yours because no woman will have you?"

The two men started to laugh, knowing their friendship would withstand all insults and their conversations would never change. The number of times they had saved each other's life in the SEALs fortified a bond that would never be broken. They were truly brothers-in-arms and who would lay down their life for each other.

Dawson was about to retaliate with another offensive line when he heard Nick tell him to secure the call. For a second, it caught him off guard, but he immediately reached down and flipped a small toggle switch on the side table. The attached box began to transmit a low frequency through the room that caused the phone participant's voices to be muffled to any hearing devices, either through the line itself or within the room.

"Ok, we're good. What do you need, Nick? What is this all about?"

"Seriously, Dog, what are your plans tonight, and who are you getting ready to take down? I might want to tag along." 'Dog' had been Dawson's nickname given to him by the team. It was short for 'Destruction On Going'.

"It isn't going to happen for you, West. This isn't your kind of work, and right now, I'm just busting a few heads for Makura. A couple of punks harassed his daughter one too many times and I just want to stop it from happening again."

"Makura? The guy who always volunteered to take point for our team? Did they hurt his daughter?"

"No, just one of the guys scared the hell out of her by running his hand up her skirt. The poor girl was so scared she couldn't move, so the guy's buddies decided to have a little fun, too."

"Any problems with the law ever getting into your business?" Nick asked.

"Just the usual. I'm always getting pulled downtown to answer a few questions, but nothing more than that."

"Do you know where these guys are now, that fondled the girl?"

"Off of Concord and 30th. But Nick, I'm telling you, this isn't anything you need to be concerned about. I'm heading over tonight to crack some balls, then I'll be done with it."

"I need to test one of my hunches out and this sounds about perfect to get me the answer I'm looking for. There's an extra two grand in it for you if you wait for me."

"Damn it, Nick!" Dawson thought about the money for a few seconds and how it would be useful for one of the purchases he wanted. "Make it three and be at my place at ten sharp. You're strictly an observer. Once I start busting on these assholes, I can't take a chance of you getting in my way."

"Ten sharp and I'll see you then." Nick ended the call and placed another to Baker. When Baker answered, Nick asked him to research and find out who was assigned patrol duty that night in the Concord neighborhood after ten o'clock.

Baker was still trying to fight off sleep from having spent all night getting a jump on patching any open firewalls of his network. Although this was his normal daily routine during system checks, he decided it was necessary to individually test each one and to add additional protection. The alerts he put in place would notify him immediately of any attempts to penetrate the firewall, capture the offending IP address or addresses and block the attack. With a captured IP address, his program would resend a small application that, once inside, would cause the sender's system power source to surge and begin frying sensitive parts of the motherboard.

"What's so important about the Concord area? That's not a particularly safe neighborhood, you know? Lots of hookers and drug addicts." Baker's mind was amusing itself with the thought of some poor guy mistaking Nick for a male prostitute, trying to score some cocaine or other pleasure.

"When you find out who the cop is tonight, I want you to place an untraceable distress call around 10:15 and give them my birth name as the person in trouble. Don't give them any more information than that and hang up. Got it?"

Baker couldn't believe Nick was being serious. "Wait, Nick. You think anyone is going to believe you need help with a couple of potheads and drug addicts, if they decide to pull a background check on you first?"

Nick appreciated the comment, but continued. "That's not what this is about. I need to see if my immunity goes beyond Ireland. It will let me know if I really have been tagged or if the cop in Ireland was simply a plant."

"What if you haven't been tagged by them and the cops in America arrest you? Do you have a plan B for getting out of jail?" Baker was sitting up straight in his chair now, having thoughts of Nick sitting on a cot looking out a set of iron bars. It wouldn't take long for them to find out who placed the call and he knew he would be sitting along beside him.

Nick's patience was running thin with Baker's line of questioning. He knew he was tired and the lack of sleep was beginning to take its toll on him. "Look, Baker. If you are as good as you say you are, that won't happen, now, will it? I'm leaving that part up to you." Nick could hear Baker cursing under his breath.

"Just please tell me you're not going to kill someone. If I have to break into police files and purge your arrest, I don't want to be facing 25 years for doing it." Baker started to cough.

"My guess is it won't be necessary. I'll call you if anything changes. You just don't forget to make that call."

At 9:45, Nick pulled onto Concord Ave and drove an additional six blocks, finally pulling up to the corner adjacent to 30th Street. One block away was the entrance ramp to the interstate. Looking around, he saw the buildings were in decline from what looked like was once a suburban neighborhood. He could imagine kids playing in the streets, barbecues and pool parties on Saturdays. Now the street was littered with garbage, broken bottles and lost dreams.

Straight ahead, a four story open garage rested against an empty eight story building. The building's windows were shattered and its doors had been pulled completely off or hung loose by only a single hinge. Graffiti and gang symbols were painted on the large walls and used condoms were visible through the open doors, lying scattered next to filthy mattresses and soiled sheets.

On the ground floor of the garage were four highly customized vehicles, three sporting twenty-one inch rims with suspensions that raised the body of the car at least a foot and a half off the ground. Standing next to one of the cars was a lone figure, holding a large weapon of some type, watching and waiting for the negotiations to end before an exchange took place. His back was to Nick's approach and his head was turned upwards, listening to make sure the voices remained calm. Nick now realized he was about to walk into a drug buy and knew these men would probably be carrying a lot of hardware.

As he began working his way through the garage, Nick could hear the same voices coming from above and he guessed the men were busy bargaining on the second floor. The man continued looking away as Nick slipped in behind him and applied a chokehold. There was a short struggle as the man went down and his body went limp. Nick dragged him around to the front of the first car and out of sight. It would be at least an hour before the man regained consciousness.

Reaching for the handle of the first car, Nick slowly touched it and pressed on the release. The door opened to reveal a twelve hundred dollar stereo and DVD player in the dash and several large speakers in the backseat. In between the speakers sat a gold and blue striped duffle bag, its sides bulging outward from its contents.

Nick slowly slid the zipper down its track just in case the bag contained a trigger switch. From his past experience in SWAT, he knew that there had been drug gangs that would have filled the bag with explosives in hopes of eliminating their rivals. There was a small fraction of those that would take the money without looking and open it later in a more convenient place. The frags would kill anyone standing nearby. A simple trip of a switch could disarm the trigger in case the dealer had to open and reveal the contents themselves.

Inside the bag were bundles of cash, each showing a wrapper in the amount of ten thousand dollars. After doing a quick count, he determined the bag held at least two hundred and fifty thousand dollars, maybe a little more. He closed the bag and went to work.

Sliding in behind the driver's seat of the last car, Nick reached underneath and attached a very small rectangular package in the open paneling, sliced the ignition wires and placed both ends into the soft material as he had done previously to each of the other cars. As he sat up, the back of his head suddenly came into contact with a .45 caliber Beretta. He froze for an instant and then turned his head towards Dawson.

"God damn, if you could see your face right now, it's the funniest thing I've ever seen. You piss your pants?" Dawson's face was contorted from the muscles pulling his smile to its max.

"Are you ever going to grow up? I taught you that trick and now you're trying to use it on me?"

"Nick, I couldn't resist. Hey, you should be proud that I could pull it off on someone like you."

"Nice try buddy, but not quite. You stepped in dog shit thirty feet back. Check your left shoe. Not only did I hear you coming, I smelled you, too. And man, when was the last time you showered?"

Dawson cocked his left shoe sideways and saw the crap embedded in the slits of his sneaker. He mumbled a few words under his breath as he turned back to Nick. "Did you bring me the money?"

Without stopping as he checked the remote switches, Nick reached into his side pocket and handed him the envelope. As Dawson reached for it, Nick pulled the envelope back. "We are going to have a little company shortly. Don't stop whatever you are doing. Just keep busting heads as if they aren't here. If it's necessary I join in, again, don't stop."

Dawson protested. "I don't like this Nick, because I don't know what you're up to, and I don't like surprises. Do you want to give me a hint?"

"I can only tell you that we are either going to help our friend Makura tonight or we are going to be in jail for a while." Nick kept his eyes on Dawson, anticipating a physical reaction.

"Thanks for the warning, but that's not anything I'm not used to. I'm going to trust that you have my back, as you always have had in the past. Whatever you are up to, there has to be a good reason. I just don't like you springing this on me at the last minute."

"I'll explain it later if needed, but thanks for your trust. Now, shall we get the party started?"

Chapter 12

At 10:00 pm, Olexia was still at her desk, finalizing assignments and reviewing the latest updates on Ahmad's whereabouts. The last fax had been received only seven minutes earlier and contained 28 pages of data and imagery. The satellite photos had been taken the day before of a series of buildings and the immediate surrounding area. In sequence, they displayed a small building exploding, followed by images on each successive page and finally, the aftermath. On the ground, people lay dying, their arms and legs twisted at grotesque angles.

Appearing as single frames from a movie reel, she could see people scattering, dropping their belongings, pushing people out of their way and not looking back. Those that chose to stay and help others, began falling beside those already dead.

After viewing the images in order several times, she couldn't understand why she had received so many pages, when only a few would have been sufficient. Reaching for the phone, she suddenly stopped, picked up the fax once again and quickly shuffled through each page.

There it was. What appeared as a shadow across the street, remained in place the entire time. He or she had never moved, but continued to watch as the hysteria grew around them. None of the images allowed her to see who the person was, and she began tossing the pages aside as she tried to find one that gave her the best visual analysis.

Frustrated, she placed a call to the name on the bottom of first page. On the first ring, a female voice answered, startling Olexia, who had expected a man to answer based upon the name listed.

"Major Sam Pierce speaking. How may I help you, Ms. Syshchenko?"

"I need a 10x copy of image 5567 sent to my screen immediately. Please concentrate on section 725 through 820, and this is for my eyes only, do you understand?"

"Understood, Ms. Syshchenko." A moment later, the image appeared, and Olexia could see the technician zooming in at 10 times the size for the quadrant requested. Within seconds, the new image was brought into detailed focus, and Olexia stepped back to take in the entire image, letting her eyes adjust.

"Please rotate the image 30 degrees North and 90 degrees center. Fill in the pixilation and compile in 3D." Olexia waited for another 15 seconds before Ahmad was staring right at her. She didn't need for the rest of the compilation to complete.

"Get me Coats, now. I need wheels up in 60 and a crew of three. Feed over the exact coordinates of image 5567 and the image on my screen, as is."

Forty seconds later, Coats' incoming call was directed into her private line.

"Have you found everything to your satisfaction, Mr. Coats?" Olexia knew that a certain protocol had to be followed before she could make the assignment. Trust was of the utmost importance and if payment had not been made and promises kept, her elite team of assassins would no longer have a need for her. They would take their services elsewhere with the possibility of those skills being used against her at a later time.

"Yes, and thank you." Coats hesitated, waiting for Olexia to respond. But when no reply came, he continued. "Since you called me, I have to assume the target has been located?"

"Hangar 17. Be there at 0130 ready for engagement. Your target has been identified and you will get the full details once you are in the air. There will be no drop. Once your wheels are down, you will have forty-eight hours to complete the kill. Do you have any questions?"

"Just one. Why no drop?"

Coats could hear the amusement in her voice. "It's kind of hard to do a parachute drop of someone onto the streets of California and not bring attention to yourself, don't you think, Mr. Coats?"

"California? My target is in the United States?"

"We had intel that he had returned to Afghanistan, but recent video shows otherwise. From the footage I am witnessing, if he is responsible, he is extremely dangerous to a great many people. In fact, if you are capable, we need for you to capture him alive." Olexia knew the response she would receive from Coats and also knew the request would be impossible to achieve, but pressed her luck anyway.

"That's not our deal lady, and it's not what I am paid for. I look a man in the eyes and I take his life. Period. If you want recon, you need to call someone else, and I thank you kindly for your initial deposit."

Olexia knew she didn't have time to find someone else. "If my suspicions are right, he has a chemical agent that he plans on releasing within the United States. If he hasn't by the time you reach him, it is imperative we find out where the toxins are and where they were made. Once we know that, you may do what you wish."

"Are you giving me permission to use extreme physical force in obtaining that information?"

"My guess is that you already have that in mind, Mr. Coats. We are wasting time. Will you at least try to either bring the man in or get the information we need before you kill him?"

"If it's possible, I will. If not, you'll get what's left of the man."

Chapter 13

Nick flipped the switches one more time on the remote to make sure all were working properly before activating them and turning back to Dawson. "I'm going to let you get your pound of flesh, but you follow my lead. I don't intend to get involved other than asking a few questions. Are you ready?"

Checking his watch, Nick decided now was a good a time as any. He wasn't worried about mixing it up with a few punks, he just wanted to see how the local police would react. Picking up a discarded two by four, he raised it above his head and slammed it down on the hood of the first car. He repeated hitting the car until he heard screaming above him and footsteps coming down the first flight of stairs.

As the first man sprinted towards Nick, Nick pulled the P250 from its holster and pointed the weapon at the man's head, stopping him in his tracks. "Hey, what's up?" Nick said. Nick was relieved they weren't carrying any large weapons and that they appeared to be at least considering their odds against him.

"What's up, mother fucka', is I'm about to punk your ass and your boyfriend, too."

Nick looked at Dawson, then back at the man. "Are you sure that's what you want to do? I mean, I'm only here to observe you getting your ass kicked, and ask a few questions."

By this time the rest of the gang members had arrived and were standing next to their leader, just waiting for a signal. "I'd say the odds are that you two are soon gonna' be my bitches." The rest of the gang laughed at the remark.

Dawson was getting anxious to drop the guy and Nick knew the situation could turn if he didn't continue staying on the offensive. He turned to Dawson and asked, "Which one is the guy who decided it was OK to fondle a fifteen year old girl?"

"The one talking out his ass." Dawson took a step forward and the man flashed a barber's razor he had hidden in his right hand, having held it previously out of view. Dawson stood his ground hoping the idiot would take one more step towards him.

"Seriously? I'm pointing a gun at your head and you pull a knife?" Nick started to laugh.

"He ain't got nuttin'." The man protested.

Nick looked at his watch; any minute now. As if having willed it, three police cars appeared out of nowhere, slamming on brakes and coming to a screeching halt as they entered the underground level of the garage. With doors flinging open, each officer jumped out, slid a shotgun over the edge of the window frame and pointed them at all of the men. Everyone froze except Nick, who began walking towards the man holding the razor.

As he walked, the highest ranking officer yelled out. "Which one of you is Nicholas West?"

Nick continued walking, raising his right hand as he went. One foot from the man, Nick stopped. "Those cars you are driving are all stolen. I ran the VINs (Vehicle Identification Number) that you thought you erased, but didn't. The stereos and other items I would assume are also stolen. I would like for you to hand over the keys to these officers so they can be sold at auction to help fund the college education of the girl you scared half to death."

The man pretended not to know what Nick was talking about. "What girl?" Slowly a smile appeared across his face. "Oh, yeah. That cute little piece…"

He never finished the sentence as Nick threw a right hook into the man's ribcage, sending him to his knees and gasping, trying to take in long deep breaths of air. Dawson turned his head towards the police and waited, but there was no reaction from any of them.

"I asked nicely, remember that." Nick turned to the stunned members and asked which car belonged to the man on his knees. When no one spoke, Nick held up the remote and said, "Gentlemen, we are going to play it your way," as he flipped the first switch on the remote of the car containing the duffle bag.

The yellow Camaro's doors blew off their hinges and the top peeled back as glass fragmented and exploded. Nick had set the charge to direct the released force to implode within a confined area, so no one would be injured by the flying debris. As the car's interior began to burn, a voice from behind screamed. "That was my car, you fuck. His is the blue Corvette."

As he said this, the man ran towards Nick, whose back was turned away from the attacker. Nick heard the footsteps coming but did not turn around. A large pipe was raised high in the air as he leaped towards the man holding the box with switches across the top.

Reaching down, Dawson grabbed the razor from the man still on his knees, pivoted, and swooped low to the ground, spinning in a three-hundred and sixty degree turn. As he spun inward behind the runner, he swung his arm in an arc and bent his wrist at the exact angle needed as he passed the blade cleanly through the man's Achilles tendon. Two steps from Nick, the man fell, screaming in agony, clutching at the severed tendon as the pipe bounced across the concrete pavement.

Dawson resigned himself in that instant that he was going to prison, having disabled a man who had not been a direct threat to him. In amazement, he watched as none of the officers moved, but continued keeping their eyes fixed on the gang.

Dawson looked at Nick. "Are you OK?"

"I will be, as soon as these men turn over their keys."

By now the members were reaching into their pockets and tossing the keys at Nick's feet, all except the man on his knees who felt he still had some chance of holding onto some dignity.

"You can kiss my ass, you mother fucker. You ain't getting' my keys. You're gonna' have to shoot me in front of all these people first before I hand them over."

Nick had not wanted to hurt anyone, but now was the time to find out if he was correct in his hunch about having immunity. If he was wrong, he and Dawson would be cellmates for a long time.

Stepping one step forward, Nick pulled the P250 from its holster, placed the barrel against the man's shoulder and fired. Dawson was startled by his friend's action, knowing that Nick had now gone over the edge, shooting the defenseless man in front of all these witnesses. Bending down, Nick reached into the man's pocket and pulled out the keys. Dawson turned towards the officers, hoping he could plead his case and the insanity of his friend.

Instead, the men kept their guns level and did not move. Nick, holding the keys, walked towards the senior officer and handed him the entire set. "These are all stolen cars. Please see that they are impounded and the insurance companies are contacted. Also see to it that those two get medical care."

The officer shook his head, but kept his mouth shut. With that, Nick and Dawson began walking back to their cars. Passing a trashcan, Nick reached inside, grabbed his carry bag and kept walking. Twenty feet from their vehicles, Nick took Dawson by the arm and turned him around to face him. "There's almost three hundred thousand dollars in here. You give it to Makura and tell him it's for his daughter's college education. You do not need to explain any of what happened tonight to him, understand?"

"Hell, Nick, I don't understand what just happened. You and I should be in jail right now. We are damn lucky we didn't get killed by the police or those assholes. What the hell is going on?"

"The answer to my question, that's what."

Chapter 14

The flight from Ireland to California would give Darryl Coats enough time to plan a strategy that would allow him several options for capturing his intended target or, worst case, make the kill and let Olexia's team dispose of the body. It had been years since he had turned over a warm body to his employer and he swore he would never do it again.

Whatever plan he put in place, it would have to appear as if he had no other choice but to kill the mark and be done with it even if it meant putting a bullet in himself and making it look like self defense. He had no intention of letting anyone live regardless of the assignment instructions. If questioned later, he would have to concede the options he had considered and intended before he took Ahmad's life.

After several hours of mental skirmishing to finalize the selected options, fatigue began to set in. He could feel the burning in his eyes and fought the urge to close them, but it was useless. He had been awake for thirty-seven hours and needed sleep. He buzzed for a cocktail, grabbed a pillow from the overhead bin, sat back down and stuffed the pillow behind his head. Finishing the drink in one long gulp, he stretched his legs as best he could, rested his head back on the pillow and closed his eyes.

The chime of a bell awoke him from what had felt like only a few minutes of sleep, but checking his watch, it had been nearly four hours. Over the speaker he could hear the captain giving instructions for landing and asking everyone to fasten their seatbelts. Looking down the center isle, he could see the stewards and stewardesses checking to make sure the passengers were complying and shutting any trays that were still in the down position.

He caught the eye of a cute redheaded stewardess as she passed, and pointed towards his watch. "How long do we have before we land?"

"If we are cleared to land, it shouldn't be more than ten minutes, but other than that, I can't tell you for sure."

"Any chance I can hit the john before we touch down? I fell asleep and I'm not sure I can wait until we land and I can find one in the terminal."

The stewardess looked back towards the cockpit and saw two passengers standing in the aisle, trying to put some belongings back in the overhead. "You've got to hurry. I will check back with you in a few minutes, after I get those people back in their seats."

"You won't even know I got up." Unbuckling his seatbelt, Coats bolted for the bathroom door. Once inside, he slid the lock and pulled out his phone. Slipping the back off, he pulled out the small wire that had been tucked along the inside and inserted it into a slanted slot, barely visible to the human eye. It was like threading a needle with a ballpoint pen, he thought. Gently tugging on the wire, he felt it grab, and a tiny green light displayed. He slid the back of the phone in place and exited. There would be no chance of someone intercepting his communications now.

He was snapping his seatbelt as the stewardess began walking back towards him. As she passed, he winked and thanked her. She smiled and continued checking on the remaining passengers.

With that done, Coats was ready to receive the coordinates and additional information he expected would be coming as soon as he departed from the airport. He wanted to complete this assignment and get back to living the rest of his life down in Biloxi with his new twenty-two year old girlfriend.

The 727 bounced twice as it touched down, but not enough to unsettle any seasoned passenger. Following the instructions from the tower, the plane eased down the runway, making its way toward the arrivals terminal. Once it stopped, almost all of the passengers jumped from their seats and began pulling down their overloaded carry-ons, trying to make sure they didn't strike those waiting their turn. Some didn't care, as long as they got their luggage and could make their getaway as quickly as possible.

Coats waited in his seat, pulling his arms in tight, and watched as passengers made their slow trek towards the cockpit and out the opened side door. The pilot wished everyone a good day and Coats caught him flipping his eyes towards the redheaded stewardess on occasion. Lucky bastard, he thought, wishing it were him instead. But business needed to be taken care of first.

Having packed only the essentials, Coats made his way towards the car rentals, not needing to stand in line and wait for the luggage tram. After giving his name and confirmation number, he was handed the keys to an SUV and asked to sign all waivers. Outside, he found the rental fairly quickly, dropped his bag in the back and climbed into the driver's seat.

Once situated, he pulled out his phone and slid the activation bar and he pushed the earpiece into his right ear. Punching in the number, there was a slight delay before Olexia's voice could be heard. It was a prerecorded message, giving the location of the last sighting of the target and what additional information they had been able to find since he had left.

The information was detailed, but not enough to allow him an opportunity to create an advanced plan for the kill. He would need to do some additional research on his own. Pushing the pound key, an image appeared on the screen, showing the last confirmed photo of Ahmad. A shadow loomed over the image, but the technician was able to clear it enough to show the outline and features of disfiguration. A second photo showed what that side of the face would have looked like prior to the assault. It was enough for Coats.

An address had been included in the phone message. Coats entered the address into the dash-mounted GPS and began to drive. It would take almost three hours with the California traffic but the sun was shining and the sky was clear. He noted that the route would take him along the coastal highways, so he anticipated a chance that he would see a few beauties before his arrival.

Two hours later he began to feel his bladder and wished he had taken a few minutes to empty it before taking his seat at the end of the flight. He would go ahead and fill the tank and grab a bite to eat as he continued his drive. Pulling into a roadside burger joint, he shut off the engine as he checked for messages once again. His email account pinged, but he ignored it. There were two cars parked outside, along with a pick-up truck and gas-hauler. Music could be heard coming from inside, but it was Aerosmith instead of The Beach Boys, as he had expected.

At the counter, he ordered a large burger with the works, onion rings and two tall cans of imported beer. As the order was being filled, he walked back outside and lifted the gas hose and began filling the tank. Placing the hose back on the pump, he heard a voice asking which direction he was headed. Turning his head, he saw a girl standing in shorts and a bikini top. The top barely held what it was meant to contain.

"I'm heading up the coast for about another hour."

"Any chance I can get a lift for a couple of miles? That's my car there, but it won't start, so I just need a lift to my Dad's house, and he can bring me back."

Coats wished he had ordered fries now instead of onion rings. "Sure, hop in. I'll be back in a minute, just grabbing my food and paying for the gas. You need anything?"

"No, I'm good. Let me grab my purse and bag and I'll wait."

Paying for the bags of food, Coats grabbed them and trotted back to the SUV. He dumped the bags and drinks onto the center console, climbed in and started the vehicle. Making sure he was clear, he pulled back out onto the road, as he fumbled with getting the burger out of the bag. "There's a couple of beers and onion rings there if you want some," he said.

"No really, I just ate, I'm good."

"Suit yourself, but if you change your mind, you don't need to ask." Coats moved his eyes down to her cleavage. She caught him looking, but pretended not to.

Ten miles had passed before the girl spoke again. It was small talk and Coats answered her, just to answer. As she talked, Coats could see her working her top loose, but said nothing.

"This damn thing is my younger sister's, I knew I shouldn't have worn it. Would you mind pulling over so I can change into something from my bag?"

"How close are we to where you need to be? Can't it wait?"

"I guess it could, it's just so uncomfortable. I suppose I could take it off?"

He watched as the girl placed her fingers around her back and started undoing the tie string.

"Hold on, I'll pull over, but you need to make it quick." He now regretted having picked her up in the first place. The conversation had been boring and other than the great looking tits, it had been a monotonous trip thus far. The only good thing to this point had been the fresh salt air and the beer. The burger and onion rings were already beginning to play on his digestive system. He wished he had a good stick of that long lasting flavored gum.

Pulling onto the shoulder, he turned to the girl to tell her to please hurry. Before he could open his mouth, she slammed a hard wooden object into his throat. Training had taught him to turn his head sideways so the trachea would not be damaged, but he had not seen the attack coming in time. His hands grabbed at the partially collapsed airway, trying at the same time to suck in air. He watched as the girl pulled away and placed her back against the dash and door frame. In her hand was a 50,000 volt taser, pointed at his chest. He reached for her as she pulled the trigger.

The next morning when Coats awoke, his hair and eyelids were matted with dried blood. He could hear noises around him but could not determine their origin or who they belonged to. There was a constant knocking on a door some ten feet away. His hands were numb from the rope tied around his wrist, used to suspend his naked body a foot from the dirt floor. Underneath, he could not see the blood that had poured, then dripped, from his wounds, darkening the soil black.

His head began to clear and he remembered. The knife had cut deep into his buttocks, the tip hitting the pelvic bone, then the inner thighs. His calf muscles had been filleted to the bone, peeled back and laid against his heels. For the moment he felt no pain, only fear.

With great effort he tried several times to open his eyelids, finally breaking loose the dried layers of blood. It was dark except for a very slim sliver of light coming from underneath the door that was being pounded incessantly. As the light flickered in, he could see the girl lying on the ground, her throat cut and her left breast removed. He silently prayed her throat had been cut first. No other injuries appeared to have been inflicted on her.

He had talked. They had hung him from the ceiling, stripped him of his clothes and waited for him to think about what would be next. First it was the fists, then the metal rods. He felt his ribs being cracked and his jaw separated as they moved upwards and started hitting him around the neck and face. When they did not get the answers they were after, they moved down his body. After being struck in the testicles for the sixth time, he passed out. When he awoke, they began again.

Hours passed. Finally a knife was driven into his right buttock, pulled down, extracted and driven in the opposite one. As he screamed, it was yanked free and pushed slowly into the inner thigh. He began to talk, answering every question they asked and volunteering information they didn't. When he hesitated to answer, they found a new place to cut. He begged for them to kill him. Each time they laughed.

That damn knocking, he thought. Got to stop it. At the top of his lungs, he began to shout. "Stop it, you fucker!" as the sobs began. His voice was barely audible. The knocking continued. He had to make them stop. Unable to move any part of his body, he shifted his head backwards to see how he could release his hands.

Attached to his head was a thin wire, wrapped around the top, which he had not felt before. As his head moved backwards, the wire loops constricted and became tight, the tension at last registering in his brain. Overhead a light came on, flooding the room with a bright beam. Below he could see clearly now. At the same time the light switched on, he heard a click as the small trap door banged against the wall and opened. In the short distance, he watched as hundreds of rats poured into the room, frenzied by the smell of blood. Reaching the girl, they bit into the dangling flesh from the open wound and began tearing it away. Her body was soon covered and disappeared below the carnage.

Soon they found his legs. He was unable to kick them away as the severed muscles no longer allowed them to work. Although the muscles had been cut, the nerves had been left intact. He now realized that the purpose of the wire had been to turn on the lights and send a trigger to the door to open. It had been meant for him to witness his own death coming. He screamed once again as a cat sized rat gripped his thigh muscle between its teeth and began to pull it loose.

His screams lasted for almost twenty minutes before a sizable hole had been eaten through to his stomach. Pushing its way in, a single rat crawled up into the chest cavity and began to feast.

Chapter 15

Ahmad listened as the details of the girls' death and torture of the man were explained. The man had been sent to kill him by persons unknown, for the moment. The girl had hitched a ride with the man after being paid two thousand dollars by his men, and threatened with the loss of her eyes if she did not succeed. She had been instructed to have the man drive out of town, then make him stop at any remote area she felt comfortable with. Whatever she had to do to stop him, she would have to do. They only needed a few minutes. Ahmad's men had given her a quick lesson on how to use the taser and where to point it as she pulled the trigger. She had done her job well and was no longer needed.

The man, on the other hand, had been extremely valuable. Ahmad had wished he could have been able to interrogate the hired gun himself, but there were too many other necessities requiring his time. He was very proud of what his men had been able to obtain, though, and congratulated them on their efforts. He would see to it they were rewarded appropriately.

It had taken hours for the man to talk, lasting longer than all of the others he or his men had ever interrogated. It had been necessary to make him watch as the girl's throat was slowly cut in front of him, then watch as the men continued to cut as she lay dying. He had been told he was next, but the threat did not seem to bother him, infuriating at least one of the men. Earlier, Coats didn't remember the killing of the girl.

Without mercy, his man began to beat the infidel into unconsciousness on multiple occasions. Not until he drove a knife into his left thigh and begin to carve out the muscle, did the man begin to talk. It was remarkable how a man could stand so much pain, yet hold fast to his beliefs. At some point, any man gave up all hope.

Coats had been sent to kill him. Many questions had already occurred to both him and his men. How did they know he was alive? How did they know he was here in California? Who had sent the message to the assassin on the coordinates of Ahmad's whereabouts? Who had the knowledge and resources to put together a sanction so quickly? Each question had to be answered, and quickly, before another attempt was made. The first two questions didn't matter as much as the third.

But most importantly, who had sent the message of the coordinates his technician had been able to lift from the satellite transmission and had relayed directly to him? Like the FBI and CIA, they listened to specific language and words being sent across the telephone lines and airwaves. Once his name was mentioned, it triggered an immediate recording and interpretation. Someone had spoken his name after all of these years as if he were still alive, knowing for certain he was still alive. He knew of no one he had left living or did not trust completely, who knew he had not been buried in that rock grave years ago.

Ahmad turned to his most trusted guard. "Get me the entire message that was sent earlier. I want all of it. I was told there was a voice message that preceded the transmission. Make sure it is included."

The guard started to relay the message to one of his own men when Ahmad stopped him. "No! You will get it for me. I trust no one else. Get the recording and bring it back quickly. I do not want it transmitted again."

As the commander left, Ahmad dismissed his other men and went into his study. Somewhere from his past, someone was still alive, looking for him and wanting him dead, enough to pay a large fee to complete the task. Perhaps it was an organization, and not an individual, as he had originally thought. But then again, who would be alive to know of his past, know that he was still alive, and alert this organization? Who would keep the secret to themselves and not alert all of the authorities? He needed that recording!

Three hours later the guard returned with a digital copy of the recording. He was winded as he entered the study and found Ahmad on his feet, already approaching him as he closed the door behind himself. The look on the guard's face told Ahmad the news would not be pleasant.

"The technician gives his apology as he erased most of the message prior to recording the coordinates. The voice was sporadic and did not contain what he felt was useful information. There were only a few words left on the end of the verbal recording."

Ahmad began to curse at the guard, a fury that always left the man he was speaking to, dead. The guard fell to his knees, begging forgiveness for not killing the technician before he left, as he knew Ahmad would want him to have done.

Reaching down for the guard, Ahmad drew his pistol from his holster and placed the barrel against the man's head. Pulling the guard to his feet, he ordered him to take his gun, kill the technician with it and drag the body in front of the rest of his men. "Make sure they know what he did and that they understand the consequences of what will happen to them if they repeat this man's stupidity and disloyalty. Now leave me the recording and go!"

The man, relieved that he would live for another day, took the gun and left, taking with him several men.

Ahmad returned to his desk and sat down. Disappointed with the news, he nonetheless opened the bay door on his computer, dropped in the disc and clicked on an application to begin listening to whatever was left of the voice recording. As he was told, the voice was garbled and sporadic. To his surprise, he was able to determine it was a woman. Words were lost between sentences and, of those that were audible, only a few were understandable. It did not matter, it was the voice he needed to recall. He adjusted the volume and listened for the third time.

There were only five words that he could comprehend, but it was the voice that began to haunt him. It was a voice he knew, but the constant gabble and high-pitched sounds on the tape made it almost impossible to grasp. For the sixth time he played the recording again, beginning to agonize over the rhythmic voice and, then at once, he knew.

How could she still be alive? he thought. Then he remembered.

Chapter 16

It had now been almost three days since Nick had touched back down on American soil from Ireland. He had expected a follow-up from Olexia, but had received none. Had she really allowed him to just walk away with the knowledge that Ahmad was still alive? What did she expect him to do? Little had been learned from the newscasts, and what information was being released was all a lie by the media in hopes of not panicking the population.

Their lies had been lessons learned from 9/11 when America shut down for days before it realized it was a single act of terrorism, and not a war, that had been brought to its shores. Most businesses and peoples' lives returned to normal, except for those who had lost loved ones. Promises of retribution and compensation had been given, but not fully realized after all of these years.

Now a single act of terrorism had been brought again and this time there would be precautions taken. Billions in revenue and thousands of lives lost at a cost of a discouraged nation. Time had not begun to heal the wounds, as expected, but instead had festered into a nation of distrust. Distrust of its neighbors, its government, its local leaders and worse, a loss of pride the country had always known. All things had changed.

Constitutional privileges to those born in the United States were now examined by every branch of government. New laws were passed protecting only those with wealth. All others would fall under suspicion until they could prove otherwise. Investment in a home now meant eventual bankruptcy instead of a nest egg for those who had hoped to retire someday. Benefits, once guaranteed by the Social Security Act, were now forever questionable.

Congress misread their own American people at every turn, believing they were starting to break, to lose faith in all things around them and that they could not take another blow. They must lie in order to protect them and themselves.

Reclining on his couch, Nick took a long swig of a Harp Lager beer before punching in the number Olexia had given to him for calling her directly. The conversation would remain between them. The audio filtering would assure it. After several rings, Nick began to hang up, when he heard a voice on the other end.

"What do you need, Nick? I thought we made it clear there were to be no calls."

"Your seventy two hours are almost up. We also need to discuss why you felt it necessary to give me immunity under your protective blanket. I don't want it, as it makes me appear to be one of you."

"Being one of us is not a bad thing, Nick. You may want to remember that. Besides, you play by your rules and I can't take a chance of you running into trouble right now, at least not for a few more days."

Nick could hear the tension in her voice. "At least for a few more days? What do you mean? What aren't you telling me?"

"It is not your concern. I will lift the protection once I have confirmation the issue has been resolved. Until then, I must ask you to try and stay out of trouble and simply continue your search."

Getting into trouble was the least worry on his mind right now and he pushed forward. "I need whatever information you have on Ahmad. Baker has pulled his data. I just want to review what you have as well, and maybe we can track him down together more quickly."

"That's not necessary. We have his last known location already."

"Where, from Wyoming, when he shot Brighton?" Nick listened to the silence, realizing she must have the additional information Baker had already given him.

When she did not answer, he knew for sure. "You know he's in California, from the explosion footage. Is that right?" Again, she did not answer.

Nick began to replay the conversation over in his head, trying to pull out little hints of information Olexia was not trying to tell him. What was she hiding? Then a thought occurred to him.

"You've sent one of your people after him, haven't you?" Nick was screaming into the phone. "You've sent a foreigner onto American soil to kill a terrorist that is getting ready to release a chemical agent on us. Do you have any fucking idea what will happen if Ahmad finds out, and you know he will? You just stepped up his timeline!"

"What chemical agent? He blew up a shop!"

"It wasn't the explosion that killed all of those people. It was the chemical compound released into the air by the explosion and it is the deadliest any of our people have ever seen."

Olexia could not talk. She was trying to race through the possibilities of why she had not heard from her man in over 24 hours. They were to talk every twelve hours, but now it had been a full day.

"I didn't know. I only saw the footage released by your media and the explanation they were giving. There was no mention of a toxic chemical other than some nearby boat having a small accident. I had the footage enlarged and recognized Ahmad, that's all."

"How are you contacting your man, and what's the schedule? Please don't tell me he has gone dark."

"No. He is supposed to call me every twelve hours for an update." Olexia now wished she had said that differently.

"Supposed to call you? He hasn't stuck to the schedule?"

"No. It's been almost 17 hours now. I was thinking of sending in a second team."

"Your man is already dead and you know it. There's no question Ahmad knows as well, if he wasn't the one who actually killed him."

He could hear Olexia starting to argue, but he didn't have time for it.

"Send me what you have, and I need your people working with Baker. You open all of your databases to him, total access and no tracking or tracing his movements. Your technical people work with him on this now, do you understand?"

Olexia knew she had little choice. If her superiors were to find out that she had ordered a personal sanction for her own reasons, she would be next.

"Alright, but you are responsible from this point on. You must find Ahmad. I am redirecting the sanction for you to make the kill. It is necessary in order to give you full international immunity from all prosecution."

"I don't want it. You've already given me some kind of security level way beyond what anyone else I know has, and I didn't want that either."

"You have no say in this decision. There have only been four people ever given this status under my directive, and every one of them eventually needed it. Without it, you are an open target. I have the authority to do this and I am the only one who can take it away, ever."

Nick did not like knowing he would be listed as a terminator in anyone's book, but knew what she was saying was necessary. If the chase took him out of U.S. protection, he would need all of the help he could get. Being able to call for backup and have it there quickly would allow him to move in and out of whatever countries might be required to follow his quarry. Having access to whatever he needed was also a plus.

"Get me the last coordinates your man called in from. I'll start there. I am going to bring in my own people on this, so you make sure you have identified them properly in your system. I don't want someone putting a bullet through their heads by accident."

"No!" Olexia began to panic. "No one else knows of this sanction outside of yourself and me. You cannot employ any of your own people. This must be kept quiet."

Nick was trying to remain calm. "You sent your man in without any backup, didn't you? Left the guy open to whatever risk he might encounter, all by himself. Is that what you are going to do with me?"

"I had hoped the other man would not need any help. He has performed several other jobs for us and was always very quick in getting results. There was no reason for me to assign other men for support. We are or were aware of his location at all times."

"Had you made any plans to send in someone for his body if he failed?"

"If he failed, there would not be any parts of his body worth recovering, or possibly, even finding." Olexia had become tired and irritated with the conversation and wanted it ended. "Enough. Please!"

Nick would not relent. "One man is all I need and he is going with me. I understand you not trusting anyone else, but I trust him. He either goes with me or you contact someone else. I need your cover of immunity this once, but after it is over, I want it lifted."

Tears began to roll down Olexia's face. She had never lost control of any situation since she had taken the helm of the organization and realized this could be the beginning of the end of her reign. If West failed to kill Ahmad or keep the details secret and take them to his grave, the reprisal would be swift.

"Mr. West, you must know that whatever the results of this sanction, no one can ever learn of it. By you bringing in another operative, you and I run the additional risk and possibility of that information being disclosed and learned of by my superiors. If that happens, you and I will be disposed of. If you and I are near anyone when that happens, those people will also be killed. Now, do you understand why I only want you?"

"And I need someone I trust totally watching my back. Again, it's either both of us or neither one of us." Nick knew what Olexia was getting at, but decided he would try one last time before giving into her demands.

"One man, and you had better make sure it is someone who will never speak of this. I cannot emphasize enough the extreme danger you will put us in if that person talks." Olexia had already made note to arrange an accident for the man, whoever he was. For Nick, she would need to be more careful and make his death appear due to natural causes.

"Send me his last known coordinates and I'll track it. That will give me a start on finding out who got to him or at least, hopefully, finding his remains."

"You will have the coordinates in the next couple of minutes. If he is dead, leave him and continue tracking Ahmad. That is the only important thing here."

The remark shocked him. "Olexia, if I find your man or what is left of him, he's coming home with me, I don't leave anyone behind. This goes deeper than what you have told me. When I get back, you and I are having a long talk."

"Just find Ahmad and then we will talk." Olexia hesitated for a moment then said, "Yes, it does go deeper."

"How deep, Olexia?"

"Deep enough that I'm coming to you. It must be discussed where only you and I can talk face to face. I will depart in 30 minutes." With that, Olexia's phone went dead.

Chapter 17

She finished filling the 20 polished insulated aluminum containers Ahmad had requested and was standing by the glass panes in front of freezer, taking final notes on the deformation of the bodies. Once the muscle spasms ended, the bodies had begun to settle back into their normal form and shape, except for those places the bones had snapped. With no skeletal support, the muscles elongated and the skin took on whatever shape gravity forced it into.

Other than the liquid trails that oozed from the orifices, there were only small telltale signs that the men had died from a toxin. The flesh no longer showed evidence of burning that had initially occurred when the chemical came in contact with the skin. Now the color of the affected skin appeared more like a light sunburn. These changes were completely unexpected. She had lowered the temperature to five degrees above freezing, enough to keep the limbs from becoming hard and stiff but enough to keep them from putrefying.

Laying the notebook aside, she turned on the air blowers in the freezer first, then stood outside, checking her suit to make sure there were no air leaks. Content, she picked up the other instruments and pulled open the door. In her hand was a scalpel used for cutting thin layers of skin. In the other were several capped test tubes.

The layers would be used to perform biopsies in order to determine the acceleration of spore division by the chemical enhancements. She hoped the counts would exceed, at the minimum, eight times their normal divisions. If they exceeded that, then that would have meant the spores continued to divide even after the death of the victim despite the need for oxygen or other living tissues. Her excitement and anticipation of what she might discover caused her to quicken her pace through the door.

It had been three days since she last spoke with Ahmad and she knew he would be returning soon. He had already been very pleased with the results of her experiments and had promised even more reward than they had first agreed upon. If she could prove the agent was even more potent than believed, she felt that he would finally allow her to partner with his future plans. She knew she was playing a dangerous game, but could not find any reason he would not partner. Had he not almost kissed her upon seeing the dying men?

Approaching the first cadaver, she stood for a moment, looking into the hollowed eye sockets. The chemical had been absorbed into the eyeball and eaten away at the outer membrane. No longer able to contain the contents, the eyeball ruptured and the fluid poured out upon the man's cheek. Raising the scalpel, she began to scoop the liquid and interior socket, scraping the matter into the first tube and resealing it.

Next, she cut away a square inch of skin under the eye, rolled it and placed it into another tube. Placing the scalpel's sharp tip against the man's trachea, she pushed it in until she felt no resistance and began cutting downward. With the trachea exposed, she inserted the blade, again scraping the layers of skin and filling a third tube.

Placing the tubes in the suit's insulated pocket, she stepped over the man's outstretched legs and started towards the second body. She suddenly stopped and turned towards the freezer's door. There had been a noise, the sound of someone's voice. She was sure of it, but the door remained closed and she did not see anyone through the glass panes. She turned back to the second man and began the same biopsies as she had performed on the remains of the other man.

Satisfied she had all of the tissue samples she needed, she retraced her steps back to the freezer door and pushed in on the handle. The handle pushed inward, but the door did not open. She could feel the adrenaline levels begin to rise in her body and her breathing rate rose slightly. Someone had locked her in. Putting her weight against the door, she placed her feet square on the floor and began to bounce her body against it, pushing in the knob handle each time she struck the door.

Now she began to panic. Being in tight spaces did not bother her. Being concealed and locked in tight spaces did. At once, the memory of her and her bastard half-brother being locked in a discarded refrigerator flooded back into her consciousness. The same feelings and anxiety she felt when they pulled his body out started to overwhelm her. She had not cared that he had died, only that it could have been her.

She had practiced many times over the last couple of days, easily getting in and out before she finally lured the tattle-tale pecker over. It would have been so easy if it hadn't been for pesky Josey closing the latch, not knowing they were inside. That was to have been her bit of fun.

Taking in large gulps of air, she only concerned herself now with getting out alive. Slamming harder into the door, one, two, three times, she felt it give. As it flew open, she lost her balance and fell forward onto her right side.

The angle of the impact caused her arm to bend underneath, pushing the elbow straight into her ribs, dislocating the shoulder and bending the wrist backwards. With the door still open, she bent her legs upwards, then quickly straightened them to kick it shut. As the bolt caught hard, she once again heard the voices just outside the lab's entry doors.

Sitting up as gently as possible, she stood, slipped out of her HAZ-MAT suit and made her way towards an unlocked cabinet that contained all of her supplies. Her shoulder was pushed outward and the pain was worse than she had ever felt from her past injuries. No matter what pain she felt, she would have to make it to the cabinet, she told herself.

Outside the doors, she could hear the conversation getting louder as one man would not stop screaming at the others. She was not able to understand all of the conversation, but understood enough to know the man believed his brother was inside and he wanted to get him out now, regardless of what evil was on the other side of the door. She took longer steps towards the cabinet.

Opening the cabinet door as silently as possible, she pushed her hand underneath a set of lab coats and fumbled for the object she hoped was still there. Just as she felt the grip of the .380 handgun, the lab door burst open and a man jumped through, looking around frantically as if Satan himself were standing on the other side. The two corpses inside the freezer caught his attention and he slowly approached them.

He began to weep at the sight of his brother, now almost unrecognizable from the deterioration of his remains. Turning towards the woman, he raised his arms and sprinted at her, disregarding the gun she had pointing at him. She heard him ranting obscenities in a language she did not comprehend, and pulled the trigger. The bullet missed by six inches as the man was now within three feet. As she fired again, the man spun and fell against the table she had laid the first set of biopsies on. As he pushed off, the tubes fell to the floor, shattering the glass and spraying the contents across the tiles.

With one last leap, the man grabbed her around the throat, placing his thumbs hard against her throat and began pushing them inward as hard as he could, hoping to end her life quickly. She placed the gun barrel against the man's chest and fired twice. His body fell against hers and she pushed him away, dropping the gun. Her life now depended on the ability to keep the chemicals from entering her body. Hopefully, she would not sustain any permanent facial scarring the chemicals would undoubtedly inflict.

She turned and ran to a far wall, slamming her fist against the large red knob, plunging it in as far as it would go. Immediately she heard the overhead vacuums erupt as they began sucking all loose matter into airtight bags. An air mask popped from a container next to her face and with her one good hand she struggled to put it on. Finally, with the mask in place around her face, she began inhaling the pure oxygen. Keeping her eyes shut as tight as possible, she waited. Moments later, she began to cough.

The attempted strangulation had caused swelling in her trachea, making it difficult to breathe without an occasional clearing of her throat. Each time she did, she hesitated to make sure there was no burning. For whatever small amount of time the toxin had been released, the lab was now contaminated. She could no longer confirm the findings of her research or why the men's skin began to heal. Ahmad was due to return in two days and there was no time to cleanse the room and equipment. The lab would have to be destroyed, but there would still remain minute traces of the chemical. No matter what she tried, it could not be thoroughly cleaned even if she had decades to do it.

The pain from her shoulder and sprained wrist was beginning to impair her judgment, making it almost impossible to think clearly. The bottles needed to be cleaned on the outside and removed from the lab before setting fire to it. Whoever was in the building would perish, but she didn't care. They would die anyway once the airbags burst from the heat, releasing the chemicals that had been vacuumed into them earlier. By then, though, she would be far enough away that it wouldn't matter.

Lifting the mask slowly, she took a very small breath to test for any burning, waiting. When there was none, she took it off completely and walked to where the canisters were concealed in a box. Taking the lid off of the box, she counted five rows across and four deep. There were twenty bottles in all, just as Ahmad had requested. It would have to do for his purposes. He had wanted much more, knowing there would be additional requests or even American retaliations, but under the circumstances... well, she would probably die by his hand anyway. No use worrying now.

For the next hour the bottles were removed and sanitized as well as possible. Most likely they were never contaminated at all, but it was worth the painful effort. It was better than having your body eaten away from the inside out, she thought.

Towards the back of the lab, there was a large closet that held an assortment of janitorial items, including sixty five gallon containers of gasoline used for filling the tanks of the different SUVs around the compound. She would take the chemical containers outside first, put them in one of the vehicles, and return. Laying down a trail of gasoline, she would light it, then drive away. She estimated she would have roughly ten to fifteen minutes driving time before the other gas containers exploded, bringing down the entire building and everything in it.

Once she was safe, she would contact Ahmad. He would understand what she had needed to do. He would be furious that she had failed in making the additional chemicals, but his primary plans could be carried out. He could reduce the amount of bottles to five per plane and still obtain the desired effects. The last five he could hold for backup and sell them to the highest bidder.

The gas containers were heavier than she thought they would be. Within an hour she had piled them into the center of the room, except for one that she placed in a cart, along with the box containing the 20 aluminum bottles. Riding the elevator down the three floors, she pushed the cart through the makeshift garage, looking until she found a vehicle with keys in the ignition. Releasing the hatch, she loaded the items into the back, closed it and sat on the tail bumper for a few minutes. The effort had exhausted her and she needed the short rest.

Not wanting to wait until later as was her original plan, she took out the phone from her side pocket, flipped open the cover and placed the call. When she heard Ahmad's voice, she took a breath and began.

"You fool. You ignorant bitch!" Ahmad screamed back at her. "Do you realize that we will have no way of fulfilling our obligations now? If we cannot deliver the additional chemicals once the sale goes through..." His voice trailed off. "If you destroy whatever is in that lab, I will kill you myself!"

It was not the response she had anticipated. Instead of praising her for saving what was already produced, she was now being threatened by the man she had grown to love. All of the times he had commended her on her intelligence and loyalty, it had not been a sign of his affections, but rather a manipulative design to play on her womanly needs and desires.

She remembered the other men as well, who had called her names after she wouldn't give in to their demands. Her studies had taught her about diseases like herpes and syphilis, and, much worse, AIDS. She would have only allowed one man to ever touch her there and now he was threatening her life. They were all bastards, only after one thing. Her error was now fully understood. *Screw the capsules*, she thought.

"Don't threaten me! You are the fool, because the formula is in my head. Did you forget that? Without me, you have no way of creating more. We can build another lab and, yes, it will take time to manufacture another supply, but you need me, you fuck!"

Anger had taken hold of Ahmad and he found himself saying words he did not intend. She was right. Without her, the plan was useless. There would be no place he could hide if he couldn't deliver. Without reasoning he responded, "If I have to start over, there are others that can produce what I need, even faster."

He had meant for the words to scare her into changing her mind, realizing that what she was about to do would not benefit either one of them. Instead, it had the opposite effect. He stood motionless as the last words he heard before the phone went dead were, "I'll see you in hell then."

With a renewed vigor, Gabrielle pushed the cart aside and raced directly towards the stairs, not wanting to wait for the elevators. Once inside the lab, she took off the lid from one of the containers and began pouring the gas over the other containers, making her way slowly out the door, leaving a small trail across the floor as she went. Outside, there was just enough gas left for her to place a piece of cloth inside and light it.

She started the SUV and pulled alongside the can. With one flick, the flame caught on the lighter and she bent out as far as she could through the window. Ever so slowly, she inched her hand further down towards the cloth, extending the lighter with her fingertips. Two inches away, the fumes ignited and she recoiled, dropping the lighter onto the gas trail. Instantly a ball of fire erupted and she stepped on the gas pedal.

As she shot out the exit, she knew she would have less time now to get as far away as she could before the decisive explosion released the deadly toxins into the air. It had not been the first time she had used the vacuums, so the airbags were full of the spores by now. Up ahead, she watched as heavy winds blew dirt and debris across the unpaved path she was heading towards. Road signs twisted and shook as the storm grew closer.

Chapter 18

Three minutes after Nick hung up with Olexia, his phone vibrated. It was a text message with the last known coordinates of Coats. He punched them into Google and waited. As his phone pixilated the map display, he could see the location was near the edge of Partington Canyon.

A few calls later, Nick's arrangements were set for a quick pick up and landing within 3 hours. From there, he would be dropped into the Big Sur and would have to make his way across a half mile of terrain. Any closer and he took the chance of being spotted.

With his equipment checked and loaded into the passenger seat of the McLaren, he pushed the garage door opener, dropped the gear into reverse and held out just long enough for the door to open and allow the car an inch of clearance. The drive would take less than fifteen minutes.

After passing through the airport entrance, Nick took a sharp right and headed towards a sign that read 'Authorized Personnel Only. Violators Will Be Prosecuted'. The second part of the wording was printed in bold red letters and underlined. The McLaren passed it going ninety-three miles per hour.

Up ahead was the hangar. Nick could see the jet pulling out as he approached, then come to a dead stop. Scrambling out, he grabbed his bags and raced towards the plane as the side passenger door descended and touched the ground. Looking up the stairway, he saw Dawson pass by, heading towards the cockpit, then abruptly stop and poke his head out the open door.

"Jesus, nice set of wheels. Too bad my Mustang got me here faster." Dawson couldn't help but let out a laugh.

"Don't hand me that crap. You were already here at the airport waiting on that stewardess from Washington, who, I am only guessing, never showed. Word really does get around about that short dick of yours."

Dawson gave him the bird finger and headed back in, not waiting for Nick to ascend the staircase and pull the door closed. Sitting across from Dawson, he pulled out his laptop and Google'd the map coordinates once again, turning the display around towards Dawson.

"We are going to drop here and traverse across this ridge. Once we are within 300 feet, you are going to set up and cover my entry. I don't know if anyone will be stationed out front, but it looks like the building only has one entrance and exit point, both being the same. I'm going to put eyes on the perimeter before I head in. Any movement, you don't hesitate to eliminate any threat, and I mean only headshots. I don't want them to have any chance of getting off a shot and warning those inside. Got it?"

Dawson looked back at Nick and shook his head. "Once we have cleared the perimeter, I will follow you," he said.

"No. I need you watching for anyone who might show up unexpectedly. When you drop a target, you clear it. I don't want someone spotting any bodies lying around, in case of a flyover."

"Understood." said Dawson.

Nick could see Dawson's disappointment. "Most likely I'm just going to find a body, nothing else. It's a fairly large complex, but there have been no signs of activity in the last thirty-six hours."

"I understand, Nick. But I have to ask. Why me? Anyone on the old team could cover you. Why this sudden hook-up again after all of these years?"

"Did you give Makuro the money I told you to give him?"

"Of course I did. He was none too pleased, but took it anyway."

"Did you keep any for yourself? I know you could probably have used a few bundles."

"No, I didn't. You're right, I could have used some of that money, but you gave me a command and I followed it through."

"That's why. I can trust you to do what I ask and cover my back no matter what. There's no one else I can do that with. You had almost three hundred thousand dollars that could never be traced and you did the right thing with it."

Nick turned the display off and closed the laptop. "Check your gear and then get some rest. Once we are on the ground, we have one hour before recon, whether we have a body or not. We miss and it's a twenty mile trek out of there."

An hour and half later, both men were being woken from a light sleep. Nick stood first, grabbing parachute straps and running his arms through before snapping the harness in place. Dawson watched, thinking it was a joke. Nick caught his stare.

"What? I told you it was a drop, so you better get your ass moving."

"Fuck! I thought you meant we were going to land and be dropped, not this."

"Times a wasting. You forget how to pull a cord? Three minutes, buddy or you go out that door hanging onto me."

Dawson knew this wasn't a joke. "Next time, you cock sucker, you tell me all the details. I'm too fucking old for these surprises."

"Next time, don't say something about my wife you know I won't like." Nick was grinning from ear to ear. He loved payback.

The plane dipped behind the mountain range and leveled at 1200 feet. Nick attached a line and made his way back towards the tail section. He watched as a bay door began to open, and motioned for Dawson to get ready. On command, both men did a nose dive out the open hatch, their chutes deploying shortly after they exited.

Maneuvering, they landed within twenty-five feet of each other and immediately pulled in the chutes' fabric. As soon as they reached the coordinates, they would signal the plane and would have forty-five minutes. Looking around, both Nick and Dawson knew it would be hard times ahead if they missed getting back on time. The pilot of the helicopter had been given instructions to wait no more than 3 minutes.

Seven minutes later, Nick was looking through binoculars at a deserted home built sometime in the late 1930s, approximately thirty-eight hundred square feet in size. It could have been mistaken for an old depot had a garage not been attached at the rear. All of the doors and windows were sealed by wood panels, except for one entrance. Some of the panels seemed fairly new in comparison to some of the others that had been nailed in place years earlier.

Tire tracks and footprints were new as well. There had been a lot of recent traffic going in, but only a few shoe patterns leaving in the opposite direction. Whoever was in the house was still there. Nick decided this would be a good vantage point for Dawson to keep an eye out for any activity while he descended the ridge and checked on the interior.

Fifty feet from the house, Nick took a knee and listened for any voices that could be audible over the winds passing through. Keying his mike, he asked Dawson if he was clear.

"Looks good," replied Dawson.

Just as Nick stood, there was a large crack as a board splintered to his left and high-pitched sounds came echoing from within. An unmistakable odor of death escaped the opening as dozens of rats poured out, running in different directions. Some ran up the walls, while others followed the edges of the exterior and soon ran into the woods. Several of the more aggressive ones ran straight for Nick.

Nick pointed his silenced P250 at the head of the closest rat and fired. Its body twisted around, becoming a meal for the rats that had followed. Three more shots and the remaining vermin would have enough to eat on while Nick made his way towards the opposite end of the house that had the only human entrance. Pushing open the door, a dozen more rats made their way out as he stood aside to let them pass.

The smell was coming from a back bedroom. Covering his mouth and nostrils with a cloth, Nick made his way straight ahead, looking at discarded cans and documents that were scattered about the living room. Finally reaching the bedroom, Nick used the tip of his boot to push the door inward. Hanging, tied to the ceiling, was what was left of Coats. On the floor, only the skeletal remains of a small woman, based upon the shape of the pelvic bone.

Nick checked his watch. Twenty one minutes left before they had to head back. All around the room lay instruments of torture: batteries, cables, hammers, pliers and a large serrated knife. On the blade was dried blood. Spreading out an open body bag underneath Coats, he picked up the knife and cut through the rope as he held one end tight, slowly letting the vestiges drop to the ground before zipping the bag shut.

Now down to seventeen minutes, he took out his phone and began photographing the documents that were strewn around the rooms, then scooped them all up and placed them in his backpack.

Reentering the room where he had left the bodies, he had just bent down to lift Coats when he heard Dawson in his earpiece. "Better move it, we've got company. You've got maybe one minute. They are coming fast. I count five heads."

"I'm on my way out." With that, Nick picked up the bag and threw it over his shoulder. "Sorry buddy, no time to handle you delicately." The girl's remains would have to stay.

Grabbing his rifle, he made his way to the only door and kicked it open, shifted the weight of the body and began to sprint through the exit. Three steps out the door, a track of bullets cut off his run as they exploded just in front of him, spraying small chips of rock and dirt that cut into his face. He had no choice but to turn quickly back towards the house, dropping the body as he maneuvered.

Turning his head towards the vehicle as he ran, he saw two large caliber bullet holes punch through the drivers' windshield as Dawson began to reduce the live body count. Three men scrambled from the bed of the truck as it began to slide sideways. A third shot caught one of the men in mid-air, spinning him three hundred and sixty degrees before he came to rest hard against a large rock. The snapping of his spine could be heard.

The other two men made it to the side of the house before separating and going in opposite directions around the perimeter. The thought was that if the target had not made it back inside, he would be caught in the middle and regardless of which man he tried to defend himself against, the other man would be able to kill him easily.

This was old school and Nick did not want to wait for the men to have time to make it around to him. Knowing that Dawson would not be able to get the angle required, he would need to surprise the men, hopefully giving himself that extra split second he needed. He ran along the outer edge towards the first man and squatted as low as he could, listening for the first assailant's approach. Right as Nick arrived at the corner, he saw the barrel of a rifle inch its way past the edge. With the P250 in his left hand, he swung it around the corner and fired two shots. A man fell forward, clutching at his stomach and upper thigh. A third shot ended his pain.

Nick moved along the wall towards the open door. Once inside, the other man would have to follow him through in order to attempt a kill. It would give Nick the full advantage of waiting on his prey and giving him a clean shot as the man came through the door. It would provide Dawson with the angle he needed to make the shot, as well.

Having made it around to the door, Nick entered and found a dark area in which to wait. It did not take long. The silhouette of a man passed quickly by the door frame, firing a shot into the room as he passed. The bullet missed by inches and Nick moved towards the center of the frame, but still remained within the shadows. Pointing the gun in the dead center of the frame, he waited once more.

Why hadn't Dawson taken the guy out? The door and the adjacent wall were in plain sight of where he was positioned. A simple squeeze of the trigger would have already finished this.

This time as the man made a second pass in the opposite direction, Nick fired three very quick shots in succession. The first ripped through the man's left arm before penetrating the rib cage. The second missed, but the third hit him in the neck. The momentum caused him to fall and hit face first, followed by the rest of his body.

That was four down, one to go. Nick keyed his mike for Dawson to respond. Instead, there was another voice he recognized immediately from the interrogation tapes Baker had provided him.

"Mr. West, it is nice to see you in action. What I have read about you is quite accurate. Your skills are superior, just like your friend Mr. Dawson here. Unfortunately, you know little about me, except, of course what Olexia may have already told you." Ahmad was smiling to himself, knowing the last statement would come as a surprise to Nick.

At the moment, Nick's concern was only that of Dawson's safety. "The man you are holding, let him go. I know a great deal about you, of the plane you blew up and the chemicals you released. I also know you killed Senator Brighton." Nick took out his binoculars and panned up towards Dawson.

On the ridge he could see Dawson on his knees with Ahmad standing behind him, holding a gun pressed against the upper part of his spine, just below the skull.

"That is all true, Mr. West, and you also know I intend to do more. Another day or two and I will have accomplished my goal. However, right now you must be worried about your friend."

"Release him now, Ahmad, and we can talk about how much more time I will give you before I kill you." Nick already knew Dawson was dead, he was just trying to stall long enough for Dawson to figure out any way possible to break away long enough for Nick to get a shot off.

"Not going to happen. This man killed my men and it is only right I take his life after we have talked. Perhaps later you can retrieve his body like you are doing with Olexia's man, Mr. Coats."

"He has no useful intel that you can use? If you want someone, take me, instead, for whatever your purpose might be." Nick looked over at the body bag. "I'm sure whatever information you need, though, you've already obtained from Coats."

Ahmad laughed and pressed the gun harder into Dawson's neck. "Mr. Coats provided me with a great deal of information. Had it not been for the transmitter in his right eye socket, I would not have been able to verify whom he was working for or the fact that you were coming to his futile rescue. Are you aware you, too, have a transmitter running off of the same frequency?"

How is that possible? Nick wondered. He had checked his and Dawson's equipment to make sure there was no way anyone could track their movements. He had field stripped all electronic gear, except for their individual communication devices. Those signals would not have been strong enough to transmit a location to anyone outside a one hundred yard perimeter.

"Mr. West. You have eight minutes to make your way back to the ridge for pick-up. Take Mr. Coats' remains back home and bury them. And, oh, yes, before I fail to mention this. Be very careful who you are becoming bed partners with. She is not what she seems. She is coming to see you, Mr. West, and should be arriving within the next couple of hours."

"How do you know that, Ahmad?" If he knew that, what else did he know? thought West.

"My technical people are as sophisticated as hers, Mr. West. Her people can be bought just like anyone else. When she arrives, I will be in contact with you. I will exchange her for your friend, otherwise, I promise you, there will be no need to come after Mr. Dawson. You have twenty-four hours, otherwise you will be responsible for many deaths, and I will continue killing until you comply." With that, Ahmad jerked Dawson to his feet and pushed him towards the awaiting truck.

By the time Nick made it to the edge of the ridge, the SUV was gone. Only Dawson's rifle remained on the ground. Holding tight to Coats' remains on his shoulder, he bent down, retrieved the rifle and double-timed it towards the pick-up point.

As he made progress towards the point, he continually checked his watch and tried adjusting his stride so he would make it on time. As the time ticked away, he knew he would not get there and began making alternate plans. Reaching the crest of the final hill, he looked down and saw the outline of the chopper's blade pattern and knew it had already come and gone.

He would have to bury Coats' body and come back for it later. Just as he began to dig a shallow grave, he heard the sounds of the rotors spinning in the distance, coming closer to where he was standing. Five minutes later, the chopper sat down forty yards away and Nick hoisted Coats onto his shoulder.

As he dumped the body through the open hatch, he yelled up to the pilot. "I told you to leave after three minutes!"

"Yes sir, you did. But you didn't tell me not to come back. This is my fourth pass." The pilot showed no expression, but Nick knew what he was thinking. It was what all service personnel knew in their hearts and it bonded them all together as brothers and sisters.

Chapter 19

In her rear view mirror, Gabrielle saw a brief flash as the cans of gasoline ignited, then a small ball of flames rise into the air. She had anticipated it to be much more and was disappointed that the fire was not spreading as quickly as she had hoped. How could almost one hundred and fifty gallons of gas not create the fireball she had expected?

Around her she could hear the wind whipping against the truck as she held tight to the steering wheel, pushing the gas pedal almost all the way to the floor. The truck strained against a force that was doing its best to flip her over and push her along, as it was doing with whatever trees had previously stood in its path. The hood cover was now bare of the original olive green color, stripped away by the hammering sands. Then, as quickly as it had caught her in its grip, the storm was gone.

She pulled to the side of what served as a road and started to shut the truck's engine off. If the carburetor was clogged, she wouldn't be able to restart it, she thought. Changing her mind, she sat up and looked back towards the building, now slowly burning, the roof having already crumbled into the interior. Had the airbags burst, releasing the toxins as she had hoped? Had she been wrong that the fire might have incinerated most of the spores, leaving only a few to rain down on the surrounding landscape?

Raising her hand and pressing it against her eyebrow, she tried to block out the sun's rays that were beginning to pierce through the skyline, now that the storm had passed. Squinting, she could see several small animals lying on the ground, not moving. A lone man made his way towards the building, looking up to make sure nothing was falling down upon him. Twenty feet from the fallen animals, the man began to stagger, pawing at his face. She shifted the truck into first gear and released the clutch. The toxins were airborne, but the currents would not carry them as far as she had hoped.

Two hours and sixty miles later, she found the main highway and turned South. Up ahead was a gas station where she could top off the tanks and clean the sand from underneath her clothes. The sand in her shoes had scrapped away several patches of skin and it stung like hell. It would require medical attention before she drove on.

After checking and securing the aluminum bottles, she grabbed a first aid kit and headed for the washroom. Locking the door behind her, she took off her shoes and clothes, standing nude in front of a cracked mirror. She was beautiful, she thought. Why hadn't Ahmad taken advantage of her? She would have let him. In her mind, she could see his hands tracing the outside of her soft breasts, his tongue moving in and out of her mouth, her hands slowly moving over and down the muscles of his abdomen. She stood for a moment, letting the sinful thoughts tease her.

Finally, she pulled out a handful of paper towels, wet them and began cleaning off the sand sticking to her flesh. She winced as she sprayed the disinfectant on her injured skin. The gauze felt good as she wrapped it around her feet and applied the clips to hold the bandages in place. For the remainder of the ride, she would keep her shoes off, allowing for the dry air to begin the healing process. Whipping and snapping her clothes in the air, she was satisfied that she had dislodged enough of the sand to put them back on. Picking up her shoes, she exited the washroom and headed back towards the truck.

Having topped off her tank, she climbed back in and tried starting the engine. It sputtered each time she turned and held the key. She finally released it before she flooded the engine. She wished she had spent more time with her brother now, learning what she could about cars and engines. Instead she had no interest in anything except biology and microscopes. It was a world that had fascinated her since she first looked down the long magnified tube at the microorganisms and bacteria that could heal as well as kill.

She kept her foot off the gas pedal and turned the key several more times. The engine finally turned over, coughing and nearly stopping again before revving to life. When the engine settled into a rhythm, she popped the clutch and hit the pedal. The truck lurched forward and began to cough once again. She quickly pushed in the clutch, waited for the engine to steady, then eased it out this time, slowly pressing down on the gas pedal. Although there was an occasional pop, the truck continued moving forward.

From inside the gas station, a man had watched as the woman tried starting the truck a number of times and finally succeeded. He did not know the woman, but he did know the truck and the license plate. He had driven it before on several occasions and knew where it had come from.

Turning back onto the highway, she kept in the right hand lane and watched her speed, making sure she did not go over the limit. Any call placed by the authorities could result in Ahmad's people picking up the transmission, let alone that person being associated with his group.

As she drove, she began to wonder how her life had come to this. There had been numerous high profile hospitals and labs that had begged her to work for them, but she had declined their offers. To the disbelief of her mother, she had turned down the money that had been offered to her, money that could have kept her comfortable for the rest of her life. Born out of wedlock, she had rebelled against her mother from an early age, embarrassed that of all of her friends, she was the only one who never had a father show up at her school recitals, or stand and cheer as she graduated as valedictorian from Kent State University.

Over the years she never dated or had interest in any men until her meeting with Ahmad. The scars on the right side of his face intrigued her and made her want to know more about him. They first met in an out-of-the-way diner while she was vacationing in Greece, and she bumped his table on purpose, so he would look up and notice her. When he did, she could not take her eyes off of the scorched tissue.

"Most people look away. Why do you stare?" asked Ahmad in a tone that was neither sarcastic nor uncomfortable for either of them.

"I'm sorry, I didn't mean to. I don't know why, but I can't seem to not want to look. May I join you for a moment?"

The request took Ahmad by surprise and he motioned for her to sit down next to him. Over the course of the next three hours, he had charmed her, expressing a discontent for what was happening in the world and his peaceful plans for changing it. The part regarding the 'peaceful' plans, he lied about, but he would never let her know that. When he learned that she was a biochemist, he asked that they continue to meet. She was in love already, but love was the most distant emotion from his mind or his heart.

Now she knew he had merely used her mind with no intent on satisfying her other needs. There had been no purpose other than to obtain a set of skills, like he had done with so many others. She had watched, over the years, as he had disregarded people once he had what he needed. It would be the same for her once she had delivered the chemicals to him.

Being discarded once again would put her over the edge and she knew it. The suicidal thoughts she had had all of her life, were always present. This time, though, it had to be different, she told herself. She had to make Ahmad realize she had been angry, that's all. He would forgive her for her act of sabotage. He had been angry, too, and didn't mean what he said. He, of all people, would understand. She could make him love her.

Pulling off to the side of the road, she kept her foot playing with the gas pedal as she retrieved the phone from her pocket. A search of the directory displayed the men Ahmad had contacted to sell the chemicals to once the supplies were ready. Each man had paid a deposit of five million dollars for five bottles containing the weapons of mass destruction, as they come to be called. Given the right weather conditions, each bottle held enough chemical to wipe out dozens of neighborhoods, even a small city.

A plan began to form in her mind. She would contact each man and deliver the chemical bottles herself without letting Ahmad know what she was doing. The monies would be deposited into the offshore accounts that had been set up by Ahmad when he robbed his father's company's assets years earlier. Unknown to Ahmad, she had been able to record all of the account numbers and pass codes when he had mistakenly given her access to his computer to do research. A quick download had also given her Ahmad's valued list of contacts and buyers, as well as their addresses and unlisted confidential phone numbers.

She had been present during many of the meetings Ahmad had with the buyers, so they would trust her. Her attendance at the meetings, however, had been only to answer questions about the chemicals, necessary storage, and transport. However, those few questions had been asked through Ahmad himself, as none of the men would break custom or lower themselves to speak with a woman.

Regardless, they would speak with her now, or lose their deposit. She would threaten to cut them from the deal and provide their share of the chemicals to the other buyers. She would have to make them realize she was speaking for Ahmad. Once she had delivered all of the bottles and collected the remaining payments, she would surprise him with her grand scheme. How could he not love her then and want to be with her for the rest of their lives? She began to make the calls.

Chapter 20

West sat in the chopper, looking at the bag containing the remains of Coats, as it headed towards Camp Pendleton. Once on the ground, he would make plans to contact Baker and bring him up to speed, but he would first make a detour to see the base hospital optometrist. Once Baker arrived, they would set up a new base of operations.

As they approached the base, the pilot transmitted the appropriate call signs, along with Coats' dog tag number and Social Security Number. They would need a coroner standing by as soon as permission was granted and they could land on military soil. The thought of having been a SEAL, and the standard requirements that forced him to retire from his last assignment, disturbed him beyond the normal regrets. He began to question why he made his decision to not continue in, perhaps, a different capacity.

The chopper touched down and was immediately surrounded by the MPs. West exited and pointed towards the black body bag, handing the officer in charge the dog tags as he stepped forward.

Nick spoke first. "Thank you for the courtesy, Lieutenant. What you are going to find in that bag is not very pretty. Because of the dog tags, I can only assume he was once military personnel, so that is why I requested permission to dispose of his remains with you. I do not know if that is his current status. The only way you're going to be able to identify him is through dental records." West watched as the medics removed the bag and placed it on a gurney.

"We will establish his identity, and thank you for bringing him home." Even though the expression was used to convey the sentiment of bringing a fallen soldier home from battle, West appreciated the officer's intent, and let it slide. Deep down, he knew the man was most recently a paid mercenary, but hoped that at least at one time he had served his country faithfully.

"I understand you had another team member with you. Where is he?" asked the Lieutenant.

Nick didn't want to disclose the circumstances of his meeting with Ahmad, nor the firefight that took place. As far as anyone needed to know, it was a recon mission for a missing soldier's remains, lost in the Big Sur. "Gathering additional intel. We will rendezvous at a later time."

With that, the lieutenant saluted and gave the order for the medics to begin transporting the body to the base's hospital morgue.

Before they could leave, though, Nick turned to the officer. "Lieutenant, I would like to request a ride with the medics to the hospital. I need to have a quick check done by one of the senior staff before I head out."

"I thought you weren't injured?"

"I'm not. I just want to have something important looked at."

The lieutenant looked at him for a brief moment. "Make sure you check back with me before you leave. If we find out anything on those remains, I can let you know then."

"Roger that." said Nick.

One hour later, Nick was sitting on top of a table trying to enlighten the doctor of his suspicions. Without telling him what the particle might be, he indicated there was something in his right eye. He could feel it, but it wasn't interfering with his vision. It was all a lie, as he felt nothing, but couldn't forget Ahmad's words about Coats having a transmitter in his right eye socket. The fact that he knew he had nothing on him that would transmit a signal, Ahmad's mention that he was transmitting on the same frequency meant there might be a similar object somewhere either near his eye or in his body.

"Well, let's take a look." The doctor began examining Nick's eyes one at a time, first beginning with the iris, then working his way around it in a circular motion until he came to the edges.

"They look fine to me. No signs of cataract formation or glaucoma in either eye."

"Doc, I need you to look at the interior of the eye socket, perhaps with something that has more magnification. Look for a small opening where an object might have been inserted."

The doctor stood back and looked at Nick quizzically. "Tell me what I'm looking for. It might make it easier for me to find."

Nick now wished he had waited to have the exam done by his private doctor. "I don't know what you're looking for other than a small tear that would allow something to penetrate and leave a minute electronic device between my eyeball and skull."

The doctor pursed his lips and shook his head slowly. "I'm going to take what you're telling me to be highly classified, so don't say another word. If I find something, I won't be able to remove it."

"Just tell me yes or no. I'll make the necessary arrangements for its removal later, if something is there."

Three minutes later, the doctor looked at Nick and said, "I would suggest you contact an eye surgeon."

The lieutenant had been good enough to arrange overnight accommodations for Nick once he followed up on his promise to re-establish contact once he had finished at the base hospital. Normally, most of the visitors just skipped and were never heard from again, causing the lieutenant a number of headaches he did not need.

Nick continued to run the different scenarios and possibilities of how the object could have been inserted next to his eye without him knowing it. It was a transmitter, for God's sake, and small enough not to be felt by one the strongest nerve systems in the human body. The tiniest speck of dirt in one's eye was enough to bring tears to any man or woman. How could a transmitter be lodged in there and he not know it?

He was exhausted, but there would be time to catch a few hours sleep later, once he notified Baker, but hopefully before Olexia arrived. Sitting on the edge of the cot, he pressed the speed dial on his phone.

Baker answered after the first ring. He listened and typed as Nick gave him instructions. Olexia was arriving in a few hours, but before she did, Baker would be doing a lot of research once again. Olexia already had the address of the operations center and Baker was relieved that he wouldn't have to pick her up from the hangar and taxi her there, once he found out she was going to see Nick directly.

As soon as they hung up, Baker took a moment to think about where he wanted to begin and what information he needed to target first, should he have to bail in case the intrusion was spotted. Hacking into the CIA databanks at a time when their techs were already on full alert from the chemical release, could prove to be extremely dangerous. He would first need to enter using a circuit level gateway to hide his IP address, and establish a rootkit to bypass security authentication. Once that was done, he could begin the search on Olexia Syshchenko while monitoring for any alerts that would notify security of a breach. Time was definitely not on his side.

The hack took longer than expected. Alerts kept going off that he had to maneuver around by sending fake packets that would re-route the search off into other directions. By the time the alert had processed all of the scenarios, his incursion would have already passed and he would be elsewhere.

He found the information Nick had requested, then turned his attention to Olexia's data. The search turned up nothing under the name Olexia Syshchenko. Either CIA had nothing on her or she was in under another alias. Another possibility would be that her team had already filtered through the data banks and had purged all records of her existence.

Baker created a bogus record and updated the primary table. He would test his theory. Once the record updated, he closed the file and reopened it. Searching quickly through the database, he saw that the record was gone. Somewhere in this vast network, a single script was being triggered to eliminate any records containing her name. How could it go so undetected?

Chapter 21

Ahmad sat up in his bed while taking the call from a man at a gas station. The man reported that he had seen Gabrielle leave the station ten minutes earlier, heading North. In the bed of the vehicle had been twenty cylinders, sitting in a box. He had counted them himself and had seen Ahmad's brand logo that was used in sealing each one.

He continued to listen as he was told of the news of the explosion that the man had heard on a news podcast through his phone. That was something he would never have believed Gabrielle capable of doing. They had fought, but she would never destroy her own work to get back at him. He knew she loved him. He had seen it in her eyes as he had seen it in so many women before her.

When the conversation ended, he continued to sit, trying to understand her motives and what she would do next. Where was she headed with the chemicals, and what were her plans? They were useless to her. She had no means of distributing them and no one who could assist her in selling them to another party. She had simply been the creator, and only he was the true brains that could bring about the full potential of her creation. Then another thought occurred to him.

He would need to contact the buyers and delay the sale for at least another twenty-four hours, enough time to find Gabrielle and get the toxins back. Each buyer had already made a deposit and was expecting delivery tomorrow. If he couldn't deliver the chemical exactly as he had promised, he would need to make other plans. He would have to travel where no one would ever find him.

Slipping out of bed and walking naked across the bedroom floor, he entered the adjoining room and sat down at his computer. Tapping the spacebar, the screen quickly displayed a password login prompt. With a few keystrokes, a list of folders displayed and he selected the one containing the buyer accounts. Finding their phone numbers, he punched the first one into his cell phone. While he waited for the call to be answered, he suddenly realized that his own phone could be tapped, and abruptly hung up.

Gabrielle needed to be found without anyone learning of her act of espionage or stealing the chemicals. Any thoughts that he was not in total control would end all business dealings with any and all buyers in the future, even if he were able to deliver the chemicals without any delays or endangering his customers.

He did not know how close or far away her current location was and he did not want to run the risk of exposing his location while exiting the compound for a hunt. If satellites caught an aircraft crisscrossing the same grids numerous times, it would send up a red flag. He saw no other choice but to bring her to him.

Standing once again, he slowly walked to the door, wondering if he should clothe first, then decided against it. Grabbing the handle, he swung it open and screamed at his men, anyone, to get him a phone. Two of his men reached into their pockets simultaneously and extracted their own, handing them to him with nervous hands. Without uttering a word, he took them and shut the door. His men knew what they must do next.

Flipping open the first phone, he noted the battery was almost spent and tossed it to the floor. The second was more promising, as it must have recently been fully charged. He did not care for the image of the man's wife, though, and pitied the poor man. Certainly, the man must have turned off all lights before fornicating. May your God bless you for your courage to wed this woman, he thought.

Slowly he dialed the number, secretly hoping she would not answer, but knew she had to. There was no other way and he knew it was his only chance of reconciling. He had to talk to her. He listened to the ringing on the other end. On the fifth ring it stopped. The phone, however had not disconnected, and ever so faintly, he could hear breathing on the other end. It continued for a moment until he heard her speak his name.

"Ahmad?" she said. She had been in the process of hanging up with the last buyer and was shocked by the timing. It had to be an omen beyond her understanding. Had one of the buyers called him after she had given explicit instructions that they not do so?

"Yes, it is me. I am sorry for the words I said. I ask that you forgive me." Ahmad was doing his best to sound sincere.

"Please don't ask me to forgive you. After all I have done, you called me those names and threatened me. How am I supposed to forgive you? Tell me!"

"I don't have an answer other than to say I made a terrible mistake. I know how important you are to me, what you have done for me, and I spoke without thinking. Us being together is all that matters."

"No! You are lying and I was foolish to believe that we could be anything other than what we are. We have created something monstrous and I let you make me do it. I believed that you loved me with all the things you said, but you don't. You still love that other woman and nothing will ever change that!"

"That woman is my past and is gone forever. I was horrified when I heard of the explosion. I prayed that my life be taken in exchange for yours. I feared that you might have been trapped inside."

She hesitated. "You know about the explosion and how it happened?"

"Yes! You were angry for the things I said, and I don't blame you. You escaped with your life. That we can be together again, is all I ask."

"I want to believe you, but I just can't. I am afraid to trust you." The tears had begun and Ahmad could hear her beginning to sob. He needed to convince her now.

"Be with me tonight. We will make love and I will show you how much I care for you. If you still don't trust me by morning, I beg you to leave."

There was small rap on the door and a man slowly entered, gesturing that they had triangulated the signal. Her current location was only two hundred and eighty-three miles due east. Ahmad raised his index finger and jabbed it in the air. Placing his hand over the phone, he exaggerated his mouth's movements. "Go get her!"

Without waiting for her to respond, he asked. "Where are you? We will come to you." Ahmad already knew the coordinates, of course, but it was a test. If she lied, he would know he would have to kill her immediately without getting the formula. The bottles he could obtain, if she did not run and dispose of them before his men could get to her.

"I'm about 200 miles due east of you on US 89. I'm in one of the company trucks." She had not lied.

"Stay where you are. My men will come in by helicopter and be there within the next hour. Will you be comfortable waiting for them?"

"Yes, but only if you come as well." It was her turn to test him. If he said no, then it was very likely he had instructed his men to kill her once they had picked her up. Once they were over the mountains, a quick push and she would be falling thousands of feet to her death and no one would ever find her body.

He could hear her breathe a sigh of relief when he said, "Yes. I will come to get you." It was the last thing he wanted to do, but he saw no other way.

Forty-seven minutes later, he could see her through the canopy of the chopper, stepping out of the truck, as he descended. She looked different, he having last remembered her wearing a lab coat loosely around her body, and a breathing mask pulled tightly over her face. She had removed it when they were certain they were no longer in danger of inhaling the spores from the lab's air.

He began to smile when he thought of the two men and their painful deaths. They were idiots and he was convinced the world was full of them. He would happily lead them to their deaths once he was through with the exchange. His plans were to release a small dosage of the chemical on his departure. The blades from the aircraft would force the pollutant down upon them and they would all be dead within the hour. By the time they were found, their bodies would be fully decomposed.

As the chopper's railings touched the ground, two men exited and ran quickly towards the truck. Undoing the latches and chains, they pulled the bed door down and reached in, grabbing the case containing the bottles and lifting it straight out. Holding the case tightly, they sprinted back to the craft and placed the case into a welded compartment, just as Gabrielle fastened her seat belt. If they intended to throw her out, they would have a brief fight on their hands in order to do so.

The blades began to speed up on the bird as the men climbed aboard, then the helicopter lifted with a quick jerk. Gabrielle looked down at where the vehicle was parked, its hood up in order to make passersby think she had broken down. No one had stopped or even slowed down. She hoped that neither Ahmad nor any of his men noticed the double set of tracks in the dirt.

Uncertain of Ahmad's true intentions before they arrived, she had made a u-turn and reversed direction, traveling the twenty some miles back to the FedEx office she had passed earlier. There had only been a few cars in the parking lot previously, so she felt she would have time to make it there and back before they put down.

Quickly selecting a label and envelope, she scratched out the recipient's name and address on the white sticker, dropped the item into the bubbled interior of the envelope, paid the postage due and returned just minutes before she sighted the chopper.

Chapter 22

Dawson had heard the chopper take off and listened as the men in the next room began to talk amongst themselves. They could not believe Ahmad would jeopardize the mission for a woman, especially for one he cared so little about. What was she to him?

The ride back to the compound had not been as unpleasant as he thought it would be. The men had been given instructions not to injure him, as he would be needed later for an exchange of another person or for demonstration purposes if any of the plan failed to come to fruition. There had been some rough handling, but little else. Once they had blindfolded him, he was left tied in the back of the truck.

At the compound, he counted off the steps as he was led exactly fifty-seven paces from the vehicle to a door. From the door it had been seven steps straight forward and four to the right. A chair was pushed against his back legs and he was gently pushed downward to sit.

A gun barrel was placed against his head as his hands were untied from behind his back, repositioned in front, then re-tied. When the men were satisfied he was secured properly, the gun was taken away. Water was brought to him, along with a several pieces of cut dried orange. Once they had placed the items on the floor next to him, the men left.

Pulling the blindfold down, he looked around the room in hopes of seeing some kind of communication device. There was none. The room was empty with the exception of the chair he was sitting on and several electrical outlets. From one of the outlets hung a long cord that was looped around a hook in the ceiling, then drooped down over it. On the end of the cord was a light socket and a single lighted bulb.

There were no windows and he ascertained very quickly that this served as the interrogation room, perhaps even as a torture chamber, if needed. He would not allow that to happen, if at all possible.

Listening once again, he counted three distinct voices, all male and very anxious. They continued to talk quickly and as they did, their tones became more agitated and aggressive. Remembering the voice that had given the majority of the commands as he was brought in, he focused on what he was saying, trying to eliminate the long-winded words of the other two.

"It is not important what you believe, only that you do exactly as Ahmad instructs you to do. You are being paid well, and once the exchange is made, I am sure he will see to it that we are compensated fairly."

The second man interceded. "What exchange? It will do us little good if we are caught, or worse, dead. He has lost his mind going after that woman. He has left us three to guard everything while he is gone."

"Ahmad is going to exchange this man for a large amount of money once he has sold the chemicals. This man is United States military."

The third man looked at them both as he had reached his limit of putting up with their whining and bullshit.

"You're both wrong. Ahmad plans to use the man as a demonstration for the buyers. Once they see what the chemicals are capable of, they will pay whatever he demands."

From what West had told him, Dawson already knew what the chemicals would do. He had also seen the news, although it had been reported as something else. Dawson mumbled as he took a deep breath.

"Time to save my ass, West."

Chapter 23

On the flight back to the compound, Gabrielle waited for the moment of attack, but it never came. Her mind continued to play out the different scenarios of how it would happen and how long she could possibly keep them from undoing her seat belt. She saw herself falling to the rocks below. Ahmad had sat with a hand clasped around her knee, on occasion giving it a gentle squeeze and flashing a brief smile. She wondered how genuine his feelings were.

"It's going to be alright," he said.

But would it be? The lab was gone, and along with it, all of the extra materials and pre-production spores that she had cultivated for months. It would be a setback to his plans and to the buyers who had anticipated additional supplies once they had unleashed the first batch of toxins on their chosen targets. She wondered what countries her little creation would be released upon to wipe entire generations of families from the face of the Earth. Who would be the first?

Gabrielle looked out the side of the chopper as it began to descend into a deep basin surrounded by tall trees that could hide a small army, if needed. As they passed underneath the edge of the tree canopy, the chopper banked left, then hard right. Straight ahead, several buildings stood. In the center was the largest, but no bigger than eighteen hundred square feet, by her guess. To the right of the house stood three men, looking as if they were in an argument of some sort. They stopped as soon as they saw the chopper coming in. Dust and dirt flew everywhere as they set down, forcing the men to cover their faces and turn their backs to them, with the exception of one. He was much older and shielded only his eyes with a tight fitting pair of sunglasses.

The men in the chopper waited for Ahmad and Gabrielle to climb out before moving towards the side exit. Taking her hand, Ahmad walked towards the center building, pulling her along at a slow and steady pace. She followed without speaking.

Inside, he offered her a glass of wine and pointed out the shower, where she could bathe and prepare herself for the evening. She declined for the moment, but took the glass of wine and sat down opposite of where he was still standing. He followed suit, pulling up a chair and sitting.

"I'm sure you have questions, so please, let's talk. I won't give you any excuses." Gabrielle's nerves were on edge and she moved her open hand underneath her leg so Ahmad would not see it shaking.

Ahmad looked at her without expression. "I have no questions, other than wanting to know if you are OK. I know whatever caused you to destroy your work, you had good reason and would have not done so had there been another choice."

"I destroyed the lab because you angered me. You threatened me even after I told you I had been attacked and the lab had been contaminated from the spores and mucus I took from the two guards. If I hadn't, the contamination would have leaked."

"I understand the explosion released thousands of spores into the air anyway. Did you not think that would happen once the gas cans exploded?"

She now realized he knew everything she had done. "I was angry. I didn't think everything through." The truth was, she had.

After several minutes without a word, Ahmad stood and stepped towards her. "You are tired and I have begged you for my forgiveness several times. What is done is done. We still have the buyers for the existing canisters, and when we are out of the country, we will simply start over. It will be several months before a secondary supply is needed anyway."

They stood in the shower together as the hot water ran over their pressed bodies. His left thumb played with her nipple as her hand moved slowly down across his abdomen, continuing until its fingers touched his pubic hairs, then found what it had been searching for. As her fingers wrapped around his organ, she felt it begin to enlarge and stiffen. Their breathing quickened as her hand gripped harder, then gently began to stroke him.

His tongue began to search her neck and jaw line as his hands moved from her breast, down her back and around. She felt his fingers moving up her inner thigh and she repositioned herself, spreading her legs more, until she felt his touch. A quick breath escaped as his fingertips continued to find and play with her most sensitive area. Her hand quickened its pace.

Grabbing the shower curtain with one hand, Ahmad pulled it back, reached around Gabrielle, lifting her in his arms and walking towards the bed. There he laid her down and moved on top. She wrapped her legs around his waist. The sheets were already soaked from absorbing the shower's water droplets.

His mouth found her breast and he once again placed his hand between her legs. They continued exploring each other until Ahmad could no longer hold back. Raising his body over hers, he entered and began a rhythmic stride as her fingers curled around his buttocks and she let them move with him. He listened to her breathing and soft moans as the sounds told him everything. If a man listened, he could learn to pleasure them both. Her body began to quiver as her fingers dug in deeper and she fell into their harmonious movements. Ahmad drove into her until at last his body stiffened and a primal timbre escaped his throat. He felt her body go rigid as she released and pulled him in as tight as she could.

They lay next to each other as their hearts continued to race, their mouths taking in large amounts of air while trying to mentally embrace the last few minutes. He turned to her and began to kiss up and down her back as she rolled onto her side. Clasping his hands around both her breasts, he moved in behind her. His breath was on her neck now, his hands were beginning to explore once again. He was not finished.

Pulling her tenderly onto her back, he slid lower down the bed and slipped his head in between her knees. Finding the spot, he began. When he felt her arch, he coupled his arms underneath and around her hips, holding her in place. Her body would soon shake uncontrollably as it had done several times before.

As Gabrielle slept, his mind thought of nothing but tomorrow's meeting and the arrival of the three buyers. Soon he would be rich enough, by his account, to change his life for good, and live it without ever looking back over his shoulder again. This woman had almost spoiled it for him.

By sunrise, he had showered and was stepping from the shower when he heard her stir. He wrapped the towel around his waist and walked to the side of the bed. She reached out and he took her hand and kissed it.

"How did you sleep?" he asked.

She didn't answer, but instead, smiled back at him. He had made love to her and it had been the happiest moments of her life. Her imagination of how a man would please her, had never been this realized in her dreams. He never said it, but she had told him several times during their love making, that she loved him. In time he would tell her as well.

"You're up early. Why?"

"Is it important that you know my business?" There was an irritation in his voice that had not been there before, and she delayed her response.

She could not let him know that she knew he was about make the exchange with the buyers she had already contacted. They had all refused to talk to her and made it clear they would only deal with Rafael, the name he used as a cover during all business transactions. It could never be known that he was still alive to anyone other than his most trusted associates.

If he had found out she had originally planned to sell the canisters to the buyers on her own, he would all but suspect that she had betrayed him. That had not been her intent, but there would no chance of convincing him otherwise. A chill ran down her spine as she thought of the consequences.

"Why are you angry this morning? I thought I made you happy."

His eyes met hers as he asked, "Where is your phone?"

"It's in my purse. Search it if you want."

"I already did. It's not there. So tell me, where is it?"

She had to think fast. "I don't know. If it's not there, I must have dropped it or left it in the truck. Did you search your helicopter. Maybe it fell on the floor and one of your men has it."

He paused, then smiled back at her. The small hesitation in her expression had betrayed her. She was lying.

Ahmad shook his head as if believing her and said, "Yes, you must be right. Once again I find myself begging you for forgiveness. I didn't mean to question you like that."

He came closer and sat down beside her, beginning to rub her shoulders and kiss the nape of her neck. Removing his towel, he got on his knees behind her and pushed her forward. She responded by allowing him to enter her. This time, however, it was different from the night before.

Gripping her hips with both hands, Ahmad thrust hard, then hard again, over and over until she pulled herself up and tried to move away. Her head was now where he had wanted it to be and turned in the exact position. His right hand clamped around her chin as the left grabbed the top, together both twisting and pulling in unison.

In that instant, her neck snapped and she fell forward, her body tumbling off the bed onto the floor. The technique had been exact, leaving her for the moment paralyzed, not dead. Her eyes followed as he walked to the urinal and relieved himself. In minutes her organs would begin to shut down and her heart would stop, but for now her mind would live in horror at the realization death was coming, and very, very soon.

Ahmad returned and bent down next to her, placing his lips next to her ear. "I know you wanted me to love you, but know that I never did. I look forward to seeing you die slowly, whore."

He knew that final word would be the last she ever heard and he wanted her to suffer until the end.

In fifteen minutes, he was fully dressed, and stepped out the door, telling his men the woman was still asleep and not to disturb her.

Checking the time, he gave his men final instructions and stepped aboard the chopper. Within two hours, this would all be over and he would be gone.

Chapter 24

The refurbished Boeing 707 landed in Maine, refueled, and took off for California. West had contacted her as they were departing from Ireland and told her it was necessary for them to reroute their flight plan. Several calls were placed as she contacted those who needed to know her whereabouts at all times, including her round-the-clock team of bodyguards. She never traveled outside the organization's boundaries without them.

Her most important call, however, went unanswered. A voice asked her to leave a message, but Olexia hung up. A minute later, she keyed the same number again, this time simply leaving an address and nothing more. She began to worry.

West had been adamant about her getting to California immediately. He was angry and wanted answers. Coats had been found, but one of West's men had been taken hostage. He had been told it was for an exchange, but he had his doubts. He had not told her he had spoken with Ahmad. That he would do face to face so he could witness her expression.

She needed to know what he knew first before deciding to what extent she could acknowledge his questions. Four years of planning would be wasted if he pressed her too hard and talked with others. She had not wanted him to bring in additional personnel, but he had insisted. If Ahmad did not kill West's man, she would, if only to make sure her secret stayed a secret.

Shortly before noon, the plane touched down, and she skipped through security and to the waiting limousine. Two black SUVs escorted the limo as it pulled from the curb and headed towards her hotel. It would have been thoroughly searched and debugged before she arrived. West had insisted she come directly to what he called his 'base of operations', but she had her reasons for not wanting to do so right away. He could wait an hour for her to refresh, she said.

Entering through a private door of the hotel, she stepped into a glass elevator that ascended fifty-seven floors in eleven seconds. The guards stepped out first, and she followed. At her room, they positioned themselves on either side as she slipped in the pass key. Once inside, she let the door close behind her and walked towards the enormous window overlooking the bay.

Below, she could see sailboats entering and exiting the harbor. A mile down the coast, the large commercial vessels made their way slowly into port. She began to wonder if this was how Ahmad had entered the United States illegally. With the entire California coastline, he could have entered at any point. If his contacts had already been established before his arrival, he would have been able to slip in undetected.

Turning back towards the kitchen, she passed the dining room table and noticed the Federal Express package. The delivery had been made within the last hour. She closed her eyes and said a silent prayer.

Peeling back the tear-open label, she extracted the note along with the phone and held them for a moment before pressing the 'on' button and reading the note at the same time. She recognized the handwriting at once, and already knew who had written it.

It was a simple message. "Forgive me, Olexia. I love him. He is not the man you think he is."

It wasn't supposed to have been this way, she thought. Gabrielle had been trained to leave all emotions out of company business. No getting close, they had been told over and over, but Gabrielle had been weak in that one area, as the psychiatric evaluation had discovered. It had been a highly volatile risk, but Gabrielle was the only one qualified. No one else had come close. So, Olexia had given the order to proceed.

By this time, the phone displayed the opening screen and Olexia immediately selected the message icon. There were four. The first looked like garbled letters and symbols with spaces inserted here and there. It made no sense until she spotted the 'equals' sign and a chemical compound she had learned in physics. "Shit," she said out loud. "It's the formula." The second message listed several numbers, times and names. It also listed three longitude and latitude coordinates, with all locations very close together.

Scrolling further down, she pressed for the next message. Her smile grew broad as she read through it. "Thank you, Gabrielle," she whispered. Seconds later, she had encrypted the message and forwarded it to her personal phone. When she heard the chime go off on her phone, she erased the message from Gabrielle's.

A quick rap on the door told her it was time to leave and meet with West. Closing the phone, she placed it in a zippered compartment of her purse and handed the FedEx envelope to one of her men as she exited. It would first be shredded, then burned to ash, before they returned to Ireland.

The 'base of operations' was not what Olexia had expected. A single laptop sat on a desk, along with a modem and some kind of antiquated box that actually had a turn dial on it. Great, she was dealing with some kind of hard ass American Cowboy, she thought. *Maybe I shouldn't be judging a book by its cover.*

West looked up from the keyboard and saw Olexia standing, looking at him with a puzzled and inquisitive look. He knew what she was thinking.

"It works, and that's what I care about. I'm better equipped in Atlanta, but my IP address is hidden and once you're on the internet, it comes down to your skills, not your equipment."

"I'll take your word for it. But for right now, we need to talk."

Nick stood and approached her. "I agree, and you have the most explaining to do. There's more to your story than you have told me and I have a feeling that no matter what, you're not going to tell me whole truth."

There was a worn chair that had been placed next to the desk and she sat. When she finished brushing away the dust particles and smoothing her skirt, she replied. "Ask, and I promise to tell you the truth, no matter what you ask."

"If that's true, then let's start at the beginning and bring me up to the point of you chasing Ahmad, and your reasons.

"You may want to sit," she said.

"I'm good right now. The truth, please."

Olexia looked to make sure her men were stationed at the door, then sat up straight, looking directly at him. "For the last twenty years I have worked for an organization that protects the interests and safety of all domestic and foreign countries that do not have the capabilities or training to legally protect themselves against a threat. In most cases, we are reimbursed by monetary means. In some cases it is through other resources that are beneficial to both parties."

"In other words, you are paid mercenaries."

"We don't see ourselves that way. We are talking about threats that are specific to the internal core of the country that we assist. We do not assist in the elimination of a threat for those who are seeking revenge or political gains. It's only if the threat endangers the citizens of that country."

"Tell me about how you began tracking Ahmad."

"To what extent?"

Nick was mildly shocked. "To what extent? I need to know everything, if I'm to figure out why he wants me to bring you to him. He took my man and wants you in exchange, or I can pick up what's left of his body when he is through with it!"

"You spoke with Ahmad? You had direct contact?" Olexia was angry that Nick had not told her sooner.

"Are you kidding me? I have about three more hours left before I have to turn you over to Ahmad, or my friend dies. He told me he would have accomplished what he needed to do in another day or two and it would be over."

"Then whatever he is planning, it will happen soon. My guess is his buyers will have already arrived, or will, very shortly."

"Why do you think I wanted to talk to you in private? I couldn't exactly say that over a phone." Nick could see he had succeeded in completely catching her off guard.

"What did he say?" Olexia had scooted so close to the edge of the chair, the back legs raised and she almost fell forward, but gracefully sat back.

"You first, then I will fill you in on what I know."

"Almost ten years ago, we were contacted by Prince Sahid, of the royal family. There had been an accident aboard his yacht, in which it was believed he was the target. Prince Sahid had his suspicions and asked us to investigate. He had presented the boat as an anniversary gift for loan to a very close friend, who also happened to be a very successful arms dealer. Their friendship had begun many years earlier. It was Ahmad's father."

"I know about the accident from Baker's materials."

"Then you know that Ahmad's inherited his father's business?" asked Olexia.

"I'd say more that he aggressively took over his father's business."

She ignored the comment, but understood what he meant. "Things were good until your President Bush declared war against his country. A lot of his buyers began going elsewhere to find other suppliers and Ahmad's partners began to worry about their own necks."

"That's pretty understandable, based upon what happened on 9/11."

"Ahmad became a target of their own greed and he fought back. There were those who felt that if they could become favored by the United States, they might escape a swift death, so they turned on him by divulging information on his clients."

"Where do you come into all of this?" Nick wanted to get right to it by asking what he really wanted to know.

"My father was a member of the IRA, specializing in bomb making. By the time I was fourteen, he had taught me everything he knew. Two days before my fifteenth birthday, there was an accident, and he was killed. I was recruited to take his place."

"So you have been killing people since you were fifteen?"

Olexia hesitated for a brief moment, then continued. "I have been making bombs since I was fifteen. Who they killed or how they were used, I don't know, as I was kept clear of that."

"OK. So that explains how you have the knowledge to get you involved in this business. How did you learn of Ahmad?"

"I was recruited by the organization when I was nineteen and had been working for them several years as an explosives expert. I also received lots of additional training, along with learning to shoot and break down just about every weapon there was on the market."

Nick understood now why she had handled Simon's rifle so easily.

"Anyway, they learned that a supplier was trading heavily in weapons and selling them to anyone who could pay the highest price. He sold them to anyone who wanted them, and that made a lot of our people nervous. I was sent to try and determine who his buyers were."

"That means you would have first needed to come to his attention and gain his trust."

"It wasn't easy. Fortunately we heard that he was only interested in those who could do the job, not their gender. So for a year I blew up a lot of empty buildings, eliminated a few of his adversaries and waited for an opening. By this time, he was in need of my type of services, so I was planted. I lived in his camp for several months until it was time I had to prove myself. He wanted to set an example by bringing down a five story bank building full of customers that his old partners had dealings with."

"There was no way to avoid it?" asked Nick.

"No. If I had showed any hesitation, he would have found me out and killed me right there."

"So how many people were killed?"

"I wasn't told, but it was probably close to one hundred people."

Nick looked at her for a long time. "Your organization let a hundred people die to get to one man?"

"It had gotten complicated. It was necessary that I leave for a while due to an illness but to get back as quickly as possible upon my recovery. By this time we had become close and I had been instructed to do whatever was necessary to keep him believing I was totally devoted to his cause, and would do whatever he asked."

"Olexia. Are you saying what I think you're saying?"

"Yes, I had to become his lover, if that's what you thinking. We knew by the way he was increasing his activities, he was planning something very big, and I couldn't risk any suspicion by not returning."

"What happened then?" Nick moved to the chair behind his desk and sat.

"We knew that he had discovered the whereabouts of several of his past partners, and he planned to kill them. We needed their information, so I was pushed to try and get whatever information I could and relay it back. I was caught, though, by one of his men when I was going through Ahmad's desk. He said he would tell if I didn't do what he wanted. I didn't have any choice."

Nick didn't want to imagine what that was like. "What happened with Ahmad?"

"The man told anyway, and Ahmad believed I had betrayed him. I was beaten and left to die. My people got me out and cared for me. I thought that I could make amends and continue with the plan. I contacted Ahmad and was told to meet him in Germany."

"The plane explosion. You were there?"

"Yes, I was there. By the sound of his voice and the way he responded during the call, I thought that he had wanted to reconcile, but he didn't. After arriving in Germany, I was brought to a house outside the airport."

"Is that the house he used to watch the plane's arrival?" asked Nick.

"Yes. We had just pulled up when he triggered one of my devices that I had designed and built for him. I didn't know who was in the house at the time."

"There was a man and a woman and their child. Do you know who they were?"

Nick watched as her shoulders began to shake and saw the tears streaming down her checks.

"They were my sister and her husband. He shot them point blank while his men held me and made me watch. Then he went into the baby's room and shot him."

"I'm sorry, Olexia." said Nick.

"Ahmad had them brought there to punish me. He had the bodies taken outside, after we left, and had them burned. We were never able to identify all of what was left."

Nick remained silent and let her continue.

"After the funeral, I went back to work. They hired Simon to find him and that was when I met him for the first time. We spent the first few weeks going over details about Ahmad, then one thing led to another and we gradually fell in love."

Nick watched as she dabbed her eyes. "So Simon thought he had killed Ahmad, but apparently hadn't?"

"We thought it was all over until we started hearing rumors a few years later that Ahmad had survived, except instead of using bombs now, he was experimenting with chemical weapons."

"How did the organization handle that?"

"We sent a woman in, undercover. Her name was Gabrielle Innarelli. She was a biochemist working for the CDC." Without warning, Olexia stood and reached into her purse, undoing a small compartment and extracting a phone.

Handing it to Nick, she said, "Oh my God, I almost forgot. I received this just minutes before I left to come here. It's from Gabrielle."

Nick grabbed the phone, hitting the 'On' key. "Did you get a chance to look at anything? Any messages or recordings? How did you receive this?"

"There were three, I think. The phone came by carrier and was in my room when I arrived."

By this time the phone had activated and Nick began to read through the first message. Recognizing it as some type of formula, he looked at Olexia. "Do you think she is the one responsible for supplying Ahmad with the toxin he now has?"

"She would be more than capable."

Nick reached over and grabbed his own phone, selected Baker from its contact list, and waited for him to pick up. When he did, Nick gave him Gabrielle's phone number and told him to download any data, including messages, contacts, voice mails, etc., that was on it. He also told him to send the formula to CDC immediately for an analysis and get back to him as soon as he was finished.

When Nick hung up the phone with Baker, he turned back to Olexia. "Where's Gabrielle now? Have you spoken with her?"

"That is the first time I have had contact with her in two years. We all thought she was dead until you told me about the toxin, and Ahmad being the one who used it. It all made sense then."

Nick suddenly thought about the senator. "Why do you think Ahmad killed the senator?"

"Best guess is the senator was supplying him intel. What kind, we don't know. When the senator found out he was under investigation, he probably had a change of heart and refused to give Ahmad any more information. They argued over it and Ahmad killed him."

"Anything else I should know before Baker calls back in a couple of minutes?"

"If Gabrielle sent me her phone, then she knows she has no more use for it or has decided to help Ahmad and cut ties with us. If she has decided to help him, then America won't be the only target. She can manufacture the chemical for him and he will use it on anyone that will pay him what he asks."

While they were waiting for Baker to call back, Nick had one more question. "What's this between my eye and skull? How did you get a transmitter placed without me knowing it?"

Olexia did not look shocked that he knew. "When you placed your eye against the scanner, it was shot directly into the skin's lining. You probably felt a small stinging sensation. That was it going in."

"Why a transmitter, and what is it for? I know the answer already. I just want you to tell me."

"Just like Coats. If you go missing, we can track your current location and come find you. If Coats hadn't had it embedded, we wouldn't have known where to start looking."

Nick considered her response. "That's one option."

"What's the other one?"

"When it comes time to eliminate an operative, you know exactly where to find them."

Olexia did not respond.

Two minutes later, Nick's phone rang and he saw that it was Baker. "What have you got?"

"CDC is studying the formula now, but I'm guessing we won't hear back from them, as I forwarded it anonymously. You didn't tell me how to handle that, so I used precaution."

"Good thinking. What else?"

"There are a few things. The strange numbers are call signs assigned to a fleet of corporate jets, three different companies. None appear to have filed flight plans, but one of the planes is not in its hangar, according to the flight deck crew. If they know anything, they aren't saying."

"OK, what's next?"

"I ran a search on the coordinates and they are all locations just a few miles from where you are. One is a small private airport owned by Lexington Airways."

"Is the airport big enough to land that missing jet?"

Baker replied, "With a very skilled pilot, no problem."

"What about the other locations?" Nick was beginning to see a how Ahmad may have coordinated his plans.

"The second one looks like it's just some vacant warehouse."

"What about the third one?" Olexia chimed in.

"Who is that?" asked Baker, not realizing Nick was not alone.

Nick cut her off before she could answer. "Where's the third location, Baker?"

Baker did not answer right away. "EarthStat shows it to be a compound of some sort. A few small buildings."

"EarthStat? You're searching with a damn internet site?" Nick was furious.

"Nick! They have highly accurate feeds and you said to keep this quiet for seventy-two hours. I start moving satellites around and ..."

"I'll take care of it. Give me your IP, Nick." Olexia already had her phone out and was placing the call.

"Hey, you're those people who stole my algorithms, aren't you? Are you working with them, Nick?"

"Not now, Baker. I need you find out what you can on any and all flights coming into both private and commercial airports in the last twenty-four hours. Call me back when you have that for me and use whatever tools you have at your disposal. Consider the seventy-two hours as already having passed." With that, Nick disconnected with Baker.

"Three minutes, Nick, and we should start seeing some live video feed."

"Anyone else going to be able to read his transmission?"

Olexia shook her head no, but still replied, first covering the mouthpiece of her phone. "Unless they are already reading your address, it's not likely."

Nick waited as she continued to give instructions into the phone. There was a brief flicker and they both watched as the image increased in magnification until Nick recognized the building they were standing in.

"I need you to feed us the video on the following coordinates." As she read them off, the screen went black, then images of the new locations appeared. The screen was now split into three different grids.

Nick looked at Olexia. "Can they pan out on the airport?"

The technician heard Nick's request before Olexia could communicate it and the image slowly shrank, showing more planes parked around a single tower. One plane stood out due to its size.

Nick pointed to it, but Olexia had already seen it, as well. "Read me the call sign on the Lear jet." As she flipped back to the text message on Gabrielle's phone, Nick felt the adrenaline rushing as he saw her smile.

Another voice broke in over the speaker of Nick's laptop. "We are tracking on the number three grid and there is an aircraft approaching that locale. One moment, please."

Nick and Olexia could see a constant blip as it crossed the screen. This time the image continued to enlarge until a chopper could be clearly seen, banking to begin a descent into a multi-building complex. The image continued to track the chopper until it landed. In all, they counted seven men exit the chopper, then each disappeared on foot under a large canopy of trees.

Nick could hear her firing off instructions into the phone, then she hung up. "Our ride will be here in eight minutes. Follow me. Whatever Ahmad's plans are, he's executing them right now!" she said.

Once outside, Olexia introduced Nick to several men. They listened intently to what she was saying, then escorted

Nick to the rear trunk of one of the SUVs. Turning to face Nick, Olexia opened the hatch and lifted a cover liner, hooking it to the back of the last row of seats. Lying inside of the compartment was the case he had given her days earlier.

"You're going to need it to lead this team into the compound. The scope has several options. Tap the trigger very gently to change and cycle through them. Hopefully, you won't need to use it."

"And if we find Ahmad and the chemicals?"

"Obviously you secure the chemicals first, then we will worry about what comes next."

The Chinook was on them before anyone heard it coming. Approaching in whisper mode, it covered the last several hundred feet in seconds, setting down fifty feet from the team. Nick reached in, grabbed the case and armor from the SUV, twisted around, and followed the escort team through the open doors of the chopper. In all, the pick up took less than two minutes.

Nick attached a harness and leaned through the opening. His missed being a SEAL, and he wanted back in. Around him were highly trained men, risking their lives to protect and defend against whatever enemy they faced. The freedom of their homeland was all they cared about, with the exception of protecting their brothers. If they lost their lives doing that, so be it.

For the first time, Nick looked hard at the men who were already aboard when he and Olexia leaped inside. He smiled, seeing one of the sons of his old friend and teammate. The last time he saw Blake O'Brien was when the kid was only twelve years old. The kid was a spitting image of the old man.

Nick could see the man looking back at him. "Hello, CO. My dad said to say 'hey' if our paths ever crossed."

Nick reached out his hand and shook O'Brien's. "Your old man was a hell of a soldier and good friend. You know that, right?"

"He said the same about you, sir." O'Brien pointed to the other two men next to him. "This is Canaan and Levi. Best damn shooters I have ever had the pleasure to team with, excuse the language, sir."

The men extended a courtesy and went back to their lookouts.

O'Brien looked back at Nick. "Any orders, sir?"

"Any immediate threat, you take it out. Protect yourself, team and Olexia, that's it."

"CO, sir, you have obviously never been in the field with Mrs. Syshchenko before."

Chapter 25

Each man had brought with him a bodyguard and his personal bank account numbers and password IDs. If the chemical proved to be as lethal as Ahmad had promised, then the transfer of monies to his account would be swift. They would each possess enough toxins to either threaten a potential enemy or eliminate them altogether. The collateral damage was an afterthought.

As they made their way into a small theater, Ahmad followed the group in and shut the doors behind them. Once they were seated, he began.

"Gentlemen. I apologize for the informality and that I could not arrange better accommodations, but under the circumstances, it is most important that we complete our meeting as quickly as possible."

Ahmad waited to hear if there were any complaints, but heard none, and continued.

"By this time, you have all seen the news of the explosions on Freemont and are aware of the closing of a fifteen block radius. It was reported that a highly toxic chemical was accidentally released from a cargo ship docking nearby. I can assure you, the chemical release was not accidental, and it was from no ship. Please watch the screen in front of you."

Ahmad pressed a button and a video recording began to play as the theater lights dimmed. The men stared at a video taken from a camera placed directly across from the hat shop. In the video, Ahmad could be seen leaving the store and walking directly towards the camera, soon disappearing as he stepped out of view. There was a short delay before there was a flash coming from within the shop, followed by windows exploding shortly afterwards.

One of the men spoke. "This doesn't look like anything out of the ordinary. Are we missing something besides a few people on fire?"

Looking at the man, Ahmad smiled. "Please be patient. Pay careful attention to the pedestrians walking by."

All of the men leaned forward and watched as the first person came into view, struggling to maintain his balance. They were fixated as the individual began to wipe his face, quickly bending his fingers and scratching harder at the infected flesh. The scratching turned into clawing, ripping layers of skin away as he started to vomit, violently jerking his head from side to side. Ahmad could see the men starting to squirm in their chairs as bones began to break and protrude through the man's flesh.

Jumping to his feet, the Canadian shouted for Ahmad to turn it off. "Enough! You said this chemical would kill instantly, but nothing about the effects of what it would do beforehand. I assumed the chemical would simply cause a person to become comatose and pass away silently. I would not use this on my worst enemy."

Ahmad stared back. "I did not misrepresent the facts. It kills quickly and very efficiently. It will also leave the affected area uninhabitable for years to come. Is that not what I said?"

"Yes, but I will not kill this way. It is too inhuman and cold-blooded!"

"Does anyone else here feel the same way?" Ahmad asked.

When no one responded, Ahmad walked towards the man, sending a small pre-arranged signal to one of his men. On cue, the man lifted his rifle and shot the man's personal guard before he could react. Red laser dots displayed on the other guards' foreheads, each knowing they showed on their own as well. No one else moved except Ahmad.

Extracting the gun from inside his coat, he placed it against the man's temple and pulled back on the hammer. "You are not allowed to change your mind and you are not about to walk away. There was an agreement and you will honor that agreement, or die right now."

The man began to sweat as Ahmad looked at the others. "Gentlemen, if you would be so kind as to begin the transfers. You will each share this man's allocation of the canisters and you can thank him for his generosity. Once the transactions are complete, we will have concluded our business."

When there was no movement from the buyers, Ahmad took the man by his hair and began pulling him towards a small glass enclosure. "Perhaps you need a demonstration." Ahmad had planned on using Dawson, but this would be more entertaining, if only for him.

As they approached the enclosure, the man began to try and pull away, but Ahmad kneed him in the ribs several times as he continued to pull him forward. With the door already open, the man was pushed inside and sealed in tightly. Attached to the top of the enclosure was a single hose feeding down to one of the canisters on the outside. Ahmad reached for the valve and turned it. There was a small hiss and the man began to scream.

The others watched as the man pounded his open palms against the shatter-proof glass, begging for help. When all he saw were empty stares, he pulled a gun that had been strapped to his ankle, placed the barrel in his mouth and pulled the trigger before the chemical could take full effect.

There was second shot and, at first, they all believed it was a reverberation echoing off of the walls from the interior of the chamber. When the shots continued, everyone began pushing towards the room's outer doors as two of Ahmad's men rushed in.

"We saw five men rappelling on the far North ridge from an American chopper and we opened fire. They were too far away, though. We never heard them coming."

"Who are they, and where did they come from?"

"We don't know yet, but we heard a shot coming from this room and wanted to make sure you were safe first before we went after them."

The tone in Ahmad's voice changed dramatically, as did his demeanor. Raising the weapon to the next buyer's head, he shouted, spitting drool as he did. "Transfer the fucking money now, get your goods, and get the hell out of here, however you can."

There was no hesitation this time as the men quickly punched in their account codes, passwords, and dollar amounts, and waited briefly while the transfers were processed. Grabbing only what they could personally carry, their guards seized the remaining canisters and headed for the doors a second time.

Outside, Nick, O'Brien, Canaan and Levi had already found their positions and were scoping the compound. Olexia had continued working her way down towards the buildings, staying low behind the tree lines. Nick's team, by now, had spotted nearly a dozen men outside running for their weapons or cover, upon hearing the shot.

Having pulled the end caps off of Simon's rifle, Nick remembered Olexia telling him to gently tap the trigger to test the options of the scope. He pointed the rifle at one of the men in the compound and centered it on the man's chest. He tapped it once.

The visual changed to a thermal scan and zoomed in so that his entire body was the only object visible in the scope. In addition to the thermal scan, Nick could see the heart beating and outline of the internal organs. The graphics were incredible.

On the second tap, only the organs displayed. As Nick moved his eye from one organ to the next, a small red dot moved with it, pinpointing the exact spot he viewed. As the dot moved, Nick could feel a small vibration in stock as the aiming mechanism self adjusted. "Oh my God", Nick thought.

A third tap started a recording and Nick saw the 'Rec' characters displaying in the top right corner. In addition, the scope displayed the exact distance and coordinates.

Once again, he tapped the trigger. On top of the scope, he saw a small circular half-sphere raise just above its center. The image inside changed to a 360 degree panoramic view of Nick's entire surroundings. He could see all of his men positioned and what they were doing without him having to move his head.

On the next tap, the word 'Override' appeared and below it, the words 'Password Required'. As he continued to tap, the scope displayed additional options until it cleared and he could see clearly once again. He redirected the rifle back towards the direction of the shot and placed the scope back in thermal view.

To his surprise, the optics displayed the men inside. The instrument was so sensitive, it had actually penetrated the exterior wall and had picked up the heat signals from within. More importantly, it continued to show the same options as if there were no walls.

Nick tapped the trigger once again and saw the outline of a man's organs. As he moved his eye from the heart to the man's head, he blinked. The rifle fired. A .50 caliber round struck the exterior wall, passed through it and hit the man just above the lower jaw line.

"Shit," yelled Nick. He now realized the rifle, when it was in this mode, synced with scope's red dot and that his blinking action caused the rifle to fire the same as if he had pulled the trigger. Nick moved to the next man, redirected his eye and blinked. The impact flipped the man head over heels.

The whisper in Nick's ear was coming from O'Brien. "Sir, what are you shooting at? Do we have permission to engage?"

"I guess there's little choice now. There are nine men in that house, total. Two are down. Count them off so we know we got them all. They are preparing to run, so get ready." Nick could see the men looking back and forth at one another, with a curious expression on their faces.

Suddenly the door burst open and the men began running through it. As the first man exited, Nick took aim from eight hundred meters away, held his breath, placed the dot and blinked. In less than a second, the guard's head exploded, painting the green door a bright red color. The next man barely had time to take a step forward when Nick blinked again.

Other doors began to open around the compound. Not understanding what was happening, the occupants started running in different directions, trying to find a way to flee. Instead of giving up, each man had decided to make a run for it. Their logic had given way to panic. It was almost comical to see men cross paths, running the in direction the other man had just fled from.

O'Brien tracked a figure running across the open square of the compound, letting the man believe he was about find safety. The round drove the man sideways into a wall.

Canaan and Levi held up fingers, adding to the count each time they pulled the trigger. Below, men began firing back at anything they perceived to be moving from above. Their shots went wide. They began to fall one by one.

Dawson had heard the commotion and set his plan into motion, as he knew they would be coming for him any minute. They would kill him simply for the fact that he would be added garbage, holding back his kidnapper's escape.

Undoing his fly, he began to urinate on the floor around the door and walking backwards to the chair. Standing in the chair, he un-looped the light cord and pulled it down. Striking the bulb against the back of the chair he heard it shatter as the chamber became totally dark. Now he would have to wait, but not for long.

He heard the door open and watched the light stream in. In front of him was one of the guards he had heard arguing earlier. As the man came towards him, Dawson tossed the broken light at his feet. The man's body began to jerk as the electricity ran through it. Finally the man fell, dropping his weapon. Dawson jumped to the ground, retrieved the gun and ducked as he ran out the door.

Almost as quickly as it had begun, it was over, as far as anyone could tell. The compound fell silent and the snipers began their trek down to the complex. Making their way across the open entrance to the buildings, they approached with caution, eyeing the windows and doors.

Lying on the ground, a wounded guard made a move towards his weapon and Levi countered. The round tore through the man's heart, digging two feet down into the hard clay. Blood quickly filled the hole the bullet had made, then began streaming out across the dirt.

Nick moved towards the doorway, pushing hard against the doors as a corpse rolled away. Inside were the canisters. Some were still boxed, but most were lying next to the dead bodies. A count revealed them all to be there. Inside a container that resembled a phone booth lay a man bleeding from his mouth and the top of his head.

"I'm going to check the main house. I'll be back in five." O'Brien pointed towards Canaan to go with him, but Nick shook his head no. "I've got it. Just check the other buildings while I'm gone."

As Nick entered the house, he raised the .45 and walked slowly from room to room, checking closets and behind curtains. In one of the rooms, he passed a female body on the floor. Since the search was not complete, he pulled a sheet off the bed and tossed it over her, then continued down the hallway.

Coming from inside an adjacent wall, he heard a noise, but there was no door to enter through. He would have to backtrack and re-approach from the outside.

The doorknob turned easily, and he pushed open the door. Inside, it was so dark he could not make out any objects. He inched forward, placing the small flashlight in his mouth, leaving his hands free. Three steps in, he heard the sound of a gun cocking and the touch of the gun barrel as it was placed against the back of his head. He closed his eyes and thought of Laura.

"Bet you pissed your pants this time, huh?"

"Fuck you, Dawson, Jesus! I don't know if I want to hug you or knock that shit-eating grin off your face. You bastard!"

Suddenly, in the distance, an engine started. The men raced out the door as they saw a truck crash through a set of bay doors and fishtail its way onto a dirt road. They could see two people inside. Both Canaan and Levi dropped to a knee, slung their rifles and fired shots as the truck took a hard right around a bend and disappeared.

The three snipers could hear Nick yelling as he and Dawson ran towards them. "Did anyone see who was in the truck?"

"Affirmative. It was Ahmad and Olexia. It looked like Ahmad was driving." Levi responded.

Immediately, Nick had a bad feeling about the answer. Olexia had played him all along, he thought.

"Secure the chemicals!" screamed Nick. "I'll call for the bird, we'll catch them from the air."

It took nearly twenty minutes for the chopper to return, load the chemicals, and for the men to climb aboard. In that time, Nick knew the pair could be anywhere. They could have gone off in a different direction or even have a remote hideout where they wouldn't be visible from the air. Doubts of finding them started to filter through Nick's mind.

As the chopper lifted, they all looked down at the bodies. They would have to be left for now and retrieved later, once Olexia and Ahmad had been found.

Chapter 26

For the next thirty minutes, the pilot crisscrossed grids covering a twenty mile radius. With the exception of a constant flow of cars on the highway and an occasional off road vehicle, there were no other vehicles to be seen.

Nick was starting to wonder if the two had stopped and reversed direction, returning to the compound once they saw them leave. There was enough dense brush to hide a bulldozer in, let alone a truck, and it would not be seen from the ground or air. If they had, then what was so important that they would take the chance of returning and being caught while doing so?

Nick tapped the pilot on the shoulder. "How's our fuel?"

"Fifteen minutes and I will have to return to base."

"What's the chance of doing a flyover of the compound where you picked us up?"

The pilot did a quick check of the coordinates. "I can give you one pass, otherwise I'm going to be coming in on fumes."

"Let's go!"

With the stick pulled to the right, the Chinook did a one-eighty, heading back to the compound.

Levi continued to look down, watching the treetops and landscape pass underneath. His training had taught him to recognize and remember the terrain patterns, plants, weather changes and food supplies with which he came into contact during maneuvers. It was only one of the many skills he excelled at. It could mean the difference of his team returning or not, and he took it damn seriously.

"We're headed back to the compound. Why, sir?"

"I don't think they ever left. I think they returned for something and waited it out until they saw us leave."

Dawson spoke. "Any chance it might be for one of the buyers? Maybe we missed some of the canisters?"

"Intel said there were twenty canisters and that's what we have on board."

"Maybe the intel is wrong. Maybe there's more and we just don't know it yet."

There was a clicking sound in Nick's earpiece and he reached up to tap the receiver and volume switch. At first, all he heard was static and a few truncated words. "Th.. .. ..ker, can you ..er me?" Nick could not make out the full sentences, but he knew the voice.

"Baker. Can you repeat what you just said?"

It came in clearer this time, but there was still garbling that Nick tuned out, trying to fill in the missing words as Baker spoke.

"I've been tracking you and listening to your communications for the past twenty minutes."

"Cut to the chase, Baker. What have you got?"

"You asked me to track all planes landing in the last twenty-four hours at the local airports. Olexia arrived five hours ago, but there's no flight plan listed. I checked all active airports and there hasn't been a 707 landing in almost a month. Didn't she say that's what she was coming in on?"

"She said she was coming in on her personal plane. If so, that's the only one she has registered."

"So either she lied, or she isn't at an airport. Where can you land and hide a 707 commercial jet?"

Canaan looked around at the men, not sure if he should mention another possibility. He used to race his Mustang against the other guys on Friday nights and paid his insurance bill every month with his winnings. It hadn't been used in over 10 years. It wasn't the ideal place to land, but it could be done.

"How about an old abandoned shopping mall? The parking lot covered over three square miles and the buildings were leveled years ago. A lot of us used it as a drag strip before they started putting up a few warehouses."

"Yeah, I remember that place," added Levi.

Canaan continued to talk. "Anyway, the locals petitioned against it and the project was abandoned. The property has been sitting vacant ever since. The last owners paid in advance on a twenty year lease, so no one can touch it until it runs out."

"Can you find us the coordinates on this area, Baker?"

"Don't have to, they were already recorded in the messages from the phone link you sent to me."

"Gabrielle's?" asked Nick quickly.

"You didn't give me a name, but yes, it shows her name in the cross reference."

"I'm transferring you over to the pilot. Give him the coordinates."

Nick could feel the chopper turning almost immediately as the pilot set the new course, then heard the pilot calling to him.

"I can only get you within a few miles of those coordinates. If I don't start heading back real soon, I won't be able to return to base."

Nick was weighing the options and it came down to only one logical choice. If his team got there too late, Olexia and Ahmad would already be on the plane and in the air, in which case there would be no hope of catching them. He certainly couldn't have them shot down over California.

"I need you to set down as close as possible without them seeing us. If that means you have to park this bird for a few hours, then you do it! We'll get you refueled and back to the base when we can."

"Roger that, sir." The pilot checked the gauges once again and thought of reducing speed to decrease the fuel consumption, but decided against it. Instead, he did the opposite and radioed back for the men to hold on.

Three miles from the location, Nick could see the tops of several buildings, all large enough to hangar a plane the size of the 707. The land was flat and Nick keyed the earpiece for the pilot's attention.

"Get as low as you can without creating a dust trail. Set us down about a mile out. How's your fuel?"

"Good thing I have some reading material, sir."

"Beers are on me when we get back." Nick meant it.

"That goes for us too, sir?" interrupted Levi.

"Until you can't walk and have to piss on yourself," replied Nick.

The team felt the chopper slowing and readied themselves for an exit.

"No! Just Dawson and myself. You two stay here and watch our six. If we can't stop them, then you will need to stop the plane before it gets airborne, but only on my command."

The three snipers gave a 'thumbs up' sign and moved back into the chopper's bay.

Feeling the chopper touch ground, both Nick and Dawson jumped and started a quick jog towards the buildings. In just under a mile away, they both lay prone, with Nick looking through the scope while Dawson spotted him.

Slowly they tracked the horizon until Nick heard Dawson clearly.

"Seventeen degrees."

Chapter 27

Ahmad was on his knees. There was already swelling around his eyes and blood dripped from the corner of his mouth, ears and nostrils. The steel tipped boots caught him in the kidneys and he fell forward, twisting his body at the last second so he didn't hit the pavement face first.

His hands were tied behind his back with a plastic strip that, should the user be so inclined, could easily cut off all circulation to the hands. He rolled to his side and was rewarded with a kick to the groin.

"How's it feel? Remember your men doing this to me after you thought I betrayed you?" Olexia was pacing in front of Ahmad, trying to figure where to place the next kick. She decided on a kneecap.

Through the scope, Nick relaxed a bit, knowing Olexia and Ahmad had not partnered, as he had originally thought. He could plainly see the expression on her face and knew that at any moment she would end Ahmad's life. In her hand was Ahmad's own gun and he wondered if it was the one he had used on Olexia's sister, brother-in-law and the baby.

Around her ear, Nick saw that she was still wearing the team's communication earpiece. Nick clicked over to a secondary frequency that only he and she had preset in their gear. He did not want the rest of the team listening in on what was about to be said.

"Olexia, this isn't the way you want this going down."

He watched as Olexia stood up straight, looking around for him. She was turning her head from side to side, at the same time placing the gun against Ahmad's temple.

"Where are you, Nick?"

"Turn thirty degrees South and I'm right in front of you. You won't be able to see me, though."

She followed his instructions and turned as he had directed. "Can you see me? Can you see my face through the scope?"

"Every bead of sweat on your forehead. Now you need to let him go. We'll make sure he is turned over to the authorities and pays for his crimes."

"It's not going to happen, Nick. This is payback, here and now."

"I can't let you do it. If you shoot him, I'll have to shoot you, and I don't want to." Nick placed his finger around the trigger.

"This man killed over two thousand people, including my sister and my child. That little boy would be seven years old now. He never had a chance, Nick. I was forced to watch as he killed them all."

"You said the boy was your sister's."

"I lied, Nick. I told you it was complicated, remember? Ahmad sent me away because he didn't want me in danger when I had our son. When I returned and was caught, Ahmad became furious and had me beaten. I could never carry another child. He hated me so much, he killed our own son."

"Olexia, I promise you he will pay. If you take that shot and I choose not to put a bullet through your head, you will spend the rest of your life in jail."

She began to laugh, almost to the point of becoming hysterical. "Nick, I have immunity, did you forget? You and I can shoot anyone we feel threatens us or our citizens and we don't have to justify it. We have a free 'get out of jail card' for the rest of our lives!"

Nick looked over at Dawson, who had heard everything. He could see him thinking, and knew at any moment he would put the pieces together. It didn't take long.

"Well, that explains why those cops didn't put a bullet in our asses. You knew they couldn't do a thing to us. Son of a bitch! When this is over, I am going to kick your ass and then I'm going to go to your house and show your old lady what a real man can do."

Nick shot him a quick glance. "Make sure you have your affairs in order first."

"You are an asshole, you know it?" Dawson shot back.

"Gentlemen, are you through?" came a voice in Nick's earpiece.

With the scope pressed against his eye, Nick could see that Olexia was reaching for Ahmad's head, pulling it back so it was looking in the same direction as she was.

"Nick, you take the shot then. It's your sanction anyway. A nice clean shot and we are all out of here. Go ahead."

"No matter what he's done, he deserves to go to trial. There's no doubt he'll be found guilty and will receive the justice he deserves. He will spend the rest of his life behind bars, most likely in solitary confinement. You have my word on that."

Again Olexia laughed. "I've watched what America does with their criminals. You send them to a cell with a nice soft bed, give them an education, give them televisions to watch, computers, let them have a lawyer that your citizens have to pay for. After years of giving them extensions, you turn them out on the streets again only to terrorize the people once more."

Nick did not reply for a moment. "Let him go. Get on your plane and go home. We will do the rest."

"No! Either you take the shot now or I will." She raised the gun, pointing it Ahmad's head. Nick placed the red dot at the center of her forehead and pulled the trigger.

He pulled it a second time and lay stunned as there was no recoil.

"Oops," he heard Olexia say. "There's a reason I gave you Simon's rifle Nick. It won't work against my face. Did you really think I would take the chance of you turning on me once you saw what I really came to do?"

"So everything you told me in Ireland was pretty much a lie, as well. You probably don't even care about the chemicals, do you?" asked Nick.

"It's your country that's going to feel the effects first, not mine. I knew it would stop here. You asked me why

Simon didn't take the shot? He knew I wanted the revenge all to myself. He knew not to take that away from me!"

"So Simon let you go this alone, all by yourself, if he couldn't return?" asked Nick.

Olexia walked around in front of Ahmad and raised the gun. "Simon loved me and he knew I needed peace. Good-bye, Nick."

The 707 began to roll out of the building, pulling within one hundred feet of Olexia and her target. The two men watched as three flashes exited the barrel of her gun and Ahmad fell backwards. Nick could hear each crack as the hammer slammed against the firing pins of the bullets.

She looked down at Ahmad's body. "That's for the family you took from me."

Turning, she ran for the extended ladder, bounded up each step and was gone. Nick saw a man grab the handle and yank the door shut as the engines accelerated and the plane began to take off down the deserted parking lot.

Switching frequencies, he started to radio for the snipers, but decided it was best to let it end. CDC had the formula, they had the canisters, and Ahmad was dead.

They stood and watched as the plane lifted into the sky.

"Are you going to go after her at some point?"

Nick continued to watch the plane. "No, it's over. Let her find the peace she deserves."

Chapter 28

In twenty minutes, they would be out of American air space, heading across the North Atlantic. She looked out the window at the ocean below. It was calm. At least it looked that way from her vantage point miles above.

She reached into her vest pocket and took out her phone. Under the listing of recent messages, she scrolled down and found the one she had transferred from Gabrielle's phone. Selecting it, she waited for the decryption code to return the message to a readable text format. Once it finished, seven separate bank account IDs displayed.

In front of her was a small fold-down tray with a laptop already open and turned on. Attached to a USB port was a cable used to transfer data and photos from her phone. She plugged it into the laptop and deleted the prompt that showed that it had found new hardware. She quickly synced the phone and typed in the bank's internet address. At the prompt, she typed in the first account and password that Gabrielle had supplied in her message.

When the balance displayed, she sat up in her seat. She typed in the next account and password. The second account displayed its balance. She began to frantically type in the next five accounts and passwords. Each account held exactly the same amount.

It was possible the program misinterpreted the characters, but not in all seven accounts. Neither would an incorrect password have allowed her access to the account balances either.

She closed the laptop and pushed her seat rest back a few inches. There had to be an explanation as to why the balance was zero in each account. Ahmad certainly already had money in the accounts, even if he had not been able to persuade the buyers to transfer funds before the attack. If he had, then perhaps the bank had not posted the deposits yet. That had to be it, she thought.

Closing her eyes, she reclined the chair the rest of the way and decided she would resolve the issue once she landed. Perhaps she would wait a few hours and check the accounts again, just before she landed. Either way, once she was home, she would have the monies transferred to the organizations' accounts and let her superiors know she had reimbursed the millions she had secretly siphoned to pay for the mission to find Ahmad. Had she gone to them beforehand, years earlier, they would not have approved.

Olexia let her body relax for the first time since the funeral. She missed Simon terribly and wondered, if he had lived, would he have kept his promise that they would be through with the organization. Instead, they would travel far away from their never ending search for those who lived to kill others. Their thoughts were constantly beset with mind games, to the point that neither could think of anything else. How do you constantly think like a killer without becoming one yourself?

He had loved St. Croix during the time they spent there on vacation, years earlier. It was the last time she had remembered Simon laughing out loud. She knew that would have been his choice of where to live the rest of their lives, secluded for as long as possible from any act of vengeance that would certainly come someday.

When she returned, she would ask for an extended leave of absence. She would take time off and go to St. Croix, taking with her the memories and Simon's remains, to rebury them in a place he loved.

She felt the plane turning to begin its descent. How long had she been sleeping or lost in her thoughts, she wondered. It seemed like only a few hours earlier they had left the United States, with Ahmad lying wasted and twisted on the ground. Olexia let the memory linger until she remembered she needed to check the accounts once more.

Flipping open the screen of her phone, she keyed in the necessary information before looking for the account passwords on her phone. One by one she brought them up, this time satisfied that the delays in the deposits were only that. The sums were less than she had believed they would be, but they were enough. After reimbursing the organization, there would be enough for her to, perhaps, never come back from St. Croix.

Chapter 29

Kandahar, Afghanistan – The 707's signature showed clearly on the screen as it descended into Ireland's main airport. It continued on a slow graceful arc that would align its nose onto runway E27. He had been watching its progress for the last three hours.

Beside him was a man who had been keeping him constantly apprised of the weather patterns, and other aircraft in the proximity of the 707, but most of all, Olexia's reviewing of the accounts. He had waited for her to key the passwords. The account numbers he already knew. They had been changed without his approval by a man he had trusted.

He watched as the technician typed in the account numbers and passwords, one by one transferring the deposits into the man's own personal accounts. The technician knew that he would never be able to live as a free man again, or leave this man's side, once the transfers went through. He would be accompanied forever by a string of bodyguards after typing in the last password. Those numbers, with so few associated words, he would take to his grave.

The thirty million dollars that had been paid to Rafael had been worth it all. In only a few minutes, he would find the tranquility he had not known for six years. The incredible pain he had endured, the loss of so many bodily functions, and motor skills he would never regain. All of it no longer mattered at this exact moment.

His hand quivered from the strong focus his mind required to move it only inches. The fingers no longer worked properly, nor did his right eye or the right hemisphere of his brain. With the ever present feeding tube and urine bag strapped to his motorized wheelchair, he no longer concerned himself with his humility or his body's deterioration.

Rafael had been the perfect choice and he had done his job remarkably well until he, too, betrayed that trust and changed the passwords. Months of surgery to alter his face and another two years to learn the mannerisms of his beneficiary, had come at a higher price than the man would ever know. Within an hour of learning of his treachery, Rafael's entire family had been slaughtered with one effortless command from the man in the wheelchair.

Ahmad had survived Simon's bullet, but the intelligence reports had been correct that he was left an invalid. As he sat watching Olexia's plane approach the airport a mile out, he bent forward, gripping the foot long attachment between his teeth. After having spent months learning to maneuver the device, he used it to either point at something he needed or to push a console button located on the wheelchair. He found the one button he desired and pressed the end of the attachment against it.

A small figure stepped from the shadows and stood next to him. "Is that one of your planes, Father?" asked the seven year old boy.

Ahmad continued to stare as he watched and waited for the 'Seat Belt' indicator light to display on the monitor in front of him. As it did, a very small smile appeared on his face as the blip disappeared. Reaching out, the boy took his father's hand in his and smiled as well.

End

FROM THE AUTHOR OF DECLARATION OF SURRENDER AND AMERICAN SANCTION

JIM BURKETT

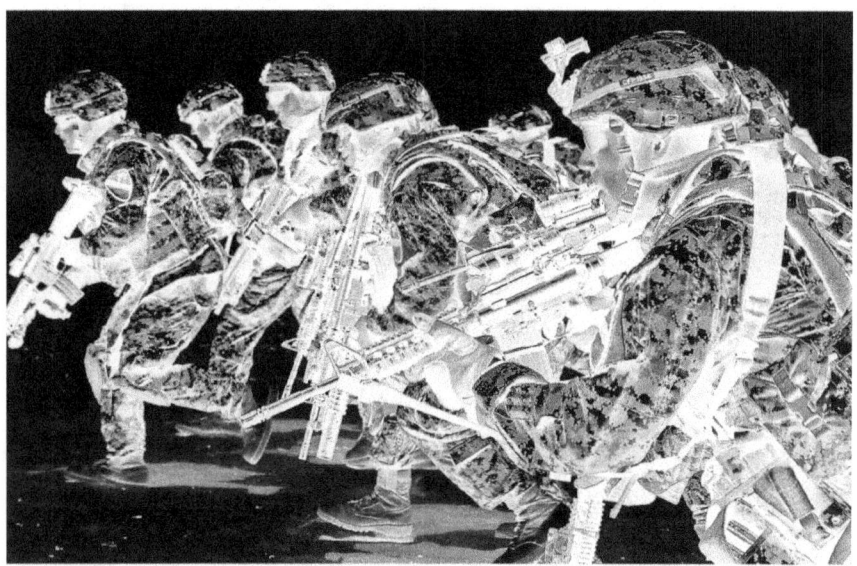

REPRISAL

A NICK WEST SERIES #3

Reprisal

By
Jim Burkett

Published by
Inknbeans Press

Accomplish great things because you believe in yourself, your abilities and your dreams. Not because of the expectations of others. Only then will you truly be happy.
Jim Burkett

Intro

Hanakapiai Beach, Hawaii, 1983.

Winter had arrived along with the powerful waves and currents that would easily drag the body out to sea. Dexter Morgan stood at the tides' edge, letting the seawater wash over his feet, occasionally pulling them loose and shifting his weight to regain his balance as they sank deep into the sand. The cigarette was positioned to the right side of his mouth as his mind remained transfixed in thought, contemplating the immoral act he was about to perform. Not to this woman, not to this incredible and loving woman, as he thought of her.

His team stood by, waiting for their final instructions. They were tired, near exhaustion from the hunt. Knowing this would not be their last, they simply killed time, anticipating his instructions to tell them that the mission was complete and to tie up all loose ends. The search for the woman had taken ten months of their lives and they were anxious to be finished and to move on to the next target. So far they had either captured or eliminated four of the eleven people on their list.

The first two had been easy, returning to the military base after decoding the cryptograms. Their trials had been short, simple and with biased representation. In the end, they were hanged and their bodies dumped in a remote area of the Everglades. The alligators and cougars had quickly consumed all trace of evidence. Families would never learn the truth behind their disappearances.

Word of their government's actions had been furtively disclosed and the remaining members of the group went into hiding, using the skills they had been taught to conceal themselves from all other humans on Earth. They had formed an alliance to try and protect one another, but they knew they were being hunted down one by one. Given the option to return and spend the rest of their lives behind bars or keep running until they were found and shot, they elected the latter.

Dr. Stephanie Pierce faced outward from the beach front, on her knees watching the tide rise higher until the water began to encircle her waist. With her wrists pulled tightly behind her back and securely wrapped with plastic bands, she waited. She, long ago, accepted that someday this would be her fate. Knowing that these people knew nothing of her family and that her loved ones would be forever safe, she had no regrets.

It was time. Morgan pulled the cigarette from his lips and tossed it into the ocean. Keeping his face turned away from his men, he let the tears stream down as he slowly walked into the surf and stood behind the beautiful woman. He raised the pistol and placed a finger around the trigger. He too was tired and his whole body began to shake. His duty demanded he put an end to her life, but for this one person, it had taken an extreme toll on him both physically and mentally. She did not deserve this ending.

"Please, Dr. Pierce. Please reconsider your choice. We can make sure you are treated with the highest respect and dignity for the rest of your life. You will be given privileges that no one else will receive. Please!"

Without lifting her head, she said, "I have already made peace with God. I will not spend the rest of my life wondering why I and the others were betrayed by our own government. We did not do what you have accused us of. We were all loyal to the end, but no one would let us prove our innocence. Did you ever think to interrogate your own peers or did you just blindly accept orders? Do what you need to do, Morgan."

The agent began to cry hysterically, his hand shaking out of control until he reached down with the other and steadied himself. "I am so sorry, Dr. Pierce. May God have mercy on your soul and mine." The bullet passed cleanly through her brain as he watched her body tumbled forward. He stepped back as the waves began to pull at her motionless remains.

Placing the barrel of the gun to his temple, he pulled the trigger a second time.

Chapter 1

New York, USA - 2012

Thomas Albright sat at the center of his large rich mahogany wood desk, watching as the three monitors ran through a series of test script he had just finished coding an hour earlier. Each scrolled uninterrupted, displaying large amounts of data returned from a search of IP addresses, and along with it, the decrypted passwords found on the corresponding hard drives. By adding one sequential number to the initial starting IP address, the program looped and pinged a new address, looking for active computers.

Once a match was found, it located the encrypted password file on the system and duplicated it. Altering the copy, the program gave it a new password assignment, then placed the copy in a hidden folder for use at a later and more convenient time. The program also tracked those systems that had no password, which so many people were simply too lazy to set up. It was too much of a hassle for most users and this indolence gave him full access to their privacy and identity whenever he wanted.

In addition, the program captured file names and sizes as it downloaded each one. On one monitor, it streamed photo files at a speed too fast for the brain to assimilate the entire image, but it was enough to know he liked what he saw. The first of the external ten terabyte hard drives began to fill, transferring the overload to the next piggybacked drive as it reached capacity. After forty minutes, he stopped the program, tabbed down to a new line of code, highlighted and ran it. The procedure began the process of moving the files into folders designated by their file type along with sorting them by their creation date. Over the past three years of running and testing his code, one folder had sat vacant waiting for the right type of file to be identified and processed. Selling the data had brought in over $200,000 a year, but he knew a big score was just waiting to happen some day.

The transfers were color coded, allowing him the opportunity to keep track of what was going where. Green files indicated the data was text or a word document, yellow meant video, blue signified it was an image file and purple was his most prized file type, bank accounts. The image files were sometimes worth a sizable amount of money if they were of someone having illicit sex in a hotel room or some other seedy location. Blackmail was dangerous but very profitable. The pedophile images, he anonymously sent to the police along with the pervert's IP address and left it to them to make an arrest and slap charges on the lowlife. In his mind, this justified his other dealings.

There were other color coded files, but he had never seen a red one come across, until now. He let out a small gasp and sat forward in his chair, watching the red icon pulsate for almost seven minutes before the pixels disappeared. Fingering a shortcut on the keyboard, the program stopped immediately and the folder opened to show the file name. There, in large capital letters, was the acronym 'DOD', standing for the 'Department of Defense.'

"Son of a bitch!" as he began to laugh. "What the fuck are you, you little bastard?" The properties of the file showed it to be 128 bit encryption and over 9.7 terabytes, filling up one drive alone. For the next three days, going on very little sleep, he tried unlocking the encryption code, using every combination key he could think of or his program could build, but neither could break it. Finally, his thought processes began to lose all logical meaning and he found himself no longer capable of thinking clearly. He decided he needed to shower and to get a good night's sleep.

Having slipped out of his clothes, he could smell his own stench as he turned the shower knobs. Placing a hand into the downpour of water droplets, he waited until the temperature was to his liking before stepping in. The shower head had cost him almost six hundred dollars alone, but it was an extravagance that he felt had been well worth it. Thomas never felt he had wasted his money if the item had brought him some type of joy, and this had certainly done that.

He heard the front door of his apartment open and figured it was his roommate stumbling in after a few heavy nights of drinking. What a waste of a human being, he thought to himself. If the man failed to pay his rent again this month, he was gone. "Hey, Charlie, is that you?" Hearing nothing, he called out again.

Through the closed bathroom door, he made out the muffled answer, "Yeah, man, it's me."

"OK, great. I'm just taking a quick shower and I'll be out in a couple of minutes."

"Take your time," came the reply.

Albright stepped into the shower and closed the glass shower door. Grabbing a bar of soap, he began to lather his body as the water drenched him. Closing his eyes, he ran a soapy cloth over his face, into his ears, then down his chest. As he moved it down towards his genitals, he heard the bathroom door open. Turning around, he shouted, "Hey, man, I told you I was taking a shower!" His eyes began to burn as he opened them, forgetting the soap was still on his face.

"Yes, I heard you the first time," a voice responded.

Albright's body stiffened and his eyes grew wider as he could see the barrel of the gun pointed directly at his forehead, even through the fogged glass.

"What do you want? Who are you?" Albright's voice cracked as his brain was trying to come to terms with what his eyes were seeing. Had he not already taken a piss minutes earlier, he would surely be doing so now.

"A couple of days ago, you intruded on our privacy and took something that didn't belong to you. I want it back and I want it now."

"I don't have it. I erased it as soon as I realized it was from the Department of Defense."

"I seriously doubt that, Mr. Albright." The man pushed the gun closer to the glass shower wall.

"I swear, I'm telling you the truth. It's, it's..." Albright was beginning to babble.

The man lowered the gun. "Please, Mr. Albright, step out of the shower, now."

Opening the door and reaching for the towel rack, Albright took one down, placed it around his waist and stepped through the opening. Placing his right foot squarely on the floor, he raised his left and began to exit. The foot sweep caught him completely off guard, lifting his entire body off the ground and propelling it downward onto the four inch concrete edge of the shower rim. The sharp edge of the lower door frame sliced deep into his back, cutting into his spine on the initial impact.

At the same time, the back of his head slammed against the shower floor. Within seconds, blood began to flow out of the shattered fragments of his skull, washing over the dirty soap encrusted patterns of the tiles, coursing downwards into the drain.

As he lay there, his mouth moved up and down, his lungs failing to respond as the brain's electrical impulses to the body's organs no longer worked. He looked like a fish gasping for its last few breaths. The man pulled the towel from around Albright's body, placed a portion of it across his own hand, reached down and cupped the mouth and nose of Albright, pinching gently to close the nostrils and airway. In less than a minute, all movement stopped. The man reached forward, placing his fingertips on Albright's eyelids and gently pulled the flesh down, closing the eyes that were staring back at him. Satisfied the exposed man was dead, he positioned the towel in Albright's hand and walked back towards the computer screens.

Bouncing around each of the screens was an assortment of images showing naked women and cars. Apparently they were Albright's favorite pastime, although the assailant had reservations believing any woman had ever stepped foot into this apartment. With the back of his hand, he tapped the mouse and the screens changed to display what he immediately recognized as a program written to translate another program's secrets. It appeared, though, that no progress had been made as the file was still intact and the other screens sat empty while the cursors continued to blink.

Running a quick search of the drive sequence and file names, he found the drive he was looking for, disconnected it and was placing it in a secured case when he heard a person placing a key in the keyhole of the front door. He quickly closed the case, dashed to the back of the door and stood against the wall with the gun pointing upwards, held level to the right side of his face.

The door opened and a man staggered through the entrance, leaving it open as he walked towards the center of the room. He reeked of alcohol, urine and vomit. Pausing, the disgusting, foul smelling man turned in the direction of the bathroom and slowly shuffled forward, taking small, deliberate steps, placing one in front of the other. Three feet from the bathroom door, he changed his mind, turned and entered a side bedroom.

Sitting on the edge of the bed, the drunken man reached down to take off a shoe, but instead toppled onto the floor. After several minutes of trying to stand, he gave up and rolled back across a shag rug, falling into a deep inebriated sleep. The man regurgitated a small amount again, but within seconds, the snoring began and the gun welding man decided it was his time to exit.

Sliding out the door, he pulled it closed behind him, checked to make sure there was no one in the stairwell and quickly descended the three flights. Stepping out into the open air, he reached over his shoulder and pulled the black wool hood of the sweater upwards. To try and shield his face from the crowd and possible overhead cameras, he plucked the Pittsburgh Steelers hat from his back pocket, placed it on the top of his head and rearranged the black hood over it. Satisfied that no one could recognize him at a later time, he moved forward, mixing in with the late night crowd as they went about searching with anticipation for their next sinful endeavor.

His car was parked two blocks away on Lincoln Avenue behind the red Buick. He had stolen it three hours earlier from an overnight parking lot and the owner would be very pleased to find out that it had been taken with hopes that it would eventually be found stripped. No matter what the insurance company would eventually pay, it would undoubtedly be more than the car was worth, having been dented so many times in the New York daily traffic. Sitting behind the wheel, he slid down in the seat as he pulled his phone from his pocket.

After several rings, the phone call finally connected. On the other end was the sound of a man taking slow, deliberate breaths, waiting only for confirmation that the undertaking had been successful. "I have the package you asked for. Please make the deposit now. You have two minutes."

The assailant tapped a new icon on his phone and waited. Within moments, he watched as the amount in his offshore account increased 400,000 dollars. Once the deposit was verified, he continued. "I will deliver your package as planned and for the full amount agreed upon. Please expect delivery within the next hour. We will complete the final transaction then."

Starting the car, he pulled out and drove the car north on Dillard, turning east onto Potomac. Another half an hour and he would be finished with this job and on a flight out of the country. In twelve hours, he would be lying between the legs of his beautiful Italian mistress, Abrielle. His nostrils flared for a brief moment, his brain's senses remembering the incredible smells of her body and dark long hair. Up ahead, the light abruptly turned red and he slowed, cruising to a stop behind the gold Hummer in front of him. Tapping his fingers on the steering wheel, he waited for the light to turn green.

Suddenly, an Asian man bolted from the driver's side and raced to back of the Hummer. Before he could fully react, three shots pierced through the front of his windshield, the last one grazing his head as he ducked and retrieved the gun from inside his sweat suit pocket. Raising the gun over the dashboard, he returned fire in the direction of where the shooter had been standing. He felt the man fall against the hood of the car and waited another twenty seconds before pulling the door handle and sliding out of the passenger side of the car.

Coming around to the front of the car, he saw the shooter lying on the ground, blood pouring from his abdomen. The dying man's eyes were still open and in a last attempt to finish his assignment, the Asian raised the gun, hoping to get off one final shot. A bullet exploded through the top of his head, ending his futile optimism. From a short distance away, the man in the hood heard another man running towards him, screaming for him to drop his weapon.

He spun and raised his weapon, aiming directly at the man's forehead. Before he could pull the trigger, though, the man running towards him began to stagger and fall forward. The man in the hood could see two red spots on the man's suit jacket as well as the badge as it dropped from the agent's left hand. He glanced around quickly to see who might have fired the shots, but saw no one.

The DHS agent had fallen to both knees, dropping his gun and shield. Looking down at the wounds in his chest, he could feel life leaving his body. His thoughts went immediately to his family: his little girl and wife who just hours earlier had told him how much they loved him and how proud they were of what he was doing.

Their kisses on his cheek, and the smiles he last saw on their faces, were what he was trying his best to stay focused on. He lifted his head and looked up at the man in the hood, locked onto his eyes and stared into them for only seconds before death took hold and he crumpled sideways to the ground.

Running to the driver's side of the Hummer, the man in the hood jumped in, shifted into 'Drive' and pressed the gas pedal down as far as it would go. There was a smell of burning rubber and screeching of tires before the wheels caught and drove the vehicle forward. Safeguarded underneath a dark overhanging café awning, a lone figure stood in the shadows, removing the silencer and placing the weapon back in its open holster.

Chapter 2

Nick West stood straight with his arms out and feet spread comfortably apart. He had just emptied the P250 of its clip and a silhouette target was being retracted, when agent Daniel Hoskins approached. Stopping short, he waited for Nick to recognize him and speak first.

Slipping in a new clip and housing the first round, Nick turned his head slightly, nodded and resumed shooting. As he finished, he popped out his fifth empty clip and laid the gun on the table in front of him.

"Special Assistant Hoskins, what can I do for you? I thought by now you would have been long gone from the service." What Nick had really wanted was to tell the man to get the hell off of his property.

"Nick, it's good to see you too. It appears your retirement hasn't changed your habits a bit. From the looks of the placement of your rounds, you're still practicing every day."

Nick let a small smile hang for a minute, then said, "Seriously. What brings you out here and what does the CIA want with me?"

"What makes you think I'm here for you?" The sarcasm was clearly present in his voice.

"If you are not here for me, then who?" Nick was already sensing that the past hostility between them was still very present. The thought that the agent may possibly be in trouble was bringing him a lot of joy.

"I'm here for Baker, if you must know. Is he around, because I don't have time to waste with you. The SA's convivial facial expressions had completely disappeared as he took two steps toward Nick.

Nick decided to try and remain courteous even though he knew neither one of them could stand the other's company. "Dan, what is this about? It looks like you're under a lot of stress about something and you're not normally one to show it."

"Just get Baker here first and we will talk. You're going to want to hear what I have to say and we may need your support as well, if you are interested. However, I couldn't care less if you are or aren't." The agent had hoped Nick would respond immediately and was disappointed when he did not reply. Nick simply watched as the agent's clean shaven jaw line tightened.

Nick retrieved a phone from his pocket, found Baker's recorded number and thumbed the digital keypad. After a brief conversation with Baker, he ended the call. "He'll be here in fifteen minutes," said West.

The agent shook his head. "Is there any place around here we can get a beer while we wait?"

Nick considered the request, knowing the agent did not drink; at least he never remembered him doing so on duty. This was not a good sign. "As a matter of fact, I do. Follow me."

Nick picked up the P250, placed it in a pistol bag and dropped the empty clips in a side pocket of his jacket. Taking out his phone again, he called Baker back and told him to stay put, they were coming to him. Baker began to object, but Nick pressed the 'End' key and shoved the phone back into his left pocket. "Let's go."

The two exited the hanger which also served as his daily shooting range. Located on his expansive private property, the sound of gunfire was never an issue with those who inadvertently trespassed in error. Those that heard the gunfire minded their own business and it worked out well for all of them. Sitting outside the hanger in the parking lot was Nick's Porsche GTS alongside the agent's standard issue black Suburban. Pressing the remote, the Porsche's engine started as Nick reached for the door handle.

"Come on! Do you seriously think I'm going to be able to stay up with that? Remember, I know how you drive. Have you ever driven the legal speed limit in your life?" Hoskins was enjoying the off hand ribbing he was giving to Nick and hoped it was really pissing him off.

"I can't say I recollect ever doing that." Nick said with a small grin. "Hop in. I'll bring you back when we are done."

The agent went around and promptly plopped himself down into the passenger seat. Stretching out his legs, he reached up and pulled down the seatbelt, buckling it tightly around his shoulder and waist. For extra measure, he pulled hard on the straps to make sure the locking mechanisms had caught and there was no chance of him being thrown out. His imagination permitted him to see the Porsche flipping over and over, with himself being ejected and his body mangled and ripped to pieces by the hard concrete.

"Are you sure you are in all comfy and cozy?" asked Nick as he waited on the agent's safety check, annoyed that the agent was taking any and all precautions.

"Just drive, and try to keep me in one piece this time, OK?" It was a jab at an accident involving both of them years earlier and the department had found Nick guilty of the infraction. In part it was true, but nonetheless, it was a pet peeve and a mark on his record that he could never expunge.

It was also a comment the agent would soon regret. Nick's earlier attempt to erase old wounds and try to be civil towards the agent was over. The Porsche was doing 110 mph down the airport runway before the agent would finally let out a breath after gravity turned loose of his body and he was able to sit up straight. "You are a fucking psycho, West! You know it? No wonder Johnson wanted your fucking ass out!" Hoskins let out a scream that combined a mixed tone of sheer terror and extreme adrenaline.

Normally not one to let emotions get the best of him, Nick could not let the last comment from the agent pass. Angered by the agent's remark, Nick downshifted, pulled the emergency brake and threw the car into a hard right as he rounded a corner while pumping the clutch and gas pedal as needed. The car drifted through the turn two inches from a railing and continued for almost one hundred fifty feet before Nick released the brake, turned a hard left and pulled the brake again, sliding through the 'S' curve.

Up ahead was the course Nick used to practice more difficult maneuvers and he headed straight for it. The first maneuver was a series of straight cones placed only meters apart and he downshifted once again as he approached. With tight controlled maneuvering through the cones, the agent was tossed back and forth, his arms and hands trying to grab anything that would hold him in place. Never having experienced car sickness before, he cupped his hand over his mouth as the Porsche slid backwards into a full one-hundred and eighty degree turn, coming to a dead stop.

The agent's head bounced hard against the headrest and he felt a sharp, stinging pain shoot down his neck and through his right arm as a nerve had been pinched by the quick snapping and recoil of his head.

Grabbing the handle and shoving the door open, the agent was just able to get his head outside before vomiting onto the asphalt. "What the fuck do you think you're doing? I ought to have your ass thrown into jail for endangering the life of a federal agent. You prick!"

"You need to get out from behind that desk and enjoy life a little more, Hoskins." Nick was enjoying the moment, but in the back of his mind, knew it would be short lived.

"When we get inside, you had better have something to wash out this taste. I'm going to remember this, Nick." The agent now realized he should have known better to mention the car incident and what would follow. He had allowed himself to think West would have let bygones be bygones and now regretted that conclusion. Already, he was savoring the moment he could get back at his ex-partner and he prayed it would be soon.

The men drove the rest of the way back to the office in silence. As they walked towards the building, Hoskins noted the absence of windows and the large commercial air conditioning unit sitting on the roof. Along one of the walls were three single bay door garages, each having its own lock keypad and finger print scanner. "Pretty high tech for a building located out in the middle of nowhere. Are you expecting some kind of theft?"

"I like keeping what's mine, mine," said Nick. "So, can you tell me what this is about before we get inside?"

"As much as I might want to, it's all going to depend upon Baker. You really are secondary in this operation, Nick. If I had any choice in this matter, I wouldn't even have you involved in this operation but, unfortunately, it's not up to me."

"Then I'll wait," said Nick.

As they came to the entry door, the same security was displayed as had been on the garage entrances. Nick quickly ran the lock sequence then placed his hand on the scanner. A digital voice told him he had been authenticated and both heard the door unlock. Once inside, Hoskins stopped cold to look around at the series of databanks, screens and computer equipment lined up in neat rows along the raised flooring. Adjacent to the equipment sat Baker at a keyboard, staring at the different large screens and occasionally typing indiscriminate keystrokes. The results of his actions were immediately shown on the screen.

"What's going on here, Nick? What are you into these days?"

"I can only tell you I am involved in other global interests, and what you are seeing is legit, completely approved by all governments. Besides, Baker needed a place to grow his skills." West waited for the agent to respond with a threat, but it didn't come. For the first time today, the agent seemed to mellow and reprise his old personality of once having been a decent partner to West.

Hoskins continued to look around as they approached Baker's station. "I don't want to know anything you are up to, West. It's probably better I don't know, and we have enough to worry about right now."

Baker saw the men coming and tapped a few more keystrokes before standing. All of the screens went blank, except one. On it displayed a logo for Nick's company.

"Baker, this is Special Assistant to the Director of the CIA, Daniel Hoskins. He wants a word with you and asked that I just listen to what he has to say. Whatever it is, this is about you, not me."

The two men shook hands as Hoskins leaned back against Baker's desk. "Less than eleven hours ago, a very highly classified file was stolen and downloaded from the DOD's computer banks. Whoever did it, penetrated a series of firewalls we thought couldn't be hacked. Only a small number of people - and I mean small - knew of the file's existence. We need to find it and we need to find it now."

"What type of file?" asked Baker.

Hoskins cleared his throat before continuing. "The file contains information about our entire informant network, safe houses, pass codes, accounts, everything in one basket. Some stupid son-of-a-bitch thought it would be less work on them to keep all of the information in one place in order to make it easier and faster to access. The only smart thing he did was use your application to make the file 128 bit encrypted. So now, whoever has it, it's going to take them a while to decrypt it regardless of how sophisticated or high-tech they are. Without keys, it could take a very long time. That's why we came to you."

"You came to me because you think I'm the only one who can break the encryption code?"

"Actually, Baker, we came to you because we need you to track who stole the file and destroy it before that someone has a chance to break it. With the keys, you can open the file and destroy its contents. We don't necessarily need it back. We just want to make sure no one else gets the information it contains."

"What about the original file? If I know what's on that, it will give me more patterns to search than just for a file name." asked Baker.

Hoskins was already prepared with a lie to this question. "Deleted by the thief on his way out, so there's only the original copy that was stolen." In actuality, the agent knew it had been moved off of the server so no one could access it now, nor ever find its new location.

"You said it has been over eleven hours. If it was a theft for profit, then whoever took it, I'm sure they have passed it along to the customer and they already have a number of techs working around the clock on it right now. It's probably sitting on a secured dedicated server somewhere, inaccessible from the outside."

"I hope you're wrong. Look, we know that the file contains your brand signature and that only you know how to trace it quicker through the internet networks than anyone we have. You know how to open the encryption and obliterate the contents. Our techs would only be making educated guesses at this point. We have tried breaching your code, but no luck. It's proprietary, but the algo…, the alget, whatever it's called, it's in your head."

"Algorithm?' asked Baker.

"Yes, that's it, along with the keys needed to crack the encryption."

Baker turned to Nick, then back to Hoskins. "You forget that I work for Mr. West now, and I am very happy where I am. Because of DHS once tagging me as a threat to national security, you can only guess that I am not to keen on helping you out. You guys were stupid enough to get it stolen from you, you find it."

Hoskins paused for a moment, trying to decide if he really wanted to make the next statement, and found he had no other option. Time was critical. "I have been authorized to have all past and remaining charges against you dropped and to purge your records of anything involving that episode of your life. In addition, you will be fully reinstated, along with a sizable jump in grade and the title of 'Associate Director of Strategic Development and Analysis.' You will only have to answer to the director, who only has to answer to the President. Whatever you need or want, will be at your disposal."

For a moment, Baker was speechless. "Only if I help you find this file, right? I have full authority and access?"

"Yes, if those are your conditions."

Once again Baker turned to Nick, then back to the agent. "You just want me to pack up and come back to Arlington immediately? What about my commitment to Mr. West here? I can't have ever asked for a better man to work for and I'm damn sure he won't screw me somewhere down the road like you guys did."

Hoskins face was beginning to redden as he stood up straight. "Make a choice, now. Mr. West is going to be busy tracking down the killer who shot his friend Paul Davis and he's going to do it with our full blessings!" The agent closed his eyes, realizing he had never had the chance to tell Nick that information before this moment.

"What are you talking about, Hoskins? Laura and I just had dinner with Paul six nights ago at his home in Virginia. For Christ sakes, he has a daughter that just graduated from Yale." Nick was recalling the hug the girl had given him as he left. "Laura and I are her Godparents!"

"Nick, that's not the way I wanted you to hear it. Whoever stole the file, shot and killed him as he was coming to the rescue of another man. We don't know all of the details yet, but I need to know if you are both 'in' before I can tell you any more."

"Give me ten minutes to get my belongings together and make a call to Laura. She needs to hear this news from me. It's up to Baker if he wants to do this, but I'm 'in' for my part."

Baker didn't hesitate, either, and grabbed his computer bag, tossed in a laptop, a couple of other items and shook his head that he too was on board with whatever Nick was about to become involved with.

"Glad to hear it," the agent replied. As Hoskins turned towards the door, he shouted back at Nick, "By the way, I'm riding back with Baker; I'm sure you understand!"

Chapter 3

On the drive to the Atlanta airport, the SA began to bring Nick and Baker up to speed on what he knew so far. There was a lot of missing information that had yet to be determined or verified, but what he told them, he made sure they understood that all he told them was classified. Until their phones could be secured, no conversations were to be made using them.

The agent checked his watch. "Approximately eleven and a half hours ago, a file was downloaded to an IP address the FBI had been watching for weeks. Over the course of their investigations, they discovered an individual had been downloading banking information and selling it along with other information he was able to export through a program he had written himself and was running on several phantom systems. They had not made an arrest yet as they had not been able to determine if the sub was working for someone else or just himself. Then this file gets downloaded and all hell breaks lose."

Baker asked, "Had he ever broken into any government facilities before?"

"From what they are telling me, he was not targeting any specific type of business or organization. It appears his program simply searched by IP address and when it found an unsecured computer, it just started downloading files, then went to the next open IP address it found and replicated the next search pattern."

"That wouldn't make sense, then, that it was able to hack a military or government system. There is so much security, there would have to be a backdoor or secondary hidden password assigned that the user would have to already know about."

"Or it was given to him by someone on the inside." added Nick.

"Yes, that crossed our minds, but we did polygraphs on anyone who had access and checked bank records. Nothing. Everyone was clean."

"Ok, what next?" asked Nick.

"When our agents arrived at the sub's apartment, they found the guy dead. His body was still warm when they got there. The coroner said he couldn't have been dead for more than twenty minutes as the body temp was almost normal."

"How was he killed?" said Baker.

"Well, that's just it. It looked like an accident. The preliminary findings indicated the guy fell getting out of the shower, breaking his spine and shattering his skull. There were no other markings on his body that would indicate foul play. There was a very small bruise behind his left foot, but that could have been sustained when he fell. There were a few minute towel fibers around the face, but again, it could have been from him drying his face and missing his step."

"So what makes you think it wasn't an accident?"

The agent looked at Nick. "The finger imprints we found on the screens and a couple of drives that someone touched."

Baker corrected Hoskins. "You mean fingerprints, right?"

"I mean exactly what I said, imprints. The finger tips on each hand had either been burned or sanded off smooth. The only thing left are the outlines of the individual fingers. If the guy was sanding his finger tips, he had to be doing it on a regular basis as the tissue eventually grows back."

"Then this is a professional hit and not just someone sent to retrieve a file. What else?" asked Nick.

The agent continued. "One of the drives is missing, which we have to assume contains the file. The killer realigned the drives hoping that whoever found the mess would miss the fact that one had been stolen.

Apparently he did not have time to download the information to another media."

"Do you think he was interrupted or heard someone else outside the apartment?" asked Baker.

"The report indicates a roommate was in the apartment when they arrived. He didn't know anything about Albright, and based upon a toxicology screen, was too drunk to even carry on a coherent conversation even after eight hours of trying to sober him up. He is still being questioned, though."

Passing through the airport gates, everyone decided to hold further questions until they were in the air. Once in the air, the agent opened and handed a folder to Baker containing images of the apartment, the dead man on the bathroom floor and all other shots the forensic photographer had taken. Since Baker was primary on this, Nick would have to wait until he had finished before he could read the report. The agent sensed the annoyance Nick was feeling and contained the small victory he was feeling.

Letting Baker read through the file for a few minutes, the agent finally broke the silence. "Baker, once we touch down, a car will take us directly to headquarters where you will meet and begin working with Director Nathan Chau. I know you are familiar with his work and you two should get along fine."

"Yes, I do know about Chau. It will be an honor working with him and I'm looking forward to getting the chance to pick his brain. The man's knowledge of the internet infrastructure is second to none. "

"Good. You will work with him, and another assistant by the name of Dr. Mary Brandt, exclusively. She is to assist you, nothing more. You will report directly to Director Chau and only to him. Whatever you find, you discuss your findings with Chau first before Brandt is to be told."

"Who's Dr. Brandt? I've never heard of her and frankly, I don't want her around." said Baker.

The agent smiled. "Somehow, I think you're going to change your mind. She has been mentoring under Chau for almost six months and when I say she has been spending every waking hour with him, I mean it. Her intellect is like no one I have ever encountered. Her mind is like an insatiable sponge. Tell her something once and you will never have to tell her again because she remembers every word. Mathematics is her forte. She can figure out an answer in her head almost as fast as you can explain a problem to her. She's also damn easy on the eyes."

Baker looked at the agent with a smirk on his face. "I've known some of the brainiest chicks you can ever imagine and I promise you, none fit the definition of being *hot*. Intelligent, hell yes, I can agree with that. But, both hot and intelligent in this field? I'll reserve my comments."

"OK, but don't say I didn't give you fair warning. There's a reason Chau had no problem with this woman coming to work for him and providing her with all the necessary clearance that was required."

Chapter 4

He had missed his appointment and flight, which at the moment was the least of his concerns. The bullet had torn a gash in his forehead, leaving a wound which still continued to bleed. If he was unable to stop the flow, he would have to suture the two edges of the tissue together himself and place a bandage on it that could mean possible questioning by airport security. That was to be avoided at all costs. It also meant he would carry a very visible scar that could be identified by bystanders during future operations and missions.

His other fear was that the authorities would now have a sample of his DNA from the blood splattered on the interior of the car when he was hit. Although they would never find a match in any of their domestic databases, there was a very small chance they would from Interpol. He had paid a hefty amount to a highly skilled hacker to remove all traces of his personal, agency and military records, shooting the hacker through the side of his head once he was assured there was nothing left for anyone to find.

The hacker begged for his life and just as the man pulled the trigger, the hacker screamed out "Interpol!" and left him wondering if there actually had been a singular bit of data remaining on him. That was six years ago, and so far he had not been captured or had ever intercepted any information that he was a person of interest from any past job.

He never felt any guilt in taking the life of a man, woman or child as long as his temporary employer paid his fee, and on time. Only once did he ever have to set an example for other payees, letting them know what would happen should they fail in meeting his demands once the job was completed.

As he applied pressure to the wound, he thought back to the events of the last several hours, wondering how he had been discovered so quickly and who had known where he would be at the time of his retrieval of the stolen data. There had been men on his tail within minutes of leaving the apartment and they even tried killing him in view of other *innocents*, as he thought of them.

Why had one man identified himself, while the other had not? The first man began shooting at him as soon as he had exited the vehicle, the other screamed at him to drop his weapon and flashed a badge while doing so. There had been two different types of efforts to catch or eliminate him, both failing with the loss of lives. Was it possible that two separate groups had found him at the exact same time? It was impossible, he told himself.

A second explanation began to form in his thoughts. The buyer had sent one or more men to follow him and retrieve the drive once he had found its location. The rest of the orders would have been to kill him before he completed the mission and called for final payment. That would mean the buyer had never had any intention of completing the contract. There could be no other explanation. But why take the chance of buying a government man, and what was his connection to the buyer?

After making sure he would soon deal with the buyer properly, he would have to investigate further and learn who the other assailant was, and who shot him. Was it a miss by the unknown shooter or was the second man really the intended target?

Pulling the bandage from the wound, he was pleased to see the bleeding had stopped. He stood and approached the mirror to determine what he would need to do to minimize the gross appearance of the wound. Suturing would be required, but if he groomed his hair in a different style and direction, he could successfully hide the slash. He also knew, by pulling the edges of tissue and suturing them together, it would change the shape of his natural hairline, so there was little choice but to alter his hairstyle.

He selected a small curved needle from his medical kit, threaded it and meticulously connected and closed the ripped tissue. He noted his left eyebrow was raised slightly, so he trimmed the brows to give them an even appearance. Applying a very small piece of surgical tape, he stepped forward to look at the damage in the large rectangular mirror, turning the switch on a nearby table lamp for extra light.

After examining the taped wound from several different angles, he stepped back and walked towards a wardrobe closet. Inside, he selected a black semi-formal tuxedo jacket to go with the rest of his attire. With the exception of his white shirt, the rest of his clothing was black, as well. This was his normal business outfit and all his clothing had been tailored to fit perfectly around the .45 caliber Colt.

By the time he had finished visiting the current buyer and settled their misunderstanding, he would hopefully look better and well enough to pass through airport security undetected. Once home, he would need to rest and alter his looks further in order to stay as average and unnoticeable looking as possible. The eventual course of having plastic surgery to erase the scar would have to wait until he could afford the time demanded to have it performed.

Satisfied that he was ready, he closed the door behind him, exited the hotel and walked the two blocks to a private garage he had leased for one month under a bogus name. He would only need it for a maximum of twenty-four hours, but the lease would delay any search until twenty-four hour leases were completed.

Just in case someone had stumbled into the garage by mistake, he had covered the stolen black Corvette with an old tarp so no one would remember seeing it. It would also give them the illusion that whatever was underneath was probably some old car the owner had abandoned, and not worth taking a look at.

He looked at his watch and calculated the time needed to arrive at the buyer's house, settle the debt and return to get his things before heading out to the airport. With the set of license tags changed on the car already, it was doubtful he would be spotted in traffic as long as he stayed true to the posted speed limits. As he had done many times before, he had already planned and mentally reviewed the necessary escape plans required for this particular situation, should he be interrupted while collecting on the debt.

As he pulled out of the garage, he phoned the buyer and advised him of the expected time of his arrival, having added twenty minutes to the estimate. It would give him the added time he needed to look around the perimeter and determine how many additional guards had been stationed, and where. With the house's layout, he had already studied the blueprints and mapped out his exact exit strategy in advance, as this would need to be a quick visit.

Chapter 5

It had been nearly an hour since the phone call, and Julio Santiago was beginning to get very nervous. It was not like his visitor to be late or not follow the exact instructions as he had always in the past. Santiago had never met the man and knew him only through a contact number, but the man had always been professional in every aspect of their arrangements.

There was something wrong and he didn't like it. Perhaps the thief had discovered he had altered the plan by sending his man to kill him and take what he had stolen, hoping to avoid the delivery fee the man had demanded. If that were the case, he would be dead before the next hour was over.

Making his way through his home, he hesitated only briefly to view the beautiful paintings and the craftsman's intricate detail which had been carved into the dark cherry woodwork throughout the mansion. The mansion was built in the early nineteen twenties and covered over 28,000 square feet, taking seven years to complete. He had been able to acquire the dwelling from the previous owner due to an unpaid debt he had masterminded himself through his holding company.

The daily interest fees which Santiago had hidden so surreptitiously within the wording of the contract, had caused the mortgaged amount to grow at such an astronomical rate, the owner was unable to pay it back to Santiago's bank. The owner was given the choice of signing over the house title to him before foreclosure was necessary or watching the members of his family suffer in front of him one by one. Knowing how they would be tortured before a bullet was mercifully put through each of their heads, especially his daughter and wife, the owner's decision was immediate. One year later, the family perished on Safari while vacationing in Africa. Ultimately, it was ruled an accident due to the driver venturing off course and flipping the jeep they were riding in. The bullet that had penetrated the driver's head was never reported.

Santiago headed upstairs, turned right on the landing, and walked down a long corridor equipped with overhead cameras that had been built into the ceiling but invisible to anyone looking up. Now the owner, Santiago had added a family 'Panic' room after taking possession of the property. At his level of wealth, there was always the possibility of thieves making their way in undetected. He also knew that anyone could be bought and money easily turned a friend into an enemy. Many wealthy and successful men had overlooked that fact and paid for it dearly, sometimes with their lives.

Once the alarm code was set from the inside after entering, and the door was closed on the Panic room, there was no way of reentering again without the door being electronically or manually unlocked from the inside. The only override was a direct verifiable vocal communication from the owner to the security firm. The only other way inside was using a welding torch to cut through the door hinges. That method would take almost an hour, and by then, it would most likely be too late if it were a true emergency. Mounted along the inside wall overlooking a desk console were several dozen perimeter monitors showing every foot of the property and interior of the home.

Julio checked his watch one more time before entering the room and pulling the door shut. As it closed, he punched in the code and watched as the twenty plus monitors came to life and the air filtration kicked in and began to fill the room with the purest of oxygen. He would observe all activity inside and outside the home from within its walls and would exit the room once he knew he was safe. For now, he would sit back, enjoy one or more of his large selection of illegal Cuban cigars and wait.

After selecting a cigar, he snipped off one end and quickly lit the other. Dragging hard, he sucked the smoke deep into his lungs and let the aroma penetrate his nostrils, passing through and over the fine hair follicles inside his nose. It was an intoxicating smell and he was questioning why he had not enjoyed this more often. Through the smoke, he gazed as his men took their assigned positions, watching for any movement that they knew could happen at any moment.

A fist slammed hard into his neck at the base of his skull and the cigar was ejected from his mouth onto the console underneath the bank of monitors. Next he felt fingers clamp down on his shoulder like a vise, the pain ripping through every fiber of his body. He tried struggling to free himself by punching at the hand that held him, but his attempts failed as its fingers clamped down harder. Within seconds, he felt his arms and legs go numb, unable to move them in any direction. He tried to lean forward and use his head to hit the speaker button and alert the men outside, but the chair was yanked backwards before he was able to do so.

His mouth and eyes were wide open as he was spun around to look at his attacker. The man's fingers continued to clamp down on the shoulder, cutting off all impulses to the nerve endings of his extremities. He could feel his chest starting to heave and he was beginning to find it impossible to breathe normally.

"Mr. Santiago. Is there a reason you chose to hide instead of facing and telling me the truth about the two men you sent to kill me? It would have been a lot wiser on your part to have confronted me instead of cowering in this sanctuary," said the man.

Santiago began to speak, but the words were barely audible and the man leaned in closer. "I'm sorry, I had no choice. I should have kept my word. I was afraid. Please don't kill me!"

"Oh, now is when you should be afraid. If you had faced me like a man, I would have killed you cleanly, but now we are going to have to reconcile this matter less to your liking. Unfortunately, I have very little time, so let's make this quick."

"I will give you whatever you want. Money, cars, this home, but please, don't hurt me." Santiago was sobbing, his throat was dry, but his eyes were full of tears and his upper lip began to be covered with small streams of mucus from his nose.

"I'm going to loosen my grip in approximately three minutes. At that time you are going to start getting feeling back in your arms and legs. Either you have answered my questions truthfully by then or you will be dead."

Santiago saw a ray of hope. "If, if I do, you will let me live?"

"If, and only if you answer me truthfully. With regards to your money, I have already emptied your account of the two million you were paid to obtain the data. Did you not think I would know about that arrangement? Cars, I don't need them."

Saliva had begun to moisten the man's throat again and he spoke more clearly. "My house, you can have my house!"

The attacker looked at the man with a smile. "Mr. Santiago. I would never take this house from you. You love this home you stole from Mr. Martinez, and its exquisite beauty. There is nothing more precious to you. You take tremendous satisfaction in looking at its rich interiors, the paintings and seeing your family's pride as they walk through it with you. No, you may keep it."

Santiago closed his eyes and mumbled the words, "Thank you." The man was right. He loved the home more than his own family, but he would never admit that. If he were unable to see its elegance every day, he knew he would never be able to get over the heartache and would rather be dead. He would gladly give away everything he owned to possess this one jewel.

The attacker knew time was running short and it was necessary to get the answers he needed. "I'm going to ask you two questions. Any hesitation, or if you lie, I will kill you. Understood?"

Santiago shook his head quickly up and down.

"Who paid you to obtain the data from me once I retrieved it?"

"I don't know his name, but the contact information is in my wallet. It was his idea to have you killed, not mine. I was to call the number and all further instructions for the drop off were to be given to me at that time."

The man reached down, pulled the wallet from Santiago's back pocket and thumbed through it until he came upon a piece of folded paper. "Is this it?"

"Yes, that's the number!" The man could tell Santiago was telling the truth.

"Good. Now, who were the two men you hired to kill me and bring back the stolen drive to you?"

Santiago had a look of confusion on his face. "I only sent one man, not two. I don't know who the other man is you are talking about."

The invader picked up the cigar and blew steadily on the lit end, the tobacco ash turning a red hot glow. "Are you sure you have no idea?"

"I swear to God, I only sent one!" Santiago began to snivel again.

Time was up and the man grabbed Santiago by his hair, pulling his head backwards with his face pointing straight towards the ceiling. His eyes were wide open with his limbs immobile, still dangling by his sides.

"I told you I wouldn't take your house, but I will take your ability to see its magnificence." With that, he placed the burning end of the cigar directly into each eye until they burst open, before releasing Santiago's head.

Santiago was still screaming as the man punched in the lock's code, slid out the door and closed it solidly behind him, making sure the lock set securely.

Up ahead were two guards with their backs facing towards him, engaged in small talk. They would only be expecting someone trying to enter the compound, not exiting it. As he approached, he raised the silenced .45, pulled the trigger twice and strolled past the fallen men. Ten yards to his left sat the black Corvette, parked in the owner's driveway. No one had thought to keep an eye on or check the half dozen parked luxury cars. They assumed they all belonged to Santiago.

Chapter 6

The chopper ride directly from the airport to the underground facility had taken less than fifteen minutes. After going through the numerous required security checks, Hoskins, West and Baker were escorted through a series of tunnels leading to the compound and the lab of Director Chau. Once inside the main complex, Baker stopped to look around at the rows of large scale mainframes leading into a central processing area.

As they walked further into the interior, he saw a very large circular glass enclosed room where a group of technicians were moving about their daily assignments. Around the enclosure were guards stationed precisely twenty five feet apart, completely surrounding the glass enclosed structure. He glanced at West, but could see that West's indifference gave the impression that he had already been here on other occasions. They would have to talk later.

Entering through several panels of doors, Baker saw for the first time a man and a woman standing over a console, exchanging gestures and words. With their heads down, neither Chau nor Brandt saw them approach and were startled by the interruption. As Brandt stood straight and turned towards Baker, Baker fully understood what Hoskins meant. He would make it a priority to treat Hoskins to his favorite restaurant in exchange for pairing them together.

Extending his hand towards Director Chau, Baker introduced himself and the two exchanged pleasantries, along with words of admiration for one another's work. It turned out that Chau was as excited to be working with Baker as he was with Chau. They both knew they would greatly benefit from each other's experience and intellect.

Baker turned to Brandt only to find her hand already extended and showing a perfect smile that made him pause before greeting her. The last thing he wanted to do was come across boyish and stupid, so he kept the greeting short and simple, making Brandt wonder if she was losing her charm or if perhaps Baker was playing for the 'opposite team.'

West and Hoskins stood back, waiting for the formalities to be completed, then Hoskins signaled to West that it was time for them to talk. Hoskins looked at Baker and said, "We are still waiting on your credentials, so make sure you only travel within the complex with Director Chau or Brandt. Once you get them, make sure they are very visible. Otherwise, these guards will be only too happy to ruin your day."

Baker took a quick glance around the room and shook his head to Hoskins indicating he understood and would have no trouble complying with the directive. It was time for West and Hoskins to find another area to talk. Both men turned and left the enclosure.

Once they had entered another secured office within the complex, Nick took a seat across the table from SA Hoskins. Baker had been left with Chau and Brandt to begin a review of the complex's network structure. From there, Baker would start the necessary protocol of putting out sniffers and tracers in hopes of getting a hit on the file's whereabouts. If they could just map a quadrant within a ten mile radius, it would be a great start. Their hopes were high, but everyone knew it could be a very long waiting game with only a very small window of opportunity. They would have to be ready to react immediately and it would require an extreme amount of coordination and group effort to pinpoint the location.

Only by chance, if the file were being transferred to another IP address, would they be able to identify Baker's signature encryption. After that, it would be a race to catch and stop it from being fully downloaded. From there, they would have to backtrack and find the source location from which the file was being transferred in order to truly stop further attempts. Baker could kill the transfer, but the source file was what they were after.

Hoskins handed West an envelope containing what the CIA knew about the theft and who might be the buyer. Since the data had been collected by the CIA, Nick was certain that he would end up throwing the information out and in all likelihood, need to start over. To his surprise, the information was unexpectedly detailed and seemed to carry a high degree of accuracy. Also included were forensic photos of the apartment, the victim and the victim's computer and additional equipment layout. He had seen these before on the plane, but these were shot from different angles. What was missing from the bundle was any information on the suspected thief himself. There was a list of names of potential names and West recognized most of them.

West looked at Hoskins. "There is nothing here on who stole the drive."

"That's because we don't have any information. Neither does DHS, MI5, MI6, the CIA or Interpol. We can tie this person's MO into at least a dozen or so data thefts around the country and a couple of killings in the last couple of years, but hell, we don't even know if it's a man or a woman. This person, in every sense of the word, is a ghost. The closest we have to identifying who he or she is are the *imprints* I mentioned to you and Baker earlier. The size of the imprints would certainly indicate it's a man, but we really aren't sure.

West was trying to determine where to begin his questioning. "So how do I even initiate a search for this person if there is nothing we or I can go by?"

"I would say that's your problem, but the fact is, we think whoever he or she is, has more to do with this than just stealing the drive. I can't say what, but it's just a hunch based upon my experience."

"So the CIA's not interested in finding out who killed one of its agents, they just want the return or destruction of the data?" West was beginning to think his friend Paul had died for nothing and his death had no significance to the branch of government he had given his life for.

"DHS will run its own investigation and you are more than welcome to pass along any information you find on this individual. I'm sorry for your personal loss, but right now we need everyone concentrating on finding that data. We will honor our dead when the time is right, but right now you need to find this person and return or destroy what he or she stole."

West knew Hoskins was right, but there was something in the SA's voice that told him he wasn't being given the most important details. "I think there is something on that drive that you're holding back on telling me. I understand the full importance of protecting our country's information, but bringing Baker back the way you did, to this locale? There's a big piece of the puzzle you're leaving out. What is it?"

Hoskins leaned across the table and hesitated before speaking. "Your job is to find the person who stole that drive, once Baker determines its whereabouts. If you find that person and the drive before someone else does, put a bullet through both of them and call it a day. If we find the person before you do, we only care about destroying the information. Other than that, there's nothing more you need to know."

"Something has you and a bunch of other people scared. What's on that file, Hoskins? What's the reason you want it so bad that your only concern is for it and not the murder of an agent? If I remember correctly, that was always every agency's top priority once."

"Story telling time is over, West. Find the man or women and do with them however you see fit. Whoever you have to deal with or whatever you have to do to find them, I don't give a rat's ass. You said you wanted in, so find your friend's murderer. Baker and Chau will find the drive and what's on it. That is our concern, so leave it at that!" Hoskins' face was flushed and Nick knew if he continued to push, he could find himself dismissed and asked to leave. He would have to find another way to get what he was after.

"Ok, I'll leave it at that for now, but you know that if you're hiding something, I will discover what it is. If it puts me in jeopardy because you failed to tell me in time, you and I will meet again. So, before I walk out that door, do you want to reconsider your response?"

Hoskins knew that West could and would keep his word on the threat and understood what he meant by 'meet again.' With West's ability to resolve any issue his way without any government interference or consequences, it was no bluff and a deadly risk he was taking by holding back information. This was not a subordinate he could easily manipulate: it was a man who would hold a grudge forever if screwed with. Payback time was something he would fear for the rest of his career if he did not handle this properly.

Letting out a sigh, Hoskins knew he had better at least give West something to go on. "All right, shit! I'll tell you what limited information I have, but that's it. If you breathe a word of this, though, you and I are likely never to be seen again."

West sat back down. He had not wanted to threaten a man who was once his friend, but he also didn't want to go into a situation blind. Whatever Hoskins was about to tell him, he would be grateful for and try to accept Hoskins' word that what he was being told was in part the truth.

"It's very complicated. What I am about to tell you does have us all unnerved, but not for the reasons you might think. If we don't find the file and destroy it before someone else is able to obtain the information on it, it's going to be real shit storm for all of us."

"By all of us, who do you mean?" asked West.

Hoskins ignored the question and decided to start by asking West one of his own. "Have you ever heard of an operation named 'Recall'?"

"No, I'm not familiar with it," replied Nick.

"That doesn't surprise me. It's been so classified that only a few people know about it. Trust me when I say it will never be declassified. Those that had any knowledge of it have been paid very well to keep it that way."

"So tell me what this is about, or at least what you can tell me."

Hoskins nodded and took a seat again across from West. "Back in the late sixties, the US government became extremely interested in what the human mind was capable of. We have all heard about the LSD experiments, things like that. For the CIA, it was all about information and intel, who had it, how it could be obtained, how it could be used and how to keep what we knew out of the hands of other countries. At that time, information was documented either on paper, recorded magnetic tapes, or microfilm."

"Easy to steal, lose or destroy," said Nick.

"You've got it. There was a lot of demonstrating going on in the seventies with the Viet Nam War and a tremendous amount of concern that the information could perish in a fire or be stolen and used against us. There were spies everywhere including our own, and having double agents serving in our ranks was the greatest threat."

"I'm not sure why the US is concerned about information from the sixties and seventies being a national threat now. Does this have to do with the informants you mentioned earlier?" Nick was trying to read ahead of Hoskins, but couldn't see where this was going yet.

"I told you, it's very complicated, and that is only a small issue in the whole picture. Let me continue, before you ask any more questions. There are other pieces I need to explain."

"Ok. I'll shut up and listen." Nick responded.

"There are people in this world who have special abilities beyond what most humans are capable of. They can retain everything they have ever encountered because their minds never forget. With some, it's what they read. Others, it's what they see or hear. Once that information has passed into their conscious, it's never forgotten, and these people can recite that information or visual experience, word for word, decades later, even up until they are on their deathbeds."

Hoskins stopped to look at West to see if he was going to ask a question. When he saw West nodding his head that he already knew this information, he continued.

"There were eleven people in this group involved in the project. They all shared this ability. For three years, they ingested every secret the United States had on their enemies as well as allies. They were given every operative's name and assignments, their safe-house locations, the information the operatives were passing to whom, who they were getting it from, everything. They were also specially trained to defend themselves and to disappear from the world around them. Even our own government couldn't and didn't want to know their whereabouts."

"So how would they be contacted if the information they had was needed?"

"Through a series of articles placed in the newspapers around the world. Each person was given specific details on what to look for. If the subject and sequence of articles pertained to them, they knew to contact their personal handler. They were paid very well through the use of buried bank accounts and were required to hide until they were needed. The accounts were easily accessible by them, but untraceable by us. The deposits were coded for the individual person that the government had no ability to track once the deposits were sent out."

West changed positions in his chair. "I'm still not following why the government has their concerns forty some years later."

Hoskins continued without skipping a beat. "As the world advanced in technology, the information given to these people was transferred to computers where security was more available and could be easily accessed if needed or duplicated and stored off site."

"So these eleven people are no longer needed and now their lives are basically meaningless to the government?"

"Yep, or at least that is what a subcommittee thought, and cancelled funding for the project without advising anyone involved of their actions. Those eleven people went from having a nice living to having nothing and not being able to secure a living doing anything else because of the restrictions and obligations as employees of the US government. Remember, these people don't exist to the rest of the world, so they can't just waltz in from nowhere and get a normal job."

"So what happened next?" Nick was starting to get an uneasy feeling that things were about to turn very bad for the forgotten group.

"About a year after funding stopped, some of the information that had been given to them started to leak into the papers. The CIA found evidence that one of the eleven was selling secrets, so it sent out a team to find and persuade them all to come in. Two came in, but the rest went into hiding, saying they were afraid of their own government. Imagine that!"

"What happened to the two that came in?" Nick was looking right into Hoskins' eyes as he asked.

"I don't know, and I'm being honest with you. Look: if the data on that file gets out, the remaining mem-bers of that group are going to be hunted down by other governments for what they know. If those regimes can get pejorative information on their enemies which can justify retaliation efforts, they will do whatever is necessary to find them, even if the information is no longer significant."

Nick stood slowly, leaning in towards Hoskins. With Hoskins telling him straight up that he was being honest with him, it meant that he wasn't. "You know what I think? I think our government is afraid for itself because the remaining associates who are left know what happened to their other two team members, and it wasn't pretty."

"No one does, Nick. I'm telling you there is nothing in the files anywhere that mentions what happened." Even Hoskins knew that was a straight out lie, but he could not afford to let West know that information.

Nick shook his head and continued. "Our government isn't out to keep quiet the information those people were taught or learned from all of that reading. It's the dirty little secret of what they did to those people. If the file is destroyed, no one will ever know about the operation and they are hoping the rest of the team members will eventually die from old age, taking with them all details and the secret."

Hoskins was stuttering. "You're nuts, West! There's no way our government would treat their own people that way."

"Jesus, you really are stupid, aren't you, Hoskins?" West pushed away his chair and headed for the door. "I'm going to find your man or woman, but the information on that drive is going to stay intact until I find out what's on it."

"That's not possible, West! I told you before, it's encrypted. If you find that drive, you destroy it immediately. Don't even bring it back!" Hoskins was beginning to show signs of becoming extremely anxious. His face was turning red as sweat began to dot across his forehead.

West stopped and turned back towards Hoskins. As he stared at the agent, he thought back to when both men would have laid down their lives for one another and wondered what had happened to his friend. For the first time in a long while, he actually felt some compassion for the man.

"Dan, there's only one reason this file is so important. Whatever is on that drive could implicate some-one very high up of wrong doing. Who is it? There is no other explanation as to why there is so much secrecy surrounding this mission. Whatever is on that drive is history that is, without a doubt, already known by every country that had any conflict with the United States or any other countries during that time. This is the age of information and trust me, it's been shared by everyone. So your explanation is crap."

Hoskins bowed his head for what seemed to him a long time, then looked at West. "I can't tell you, Nick. Honest to God, I would tell you if I could, but I wouldn't make it out of here alive if anyone knew I told you. Go back home and start your research. The only thing I can do is send you what information I have on the remaining people in the group. From there, it's up to you to find whatever you can. Once you have the files I send you, I don't want to hear from you again until you are able to tell me you've found the thief and drive and eradicated both."

"No promises. You just get me that information as quickly as you can. I should be back in Atlanta in a couple of hours."

As West opened the door, Hoskins echoed a warning. "West, if you find out what happened to those people, just accept that what is done is done. You can't help them and if you try to pursue it, people are going to die, starting with everyone you know and care about."

"If you tell me right now that if our government silenced those people, it was done to protect our country, then I will. If it was for any other reason, then I will make sure that whoever was responsible for the deaths of those American lives will be exposed for what they did."

Hoskins knew that he could offer West nothing else and that he was also looking at a soon-to-be dead man. And yet, he felt he owed this man something. "Keep your family safe. Whoever stole that drive is injured and they are most likely looking for some kind of retaliation. If they think you were involved with the attempt to capture them, there's no telling what they will do to get even."

Chapter 7

Elizabeth Lane, '*Liz*' as most of her friends called her, looked intently at the small manila envelope in front of her as she worked at aligning the last finger on her left hand into the small opening of the latex glove. Having broken the pinky finger during a softball game years earlier, it never healed properly and remained slightly bent outwards away from her ring finger.

Even though she was their boss, she was well liked by the other techs as she was willing to put in more hours than they did and wasn't hesitant to cover a shift for them if a personal emergency arose. Along with her exceptional knowledge and uncanny ability to discover evidence the others overlooked, she was a natural beauty and a good hearted prankster, even if the joke was on her. She could 'get' as well as 'give' and the respect she received was well earned.

Picking up the airtight envelope, she recorded its size, weight and evidence number C77234-A. Peeling the 'Open' tab, she gently reached in and extracted two plastic bags. The first contained a cut swatch of leather from what appeared to be a car seat cover. The swatch was covered in a dark red gooey substance and from experience, she knew immediately it was blood.

The other bag contained several hair follicles attached to a thin patch of flesh. The edges of the flesh were elongated as if torn away from whatever they were previously attached to. Once again she recorded the size, weight and a brief visual analysis of what the bags held.

She decided to run tests on the bag with the hair follicles first. After cutting away a tiny piece of the flesh holding a few strands of hair, she placed the two separate pieces in different sterile tubes and capped the one with the largest piece, setting it aside for future analysis if needed. Giving it a second thought, she uncapped the tube with the larger piece and cut another single layer, placing into another sterile tube next to her computer.

Plucking a strand of hair from the layer of skin, she cut off the cuticle and placed the other end in a fresh tube. Squirting in two drops of solution, she capped and placed the tube in the spectrometer. Flipping a switch, she watched as it began to spin. Several minutes later, the whirling tray slowed as a printer in the far corner of the lab sprang to life.

Swabbing the swatch of seat cover, she clipped off a piece and inserted it into another tube, repeating the same process as she had for the hair. Just as the printer started to publish the results from both tests, she saw a warning light flash on her monitor, indicating there was a paper jam. With the jam, it meant she would have to rerun the tests if the results had not been automatically saved. Upon examination, she began to swear underneath her breath.

This was the third time it had happened this week and her frustration level had finally peaked. Now that she had to rerun the tests again, she was going to let that little twerp in the IT division have a piece of her mind before she did. With thoughts of homicide, she quickly snatched up the evidence containers and placed them in a holding unit until she could return and run the procedures again.

Turning off the recorder, she slammed the cabinet door shut, locked it, set the alarm and headed down the hall towards IT. Six minutes later, she returned with two technicians in tow, each trying to explain that it was not their fault. They both insisted the paper jams were due to the inferior paper quality the organization had started using in an attempt to cut the budget in all departments. It was affecting everyone and whatever white collar moron signed off on purchasing the paper, should lose their job.

"Just fix it. I've got to rerun all of my tests and get the results over to my supervisor before noon. My job is on the fucking line if I'm late! Do you understand that?"

Lane was even angrier than before and if she could get these two incompetent assholes fired or, at the minimum, transferred, she would see to it once she was finished.

Replenishing the chemicals and readying her equipment to begin, she unlocked the cabinet and opened the doors. Inside, on the shelf where she had placed the evidence, it was empty. As panic began to set in, she searched the other shelves and floor, but found nothing.

Racing back to her console, she flipped on the recorder and backtracked to the starting point of the footage. The initial analysis and the preliminary DNA sampling would be on there and perhaps she could salvage something from that. To her dismay, the recording was blank. She began to tremble. This was a priority one, "eyes only" assignment. The evidence had been handed to her personally by her boss and she had been told to rush it. The CIA Chief had trusted no one else but Lane to handle it.

She looked around and saw three other technicians urgently working on their own assignments, seemingly oblivious to what was happening. She could not get to them fast enough. "Did you see anyone come into the lab while I was gone?" she screamed as she jerked one of the technicians by the shoulder and spun him around.

"What is your problem?" the technician yelled back before realizing who he was talking to. His entire concentration had been on the sample he was looking at through the microscope.

"I'm talking to you and everyone else here!"

"I'm sorry Liz. I didn't know it was you asking." He regained his composure after a short moment of embarrassment, then continued. "Are you kidding, though? Look at the workload we all have! I haven't had time to come up for air, let alone watch your office station. So, no, I didn't see anyone come in."

She turned to the other two, but just stared as they both shook their heads in unison that neither had seen anyone either. Her temples began to throb and she felt her chest beginning to tighten. Seventeen years at this job with numerous promotions and recommendations and it would soon be embarrassingly over. Never had she lost, contaminated or misplaced a single shred of evidence and now she had lost all of it during the most important assigned task of her career. "Fuck!" as she once again screamed under her breath. Someone had come into her lab and stolen the evidence. "Why?" was all she could think of in that instance of rage.

Holding back her tears, she apologized to the technicians and made her way out the door and proceeded to her lab. Standing in the center, she would need to take a few minutes to compose herself and try to think of how she would explain this. If it hadn't been for that stupid printer or 'inferior paper quality', she would be standing in front of her boss right now, having passed along the results, and would surely be getting high praises from her superior.

There was no way of putting it off any longer. She needed to go ahead and face whatever disciplinary action was coming. Hesitating for one final look around, she bent forward to switch off the lab's computer. As she leaned in, she felt a small round cylinder under her hand.

"Oh my God," she could barely hold back a shout as elation began to replace her feeling of dread. It was the capsule containing the second piece of skin and hair that she had cut away. Somehow it must have rolled and latched itself to the underside of the computer cover, and whoever took the other evidence, missed it.

She looked at the clock and saw she still had thirty-seven minutes. The pride and dedication of putting in seventeen long years of hard work, was only moments before, about to be stripped away. Instead, those years were going to be saved by one single strand of flesh and hair.

At precisely 12:27, Lane walked into her boss's office and placed the lab results on her desk. She waited until her boss was off the phone before speaking.

"I'm sorry I took so long, but here are the results of the tests you had me perform on the hair and skin samples taken from that red Buick and shooting last night." Lane started to smile but stopped when she saw her boss looking at her quizzically.

"Why didn't you give this information to Agent Avery? I sent him down almost an hour ago to get the evidence and anything else you had processed. He was taking it directly to Chief Parker."

"No one reported to my lab and I certainly wouldn't have turned it over to someone I didn't know or didn't have proper authorization to do so." Lane's skin began to pale. "What did this agent look like?"

Marla Buckner knew her technicians better than anyone. She knew their personalities, friends and family, but most of all, when something was wrong, and she sensed something was terribly wrong with her number one employee. Grabbing Lane by the arm, she steadied her as they walked towards empty chairs.

What happened, Lane? What's wrong?" It wasn't a question as much as it was demand to know.

"Have you ever seen this person before? Did he or she have a signed authorization to secure the evidence?" Lane was enraged knowing the agent hadn't approached her and signed off for the evidence bags, but instead, took it all, even breaking into her private cabinet to get it.

Buckner was not used to being talked to this way by a subordinate. If it had not been for Lane's outstanding record and the fact that she had solved more crimes with her bizarre research abilities, the conversation would have been over. "I asked you a question, Lane. Answer me!"

"You first! Did you see valid authorization from Agent Avery for the release of the evidence?"

Buckner had to refrain herself from throwing the technician out the door and onto the street. If it had been anyone else, she would have. "Yes, I followed all protocol! Not only did I see the signed request, I also required the agent to show his credentials. Everything was followed exactly by the book."

Lane hesitated and then began to tell her everything. "The agent never showed himself to me. The only plausible answer is that he stole the evidence for some unknown reason."

"You don't think he simply went ahead and took it because he couldn't find you?"

"How many agents do you know that can break into one of our evidence containment units, bypass the alarms, take what they need and be gone in less time than it takes me to walk to the tech desks and return, without anyone noticing them? This wasn't an agent. He knew exactly where to look and what to look for."

Now Buckner understood, but couldn't believe the possibility. "Who the hell would have the knowledge, credentials and balls to walk directly into CIA headquarters and steal evidence from under our noses? They would have to know this place inside and out."

Lane stood and faced Buckner. "I don't know, but whatever he was after, he felt it was worth spending the rest of his life behind bars or possibly even shot if he had been caught and tried to run. I've got to get back to the lab and backup whatever evidence we still have and try to get a facial match from the DNA samples."

Buckner nodded and said, "I'll pull security footage, and if you get a match from the sample, we can see if it could possibly be the same person."

Chapter 8

Baker listened as Dr. Chau explained the next steps in tracking the IP address once the file's signal and name began to transmit from one network address to another. Brandt was leaning in and Baker could feel her right breast pressing into the back of his left arm. It was soft, but firm, and he made no attempt to change his position.

"Once the file begins to transmit, we will have to triangulate on its coordinates as quickly as possible. The hard part will be to determine the receiving IP address and block all transmissions to that address. Do you agree?" asked Dr. Chau.

"I agree, but I don't see that as the most important issue. If we block the file from being received for any length of time, our efforts are likely to become suspect and the sender will either disconnect or reroute it elsewhere. If they believe we are tracing it, they may find an alternative way to send it and we won't get the chance again."

Dr. Chau understood Baker's comments completely. They had only one chance to get it right. "What do you suggest is our best course once we locate the file?"

"Grab it, cloak our effort and reroute it one of our own IP addresses before the sender ever realizes the transfer wasn't complete. Let the file go through, but to one of our own secured systems. We can close the portal and then mimic the receiving address so the sender believes they are sending it to the intended recipient."

Mary Brandt intervened. "That doesn't solve the problem of the sender still having the original file. Even if we reroute the file, they will certainly use some other way of getting it to the buyer once they are notified it was never received."

Baker looked at Brandt. "A delay is what we are hoping for. If we succeed in delaying the transmission to the buyer long enough, there's a good chance the thief won't get the chance to send it out again and will be dead before then."

"What do you mean, dead? I thought we were trying to secure the file, that's all." Brandt looked at Chau for an answer, but he just nodded towards Baker.

"The man that came in with me has been asked to find the file along with the man or woman responsible for taking it. We believe the thief is also responsible for killing a DHS agent who was a good friend of that man."

"He's a contracted killer for the CIA?" Brandt was trying to keep her voice low, but one of the techs turned and looked at her before he turned back around in his chair and continued working.

"No. Nick is not a killer for the CIA! He has a special designation for this type of assignment, far beyond what other agents are granted. He also has access to a large network of information that few, if any other government agencies, have. The CIA is hoping he will be able to find this person more quickly and without all of the red tape the Bureau is burdened with."

"You said the thief might end up dead. That doesn't sound like he won't kill him, if needed."

Baker's attempt to impress this girl had gone in a different direction than he had intended and he now wished he had not mentioned the possibility of the man or woman being killed. "Look. There is always that chance, but only if Nick has no other option. Only if there is a gun pointed at him will he kill someone. Otherwise, he will do whatever he can to avoid it."

"How do you know him so well?" asked Brandt.

"He is my boss, or was."

"So, do you go around killing people, too, if they point a gun at you?"

Baker was about to say "No" to the question, but decided he would play a mystery card, hoping to get Brandt's interest. "I've done what I have needed to do when necessary."

There was a blank stare for a moment from Brandt and then she flashed Baker a nervous smile before redirecting her attention to the monitor that was beeping. "We have a hit, Dr. Chau!"

Around the lab, several technicians started typing away at a frantic but controlled pace. These were all highly trained, seasoned professionals who knew the proper methods for tracing over the internet and wasted no unnecessary keystrokes. Everyone had a specific role to play in maximizing the efficiency of their jobs and they took it very seriously. As both Dr. Chau and Baker joined in, the connection was suddenly broken as quickly as it had begun. There was only a brief flash of the sender's IP address, measurable only in a minute fraction of a second, then it was gone without their systems being able to capture it.

All activity stopped as the technicians stared at empty screens. One by one, they slowly turned towards Baker and Chau. Baker spoke first. "He knows he was being tracked. How is that humanly possible to detect us so fast?"

"It's not. The only way for him to detect us like that was to already be set-up for a sniff and was running it ahead of us. They would also have to have been targeting our classified IP addresses as the primary suspects in running the search."

Brandt cut in. "Or they didn't detect us at all and simply shut down their system as soon as the transfer started. It may have been a test using one machine to send the file, then shut that one down as he or she ran a secondary search from another system to try and see if someone was pinging that IP address."

Baker bolted from his chair and began yelling for everyone to stop their search immediately. "If that's the case and he picks up just one of us, we are done. Stop your searches now!"

Jonathan Clay D'Amore sat in his car two blocks from CIA headquarters and watched as the tiny red dots bounced around his cell phone screen, mimicking a trace from one tower to the next, finally completing a loop back to the headquarters. He had been right in believing the CIA was the organization searching for the stolen drive, and from the sophisticated search patterns, this was not a usual search and grab.

The software on his phone had worked perfectly, allowing him to remotely switch on the computer, begin the transfer and then stop it with a simple touch on the keypad. He had paid $4.99 for the software download. Since it was still in beta testing, he had simply modified the script slightly and recompiled the new code to his needs. The developer of the application had asked that any changes to the code be sent back to them for final testing and inclusion in a future version release, but this was one modification they would never see.

The altered software also notified him of anyone trying to trace or browse his connection. It listed the hacker's IP address and user name, along with their host's name. This was important and useful information that he could later retrieve for whatever course of action he would eventually take against the intruder. He watched as multiple invasions began to close from the prior connection. The list of IP addresses he had stolen from a previous client would tell him who the hackers were, but it was not necessary, as he already knew.

He had never cared before about what he was stealing. But now, with this activity, he began to wonder regarding the importance of what he had stolen, what it meant to others and what information it contained. Four men had already died trying to take it from him and another one he had blinded in order to find out who had been sent to kill him. Before, it was only important that he stole the correct data, passed it to the buyer and was paid properly and promptly. He never questioned what he was stealing and for whom. However, this buyer had sent people to kill him, and the government was spending millions to recruit the top people in their fields to trace and retrieve the drive.

He would need to back-up the files to protect his 'health' and lay low while he did further research on what the drive contained. But first, he needed to destroy the DNA evidence he had stolen from the CIA lab. The application he had loaded on Lane's computer, to record all activity, would also need to be monitored on a regular basis. If additional information was input or discovered at a later time, it could prove to be useful.

It had been a close call, as he had barely made it out the door when a lab technician and several others passed him in the tiny hallway. If he had not turned his back and faked a cough as they went by, they would all have come face to face, with dire results. The girl in front was looking directly at him as they approached one another, giving him little choice but to eliminate her at a later time if he felt she was capable of identifying him. He was certain, though, that she had not seen him long enough to describe his features accurately and make a positive id.

He started the car, checked for oncoming traffic and pulled out, heading in the direction of his rented motel room. Once there, he would drop the evidence in a small container of sulfuric acid, then dump whatever remains were left in a small wooded area of the park on his way out later.

Chapter 9

The flight back to Atlanta had been just long enough for Nick to catch a few hours sleep and refresh his body and mind. He would now be able to focus completely on what Hoskins had been reluctant to tell him. If it were true, then there would be a number of things he needed to take care of before beginning any research. Number one on the list was making sure Laura was safe.

After exiting the plane, he headed through the airport terminal towards the elevator that would take him to the parking lot. He pulled his parking ticket from his wallet as he approached the open doors and verified the parking aisle number and space where he had left the Porsche. As he began to take his last few steps towards the doors, a man, woman and three children approached from his left. Nick stopped to allow them to get on first, then followed behind them. Before he could press the required floor button, a little boy reached over his hand and began pressing all of them, one by one.

Under his breath, Nick began to mumble a few words and briefly stared at the boy. After a moment, though, he found a smile crossing his own face as he, himself, recollected doing the same thing a number of times during his youth and accepted that this small act was only his repayment from a younger generation. Nick placed his hands in his pockets and, without realizing it, pushed the sides of his coat open to reveal the handle of the P250 pistol. The little boy recoiled towards his father and pressed in very close.

Seeing the boy's eyes, Nick turned his head towards the father. "I'm sorry, but it's OK. I'm contracted by the government and have proper authority to carry it." Looking down at the boy now, he continued. "I'm also sorry that I scared you."

The father patted the boy's shoulder and reassured him everything was all right. The little boy shook his head that he understood, then extended his palm out to Nick in order to shake hands, but said nothing. After a brief moment, Nick returned the gesture and the boy smiled as they each formally introduced themselves. For the first time in a long time, Nick began to think of what it would be like having children, especially a boy to carry on his name.

After the doors opened and closed a number of times, Nick finally stepped off onto the floor that was identified on the ticket. Crossing over several aisles, he saw the Porsche sitting where he had left it. A quick press on one of the key's buttons, and he heard the engine start, echoing with a deep bass sound from the exhaust. It was a sound he never tired of hearing. Another press and he heard the programmed chirping sound of the driver side door being unlocked.

Having paid the toll, he merged into the exiting airport traffic and began to consider where he should begin his research once Laura was safe. He would also need to contact and inform his close friends of the situation. He did not anticipate that his future actions would put anyone in danger, but felt obligated to at least notify everyone of any potential threat. The friends he had in mind would understand, be thankful and ask no questions.

His thoughts turned back to Laura and what would be required in order to protect her first. Even though she was equipped to handle herself both physically and mentally in almost any given situation and could take care of herself, there was always the danger of her being caught totally off guard. He would need someone to watch her back. It was a very short list of those he felt capable of doing the job and be trusted never to leave her alone. After going down the list, eliminating each person for various reasons, it came down to only one person left, Jeff Dawson.

Nick had the utmost respect for the man and knew he would not let him down. They had served dozens of missions together over the years and not once had Dawson left his side or failed to watch his 'six' when needed. Both had protected one another during the deadliest of operations and on several occasions had come very close to sur-rendering their life for the other.

The thought of Dawson watching over Laura was a great relief. Somehow, he would have to think of a way to return the favor, although he knew Dawson would refuse any attempts to allow Nick to reciprocate.

Selecting a number from the speed dial on his steering wheel, he heard Dawson's voice come on almost immediately. After a few minutes, the arrangement was set. Dawson would be at the clinic by late evening. Now the hard part would be trying to convince Laura of the protection she would need. It was going to be a hard fight, but she would have to understand the danger she would be in if Hoskins was right. If he found something that the government did not want known, they would go to any lengths to keep it quiet.

He knew this because of his acquaintance with several people on the government's task-force whose job it was to make sure secrets remained secrets and keeping those who could and would talk, silent. It was not a part of the job that any agent wanted to perform, but it was essential in order to keep the country safe and its people unaware of what the United States, or any other country, for that matter, would do in order to protect itself.

Unethical decisions were made constantly by the people in power who felt its citizens were not literate enough to understand and believed that their own actions were always fully warranted. The decisions weren't always accepted by the people having to carry out their given orders but, for the most part, it was a necessary evil that kept the peace or someone's ego inflated and yourself alive from the threat from unforeseen foes.

After making the other calls, Nick returned his thoughts to the individuals who had been selected to participate in the project many years earlier. How had they vanished and where did they go? What did they do to keep occupied and not go stir-crazy waiting to be notified by their government? Did they simply take on a new life and merge in with society, never to be heard from again?

Nick glanced down at the packet Hoskins had given to him and wondered how many or how few answers he would find to those questions and the hundreds of others he would hopefully uncover before his search was complete. Hoskins had told him to concentrate only on finding the person who had stolen the data drive and to destroy both if necessary. However, the thoughts of trying to discover what had happened to each of these people began to take on a personal priority over that order. He knew deep down, though, that what Hoskins had demanded be done was more important for now. Nick would have to wait for the time being, and center his attention on tracking down the gunman and thief.

Chapter 10

It had been nearly twenty four hours since Dr. Chau's team had seen any additional activity on the network. The trace they had used to try and capture an IP address that the thief was sending from his location had backfired on all of them. Instead of finding his or her location, they had inadvertently revealed their own locality to an outside source who was either working for the thief or was the thief himself. It would not take long for that person to identify who the trace was coming from.

Everyone knew there would not be a second chance to run another trace. Whoever the person or persons were, they would use an alternate method to pass on and transfer the data files. If they were technically advanced enough to break the encryption, it would simply be a matter of sending the data by another chosen media type and hand delivering the information to the buyer. Almost every business person carried a laptop through airport security nowadays and it would be impossible to know who might be carrying the data.

Baker had thought that breaking the code would be almost impossible for anyone, with the exception of two or three other analysts he knew who had the capability and technical resources. However, after watching the skill level of this person tracing their movements so quickly, it made him wonder. Whoever it was, was either extremely lucky in guessing where the trace would originate from or had an inside contact that had passed along the information.

Turning to Dr. Chau, Baker wanted to know more about the file. "Do you have any idea what is contained within the file? The only information I know is that it was some type of project carried out by the government in the early seveties."

Dr. Chau looked as if Baker had struck him in the face with an open palm. Keeping his voice down as low as possible, Baker could hardly make out what Chau was telling him. "Do not discuss anything you know about this to anyone, not anyone, do you understand? Our job is to find the missing data and pass along its whereabouts. Asking questions like you are can land you in jail."

Chau looked up at Baker to see if he understood and his stern look told Baker to drop whatever further questioning he had or had intended to have. Baker didn't understand and pressed the matter further.

"Do you know what's on the file?" asked Baker.

The look on Chau's face told him he was about to explode. Leaning in so close one would think they were about to kiss, Chau whispered, "Yes. Both Brandt and I have that clearance, but you don't yet, so do not ask again until you do. If you do before then, I will have you removed from the premises permanently. "

Chau quickly decided he needed to make it look as if their conversation appeared to be a simple request and not about the project. "Yes, I agree," said Dr. Chau. "I think we should break for dinner and wait to see what develops next. If anything happens, we will be notified."

When Brandt and Baker saw Chau logging off his system and bringing up the password input prompt, they followed suit and did the same. Satisfied their systems were secure, the three headed towards the glass doors and waited for an ID check to allow them to exit the area. Having just received his credentials, it took a few minutes to activate Baker's card through all checkpoints before the guard allowed him to pass. Dr. Chau sidestepped and gestured for Brandt to lead, but stepped in front of Baker as they headed towards the main dining room floor elevators.

Once the elevators doors closed, Baker started to question why they left so abruptly, but Chau shook his head, indicating this was not the time. Baker stopped talking and Brandt looked at both of them, wondering what was going on between the two. She had never seen Chau interrupt a colleague while talking or asking questions before. Never.

They exited the elevators as two guards stepped forward, brushing arms and shoulders with all three. Baker started to protest, but decided that might lead to some kind of harassment later on and didn't want the guards passing his name around, making him a future target of a 'brotherhood' joke. Baker had nothing but total respect for what true police officers did for a living, but knew better than to cause any problems with military police officers. Even though his new title carried a lot of weight, he was new to the facility and that meant he would have to earn their respect.

Following close behind Chau, he walked down several corridors before the smell of pizza found his nostrils and started his salivary glands watering. He wanted to pick up the pace, but didn't want to annoy Chau any more than he already had, so he maintained his gait. Of course, at the moment he had no idea what he had done wrong, but knew at some point soon, Chau would either explain things to him like a patient father or give him a tongue lashing similar to that from a Catholic nun.

At the counter, Baker selected several slices of different type pizzas, a drink and a large piece of Key-lime pie. He stood waiting for Chau and Brandt to finish with the cashier, then proceeded to find a table that could accommodate them all. As Baker selected a table, Chau shook his head and directed them all towards a table further back, away from the other diners.

Once they were seated, the three began sliding their meals off of their trays and placing the empties on a table next to them. For several minutes no one spoke, making Baker very uncomfortable. Normally the conversations started right away with how they had spent their evening the night before or what they had watched on TV that the others might like to hear about, but it was very unusual for there to be no talking at all.

Having had enough and knowing the silent treatment was somehow his fault, Baker turned to both Brandt and Chau. "Look. Whatever I said that has offended you, I am truly sorry, even though I don't know what I have said to cause you not to speak to me."

"You have said nothing offensive, but I told you once before it is dangerous to ask questions about what is on the drive or about the person or persons who have it. Regardless of my precautions, you did it again and if you continue to do so, it could put us all in danger."

"How am I supposed to learn anything if I don't ask questions, Dr. Chau? I need to understand what I am researching and looking for and the only way to do that is to ask questions."

Chau kept his face looking straight on, but turned his eyes towards Baker. "You can ask any questions you like about the technological aspects, but not about the project or data that is on that file. It gives the impression we are getting personally involved in areas we have no business researching."

"But I need to ask questions in order to understand the intent of the thief. I'm told I can ask anything I need in order to get those answers."

"Yes, you can, but those types of questions bring suspicions upon us and can get us all removed from this and other future projects. Ask enough questions and it can land you in front of an investigative unit. After you have spent several days under their constant barrage of endless questioning and accusations, you are likely to say anything, and if you say the wrong thing, you will go away for a long time. I don't think that needs any further explanation."

Baker was beginning to feel some paranoia about what he had signed on to do. This was not what had been explained to him, rather that he would have full access to anything and everything and could do any research and testing required in order to track down the killer and thief. He knew his job was to find the stolen drive and delete whatever it contained, but he needed to have a lot of questions answered in the meantime that would help him understand the thought processes of the man.

This was not simply a case of tracking a signal, it meant getting into the mind of the person and figuring out what motivated the theft and his apparent disregard for the lives of anyone he came in contact with. If he could find the answers to those questions, it might be possible to get a step ahead of his quarry and determine his or her next move.

"Is there any way for me to obtain information on this guy without asking questions? Is it possible to find out what the CIA and FBI already know?"

Brandt could not hold her tongue any longer. "I know you are a lot more intelligent than you're coming off to be right now, Mr. Baker. Dr. Chau has already explained that your job is to assist in finding the location of the drive. That's it. You are to use whatever technological knowledge you possess or whatever has been given to you to use in the lab, only. Period!"

Baker was getting ready to remind her that she took orders from him when Chau told them both to be quiet. For the next ten minutes, Baker picked at his food, waiting for the other two to finish. He felt that they were waiting for another apology, but he did not feel one was due. Nevertheless, as each began to stand, he leaned forward across the table and gave one anyway with as much genuine meaning as possible. With the apology accepted, they all made their way back to the lab, with Dr. Chau leading.

As they cornered around a blind spot along the interior wall of a hallway, and out of camera view, Baker felt Brandt's hand dip down into the side pocket of his coat and put something in it. She pulled her hand out quickly and continued to walk, making sure there was no eye contact. He made no attempt to see what she had placed in his pocket and just followed both Brandt and Chau out the cafeteria exit.

At the right time he would look, but not now. After their prior conversation at the table, he knew that everything he did and said was now under the watchful eye and scrutiny of the United States government. The freedoms he once took for granted were gone and that fact was just now beginning to settle in.

Chapter 11

The day had been long and the three decided to call off the IP search for the night. They would leave the trace going, but it was time to get some sleep before they reconvened in the morning. Hoskins had made mention earlier about Baker's temporary living quarters being provided to him within the facility and that the layout should be to his liking. He had also been given instructions that a guard would escort him there in order to locate the room easily for the first time. After that, he should have no trouble finding it again.

Hoskins was right. The walk had taken less than two minutes. After leaving the lab, both he and the guard continued down a straight corridor until the guard stopped and turned to his immediate left, pointing towards a door that had Baker's name plate already affixed. "Please place your right thumb there and it will unlock. Once you have settled in and had time to record your voice, you will only need to speak and it will open. Do you have any questions?" asked the guard.

"I think I'm good," responded Baker. With that, the guard wished him a good evening and started making his way back to the lab.

Baker placed his thumb where he had been told, heard the lock mechanism click and pushed the door open, not quite certain what to expect. His first thoughts, prior to the door opening, were that the room would be small and contain only a few sparse items that were essential for a human being to maintain an existence. Perhaps similar to that of a jail cell, he thought. To his surprise, the room was extremely large, almost the size of a small house, complete with a kitchen and both a dining and living room. Mounted on a wall was a sixty inch flat screen television. Attached was an Apple iTV box and complete gaming system.

Next to the screen area was a desk, which sat a twenty seven inch iMac containing solid state drives and an iPad, both with the new retina displays. He sat down in the desk chair provided and felt the seat adjust to his posterior. The back of the chair began to adjust as well until he felt a small vibration begin to pulsate along his spine, then spread out across his back. He looked down at the arm of the chair and decided to switch off the massage mechanism until after he checked out the rest of the place.

Standing, he walked across the living room and saw a bedroom door located further down a hallway. As he walked toward it, the lights overhead turned on automatically, than intensified slightly as he passed underneath each one. Reaching the bedroom door, he looked in to see a California king size bed large enough to sleep several people. Making his way to the edge, he laid down on his back across the mattress. Perhaps he had prejudged his situation a little too harshly.

Picking up his cell, he dialed West, hearing a voice break in stating the call was being placed. No, he had not prejudged the situation too harshly at all. Big Brother was everywhere and even his private calls were being screened. If he complained, he wondered what the penalties would be, especially after talking to Chau and Brandt. He would wait it out for a few days to see if this was just a test and hopefully Big Brother would let up soon.

After a few rings, Baker heard West pick up and speak his name. "Baker, are you doing ok?"

"I would be if everything I did wasn't being scrutinized. I tried asking Chau about the project and the person we are tracking, but I got a verbal tongue lashing. It appears that my job is strictly to find the location and delete the contents of the drive. I've been sternly warned not to ask questions that don't pertain to my exact purpose for being here."

West could hear the frustration in Baker's voice. "I understand and know what you are going through. My in-structions are pretty much the same, except I had to do some threatening myself and it worked only because I have a few embarrassing things on Hoskins. He gave me a small envelope but it doesn't contain much other than a few pictures of the project team members and their names. Other than that, there is no history on anyone nor the man or woman we are after."

Baker's pulse quickened just slightly. "Any chance you can deliver that to me other than sending it over the internet?"

"You don't have a secure line that I can send it through?" asked West.

"There are supposed to be, but I'm certain they are being monitored any way. As a matter of fact, I can see where this conversation is being traced and recorded right now." The software showed the IP address of where the trace was coming from. It would be easy to track it back to its source, but he decided he didn't want to cause any problems, at least not yet.

West laughed quietly at Baker's comment knowing that some flunkey was on the other end of his line in shock, believing he was invisible to everyone across the network. It only took a five dollar software application installed on a system to trace the call back. It wasn't even considered high tech by anyone anymore.

"OK, we will meet up tomorrow night. I've got to fly back into Arlington to attend a conference with the CIA Director about some information I was able to find. Once I'm there, I'll follow-up with you and we can figure out a way to go off radar and exchange our notes."

As Baker was beginning to agree, there was a small tapping at his door. He quickly said goodbye to Nick, hung up and walked towards the front of the apartment, if that is what one would call it. He placed his thumb on the inside console and once again heard the door open. On the other side stood Brandt out of her lab coat and in something more revealing that grabbed Baker's eye immediately. He stepped back to allow Brandt to enter, then pushed the door closed behind her.

"Did you read my note?" Brandt was in a playful mood and it was hard for Baker to adjust to this new disposition. This was a side of her he had never seen before and wondered what had gotten her attention that she was now making an effort to try and get to know him.

"Yes and thanks for the heads up."

"Did the file location I gave you help answer some of the questions you were trying to get from Chau?" She smiled at him as she dived onto the couch, straightened up and crossed her legs over each other, Indian style.

"It's a beginning, but it doesn't help identify the person we are after." Baker suddenly realized how stupid that remark sounded.

"Well, if it answers any of your questions, than I at least know I was somewhat helpful."

Chapter 12

Several thousand miles away, Nick West sat at the console of Baker's collection of computers, drives, monitors and an assortment of other equipment that no one individual in the government could afford. Baker had proved his worth over and over and Nick did not scrimp on expenses whenever Baker asked for something. He had made Baker a millionaire several times over, but he still insisted on picking up the tab and purchasing anything and everything Baker requested for the company or for his own special needs if it were relevant.

West had earlier reviewed the few notes on the 'Recall' project from the envelope Hoskins had given to him. Inside were small photos taken decades earlier along with a briefing on each of the individuals who had taken part in the project. He made a note to have Baker scan the photos and age enhance each one in order to try and get a composite of what they would most look like today.

Two names had been consistently blacked out throughout the documents. West wondered if these were possibly the names of the men that had been sent to find each member or if they were the names of those people the government were trying to protect. He decided it could not be the team as a tracking team would have consisted of more than two people. A quick count however, revealed a larger number of names than the original eleven who took part in the project. He would need to find out why there were more names listed and who the others were.

He began putting a check mark on the paper beside each of the names that matched to a name on a photograph and found that all of the members of the group were listed. After eliminating those names, there were five left. Of those five, two of the names had been blacked out. The others were listed as Thomas Richard Adele, Christopher Phillip Clark and Gregory Charles

Portman. Nick turned to the console and typed in each name individually to begin separate searches. Several pages of results were found on each man and Nick sorted the list in order by dates, with the most recent result first.

He immediately took notice of his findings as each result was identical to the others. All three were senior liaisons for the Central Intelligence Agency from 1967 until 1982 when they were reportedly killed in a plane crash over the Atlantic Ocean. Neither the plane nor the bodies were ever recovered despite an extensive search by both the U.S. Navy and the U.S. Coast Guard. Nick scribbled a notation on the paper that he would need to research this further, but for now turned his attention to the list of names in the project. He would also have to come back to the two blacked out names later.

Typing in the first name listed on the project team, he hit the key to begin the search and waited. The results came back blank as were the same on each of the remaining names on the rest of the list. Their lives and histories had been wiped out as if they had never existed. In today's internet world and socially driven society, that would be impossible. Somewhere there would be a record for each of these individuals. There would have to be either a school, military or tax record in the system prior to the project's inception. Nick thought for a moment, finally realizing the obvious. The list contained an alias for each person, not their real names. The group had been sent into hiding for the rest of their lives and the list must contain their new names and identities, not their original.

Nick wondered if Hoskins had known this all along and if it was his way of getting a back at him for the ride. Or, Hoskins really did not know any more than he had proclaimed to know about the project. Regardless, the list would not do him any good. He would have to wait until Baker learned more. He began to believe it would also be a waste of time to try and identify the blacked out names.

The ringing phone startled him and he answered quickly, grabbing it off the desktop and answering in a hurried voice. It was Baker on the other end.

"Nick, it's Baker. Have you been able to find any information on the people in the project or what it was about?" It had been several hours since they last talked and Baker was just following up.

"I've gone through the contents of the package Hoskins gave to me. There is a list of the names of the members and a few details, but I have to believe the names are aliases as none of them come up in my searches. The government would have done this in order to protect their true identities."

"There may be a way to sort the file in some order that will identify them correctly. I've had some additional information given to me tonight that might help."

Nick was curious. "So Chau talked to you then?"

"No, it wasn't Chau. Someone else. You're going to have wait until you get here for the rest of the details, I don't want to mention anything else over the phone."

Unable to communicate freely with Baker was beginning to upset West. Pissed off was more like it. He had played this bullshit game for too many years to have to do it again. Once he was in Virginia, he would make sure all eavesdropping would cease and that his and Baker's conversations would no longer be monitored by any agency for any reason. He had no issues with blackmailing someone high up, threatening to release their past sexual indiscretions if he had to in order to get them to comply.

"Ok. I'll drop off the document with you to see if you're able to decipher the names properly."

As he hung up with Baker, Nick decided to take one more look at the list, from a different angle. He wondered if by simply resorting the first, middle and last names, if that would spell out their real names or if there was a pattern used for creating the aliases. If he could not discover their real names, than it would be a waste of following this course of research. He read off each one aloud.

David Lester Marcum
James Michael Bishop
Paul Anthony McGuire
Douglas Albert Scott
Jack Preston Fuller
Andrea Louise Spencer
Stephanie Anne Moffatt
Patricia Louise Pierce
Gillian Courtney Boardman
Daniel Benjamin Pruitt
Thomas Anthony Pritchet

They had seemed legitimate names, but it would be useless to search any more if they were not. He decided to check out one last idea before giving up and waiting on Baker. Entering the keywords '*memory research*', he saw over forty pages of articles display, each page number identified in order on the bottom of the screen. He narrowed the search to those articles written in the seventies. The list tapered down to six.

Going through each article, the information started to become redundant, along with the research centers mentioned. He made further notations on the centers' names and cross-referenced the alumni and student listings. When those produced no positive results, he decided to make one last attempt by looking at the yearbook photos on those colleges and research centers that had a high IQ society as part of the curriculum. He placed the photos from Hoskins envelope next to the keyboard.

Ten minutes later, he had a visual match on one of the women. The yearbook listed her as Andrea Louise Pruitt. He entered the name and password into the CIA database as Baker had shown him how to do and pressed the enter key once again, keeping his fingers crossed that his IP address was being hidden by the shielding software that Baker had programmed.

Next to the monitor, a red light began to flash, indicating a reverse trace was being placed on his request. Nick remained calm, searching his memory on what instructions Baker had given to him should this happen. With his two index fingers, he pressed both the 'Home' and 'X' keys simultaneously. The warning light turned off. Baker had told him this would reroute their IP address to another system located in a foreign country and the trace would follow it there. Some poor innocent bastard would wake up to the authorities kicking in his door and several days of uncomfortable interrogation. As long as it saved their asses from being put in jail, so be it.

The profile sheet listed her date of birth as October 30, 1947. On her twentieth birthday, she had been recruited into the CIA's training program as an analyst. Even though she was young, she had already obtained her Doctorate in clinical psychology and a Master's in mathematics. There had been many promotions over the next three years, and then her file stopped. The last entry was stamped in large red bold letters with the word 'Recall'. It was the same project name Hoskins had mentioned in the interrogation room.

Nick decided he needed to give the information to Baker and go back to work on identifying who the thief was. It was, after all, what he had been brought in to do and as much as he wanted to know all the details of the project, he could not afford to go off in another direction at this time. He also had a score to settle with the person who had killed his friend. Backing up the details to a thumb drive with the information he had found so far, he checked in with his pilot and advised he would be rescheduling take off for that evening instead of in the morning.

The pilot responded, telling West the plane was always ready to go at his request and he would meet him at the hanger at the specified time. What he didn't tell him was that he was crawling out of bed, leaving the redheaded beauty to find herself another way to satisfy her needs so he could meet his obligation to West. With the salary he was being paid, no woman was worth screwing up that arrangement.

Chapter 13

Dr. Mary Brandt sat in front of her computer making notes of the days' activities and wondering how a person or persons could have tracked their trace so quickly. There was no doubt by any of the team members that they had been hacked by a professional who was as skilled as they were. Heaven help them all if he was better. It was almost impossible to believe that someone on the outside had simply been lucky in stumbling across their efforts at the exact same time. Whoever they were, they now had their classified IP addresses and with them, they could hack whatever information each contained.

With any hope though, it would entice the hacker into logging back on and try to intrude further past the department's firewalls. In doing so, the team might be able lock on to where the search was originating from. They would have to let the intruder regain access and then work feverously to reroute his or her penetration, letting the intruder believe they were hacking deeper into the infrastructure. At some point, they would have to block him or her, but by that time, they would have a smaller parameter defined to start their own search. Better yet, if they were lucky, an actual IP address

She thought back to her after hours meeting with Baker and smiled at the memory of the look on his face when he opened the door. It was obvious even to a teenage girl that he had hoped it was for other reasons than work. Much to his disappointment, it was not nor would it ever be. Brandt knew of his history with the bureau and the fact that he had been labeled a traitor, whether it was true or not. The thought of him touching her made her nauseated.

Entering his room earlier, she had handed him a folder containing her own notes on her discoveries of the project as she passed through his door. The note she had given him earlier contained a fake website she had set up herself with only brief notations. She needed to find out if he was already familiar with the information it contained or if he really was only there to find the location of the drive, as she had been told. The idea that he had been brought in over her was all the more reason to despise him. Her feelings and emotions would have to wait for now.

After six years of research, she had been able to identify several members of the project and their backgrounds. Only one had interested her, though. If she could learn more about the last hours before the woman's death, then perhaps she could work backwards from there and identify the men involved. She did not care who the other ten people in the project were, only who was sent to find them and who had initiated the order to kill them all.

She had kept the most critical details of the project to herself and had made sure no one else would ever see that documentation. After the death of her grandmother, she had been willed the diary written by her mother that started her own search six years earlier. Once she had learned of the research Dr. Chau was doing, along with certain classified data he alone was responsible for protecting, she did everything possible to get reassigned to his team.

It had taken a lot of red tape and submitting every required document in the world it seemed, but she eventually worked her way into getting the position. In doing so, she confirmed that it really was still a man's world within the Bureau and the assignment did not come easily or without a personal and sometimes humiliating cost. When this was over, she would make sure the perverts would pay with more than just the loss of their pensions. She would use the skills they had taught her so well against them.

The call between West and Baker had been discouraging as she listened in without their knowing. Baker had thought it was the agency, but he was wrong.

Being in his room had given her an opportunity to place a small bug on the underside of a drawer of his desk. The Bluetooth device allowed her to pick up any phone call he had made or received and any computer research he did. It would also forward the personal password he was using to log on.

The information Baker and West had passed along to each other had been known to her years earlier. She was also aware of the correct sort order and names of the members of the group. Brandt decided that she would have to work outside the agency if she was going to learn anything further. This might be the only opportunity she had left to find the information she so desperately wanted and needed to know.

After running through the options that would work best in her favor, without the agency following her every move, it would have to be up to her to figure out a way to conceal her actions. She would have to become the aggressor, finding and confronting the thief alone.

Closing her eyes, she began to concentrate on remembering all of the events that had happened since Baker first started. He was very smart and if he continued working with Dr. Chau as closely as she had, they would find the person they were after very soon. It would only be a matter of the sender of the file screwing up once and they would have him. She had spent six long years trying to obtain the information everyone was now after; she wasn't about to let a traitor walk in and steal it from her grip.

The events played through her head like a movie in slow motion. Every detail was captured and exposed by her brain's process. Even the smallest of details were enlarged and analyzed before being filed away as non-essential information. It was an agonizing process as nothing was missed, not even the most boring of conversations and the information she had heard by so many people.

Giving up, she stood and reached to turn off her monitor. As the screen flicked once, there was a sudden image that popped into her consciousness, then immediately disappeared. "Oh my God, that was it."

Closing her eyes once again, she searched the far depths of her subconscious trying to bring the image back. Abruptly and very clear, it materialized. The flash of the IP address that had been so quick to delete itself that no man or machine had the time to record it. As if printed on a large document in front of her eyes, the numbers and dots displayed.

Grabbing her keys, purse and ID, she left her room and headed towards the facilities exit. Scanning her card, the doors opened and she almost ran through them before catching herself, realizing her actions would set off alarms. She stopped herself and waited for the doors to completely open before taking a casual stride past them, walking steadily down a flight of stairs to the underground garage.

Certain that no one had followed her, she started the car and drove the posted speed limit heading out of the garage and towards a popular internet cafe. The more internet traffic from a single location, she thought, the longer it would take for the agency to find her transmission if they did have her under surveillance. If all went well, she would have the drive and would be able to decrypt the data before anyone knew she had it. Afterwards, she would remotely ping the drive's offsite address so everyone would believe she had found its location, making her the hero over everyone else in the lab.

A half hour after she left the garage, she was driving down the center of town, past the internet cafe and boutiques that lined the interior of the sidewalks, displaying their latest and newest sales items for what they hoped would be a start to bringing the customers back into the stores. With the current economic status, several of the bigger stores had shut down months ago, leaving the small profitable ones behind. Many of the small stores, however, thought their fates may not be that far behind either.

After parking her car, she counted out several quarters and dropped them into the meter. Spinning the dial, she looked to see that she had three and a half hours to kill before heading back to the facility in the evening hours. She decided to do some shopping first in order to throw off any tail that the agency might have sent out after her, just to make sure she was not having a clandestine meeting with someone on the outside.

Two hours later, she emerged from a small sandwich shop holding several bags of items she had purchased at a number of stores she had visited. Most of the items she would simply store away in drawers never to be opened, but at the computer shop she had found just what she needed. The drive was identical to one described as stolen in the police report she had hacked while searching through the CIA databanks.

Finally deciding there was no one following her, she slipped into the internet cafe, handed the owner a fake id and proceeded to complete a small document with general information about herself. The photo showed her as a redhead, which she now was thanks to the wig she was wearing. Handing the man a fifty dollar bill and getting her assigned computer table, she took one more quick look around before heading in that direction.

Placing the bags down and pushing them under the table, she flipped on the screen and entered the password the owner had given her. At the prompt, she typed in a short script and exited the default screen, taking her to one that allowed more advanced options than the current interface provided. With a few more keystrokes, she was able to verify the IP address that she had in her head, was active but not transmitting or receiving. It was simply sitting idle.

A few words were all that would be needed. The message and threat she sent was straight forward and undeviating. If she did not get a response within ten minutes, she would be gone without giving another opportunity to the thief to consider additional options or alternatives. Two minutes later, she smiled as she watched the texted response display on her screen. The thief had quickly analyzed the wording and determined it was sent by a woman.

Reading the reply, she typed another message. "I found you, now you find me. You have one hour."

Chapter 14

D'Amore watched as the connection was broken between the woman and himself. He had one hour to bring the drive intact to her or she would turn over his identity to the CIA and local police. It was a bluff he knew, but how had this woman been able to capture his IP address. There was no system in the world that could have recorded it in the minuscule amount of time it flashed and was gone. There was no way of avoiding it being transmitted with his own trace, but no one had ever captured it before.

Little did the woman know he was only ten minutes away. He would have plenty of time to walk into the cafe and look around to find the person who had sent the message. If he was not able to do a visual verification, he would ping the address of the computers within the cafe and determine exactly where the person was sitting. If there was an unobstructed opening, the gun's suppressor would conceal the sound of the shot. With most of the cafe customers blasting songs through their earphones, they would be oblivious to any noise that escaped.

Placing both the drive and gun in a computer bag, he headed across the parking lot and onto the city's main street. There was a lot of foot traffic as the daily working hours for most were over and those people had begun making their way home towards their apartments and to their families. At the crosswalk, he watched as the flashing hand gave way to a countdown and switched to a little 'man' icon indicating it was safe to cross. Blending in with the crowd, he proceeded to the other side and looked down the street to see the sign for the cafe. He would be inside within two minutes.

Reaching into his front shirt pocket, he pulled out a pair of sunglasses and placed them on his face. The tinting on the glasses lightened considerably as he entered the cafe and walked towards the counter. As he waited in line facing away from the computer monitors, his eyes glanced at the small mirrors hidden inside the edges of the sunglasses allowing full view of everything behind him.

There were seven women sitting at the consoles, busy typing messages to friends or possibly lovers. That is why they came here: to hide away at the cafe so their husbands would not find their ongoing affair deep within their own system's emails, hidden away in some password protected folder. With stealth software available to anyone, it was not hard to snoop in on your spouse and find out what they were doing while you were away from home. No amount of deleting emails or defragging your hard-drive would erase your cheating from what was saved by your network provider. A few keystrokes and your internet life was on full display to anyone who cared to look.

As he was about to be called for his turn to purchase computer time, he noticed the redhead typing on the keyboard. Her fingers went almost non stop, only hesitating for a moment as she glanced at the screen for a second, than continued. He stepped to the side to allow another customer to go in front of him as he surveyed his surroundings. The tables had been staggered in order to help the patrons with privacy, so there was no clear path for a bullet to find its target. Much to his disappointment, he would have no choice but to approach her and hope he could persuade her to leave with him.

Making his way in and around the tables, he walked up behind her, bending down so his face was directly behind her head.

"I found you." he whispered just loud enough that she alone would hear him.

He was surprised when the woman didn't jump or turn around as he had expected. This woman was cool and continued to type as if she had not heard him. As he was about to repeat himself, he heard her speak. "Did you bring it? If so, please place it on the floor and slide it under the table."

"Not going to happen, at least not here," he said. "You're welcome to the drive, but you have a few questions to answer before I hand it over."

"It happens here and now or it doesn't happen at all. I'm not very keen on playing games, so don't try them on me". With that, she turned to look directly at the thief. The sunglasses blocked her ability to see his eyes, but he swallowed hard when he saw hers. They were dark blue and he had seen them on only one other person before. They were the same ones he saw in his own reflection every time he looked into the mirror.

He stood up quickly keeping his eyes on hers. "Then it's not going to happen. Whatever is on this drive, you can kiss goodbye, lady."

Dr. Brandt was good at reading faces and knew that whatever was causing this man to change his mind so quickly was not the loss of the drive, but something else. She did not have time to figure it out as her chance of getting the drive was about to evaporate.

"Help me, that man stole my briefcase!" she screamed and pointed at the man walking away from her. Several men jumped to their feet and began to converge on him, not realizing their mistake before it was too late. As they moved forward and grabbed at him, bones began to break and noses were broken as faces were slammed down hard onto a monitor or knee.

During the struggle, D'Amore released the computer bag, letting it drop down gently onto the floor. Brandt reached down, snapping it up, opening the zippers quickly and extracting the drive. She also saw the gun.

Realizing she did not have the time to make an exchange, she threw the drive back into the bag, grabbed her small purse and ran towards the exit of the cafe. As she made her way out, she looked back through the glass window only to see a man staggering away from the man with the sunglasses. He was looking straight at her as he held a tall man in his grip and was a second away from breaking the mans' kneecap with a sidekick. Letting go, D'Amore began running after her, pushing people out of the way or punching his way out against those who were stupid enough to try and make a last stand or make a final attempt at stopping him.

She had a twenty yard head start and began running towards the street, hoping she could dodge in between the traffic of cars and buses and make it to her car safely. She had purposely parked her car at the end of the street in order not to be blocked in and was thankful her training had taught her this one small trick.

Up ahead she saw her car and pressed the buttons on the keychain as she ran towards it. She was close enough to hear the doors unlock. Grabbing the handle, she jerked the door open and dove in, throwing the bag on the passenger seat. Not able to get her left leg inside in time, she pulled the door hard shut on her foot and yelped as the pain shot up her inner thigh. In her door's mirror, she could see the man only yards away and coming fast.

With the door still partly open, she felt his hand grab her by her hair as he began to try to pull her out of the car. Turning the ignition key and stepping on the accelerator, she felt the hand release her head as the wig's securing snaps broke, leaving the man holding it in his hands as the car turned a corner and was gone.

Holding the wig in his hands, he looked down inside to see the blond strands of hair he had ripped from her scalp as she had made her get away. For now, his thoughts were not on the stolen drive or the men he had left broken in the cafe, but on her dark blue eyes.

He would need to run an analysis to determine her identity by matching her DNA to that found in the govern-ment's database. There was no doubt in his mind that she was a specially trained government employee, after having watched her actions. If there was no match, then it would mean risking the possibility of exposing his existence, but it was something he was willing to do if it meant catching her. There were people who would know of her and he needed to know who they were in order to find out who she was. It was simple logic. Nothing else mattered for the moment. Nothing.

Chapter 15

Brandt sat on the side of the road eight miles out of town as the red and blue lights flashed behind her from the state trooper's patrol car. He had seen her drive by going under the speed limit, but didn't care. He just felt like he needed and wanted to fuck up someone's day. He could also see she was beautiful and blond at that. Perhaps she would be willing to barter with him with hopes of him not giving her a speeding ticket. He could feel his small penis begin to move.

After making gestures, as if he was calling in her license plate, he stepped from the patrol car and with his best swagger, walked up to her car door and tapped on the window.

"Can I see your license and registration, please?"

Her foot was aching and she was not in the mood to have to deal with a man who thought having a uniform gave him the authority to hassle people anytime he liked. She thought of showing her CIA badge, but decided against it.

"Can you tell me why you pulled me over? I was four miles under the speed limit. It's posted at sixty miles per hour and I was going fifty six."

The trooper looked at her before responding. "M'am, I asked for your license and registration. Please give it to me or I will be required to arrest you."

Brandt had several fake IDs, but not for the car's registration. If she tried to present anything other than her real id, they would not match and she knew she would be booked. Presenting her CIA badge would make matters even worse as it could and would be used to identify her later on. She could not chance getting a ticket or being arrested, not with the gun in the bag.

"If this is a shakedown, than tell me the amount and I'll pay it. You and I both know I wasn't going over the speed limit, nor do I have some busted tail light or anything else you want to make up." Brandt turned to look at the officer eye to eye.

It was at that moment he noticed the small blood streak at the top of her hairline. "Lady, you are bleeding at your forehead. Can you tell me why?"

"I stumbled getting in my car and hit my head against the edge of the door, that's all."

"Have you been drinking?" It was the one question he loved to ask as it always caused a driver to become nervous. Once that happened, he knew he would have this little bitch doing just what he wanted in a matter of moments. They always started to cry when he had them get out of the car, walk the line and tell them they were under arrest. He would be pulling down his fly soon, he thought. A small smile creased his face.

"No, I..."

"Please get out of the car, M'am." The officer opened the door before she could respond further.

Brandt was furious. She knew where this was headed as the campus police had pulled this stunt on her and her friends continuously during their college years. Every man she had ever known thought with his dick first, then his brain, provided he had one. She had envied the girls who were ugly, or so fat, the boys wouldn't pay them any attention.

The trooper had not noticed the computer bag, caught up in staring at her cleavage and fantasizing about what was underneath her bra. Telling the officer she needed to secure her purse, she instead reached in the open pouch of the bag, grabbed the handle of the gun and slid it into the back of her skirt, underneath the shirt without him noticing. Opening the car door, she exited, than stood facing the officer waiting for further instructions.

"Please walk to the back of the car and stop." The cop followed behind her, unable to take his eyes off of her heart-shaped ass. He wanted to frisk her now, perhaps run his hand over one of her breast, then apologize that it was a mistake, blaming her for moving. Soon enough, he kept thinking.

Her left foot was hurting, but she did everything she could not to sway off center. When her foot stepped onto a small uneven piece of asphalt, she turned her ankle and the pain was instant. She stumbled forward, grabbing the back of the car to keep from falling down.

"M'am, I have reason to believe you have been drinking."

"I injured my foot earlier, that's all. I haven't been drinking."

"I believe you have been, M'am. You're under arrest for 'Driving Under the Influence'." He could feel his crotch throb once again as he said this. She would be *his* any minute now. The tears would flow and she would be begging within seconds. He could already feel her beautiful pair of moist lips working him and he began to stiffen even more.

Instead, he was surprised by her sudden resignation and was even more excited when she spoke. "Let's go ahead and get this over with. Do you want it in my car or in the woods?"

Off the main road, was a stand of trees thirty to forty feet deep. They ran along the stretch of road for the next three miles, before an exit split the tree line. With the darkness, along with the woods blocking anyone from seeing into the trees, she would take care of business and be on her way.

She was certain the trooper had turned off the dash cam and faked the call into headquarters. After all, no trooper wanted any recording of their illicit activities that could possibly make them face disciplinary actions later on if some bitch caused any trouble. The possibility of that happening was remote anyway because of the 'old boy' network, but none of the officers ever wanted to take chances.

"In the woods would be fine. Just give me a minute."

The trooper walked to the back of his car and quickly placed his weapon and holster in the trunk. It was against protocol, but he didn't want it to get in the way nor allow this woman to get his gun by accident.

Brandt kept her eyes on the road noting the area was very isolated and up to this point, she had not seen any other cars pass since she had been pulled over. Perfect.

Watching the trooper close the trunk, she turned and began walking into the woods with the asshole close behind. Once they were in about twenty feet and secluded, he called to her to stop and turn around. Turning, she saw the man with his pants already down to his knees, fondling himself. "Get over here and get on your knees, now."

By the time she had approached within three feet of him, he had slid everything down to his ankles. She looked at the object in his hand that he alone thought was the desire of every woman and with it, was capable of satisfying their most erotic needs.

As she spoke, she slowly moved her hand around to her back until she felt the handle of the gun. "Seriously? I've seen bigger dicks on the two year olds I used to babysit."

The trooper exploded in anger, his face turning red as he began screaming profanities and trying to get to her. She stepped forward to meet him square, placing the barrel of the gun under his chin and placing her finger on the trigger as she did.

"You get on your fucking knees, now!" she yelled.

Shaken and stunned by what was happening, the trooper hesitated too long. Bringing her knee up with as much force as she could expend, the knee caught him solid in the groin. He tumbled forward clutching at one of his crushed testicles. She watched as he tried to stand and gasp for air. He once again started to mutter profanities in between the gasps.

This time she stepped back and swung her foot up like someone trying to kick a football, smashing it against his nose. She heard the cartilage snap and smiled as he screamed in pain and blood flowed freely from his nostrils. The trooper collapsed onto the ground, now silent.

Bending down, she placed the barrel of the gun behind his right ear, pointed it towards the interior of his skull and pulled the trigger. Next, she placed it against his temple and fired again, just like she had been taught by her mentor.

Chapter 16

Nick's flight arrived in Virginia at 11:47 that evening. The air was crisp and the temperature was in the low fifties. Stepping off of the plane, he walked across the runway towards the waiting car as Hoskins stood next to an open door. He greeted Nick with a faceless expression and a cold nod. There was no attempt to hide his displeasure for having to come out so late, but he had been ordered to pick up West and give him the latest intel, personally, as soon as he arrived.

The back of the limo had facing seats allowing them to talk directly at one another without having to turn sideways. Before Nick could buckle his seatbelt, Hoskins was handing him a small envelope similar to one he had handed him with the project information during their initial meeting at the facility.

"What's this?" asked Nick.

"It's a ballistics summary from the gun or should I say 'guns' that killed Paul and the other man."

"They weren't the same?"

"No they aren't. Each was shot with a different weapon, different caliber. The sub that we are after didn't kill Paul, but he did shoot the Asian."

"Do you have any idea who shot Paul and why?" Nick was looking over the ballistic report as he asked.

"We don't have an answer to any of those questions. The round that killed Paul is not from the Asian's gun either."

"So there was an unidentified third shooter?"

"Looks like it. Other than the bullet, there is nothing else we can trace. The person disappeared as quickly as they appeared. How they arrived at the exact spot where all of this went down is even a bigger mystery. The only way possible for that to happen is if the person had prior knowledge of where the attack was going to take place and simply waited for everything to unfold."

"Anything else new that has happened since I've been in Atlanta?" asked Nick.

"There's was another killing last night. He or she is now a suspect in a cop's murder."

"A Virginia cop?"

"Well, it was a state trooper. Shot execution style too. Looks like he or she tortured the guy first before capping him. They wanted the trooper humiliated when he was found by making him drop his pants and underwear to his ankles. "

Nick handed the envelope back to Hoskins. "I'm guessing there was a match from ballistics that confirmed this? Any guesses as to why the trooper was killed?"

"Yes to your first question and not a clue to your second. The trooper looks like he was in the wrong place at the wrong time. He didn't even have time to call in a tag number. No video footage either, we checked."

Nick thought for a minute and tried to figure out how a trooper could be involved. "My best guess is this person was pulled over and didn't want to be identified or have their mug captured. It doesn't make sense why they just didn't kill the officer and leave it that. Why would they torture him?"

Hoskins threw up his hands in a gesture indicating that he agreed with Nick and that he also did not understand why.

"Alright. Let's get going. I've got to meet with Baker to go over some things that my research found and what he needed to see me about as well."

"What things?" Hoskins voice cracked as he asked.

"Just some things we need to review to see if it helps in finding your guy and possibly some more information on the people in the project. Maybe who was involved and the names of the people that took part."

Hoskins lurched forward, almost grabbing Nick by his lapels, but stopped short. "I told you to leave the details of the project alone. Your job is to find the guy and the drive, that's it. How many fucking times do I have to repeat myself?"

Nick remained calm, but stared at Hoskins, letting the agent regain his composer and wipe his own spittle from around his mouth. At least a minute passed before Nick spoke.

"Let's get one thing straight. In order to find this guy, I'm permitted to do any research I need to do and I don't need your permission to do it. By bringing me in, I have any and all authorization that I need. The fact that this person is a threat to our national security, it automatically authorizes me to intercede wherever and into anyone's business I want. At this point, you're just a piss-ant getting in my way."

"You're gone, West! You're no longer part of this case. Get the fuck out of this car! We'll find the cocksucker ourselves, we don't need your skills. I only allowed you to take part in the search because the guy killed your friend and I thought you might want to get even." Hoskins was completely red and the top button on his shirt popped as he swelled from the extra blood flowing into his neck vessels.

"Not a problem." said Nick. "However, you will want to explain my absence to your superior who I spoke with last night and who questioned me on my progress. From the information I was able to gather, I know who your guy is and where he was last seen. But since I'm not part of this project any longer, I don't have to divulge any of this information to you."

With that, Nick opened the car door and exited, taking with him his bag and findings. His knowledge of the location of the man or woman was false, but he knew it would send Hoskins even further over the edge.

Hoskins was right behind him, trying to grab Nick by the shoulders to stop him from leaving, but Nick had moved too quickly for him to succeed.

Before shutting the door in Hoskins' face, Nick turned around facing the agent. "You had the chance to tell me what you knew, but you decided against that. You told me the drive contained the only existing file on the Project, but there is another and I found it. Once Baker and I have decrypted it, we are going to discover what really happened."

"Damn it Nick, you don't know who you're messing with! If you try to go after the people in that file for what they did, you're going to bring down a lot powerful people and get a lot of innocent people killed, starting with your wife."

"Thanks for confirming my suspicions. When it comes down to it, no one in the organization gives a shit about what happened to those people. All that the government cares about is the possibility of someone finding out who was involved in the cover-up and stopping them from spreading the truth. I'm right, aren't I?"

Hoskins sat for a moment trying not to make eye contact with Nick. Finally, he turned back around in his seat, tapped the driver on the shoulder and pulled the door shut as the car drove away.

When the car was far enough away, Nick called Baker and told him what had transpired between Hoskins and himself, letting Baker know that neither of them was required to work with Hoskins in any capacity. From this point forward, West would be independent of the agency but was still authorized to receive full disclosure from Chau's team on anything they discovered.

"What happened, Nick? Am I still allowed to work with you on my own?"

"Baker, you're working for the agency now, but whatever you find, it's important that I be in the loop. I've been doing some research and have found some things that I don't want to discuss over the phone. There's something I need for you to do and it needs to stay between you and me. Anything that I authorize for you to do will not be questioned. Understand?"

"Nick, I've been down this road before. I can't take a chance of screwing up this opportunity. I'm here because of Hoskins, not you and that's not to say I don't appreciate everything you've done for me. I need to have those charges erased off of my records so I can get on with my life. If I don't, then it looks like you will always be my employer."

It was true what Baker was saying and Nick knew it. "Alright, but do one thing for me and if it doesn't change your mind, I understand and wish you the best."

Nick could hear the sigh in Baker's voice. "What do you need me to do that I know I'm going to regret?"

"Call this number and speak to the man on the other end of the phone. Just mention your name and what you are working on. Call me back when you are done and let me know your decision."

Baker scribbled down the number and told Nick he had made up his mind already, but would call the number to appease him.

"Thanks Baker. I need you to call me back as soon as you get off the phone. I mean it."

After disconnecting, Baker stood for a few minutes trying to figure out what the man on the other end could possibly say that would change his mind. Telling Nick that he had to leave his employment, was the toughest decision he had ever made. He hated the situation he had been placed in. Finally, he dialed the number that Nick had given him.

Five minutes later Nick saw his phone display light up. "You had me call the fucking President direct? Do you have any idea how stupid I sounded talking to him? And how the hell do you have his personal number? Jesus Nick, it would have been nice if you had warned me!"

Nick suppressed a laugh. "Well, are you going to do what I'm going to ask you to do this one last time?"

"You're a real ass Nick, do you know that? I guess I have no choice now. By the way, it would also have been nice if you had told me the President had already signed an order dropping all charges and reinstating me with all privileges in my current position. He said you asked him and he was happy to do it!"

"He owed me a favor. Besides, I didn't want you to get screwed by Hoskins if his plan didn't work out."

Baker could hardly get the words out. "The President owed you a favor? Never mind. I don't want to know what you did for him." He really did, but knew Nick could not tell him.

Nick changed the discussion back to why he called Baker. "Do you know the exact size of the file that was stolen?"

"Sure. It was..."

"I don't need to know that. I only need to know if you can trace that file through the systems and find an exact duplicate maybe on another government file server?"

"It could take some time, but yes, it's possible. And provided there have been no changes to that file."

"Then I need you to get started right away. I also need you to run an audio search on any communications mentioning the word 'Recall' and I need for only you to do it. Don't mention what you are doing to anyone else."

"It sounds like you're saying a duplicate file might be on another server? I thought it was the only copy."

There was a hesitation before Nick spoke. "I ran a bluff with Hoskins and told him I found the duplicate file. I thought the guy was going to pass out. There is something he's not telling me and I think the duplicate is about to be moved from its present location to another server."

"So you don't know for sure there is another file?"

"No, but I have a gut feeling we are being played. I know this man and no matter what, he has always been honest with me before, regardless of what the circumstances were, even if it was bad news. His actions are telling me he's lying and he is really scared about something this time around."

"Any idea what he is trying to hide?"

"He's protecting someone who knows all about the project. Whatever happened to those people, the govern-ment's involvement was not good, otherwise there's no reason to worry about it becoming public."

"I'll let you know what I find. A file that size won't be hard to track if it's being stored and especially if it's being rerouted."

Chapter 17

Brandt watched as the decryption application ran against the file on the drive. In order to avoid any questions and allow her time to run the code, she had notified Dr. Chau that morning that she was having 'female issues' and would not be coming to the lab today. He wished her well and hung up without asking further questions and pressing the conversation. He had told her that, so far, they had not had any more luck with the person trying to transmit the file, so to get some rest and he would see her in the morning if she was feeling better.

As she waited, she thought about the man who had chased her, almost catching her at the last minute. There was something that did not make sense to her. Why had he not gone for the bag instead of grabbing her by her hair? With the amount of time given, he could have easily reached across and retrieved the bag before she was able to speed away.

She looked at the screen again and watched as the decryption code appeared to be making faster progress this time around. This was the eleventh pass and each cycle progressed a little further. Occasionally she would have to alter the method of decryption, but that was easy enough for her. She wondered if Baker was able to match her cyber skills that, at times, she had to hide so she didn't embarrass her superiors who thought they were the best at their job. She looked forward to the time when she would have the opportunity to show them just how ignorant they were in comparison.

She also wondered how long it would take Baker to come knocking on her door to see how she was feeling and offer to help in some way. Her initial assumption of him had been based solely on her own belief that he was some egotistical frat boy out to prove he was better than anyone else, ready to disregard anyone else's theories or input. But as she watched her own algorithms trying to decipher his, she realized just how smart he truly was. By now, she would normally have had the decoded information flowing and would have been able to read whatever she needed, but her code had yet been able to completely break his.

It had been seven hours since the program had started and she had not had anything to eat except for a few crackers and cheese she had consumed a few hours earlier. With the application still running, she decided to grab a small sandwich from the cafeteria, then changed her mind and made the choice to drive into town instead. Tonight called for a steak instead of her usual weight watcher meals. Long ago she had a made a commitment to herself that she would always celebrate the small victories in her life and this one certainly fit the bill.

She also wanted to feel the touch of a man. It had been a long time since she had enjoyed going on a date and having a man compliment her on her beauty. Even more so, with a man finding pleasure with her body. Most of the time it had never gotten that far as men found her intimidating or she found them below her intellectually and ended the night early.

Looking at the clock, she noted the hour and felt she had plenty of time to take a shower and get ready before her evening out. The car drive would only take a half hour at most at that time of night, so it would put her in town by seven-thirty or possibly eight o'clock. Standing, she began to strip as she walked towards the shower. She felt more comfortable nude then dressed, and slept that way most of the time. Her habit had annoyed her roommates in college, not because she slept that way, but most of the other girls would slip their boyfriends into their dorms late at night only to find her asleep in her bed with the covers only halfway covering her. It did not take long for their boyfriends to reset their sights on her.

After showering and toweling, she stood at her closet doors trying to decide what to wear. With her golden blond hair, it would definitely be black, regardless of whatever outfit she would eventually decide on. After several minutes, she reached in and pulled down a long evening dress. Turning towards the full length mirror, she held it against her body to see if she liked what she saw. The sides along the top portion had been cut to allow the outer exposure of each side of a woman's bare breast. Placing an arm across the middle of the dress, she lowered the top half to reveal hers in the mirror. She smiled knowing they were still firm and full.

After blow-drying her hair and applying just enough makeup, she slipped into a pair of silk panties and her dress, along with a pair of matching black high heels. Once again she stood in front of the mirror and checked her appearance. Hopefully it would grab the attention of a man who would be capable of spending the evening entertained in conversation, perhaps making it worthwhile for her to spend the rest of the night with him. Regardless of the man's cock size, if he was unable to make her laugh and make her feel as if she were more than a piece of meat, she had no interest.

Just as she was applying her lipstick, there was a knock at her door. Believing it was Baker, she ignored the knock until she heard a voice calling her name that she knew was not him. Straightening her dressed, she proceeded towards the knock, pulling the computer room door closed as she passed. Pressing the button on the monitor console, the screen's image displayed the man on the other side of the door. Perhaps there would not be a need to go out for the evening, she thought as she opened the door.

"How can I help you Mr. West?" Nick West stood looking at Brandt, having expected the woman to be dressed in something much less formal, with her hair pulled back away from her face, holding a chart in her hands. Instead he was staring at a woman straight out of a Vogue magazine, apparently getting ready for a night out.

"I had some questions regarding the project and wanted to speak to you about some additional information that I found in my research, but it appears you are getting ready to leave. Dressed like that, I have to assume it's for a date."

The mention of West having found additional information refocused her attention on the drive and what it would contain once her program finally decrypted the information. There was no doubt in her mind that once that happened, she would have all of the answers she needed, but whatever West had to say could be beneficial, as well. She had to think fast.

"Well, as it turns out, I did have a dinner date that just cancelled. So, here I am all dressed up and no place to go. If you wouldn't mind playing my date tonight, perhaps we could get something to eat and I'll be happy to answer any questions you have?"

Had she been dressed in the lab coat that he originally pictured her in, he would have immediately said "Yes." However, this was something he had not expected and was uncomfortable with accepting. She sensed what he was thinking. "Would you prefer I changed into some jeans?" she asked.

"No, you're fine. I'm the one that was feeling a little underdressed." Nick had said the first thing that came to mind. His preference would have been to decline the invitation, but he needed answers and this would be his best chance of getting them as quickly as possible.

She looked him up and down. "You're perfect! Let's go." Brandt picked up her purse having forgotten that she had transferred the gun from the computer bag to it earlier in the day. She could feel the weight of it, but if she stopped to take it out and West saw her do it, how would she explain it to him? Agents were not allowed to have weapons within the facility. She pulled the zipper of her purse closed and set the alarm before exiting.

As they drove towards town, West could smell Brandt's perfume and he thought about Laura, immediately. He missed being with her and wished it were her instead of Brandt sitting next to him. When he returned home, he would make it a point to call for a reservation at an upscale restaurant Laura had mentioned that she had wanted to go to before he left. Perhaps he would surprise her and fly them to Belize or some other exotic port for a much needed vacation. She had not taken one in years, explaining that the need of her animals came first. He would see to it this time that they had all of the proper care that they deserved and would give her no choice.

Arriving at the restaurant, Nick grabbed the ticket from the valet as he and Brandt made their way in, greeted by the owner. Nick requested a table along a far wall where they would have more privacy discussing the project, where no one would be able to overhear their conversation. They were led to a table that allowed them complete seclusion, even from roaming eyes looking to find something or someone to gossip about.

Brandt ordered a cocktail and West did the same, not wanting to appear as if the dinner was going to be boring and *all* business. He had no intentions towards the woman, but at least he could be a gentleman. After placing their order, Nick began telling her of what information he had found during his research and wanting to know if she could verify any of the findings. He explained that Baker had told him that she had some knowledge of the project, but did know how much she knew.

As she listened, she wondered how West had been able to obtain so much data so quickly, where it had taken her years. The details matched hers with the exception of a few minor differences. Those differences however, meant she would have to reconsider some of her own findings, unless the drive results proved hers to be more accurate than his.

She found it hard to lie, at least at first. "Almost everything you said is the same information I have been able to find. There were eleven people involved in the project and the project funds were cancelled after almost ten years. No one knows why, but the final decision to cancel the funding was made by Senator David Larson, not a house committee assigned to investigate the project as would normally be the case if protocol was followed."

Nick had seen the name before and it took him a minute to remember where. "Weren't Larson and his wife killed during a robbery at their home, back in the nineties?"

"Yes, but the assailant or assailants were never caught. Does it mean something to you?" She thought back to her first assignment and how she had executed Larson's wife first before taking her time with the senator. The man had died of a heart attack after injecting the cocktail of drugs she administered and before she could finish with her questioning. To cover up, she placed a two bullets dead center through his heart, so there would be no suspicion that it was anything other than a burglary gone wrong and not enough left of the organ to dissect and discover the real reason for his death.

Without responding to her question, Nick continued. "What is not the same with your findings that I have told you so far from my intel?"

"The last names of the eleven members of the project are correct, but their first and middle names aren't. Also, I've never heard of the other people you mentioned." The second part was a lie and inside, she was elated that West had given her an additional two names outside of the members she was not aware of. If the configuration of the naming convention held true, she would have their real names. With that, it wouldn't take her long to identify their true identities and what positions they held in the project, as she had done with the rest of the group.

Out of the corner of his eye, Nick saw the waiter approaching and held off asking further questions until they were served. Both steaks had been cooked as requested and the vegetables had been steamed to perfection. They had taken several bites, savoring each one, before returning to their conversation.

"Do you have a list of the group's real names, then?" asked Nick.

"Before I answer that, I'm going to ask why you have so much curiosity about them? According to Baker, your interest is in catching the guy who stole the drive. That is also what Hoskins told me, so I don't know if I should be giving you any more information about the project or the people involved."

"You are right. That is why I was asked to participate and it should be my only interest. But, from what information I received from Hoskins, I think there is a cover-up going on and he is very scared that I might uncover what it is and end up implicating some very important people."

His reply sent shivers up her spine and she nearly choked while sipping her cocktail. Taking a deep breath to clear her airway, she stared at Nick, realizing if he found the people before she could discover the identities of those responsible, her plan would be ruined and she could not and would not let that happen, regardless of what she needed to do to prevent it.

"I do have their names, but I don't know how that will help you in finding the person you are after. I think you should try and find the guy who stole the drive and killed your friend Davis, as I understand. I would think that would be at the top of your list."

It was Nick's turn to stare at the woman. "How do you know about my friend, Paul Davis?"

"Baker told me about him and that's why you are here. That you're some kind of contracted hit man for the government and that you jumped at the chance to get your revenge." Brandt knew that if she did not redirect the conversation, there was the possibility of West asking enough questions that he would catch her in a lie. If she angered him enough, he might stop answering her questions all together.

"If Baker told you that, then Mr. Baker and I have some talking to do. I won't deny that I have the authority to eliminate persons that are a security threat, but a hit man for the government, not even close lady."

The rest of the conversation constituted small talk while West tried to figure out why Baker would have mentioned his friend's death along with his reason for being there. That information was privileged for only a few who knew him, releasing it was a sure way of getting him killed. He would need to talk to Baker as soon as the evening with Brandt was over.

He looked over at Brandt as she was finishing the last few bites of her meal. Meeting her stare, the look in her eyes told him she had no plans of finishing the evening so quickly.

Chapter 18

Baker washed down the last of the chocolate donuts from a box of a dozen with a high energy drink, belched, then refreshed his search for a single file over 9 gig in size. Out of the hundreds of servers he had already scanned, only nineteen had shown promise of having a file that size or larger. In addition, all of the files had originated on the server they currently resided on. They had not been moved.

Since the projects' files had been compressed into one large file, than encrypted, it was unlikely he could find a server that had multiple files totaling the same size as the one he was searching for. In order to do so, it would mean that a person would have to know what applications were used to compress the files and what the compression ratios were for the applications.

He also knew that two separate files, originally being the same size, would be compressed into two files of different sizes depending upon the blank spaces the compressing encountered while doing so. It would be impossible to get an exact byte match. How much empty text space was removed also depended upon the version of the application at the time of compression.

Right as he was beginning to calculate the effort that would be needed to write the required code for a different type of search sequence, a small icon appeared on one of his monitors signaling a match or near match to the size of the file he was scanning for. Tagging the file with a tracer, he dialed West and waited for him to pick up.

"I think I might have found your file, but I haven't been able to verify that yet until I can copy it over. If the file is password protected, it may take me a little while to open it." Baker was already in the process of a copy as he was speaking.

"How long do you think it will take?"

"Not long to get it copied over. After that, it could be minutes or it could be hours before I could open it to see what's inside. It just depends."

"Alright Baker, I'm on my way back and should be there in less than an hour. As soon as that file is copied over, shut down any access to your system. We don't need someone tracing you."

"I understand Nick. Just get back here as soon as you can. I will have to authorize your entry though, thanks to Hoskins removing your credentials for access to the facility."

"I don't think that's going to be a problem, but do whatever you think needs to be done."

Nick hung up and told Brandt they needed to leave quickly and get back to the lab. When questioned why, Nick simply said there was a new development and his assistance was needed. Taking one last bite and gulping down their drinks, each stood as Nick threw two one hundred bills on the table. The waiter would be pocketing over a fifty dollar tip tonight and would watch for this gentleman in the future.

The valet swung the Porsche around, wanting to sit in it for a few more seconds, but saw Nick already walking around after opening the door for Brandt. He quickly jumped out holding the door for the driver. As he sat down in the driver's seat, Nick caught the seventeen year old eyes transfixed on the side of Brandt's left breast, it having nearly fallen out of her dress and showing a large portion of her nipple. When the kid saw Nick looking back at him, he shut the door, completely forgetting to take the twenty dollar bill that was being extended to him.

It took less than the thirty minutes to return. Nick did his best to keep Brandt entertained without mentioning the file and she seemed eager not to bring it up again. She had enough on her mind and the lack of some occasional conversation did not bother her. Her thoughts of getting laid that night were also erased by Nick's failure to at least take a glance or two of her breast. He was incredibly handsome and she would have easily allowed him her pleasures, but it wasn't happening and she had realized that very early on. Even hiking her dress up just short of fully exposing herself on the drive back had little effect, it seemed.

The gate attendant held up his hand as the car approached and came to a stop. Next to the attendant stood a man nearly seven feet tall holding an automatic weapon readied for use. As the car sat, another attendant rolled a mirror around underneath the car looking for concealed weapons, bombs or both. Brandt and West each waited for a laser scan of a single eye and thumb print before the attendant waived them through. Baker must have forgotten to make the call.

The housing quarters still baffled Nick as he walked the corridor to Baker's 'station' as it was called. During his tenure years earlier, he remembered being assigned a room just big enough for a bed, closet, toilet and small eat-in kitchen. Now they were luxury suites with all of the enmities needed that anyone could desire. He knocked on the door once and it immediately opened. Baker stood in the doorway, his skin tone completely white, looking at Nick as if he were about to faint.

"What the hell, Baker? Are you alright?"

"Just get in here and shut the door! You need to see what I found, Nick."

"Can't you just tell me?"

"No, I can't Nick. And just trust me on this, alright?" Baker was facing Nick, pointing towards his desk. The drawer had been pulled out causing Nick to walk over and take a closer look. Under the drawer was a small audio transmitter that had been attached against a metal slide-out.

Baker picked up a pad and pencil from top of the desk and began to write, turning his scribbles towards

Nick when he had finished. On the pad it read, '*Only Brandt has been in here. No one else.*'

With a wave for Nick to follow, they made their way back towards the back room where Baker had moved his computer equipment. He had followed Nick's instructions to shut down the router as soon as the file had been received.

Nick spoke first using a whispered voice. "Do you really think Brandt is involved somehow? Just because she was in here, doesn't mean she planted the bug."

"I don't see how it could have been anyone else. She's the only person I have allowed through that door except you. I was getting some things out of the back room when she was here and that would have given her plenty of time to place it."

"What about the possibility of the cleaning crew or someone else coming in while they were out?"

"I don't know, Nick. I'm just telling you, someone thinks I know something about this file or is waiting for me to find it and discover what information is on it. Once that happens, what do you think my life is going to be worth?"

"I think we need to confront Brandt right now and get to the bottom of this. If she is lying, I'll know. Get your things together. Regardless of what she says, there is nothing else here that we can't find out on our own in Atlanta. Make sure the file that you downloaded is secure."

"Shit, Nick. I forgot to check the file." Baker returned to the computer, clicked on the folder he downloaded the file to and waited for it to display. Once it opened, he clicked on the file expecting it open on its own. Instead, it began to self-extract into thousands. Each varied in file size with dozens of different file types listed, as well. The files were named individually beginning with the name 'Recall' followed by an eight digit number.

"Nick, the original must have been set up to self extract the files once it was downloaded. Hell, where do begin looking?" Baker began to sort the files in name order so they would begin with the oldest listed first. Looking at the date stamp, they did.

'Resort the files and let's look at the latest first." Nick requested.

The last file was dated three days earlier. All of the rest were prior to 1984. "Click on that one." The file opened and both Nick and Baker began to read it. Half way through, Nick reached over and closed the file.

"We need to find Brandt and get the hell out of here. Now!"

"If they know we have this information, they are going to kill us aren't they, Nick? I don't think they really expected us to find the project files and read what's on them." Baker was visibly shaking as he asked the question.

Nick did not respond to Baker. "Get your stuff and let's go."

West and Baker stood in front of Brandt's door, having knocked and waited for her to answer. When she did not, Baker knocked harder. To both their surprise, the door opened. Realizing the door had not locked properly and opened from the force of his knock, Baker stepped inside, followed closely by West.

They called her name again, but there was no response. West started towards the back bedroom, while Baker began a quick search of the kitchen and bath areas. It was clear no one was there. Her personal belongings were also gone. As they converged back in the hallway, Nick saw a small light coming from under a room they had not checked yet.

The monitor sat idle with only a few lines of text displaying across the top half. Underneath the text were a series of symbols Baker recognized right away from his encryption algorithm, with the exception of small coding changes. Next to the monitor sat an external drive and docking station holding a laptop neither Nick nor Baker were familiar with. Nick picked up the drive and turned it around in order to read the serial number. It matched the one they were after.

Nick looked at Baker. "I don't know who she's working for, but it's plain to see it's not the CIA. I think we just found our killer and it appears she's not planning on returning."

Chapter 19

"Who the hell else knows about this?" screamed Hoskins as he stood in Lane's office with the door closed.

"Just you and me. I was told to report my findings directly to you and no one else. Anything that I found was for your eyes only."

"Do you still have any of the DNA samples left? I want this verified by another tech." Hoskins was bluffing but he needed to make it look as if he trying to disqualify her final analysis.

"I ran the evidence a number of times through different testing procedures. The results all came back conclusive. But, to answer your question, there is not enough evidence left to run any more testing. What I had to begin with was a very small sample."

"Are you sure this is the person we are looking for because it clearly states right here, the man died years ago?"

"If that is the sample taken from your crime scene and you gave it to Buckner for me to analyze, then, yes, it's the person you're after."

"There's no way you could have switched samples, maybe pulled from the wrong tray of evidence?"

"Think about that question Agent Hoskins. If the man died years ago, then how did we get a fresh sample of his DNA taken from and splattered all over the interior of a car?"

"That's classified information, Ms. Lane. You're not privy to where the evidence comes from, it's just your job to test it and give us your findings."

"Hoskins, in this lab I have the same authority as you. If I have questions, they get answered. For me to do a thorough job, I need as many details as possible and I wanted to know everything surrounding the evidence. I asked and your people told. So, if you have a problem with me knowing more than you think I should, then you take it up with your staff."

The veins in Hoskins neck were starting to expand as before. "Well, there's one thing I have more authority to do than you. I can throw your ass in jail if you leak a word of this. One word and I'll have you stripped of your credentials and spending years behind bars. This is as classified as it gets!"

Over the years, she and Hoskins had squared off on a few occasions, but he had never threatened her. Whatever was in that folder, she decided it was in her best interest to back off.

"Alright. Whatever you want is fine."

"Good, I'm glad we have an understanding. I need for you to destroy any testing analysis you have completed that you have not given to me. There is to be no trace of this on either paper or digital. Scrub the lab if you have to, but I want it all destroyed. Understood?"

Lane was flabbergasted, but kept her comments to herself. "Yes, I'll see to it myself."

Hoskins picked up the folder, making sure nothing had fallen onto the desk or floor. "Ms. Lane, you make sure no one else is told about this. I would hate to see you spending your best years locked away." With that, Hoskins closed the door behind him, leaving Lane to stare at him as he walked down the hallway.

As soon as he turned the corner, Lane lowered the curtains in her office, than burst into tears, sitting down in a chair, trying to compose herself and hoping no one saw her. Five minutes passed before she was able to stop her hysterics. For the first time in her life, she was glad she wore no makeup as any mascara would have been streaking down her face, with long black tails running down her cheeks. There was no way she could conceal her current state if someone were to walk in now.

It did not take long for anger to replace shock. The son of a bitch had spoken to her like a father reprimanding a daughter and she was not about to have someone threaten her for a job she had done well. Exceptionally well, as a matter of fact. She reached into her top desk drawer and pulled out a folder containing the exact duplicates of the data analysis she had given Hoskins.

Twenty minutes later, West felt his phone vibrate in his pocket, retrieved it and punched the red 'Answer' icon with his index finger. He recognized the number from a few years earlier, but had not spoken to that person since then.

"Agent West, this is Elizabeth Lane. I hope you remember me."

"I do Ms. Lane. What can I do for you?"

"It's the other way around. I have information on who you are looking for that I need to get to you as soon as possible. I know you are working with Agent Hoskins on this, but he requested that I tell no one."

"Why would he do that?"

"I don't know, but his behavior tonight was out of character."

"Are you on a secure phone, Ms. Lane?"

"No, I'm using my personal cell phone, Mr. West." Lane paused for a response from West but when she didn't get it, she continued. "I have a folder that contains the identity of the man who was in the apartment of your dead hacker and who you believe stole what you're looking for. That evidence is backed up by the DNA samples taken from a car where he was later shot, but escaped."

"I'm surprised you would have this information, Ms. Lane."

"Hoskins's team was very cooperative when they learned who I was. I doubt it will happen again though once Hoskins speaks with them."

"You said man, but we believe we have already identified that person and it's not a man, but rather a woman."

"Then you have the wrong person, Mr. West." Lane made the statement as clear and to the point as she could.

Elizabeth Lane was the best at what she did and West knew it. If she was certain they had the wrong suspect, then she would have undeniable evidence and he needed to listen to her.

"OK, Ms. Lane. Meet me at Shaffer's in an hour."

The flight back to Atlanta would have to wait for a few more hours until he could obtain whatever evidence Lane had. All of the evidence they had already pointed towards Brandt, especially after finding the drive, but now he wasn't so sure. It didn't make sense.

Shaffer's had been a local haunt for nearly eighty years, once catering to every form of low life the city produced. It was a place that few talked about having visited, but everyone went anyway. During the forties and fifties, many bastard children were spawned there by the city councilmen and out of town business men looking to hide their identities for a few hours with women other than their own wives. When the real estate market started to edge downwards in the last several years, it was bought by Mark 'Chic' Allicini, converted and named after his mother. Today its clients consisted of only the wealthiest stock. One-third of the patrons were bodyguards for the other two-thirds.

The proprietor was well thought of and had many high profile connections throughout the town. He knew everyone and everyone knew never to cross him. He was often confided in by his patrons, knowing that what he knew about someone else stayed quiet. It was information only passed to protect the person he was speaking with, should they ever be caught in a predicament and need an intimidating threat to escape prosecution.

The restaurant was dimly lit as Baker and West entered. Sitting in the far back corner was Lane, with a menu propped up in front of her face. She appeared to be staring at it trying to decide on what dish to select for the evening. West had remembered the broken finger on her left hand and it appeared the angle had gotten worse over the last couple of years. He wondered why she had not had it straightened.

They made their way through the lines of tables, hoping Lane would see them coming, but she continued to stare at the menu. As Baker started to call her name that he had been given earlier by Nick, West put his hand against Baker's chest stopping him cold. They were still four to six feet away from her table. West could see a small hole dotting the spine of the menu. Looking down, West could see a pool of blood forming in her lap and watched as a new drop fell towards it.

"Back up and turn around. Walk out slowly and don't say a word." Nick was scanning the room as he spoke looking for anyone who might be taking a quick glance in their direction. Everyone seemed to be enjoying the evening with their dining partner, completely unaware of the dead woman sitting only a short distance away.

Chapter 20

Brandt sat in her car trying to get up the nerve to walk up the entry way leading to the front door of the little cottage tucked away on the Maine coast. She had found the address of the home after obtaining critical information from the drive and searching the internet further. It had not taken her that much effort.

On its south side, a long dock extended into the ocean greeting a forty foot open fishing boat that was moored to its piling. Seagulls darted in and around as a man on board threw the remains of a cleaned catch overboard.

Finally, she exited the car and walked a slow pace over the cobblestones, noting the well manicured lawn and the smell of fresh paint on the house. Stepping onto the porch, she rang the doorbell and stood back. She could hear a woman yelling from a back bedroom that she was, "Coming".

Brandt watched the figure approach through white sheer curtains covering a plain glass window in the door and smiled. She heard the lock turn and a small creak as the door opened.

"Hello, how may I he..?" The small-built woman gasped, followed by tiny tears that began to form around the bottom of hers eyes before they began to roll down her face. Brandt watched as the woman's shoulders began to shake and her open arms lift towards her.

"Oh my God! Mary!"

"You know who I am?" Gillian's response had caught her completely off guard. She never seen this woman, but within a matter of seconds she clearly knew who she was.

"Yes, I know who you are. I would know those eyes anywhere. You are an exact image of your mother. Please come in."

Brandt passed through a tiny foyer, into a beautifully decorated living room. Off to one side was an expansive kitchen with new appliances and granite countertops. Towards the back of the living room was a hallway and Brandt counted five doors. The entire floor throughout the house was made of real cherry wood, not the store bought kind that was made of simulated compressed fiber board. The photos and artwork however were that of what you would expect for someone their age.

After offering her a drink from the kitchen, the woman sat across from Brandt, fidgeting with her hands. "How did you find me? I mean us?"

"It's very complicated and a long story. I've been trying to find you for over six years."

"Why?" asked Gillian.

"To get answers, of course."

"Answers to what?"

Brandt shifted in her chair. She knew that the woman would be skeptical about answering any of her questions, but hoped that since she had recognized her, calling her by name, she would not make the questioning more difficult. She would need to gain the woman's confidence.

"I'm not here to hurt you, Gillian and I'm not here working for any government agency."

"You didn't answer my question!" Gillian McGuire was doing her best to keep her voice calm and Brandt knew she needed to be truthful.

"There was a file that was recently stolen or accidently released containing information with regards to the 'Recall' project. The information in that file listed almost all of the names of the participants, including the researchers and how to notify each of you when your services were needed."

"Yes, but we were told that no one would be able to find us or know our identities. We all stayed in contact, but after a number of years, we lost track of one another.

We had heard rumors, so we all thought it was best to cut ourselves off completely from the other members of the group and go our separate ways. We were never to contact each other again unless it was an extreme and life threatening situation."

"What rumors, Gillian?"

"There were several. We became afraid from what we were hearing."

Brandt leaned in closer and took Gillian's hand. "What were you hearing?"

"They were hunting us down, bringing us in for questioning."

"Why would they be doing that?" Brandt already knew the answer to the question, but wanted to know if any of the others had learned the truth.

"We never found out. Spencer and Fuller were the first to be contacted and returned for debriefing. At least that is what we thought, but none of us ever heard from them again."

"How did you hear they were hunting you and who told you that?"

Brandt had expected an answer, but instead, Gillian had become suspicious by this time and answered with her own question. "What was in that file and why after all of these years, does anyone care? Whatever information we have is of little importance now."

"You really don't know the truth do you? You don't know that they were killed by their own government to keep them quiet."

The shocked expression on Gillian's faced told her that she and the others had not known. It also told her Gillian was starting to panic.

"Gillian, listen to me. What can you tell me about the men behind the project? Who was involved in planning the project and who made the top decisions? Who gave the orders to come after you?"

"We don't know, honestly. We only knew our handlers. Each one of us was assigned someone who stayed with us the entire time during our training."

"By 'the entire time', do you mean they lived with you as well?"

"Yes, but it was a same sex handler, not a paired man and woman. And we all stayed in a guarded complex on base."

"Do you remember any of their names?"

Both women heard a door open and close behind them.

"May I ask who you are and why you are here?" came a man's voice.

Both Brandt and Gillian looked up to see the man wiping his hands with a cloth, walking towards the kitchen sink. The smell of fish hung pungent in the air.

"Mary, this is my husband, Donald."

Brandt extended her hand, but Donald did not take it. "Who are you and why are you here? We don't normally get visitors, only invited neighbors coming for dinner."

"I'm not sure I can tell you that. What I came for is a very delicate matter that I was discussing with Gillian."

Donald turned to his wife of twenty-two years. "What was she asking you?"

Gillian began to shake again and with a trembling voice answered. "You know I can't tell you that. I told you before, I can't discuss that part of my life."

"Get out of our house, now!" Donald grabbed Brandt by the arm and was pulling her towards the door. She could have easily taken the man down with one blow, but decided it would do no good and there was no reason to upset them any further.

Instead, she yanked it from his grip and continued towards the door.

"Wait!" yelled Gillian. "I don't know what you have discovered already, but I know Dexter Morgan was one of the handlers. Do you recognize that name?"

"Yes I do. Why is that so important that you would remember him? What about your own handler's name? Do you remember his?"

Gillian looked at her husband, then back at Brandt. "I remember them all. This curse that we all shared won't let us forget. I suppose the information on the ones that ran the project was held back from us on purpose so we could never identify them in case something went wrong."

"So why is it that you are giving me this one name?"

"Because Dexter Morgan was your father. Your mother confided in me a great deal and we stayed in contact for as long as we could. She asked me to get word to him because of her isolation. He had no idea he had a daughter."

Brandt was stunned. "Dexter Morgan killed my mother! He is not my father!"

"Oh my God!" Gillian began to stagger where she was standing and her husband saw her.

"Get out now or I will call the police!" Donald was reaching to grab her again as he was opening the door with the other hand.

A swift upper cut caught the man clean, followed by a knee to the temple as he was going down. Reaching underneath her coat, Brandt pulled the weapon from a holster, aimed it at Donald's stomach and pulled the trigger. The man twisted in agony and Brandt knew it would be a slow painful death for the man if he did not receive medical care in time. Good, she thought.

Gillian was only three steps away, frozen and unable to move or scream.

Pointing the gun towards Gillian's head now, Brandt came towards her. "You're lying! Dexter Morgan came after my mother for the sole purpose of killing her. He can't be my father!"

"You're wrong. Your mother and I were very close during our training together. That's how I recognized you. You have her eyes and I've never known anyone else to have any like them."

"No! My mother told me my father died shortly after I was born, in a plane crash. She raised me as a single parent until I was eight years old then sent me to live with my grandmother."

"She sent you away to protect you. It was at the same time we began to hear the rumors."

"Tell me who gave the orders to go after the group!" Brandt was pressing the gun to Gillian's head.

"I, I can't. They will kill me and go after those still alive. Please, I'm begging you to let this go. If Dexter killed her, then she took our secrets to her grave to protect us all. I know you must kill me, but let the others live. Please!"

Brandt could feel herself losing control of her emotions, but she didn't care. This would be the only time she would be able to learn if the other members in the group's locations were known. "Do you know where the others are, their addresses?" She pressed the gun even harder against her victim's head.

"No I swear." Gillian had hesitated with her response and Brandt knew she had lied.

Redirecting the weapon, she pointed it at the husband's tibia and pulled the trigger. The bullet tore through flesh, shattering the separating the bone into fragments. Donald screamed even louder, drowning out Brandt's threat to Gillian that the next one she would put through his head. In just over twenty seconds, Brandt had the name and addresses of three more members.

"I want those responsible to pay, do you understand that? I loved my mother so much. She was the kindest human being you could ever know and was loved by everyone. Morgan put a bullet through the back of her head, so I doubt he could have ever loved her!"

"How do you know this?"

"I have the project file with everything that I need, except the names of the people who ran the project. I know all of your friends who participated and how to get them to turn themselves in. Except it won't be the government they will be reporting to after all of these years, but me."

Gillian was sobbing. Please, leave them alone and let them live the rest of their lives in peace. They have sacrificed so much and have known so much pain. The death of your mother had nothing to do with the project."

Brandt was speaking the words, "Not enough," and already pulling the trigger as the last words from Gillian registered in her brain.

She watched as Gillian fell next to her beloved husband from the two bullets that passed through her heart. "What the fuck are you talking about?" she screamed, but it was too late.

Angry that she had not waited, she watched as Donald placed a bloody hand across Gillian's face, trying to pull himself closer for one last kiss goodbye. Brandt put a bullet through the side of his head just as their lips touched, robbing him of his devoted and final loving act on Earth.

Chapter 21

D'Amore scanned through the file he had taken from Lane just before ending her life. Passing by her table, he had reached for the file at the same time aiming from the hip and pulling the trigger. The act would have been unnoticeable even by someone looking in that direction and the sound had been muffled by the suppressor. It had been a back up weapon used only for close range elimination. The .22 long bullet would be required to hit its target precise in order to be effective immediately. In this case, the projectile had passed through the right eye and bounced around inside, tearing the brain into sections. Death had happened so quickly, her body had no time to react and remained stationary.

Inside the file were charts diagramming genetic DNA markers of several people. The findings appeared to match on a high degree of those markers. Three of the individuals were identified by name, the last two having had their names removed by 'Xs' typed over them. Two of the names he recognized but could not comprehend, better yet, accept as the final analysis. After reading through the other documents in the file, he slowly closed and threw it across the room as if trying to skip a small stone across a pond. It slammed against the opposite wall and the papers scattered onto the floor.

Turning to his computer, he logged onto Lane's computer and searched for the recorded application file that he had placed on her system earlier. Whatever information she had gathered would show. There had to be more submissions then what the final report listed in the files he had just finished reading.

Several keystrokes later, he had it. He sat mesmerized by the intricate details of what Lane had been able to gather. It appeared that she had only documented the files with the most pertinent information, leaving out important information that only he could appreciate.

The genetic markers indicated matches between all parties listed. Running the different scenarios, it finally made sense. The oldest female was the mother of the two youngest individuals listed. The oldest two males were fathers of the youngest individuals, each having born a child. The oldest female was the center of it all, meaning, she had two children by two separate men.

He stared at the displayed names again in disbelief. He had a hundred questions, but only two kept repeating in his mind. *Who were the two males that had their names removed and what was the purpose of that? And, who was Stephanie Pierce?*

Having lived in Italy his entire life, he rejoiced in having been brought up by his two loving parents, Anthony and Gabriel D'Amore. They had dedicated their entire lives to making sure he had gone to the best schools and was raised amongst the most important and influential people their money could afford and attract. He had excelled at all sports and graduated at the top of his class in each of the grade levels. There were many who had expected him to go into politics, but the car wreck had changed his life dramatically.

With the loss of both his parents, he had never been given the full details of the accident and he blamed himself for their deaths, even though a drunk driver was said to have been the cause. Had he not insisted on staying late for a practice instead of leaving on time for a weekend out of town with them, they would still be alive. The accident would alter the course of his life forever, bringing with it a dark side he had never felt before.

Living in a small town and with the inability to travel, the man was bailed out of jail by an uncle and allowed to go free until trial.

Tracking down and killing the man had been the defining moment when what he had been expected to do and what he now did, was set. The remains of his parents had been scattered over the road according to the police report and he was going to make sure his first kill would suffer in the same manner.

Having found the man in a local tavern, he continued to buy rounds for them both until the intoxicated man could no longer stand, than he offered the murderer a ride home. Driving to the location of his parents' accident, he pulled the inebriated man from the car, laying him flat on the road.

Returning to the end of the road several hundred yards away, he pointed his car at the object, pressed down on the accelerator as far as it would go and struck the man at over ninety miles per hour, tearing away the left arm and leg.

D'Amore nearly lost control of the car as the tires caught the pavement after slicing through skin and bone and sailing over the body. By the fifth pass, there was too little left to recognize of the remaining parts lying in the road, those once belonging to that of a man.

Now, Lane's report indicated that his birth right was a lie and that his real mother was Stephanie Pierce. If that were the case, then who was his real father and how did the D'Amores come to play the role of his parents? It was a lie, all of it, he told himself. But yet, genetics did not lie. There had to have been a mistake, but the overall markers were present in all of them. He would have to accept facts.

D'Amore could not take his eyes off of the other woman's name. If the markers were correct, then she would be his half-sister, given life from one of the men on the list. The hours passed as he sat, trying in vain to explain and validate in his mind the information he now possessed.

Chapter 22

Nick West sat looking through the files as he and Baker flew towards Atlanta. Having found the data drive, he was tempted to call Hoskins and let him know they had it in their possession and would destroy it if that's what he still wanted. However, he would not tell him the drive had been found and partially decrypted by Brandt, apparently for her own purpose and not theirs.

Baker looked at West as if knowing what he was thinking. "You going to let Hoskins know we found the drive and who had it?"

"Maybe I will later after we have a chance to find out what it tells us. Let him keep sweating it out. Maybe he'll have a heart attack and I won't have to let him know we know who is behind the cover-up."

"Do you think he works for the guy?"

Nick thought for a moment. "I think Hoskins either did something wrong within the bureau and has his balls caught in a vice or the man he is reporting to found someone stupid enough not to see anything further beyond their own nose."

"How do you think Brandt is involved in this?"

"I don't know, but we need to find that out as quickly as possible. She's after something and I don't think it has anything to do with helping us. Lane said she had solid evidence that the person we are after is a man, not a woman. If that is true and we are to believe her, that would eliminate Brandt as the thief, but it doesn't explain how she obtained the drive."

"OK, so what's next?" asked Baker.

"When we get back to Atlanta, I need for you to run a search on Lane's personal machine and find out what you can. You're going to have to call Chau and tell him you are researching from a different location, but don't give him any other explanation."

Baker nodded in agreement. "What am I looking for on Lane's system?"

"Lane was in forensics. Pull her findings for DNA analysis and anything that doesn't look right and whatever she may have spent the most time researching in the last two weeks. She said she had identified who stole the drive, but I know if there were more she wanted to share with me, but couldn't. That's why she wanted to talk in private."

As the plane touched down and rolled towards the hanger, Baker gathered his belongings and waited for it to stop. Before the passenger door could fully extract, he started down the stairs without looking back to see if West was following him out or was staying seated, lost in thought trying to figure out his next move. He heard West's phone ring and decided to keep moving.

"What do you want Hoskins?" answered Nick in as much a sarcastic voice as he could assert.

"Where are you? I haven't heard shit from you in over twenty-four hours."

"I don't need to answer that question, but if you really want to know, I'm sitting in my airplane in Atlanta, holding the drive you've been looking for." Nick could hear Hoskins take a deep breath and let out a sign of relief. He remembered telling Baker he would not pass on this information to Hoskins, but was angry enough that he just wanted to get Hoskins off his back and be left alone from the man. Clearly the man had changed over the years and was now just someone's puppet. Hoskins had lied to him in more ways than he thought possible and it was time to cut all ties.

"Did you destroy it like I asked? What about the person who took it?"

"Whatever your instructions were to me, they are no longer valid. Remember, you fired me? So as far as the drive goes, it's fully intact and the information on it has been decrypted by both Baker and the thief."

Hoskins did not wait to hear any more and hung up. He would have to report this to his superior, but needed time to figure out just what to say and make sure he had a plan in place before he did. As for his career: it was over and just possibly his life, as well.

Two hours later, after downing his fifth whiskey at a local tavern, he reached for his phone and dialed. The call was answered on the second ring. Hoskins waited for a short delay while the phone's software secured the line. Despite the secured line, he took no chances in speaking about the data drive itself so no one would know what the true conversation was concerning. When he heard the man's voice, he began to speak.

"This is Hoskins, Senator Brooks. The package has been found, but opened before delivery. The buyer will be contacted to pick-up the package and deliver it to you as originally requested."

There was delay, just as Hoskins had assumed there would be. At best, his termination papers were already being ordered by the senator on another line.

"Do you know if the card was read and if the receiver might know what was written on the card?" Senator Brooks was also taking precautions.

"Since the package was opened, then I would have to assume the card was read, yes sir." Hoskins knew this statement just signed his death warrant.

"That's too bad Agent Hoskins. I appreciate your efforts. As you know, I really wanted that present delivered unopened, but you did your best and I will see to it that you are rewarded appropriately." The senator was about to hang up when he heard Hoskins pleading on the other end.

"Please, sir! The man that has the drive is a fellow DHS agent I partnered with for many years. He has a co-worker who designed the protective wrapping that secured your present. I'm certain that they were the only ones who took a peek inside. They would not share what was inside with anyone."

"Where is this partner of yours now?"

"Atlanta, sir. I am sure I can persuade him to return your present immediately."

"You have twenty-four hours, Mr. Hoskins, or I will need to visit your partner personally. Do not fail this time." The senator ended the call before Hoskins could thank him.

Senator Benjamin R. Brooks sat back in his chair fully comprehending what the exposure of the information would do to his career. His campaign for the Vice Presidency of the United States was going along as planned, but in the later weeks, he had fallen behind in points to that jackass out of Montana. The man's platform was solid and the key items on his agenda were more in line with what the people wanted. If he didn't get his act together, he would fall further behind.

Brooks had spent nearly thirty million of his own family fortune campaigning and in the beginning, it looked as he would recoup his money in donations early on. His accountants and analysts had told him he would see donations of over six-hundred million by the time they went into the final days of the campaign. With the new laws, he would be able to keep it all and use it as he saw fit. With the rush to get the new laws into effect, the law contained loopholes that his lawyers fully intended to use. He would be a rich man whether he won or lost. He could not help containing a smile at the thought.

In reality, he didn't give a shit if he won or lost, only the money mattered. The Vice Presidency meant you were second, given the less important tasks that carried little weight in the scheme of things. Twenty years down the road, your name would be forgotten. Hell, half the American population wouldn't even know your name while you were in office.

He decided, after giving it careful thought, that those involved could never speak about what they knew. Hoskins, West, Baker, Brandt and possibly even Dr. Chau would have to be eliminated first. The remaining members of the project group would also need to be found and eliminated, regardless whether or not the information on the data drive was ever established. D'Amore, he would deal with in another manner.

Chapter 23

"How the fuck did West end up with the damn drive?" Hoskins could feel his blood pressure rising way above what the doctors had warned him about. Over the past week, he had forgotten to take his medications and the results of his absent mindedness were in full swing.

"He must have found it my room, but I don't know how he would have been able to gain access." Brandt said.

"Jonathan had the drive and was about to bring it back to me. How did you get it?"

"That doesn't matter. I told you, I wanted answers, but you wouldn't give them to me. So I stole the drive from Jonathan and started the decryption process myself."

"You stole the drive from Jonathan? How did you manage that? How did you even know where to look?"

"I'm not going to go get into this with you over the phone, but we met in a café and I was able to distract him long enough to grab it and run. I was barely able to get away."

Hoskins could feel the constrictions in his chest and throat. "You two met and you're still alive? You actually saw him and he saw you?"

"Hoskins, you have to be the biggest dick I know! Do you forget who I am and who trained me?"

The comment sent Hoskins over the edge. "You little over educated bitch! You want answers, than you're going to get them. All of it. You want the man who was in charge of everything? I'll bring him to you tomorrow."

"You don't know anything, you idiot." Brandt shot back.

"Really? I was there, Brandt. I saw your father put a bullet through your mother's brain. If he hadn't, I would have! She betrayed her country, just like the rest of them. They all deserved to die!" Hoskins could hear Brandt swearing at him from the other end of the line and pulled the phone from his ear until she quieted down.

After a moment, he heard her come back on the line. "Where do we meet?"

"Before I tell you that, we have to agree on a few details you're going to wrap up."

"What kind of details?"

Hoskins chuckled. "Oh the kind you did years ago when you worked for the agency. I need you to kill West, Baker and the man I'll be bringing to you, once you have all the answers you came after."

"Not a problem. Just make sure you keep your end of the bargain."

"I'll have everyone there tomorrow at 2:00 pm at the warehouse on Lexington. I know you know the place. I'll make sure all of the interrogation equipment that you *loved* so much is ready and waiting for you."

After disconnecting with Brandt, Hoskins called the senator back and advised him of the arrangements. The senator seemed annoyed at first, but quickly changed his tone when he realized everyone would be in place at the same time. This was going to be too easy. The warehouse hadn't been used in years, nor had the acid containers for dumping the deceased into. A few head taps by his bodyguard and the decades of worry would finally be over for him.

Chapter 24

West listened as Hoskins explained the details of the meet and how he was going to come clean about the project. He would answer any questions that needed answering as far as he had information on. All party names would be exposed and he could do with the information as he felt necessary. After that, he would put in his retirement papers and finally take that long vacation he had always planned.

"I'll be coming alone. Baker needed to get back to Arlington and he's already on his way." West knew this was a lie as he turned his head to see Baker busy finalizing the last of the decrypted files. Whatever Hoskins was going to tell him, he would already know going in and would be able to catch Hoskins in any lies he would try to cover up regarding specific details he didn't want known.

"Crap!" Hoskins thought to himself. He needed them all there, but did not want to alert West that the meet up was anything other than what he told him it would be. He would have to have Brandt deal with Baker later. It would have to be some type of accident, of course, beyond suspicion.

"That's fine. You can feel him in later. The meet is set for 3:00 pm. We'll see you there." Hoskins added an hour to the time in order for Brandt to extract whatever information she needed from the senator, kill him, than concern herself with concentrating on doing the same with West.

Ten minutes later, West stood, walked over to a coffee pot and poured himself a cup. Reaching into the refrigerator, he pulled out one of Baker's favorite power drinks and walked back to the console where Baker was sitting.

"Hoskins wants us in Washington tomorrow, but you're not going. All of a sudden he's had a change of heart and wants to spill the beans about everything. Does that sound right to you?"

Baker continued looking at the screen reading through the files. Without turning, he responded. "Not a chance. Something has changed in the last twenty-four hours and he's running scared. Whatever he's been hiding is about to catch up with him."

"Good, I thought the same thing. What else can you tell me that you have been able to find out from the files?"

"Well, first off, all of the real names of the people who participated in the project. And I can tell you the names of the hit team members who were sent in to track down those people, but you're going to freak when I do."

"Who?" West shifted his weight and sat up in the chair he had only moments earlier been completely relaxed in.

"Paul Anthony Davis and Daniel Jerome Hoskins."

"That damn son of a bitch. He's known about everything all along. How do you partner with someone for five years and not know everything about them. And how the hell is Paul involved in this?"

"It says here he was only nineteen when he was placed on the team, right out of training. He was responsible for the third kill. After Pierce, he requested transfer off the team once that mission was completed."

"Who did they eliminate other than the two that turned themselves in and Pierce?"

"James Michael Scott."

"What about the rest?" West was wondering if any of the others had survived.

"It just shows who next target was after Scott: Stephanie Anne Pierce. Hmmm…this is interesting."

West leaned further in to see what Baker was reading.

Baker continued. "It looks like one of the handlers, a Dexter Morgan, was brought in to try and bring Pierce in. That doesn't make any sense. Why would they bring in someone like that with no experience in this type of work?"

"None of it makes sense. Anything else?"

"Nope, that's as far as I've gotten, but I'll let you know if I find anything else that's interesting. You need to get out of here and catch a plane. For God sakes, though, West, watch your six."

"Damn Baker, you're starting to sound like me with that jargon."

"You know what I mean, Nick."

"Yes, I do. Just keep me up to date with what you find. There are just too many pieces missing."

Baker countered. "I don't know that we even have any pieces that fit together. Somewhere in this puzzle though is going to be one central piece that locks the other pieces it all together. We just haven't found it yet."

"You're right." Then West had an idea.

"We should have done this sooner, but I want you to do a facial and dental scan ID on Brandt throughout all of the agencies. Find out whatever you can. I know you're going to run into some interference, but we've already established she doesn't work for the CIA. Maybe as a contractor, but not as an agent."

"If I find anything, how do you want me to get it to you?"

"I don't. I want you to text her phone and leave any kind of message you want, maybe something about meeting her with some additional information that you have found. When she opens the file, be ready to grab her location as I have a feeling someone else will be waiting as, well. And one more thing – include the location of the meet tomorrow."

"You're thinking of bringing everyone together?"

"Like a puzzle and Hoskins is going to be the central piece."

Nick left the computer room, and trotted to another part of the building. Placing his eye against the scanner, he walked into the room as the door closed behind him. Along the walls was a vast assortment of weapons. Below, were rows of cabinets containing components for the weapons which could alter each to the user's needs.

Twenty minutes later, Nick left the room holding a bag with what he would need. He had taken the time to check each weapon's mechanisms even though he knew each was in perfect working order. The meet was to take place in a warehouse, but with Baker's most recent find, there was little chance its purpose was what he had been told.

Chapter 25

Hoskins stood in Senator Brooks' office waiting for the senator to finish his call. As usual, it was all bullshit and whatever promises were being made to the other party on the other end of the phone, it would never happen. All he cared about was that the donations continue to pour in and if it meant lying to every whining, begging, sniveling large corporate head, screw it, that was how you played the game. He would promise them his vote on anything they wanted, but in the end, his vote would only be used for his own personal agenda. "Screw them all." he thought to himself.

"Sir, if you are ready to go."

"Yes, Hoskins, I am. But before we go, there has been a small change in plans." With that, the senator pressed a button on his desk and Hoskins watched as a man entered the room.

He was extraordinarily large for an agent. His hair was jet black and combed straight back. His face was defined by a jawline extending from a neck that appeared to be restrained underneath the collar of his shirt. The suit was cut perfectly to make room for his large biceps and the weapon he was covering under his jacket. He made no attempt to introduce himself and Hoskins knew he was looking at his own executioner.

"Agent Hoskins, this is Agent Kisker. He will be joining us. I hope you don't mind, but in case you do, I really don't give a shit. You've screwed this up enough. I can't take a chance of you doing it again."

Hoskins looked at the man who was staring back at him, not moving, but showing every bit of confidence a man in his profession would. "No sir, I would be more than happy to have Agent Kisker join us. One condition though - he sits up front with me."

Both the senator and Kisker looked at each other, each knowing that Hoskins was fully aware that the agent was not who he was being introduced as. And neither of them cared

"Well, of course. It would look kind of foolish of me sitting next to an imbecile, don't you think?" The senator let out a small laugh.

With the years he had put in with the senator, hiding every secret and wrong this man had done, the insult cut to the core. Hoskins had spent the last ten years of his failing career protecting Brooks more from himself than his constituents. If they were ever to learn of his illegal activities, the senator would be spending time in jail now instead of sitting in a lush office paid for by tax payers. The thought was repulsive to him and he could take no more.

"You're the imbecile, Ben! I'm done. After today, you find someone else to cover your ass and do your dirty work. The biggest mistake of my career was ever taking this assignment."

"Watch your mouth and remember who you're talking to. You're not done until I decide you're done. Remember, you killed Davis and I can very easily leak that information. Your own agency will take you out before the night is over."

"Really Ben, you want to play that game? I did that on your orders to stop anyone who interfered with the exchange. You're the one who paid Santiago the two million to get the data back. How the hell could any of us have known your son would be his contact man?"

"Shut up! Shut your mouth right now!" Brooks was visibly shaking, the sweat beginning to form around his brow.

"No, you shut up. Davis knew all about D'Amore and Brandt and was just trying to get the siblings together after all of these years. He knew about Morgan and Pierce's relationship way before any of us. What would be the fucking chances he would find D'Amore at that exact moment we were making the exchange?"

"Enough! Davis was a romantic. He had no business being on the team and I hated the asshole. After today though, we can all stop worrying about this."

"Are you out of your mind? It's never going to be over. There people out there who know the truth and they will talk, regardless of how you hope to stop it."

The senator charged at Hoskins. "And it's all of your fault. If you would had grabbed the drive when you had a chance, that would have been the end of it. This whole mess would be over."

Hoskins couldn't believe what he was hearing. "You told me to take out whoever interfered with the exchange, not everyone involved."

"Hoskins, you're finished. Right now, it's only your career. But, I'll see to it you're out of the agency and begging for food money on the streets by the end of today. You try to screw me and I'll cut your fucking heart out myself." The thought of that made the senator begin to laugh once again.

The agent's mind was reeling. Only a couple more hours and we will see who is laughing, you fuck. For the moment though Hoskins was more concerned with how he would kill the so called agent before he had a chance to do the same to him. However it played out, it would have to be quick and without warning as he knew that his own reflexes, slowed from age, would not match that of the man who still had not taken his eyes off of him.

The drive would take an hour, give or take another hour depending on Washington traffic. During that time he would have to figure out somehow what the senator had premeditated. It was obvious the senator had planned to have him killed due to his screw-up, but how could he expect one man to take out seasoned professionals like West and Brandt since the senator knew they would be present?

Thirty minutes into the drive, he learned the answer. As a black Suburban pulled in behind at the traffic stop, he knew it contained a four man SWAT team, fully loaded for whatever would be necessary to eradicate the small group of terrorists the senator had advised them had kidnapped a foreign diplomat. It was a lie, but by the time it was over, he would say agents West, Hoskins and Brandt had failed to identify themselves properly and were killed accidentally by friendly fire. "There are to be no survivors," were his last orders to the team.

If anyone questioned why the senator was there, he would say that the diplomat was a personal friend and the terrorist demanded his presence. He doubted that anyone would ask, though. This was an elite group of men, hand selected, who never asked questions and did as he instructed.

Forty five minutes later, Hoskins could see the warehouse, tucked inside and surrounded by much larger building structures. The entire facility had once been a training complex for the CIA, later used by the military, then by a few upcoming technological startup groups that would eventually fail. Once the groups abandoned the buildings, it had been shut down permanently. The last time anyone stepped near the neglected site was years ago.

Both vehicles came to a stop outside the gates and waited, watching to see if there appeared to be any movement within the complex. In the darkened interior of the Suburban, instructions were being given to each of the men on which part of the parameter they were to cover and on what further orders they were to wait before entering. Each man did a final check of his weapon and synchronized his watches to 2:04 before exiting the vehicle.

With bolt cutters extended, the first man cut through the chain while another quickly lubricated the hinges in order to silence any noise the gates would make when pushed open and possibly alert any unknown subjects who would be inside. Brooks told Hoskins to drive through and follow behind the team, now on foot.

As he pulled through the gates, Brooks, Kisker and Hoskins watched as the man, previously holding the bolt cutters, was lifted off the ground by the impact of a bullet. Twisting in mid air, they all observed the explosion of red crimson as it exited through the hole punched through the side of his helmet.

In the open, the men were defenseless and had not expected to be caught running towards their assigned posts before being able to assess the situation further. As if in slow motion, each man fell before being able to drop behind an object that would give them any chance of protection. The kill shots had been extremely accurate and did not require the shooter to wait to see if her targets were immobilized before redirecting. In a matter of seconds, the greatest initial threat had been eliminated and all that remained, in the shooter's mind, was getting to Senator Brooks.

Slowly, a door of the warehouse opened and the three remaining men watched as a lone figure began to run towards their vehicle. Hoskins saw Kisker fumbling with his seatbelt, trying to extract his weapon while releasing its hold. Now would be his only chance.

Reaching inside his jacket, Hoskins retrieved his own weapon and placed the barrel against the side of Kisker's head, pulling the trigger and blowing the man's brains out. Blood and matter sprayed against the front passenger's side window. Senator Brooks began to scream, believing he was next and that his life would be over in only a matter of seconds.

"Shut up, you son of a bitch! I'm not going to kill you, but you're going to wish you were dead in about thirty minutes. You were going to have this asshole kill me, weren't you?"

Hoskins was putting his weapon back in its holster as he watched the woman yank at his door handle. He smiled and turned to greet her as the knife cut across his throat, slicing deep enough to open a gash one half inch wide. The agent fell out the door, clutching, eyes wide open, trying to ask 'Why' before his body hit the ground.

Before death could close the final chapter on his life, Brandt bent over the agent and spat onto his face. "You fucking bastard! You were there to kill my mother?" The agent's eyes closed before she had a chance to continue.

Furious, she opened the backseat passenger door, reached inside and grabbed Brooks, pulling him hard out through the open door. The senator fell, but was quickly snatched to his feet and pushed forward until they passed through the door the woman had exited just moments earlier.

Chapter 26

D'Amore decided it was time to return home, certain that whatever he was after, needed to stay in his past, hidden forever. With his parents dead, if they were his parents, nothing would be gained by trying to unearth the mystery. They had died in an automobile accident. It was as simple as that. Let it go. He had loved them beyond measure, so to him, they would always be his parents.

Whoever the woman was, even if she was his half-sister, he didn't care. For all he knew, the information was a lie, conjured up by some analyst hoping to bring him in or perhaps get lucky enough to expose his whereabouts.

They had sent him undercover years earlier telling him he was to remain there, that he would be protected, but never wanting him to return. He would receive his assignments as would be required of his services, but he was never to surface. The consequences would be extreme.

At the age of twenty-three, he had been recruited as a field agent to gather intel on a multitude of subjects. He easily remembered all details on every assignment and that skill would eventually get him noticed by his superiors. The psych exams were what got him noticed even more. Inside the man was a killer, waiting to be unleashed and the CIA wasted no time in training him. Once finished, he was sent into a hole deeper than any other operative could imagine or dare to go.

The assignments were of the highest classification, necessitating only a one man operation to complete. Sometimes they would be days apart, others taking months to plan and implement. There was never a 'Plan B' should the job fail. That was not an option he was given as had been to the other agents. A failure on his part would mean exposing the agency all the way to the top, of which, even the President could not escape.

Each assignment had its own risks and did not always dictate the need for a kill shot. By the time he was twenty-nine, he had already been responsible for the deaths of twenty-four men and three saves. Before his life changed once again and he went rogue, the last assignment had been to extract Abrielle's father, a diplomat and wealthy land owner. The agency needed the locations of all his global holdings, in exchange it would keep her father alive.

Aberto Bianchi had invested heavily in real estate around the globe and leased the properties to those who had the means to pay the market price. Due to the heavy demands of his time, he had turned the everyday operations over to a distant cousin to lease the properties after verifying they had the ability to pay and were legitimate tenants.

The cousin was resolute with the first demand, but never intended to follow through on the second. If the lessee had the ability to pay, that was good enough for him. Let his uncle worry about the rest. So far he had been able to lease almost eighty-four percent of the properties and Aberto had paid him huge commissions for doing so.

When it was learned that three of the properties were being used by the Russian mob and two others for Jihad training camps, they were quickly seized by the U.S. government and Bianchi was humiliated, with his resignation from service demanded by his peers. Within hours, several hits were placed upon him, his family and his cousins' lives. D'Amore was ordered to extract the father and get him to a safe zone, where he would be extradited to the United States for questioning. The rest of the family would be on their own.

By the time he arrived, the family compound had already been penetrated by a team of three mercenaries.

On the ground were the bodies of two agents and several men and woman D'Amore assumed were housekeepers and staff. There were no signs of any other protection the family had been afforded.

Standing underneath a patio ledge, he heard a woman scream and several shots. The sound of a body hitting the hard tile reverberated through the concrete structure. To the right of him was a flight of stairs and he ascended them as quickly and cautiously as he could. Looking over a sidewall of the banister, he saw two men entering through a set of French doors, adjacent to a large library.

Inside, a man and woman were on their knees with a man standing behind them, a gun pointed at the owners head. The man appeared to be demanding a combination to a wall safe hidden behind a painting that been taken down and ripped to pieces. These were professionals but also mercenaries who, by reputation, always tried to get more money when possible. The safe had caught their attention and delayed their mission, if only for a few minutes.

D'Amore took aim at the man standing over Aberto Bianchi and fired. The bullet passed through a glass pane of one of the French doors, continuing on its path, striking the would-be-assassin above the left eyebrow. As the man fell, his companions turned just as they were struck. Both men went down were they stood.

Bursting through the doors, he grabbed both the man and woman, jerked them up and ordered them to follow him back out the French doors. If they could make their way down the stairs quickly, he would be able to help both; otherwise he would have to leave the woman behind.

Halfway across the courtyard, a shot rang out and D'Amore felt the man let go of his hand, the warmth of blood splattering across the back of his neck. Pulling harder on the girl's hand, he forced her to the ground as he spun, looking back over his shoulder. Aberto's body lay twisted, a large pool of blood streaming out of his back. In the front center of his chest was a gaping hole where the bullet had exited, ripped open by the fragmentation of lead.

Raising his eyes, D'Amore realized he had not killed all of the men as he thought he had. This one mistake would now send his life into a different direction. One man had survived long enough to stand and fire a single last round before tumbling over the balcony and landing head first on a flat stone border, arranged in a box pattern around the garden below.

The girl would need to be protected. He had failed to save the father, but the daughter was still a target and would be hunted by these same men until she was found. She was his responsibility now and it would mean getting her as far away and concealed as possible. He too would be on their list and together they would need to disappear. For how long, was the question playing on his mind as they raced out of the courtyard, into the waiting jeep.

Almost five years had passed. He had changed his appearance on occasion, but insisted on leaving hers as was. She had wanted to do the same, but it was the one and only thing he would not allow her do. What he did for a living required the alterations, but that life was not hers. They would argue about it, but in the end, she would see his reasoning and decide to leave the subject alone, at least for the time being.

They would eventually become lovers, intoxicated in each other's arms. The surroundings of the small Italian village made it even more romantic. They spent their mornings shopping in the open markets, having coffee in a quaint café with the other locals and walking along the cliffs that overlooked the ocean below. They would ride horseback along the sands and she had learned to paint while he took a liking to photography.

It had taken him ten months to reestablish a new identity and work his way back into the network. His past had been wiped clean by the hacker, with no trace of his prior existence remaining. To all that had known him before, he would cut complete ties and never establish contact again. The only thing that mattered now was money in order to keep their lives hidden and safe.

The surgery had reshaped his jaw line and he had begun to sand his fingertips. It had been painful at first, but he had learned to accept the pain over the alternative of being found. He had also learned to be careful in not damaging the most sensitive of nerves. The sanding would require less and less of his time as the skin tissue no longer generated as quickly as before, but he remained vigilant in this one act.

As he sat thinking of when they would be together again, his phone began to vibrate across the table before it sounded a small alarm, indicating a message had been received. Picking it up, he read it twice to make sure he understood its meaning. It had not been intended for him, but he had intercepted it none the less and smiled. The first part of the message was meaningless and nondescript and he ignored it. It was the location address that interested him only.

A quick check determined that he could be there in less than four hours driving time. A flight would take him less than an hour, but the equipment he would be carrying would never make it past the first security point even if he flashed the fake Air Marshal credentials.

He gathered his equipment and headed out the door, tossing the bag onto the floor of the back seat. The drive would require him driving along the major highways, which he always avoided if possible, but he would do so this time. At this hour of the morning, the traffic would be heavy heading into Washington and he would have to be cautious and alert.

Starting the vehicle, he pulled out the GPS and began to enter the location address, then stopped. Entering the address would mean a satellite relay being broadcast and his car would become an easy target for the military, police and other government agencies to track. Given that the address was once a classified milieu, it would send up an immediate alert. He would have to find the route the old fashion way by pulling out a map.

Chapter 27

At 2:17, West crept through the entrance gate, seeing the carnage that lay before him. He counted six bodies, including that of Agent Hoskins. With the exception of Hoskins, each man had a single gunshot to the head. The entire SWAT team lay no more than a few feet apart from one another, making West wonder if there were more than one shooter.

Making his way around to the back of the warehouse, he could hear a woman shouting vulgarities as a man pleaded for his life. Suddenly the man's voice went silent as he was pistol-whipped across the forehead. Ahead was an open window, its glass smashed out by either vandals or vagrants trying to find a place to escape Washington's winter winds and snow of months past. West crept towards it.

Lifting himself over the edge, he moved along the walls' edge until he saw the staircase and headed in its direction. On the second floor were offices that had previously served as classrooms and training rooms. Most were missing their doors and empty of all furnishings.

Keying his earphone, he called Baker, preparing to speak as quietly as possible, almost to the point of whispering. When he heard the connection go through, he cut Baker off before he could talk. "Baker, don't say a word, understood? There are six men down outside. I need you to leave this connection open and record everything until I tell you to stop. Tap twice on your mike so I know you are receiving my message." When he heard the two taps, West spoke once again. "Roger, out."

In the short distance, he could see the woman moving a small table, on it was an assortment of surgical equipment, cables and car batteries. A five gallon bucket of water sat on the edge, next to it a large sponge. Hanging on a hook was a drill already attached to a power cord that ran across the floor to a wall socket thirty feet away.

While the woman focused on her task, West climbed the stairs and moved to the edge of the railing where he could get a better look. On the floor lay Senator Brooks, plastic bands wrapping his hands tightly behind his back, along with one securing his feet. Lifting his rifle, he took aim at the back of the woman's head, the red dot dead center. Placing his finger on the trigger, he took a slow deep breath and began to let it out.

Out of the corner of his eye, he saw movement, a shadow at first, then the full silhouette of a man. Relaxing his finger, West turned his head sideways as the man's own red dot pointed directly at his forehead. The man began using hand signals telling him to wait and that they both needed to hold their positions until the woman took action.

West watched as the man waited for his response, holding the .50 caliber steady and still pointing at him. For the time being, he would have to comply. The man appeared as professional as he was and would not hesitate to pull the trigger in an instant. D'Amore had gotten there ahead of him and was waiting for something. But what?

Without responding, West turned back towards the woman, but held his finger off of the trigger so the man knew he would comply, but at the same time indicating he had every intention of killing her if she injured the senator.

Suddenly he heard a voice in his earpiece. "If you kill her, I will kill you. All she wants is answers, give her time to get them." D'Amore had captured the frequency Nick had used to contact Baker and had now taken control of the immediate situation. Nick knew that Baker would still be able to tape all of the conversation, provided D'Amore stopped talking and didn't corrupt the recording.

"If she makes any attempt to injure the senator or kill him, I will have no choice."

D'Amore responded as quietly as he could. "She will hurt the senator, that you can sure of. But kill him before she has her answers, no. If I see that starting to happen, I will kill her myself."

"Who killed the men outside?" asked West.

"She did. Wouldn't you say Brandt is more than she appears to be?"

"I think she has had a lot of people fooled. My guess is she is highly educated and working as an operative trying to uncover something someone doesn't want uncovered."

D'Amore thought for a moment. "You're partly right in that she is well educated and an operative trained at the highest level. She is extremely dangerous and very, very good at what she does. You would not want to be at the receiving end of her skills. But what she is trying to uncover is for her own personal needs and not of the agency's."

"What about you? Why are you waiting and what are you hoping to gain?"

"The same answers she is after."

Reaching down with both hands, Brandt lifted the senator to his feet, then bent slightly as she rolled him onto her shoulder. Carrying the man some twenty feet, she sat him down adjacent to the table before reaching up for a metal cable looped through a pulley attached to a rafter beam. The other part of the cable ran downloads towards an electric winch operated with the touch of a switch.

Cutting the plastic wrap from around his hands, she placed them through the end of the open cable and tightened them once again before flipping the switch. The senator began to awake as his body elevated upwards until he was a foot off the floor. Brandt flipped the switch again and the winch stopped.

With the pain shooting through his arms and wrists, the senator became fully awake, looking around to try and establish where he was. The horror of what was happening suddenly hit him and he began to scream and once again beg for his life. He knew about Brandt and what she was capable of. The images he had seen of her work caused him to vomit and urinate simultaneously.

"What do you want? You can't do this! I'm a senator for God sake. You won't get away with this!"

Without saying a word, Brandt began to remove the senator's shoes and socks, pants and underwear. Ripping open his shirt, she used a surgical knife to slice open his tee-shirt and cut away the tie. Dipping the sponge into the bucket, she applied as much water to his body as necessary, making sure she soaked his hair completely.

When she had finished, she finally spoke. "I want to know certain answers about project 'Recall'. I already know what the project was about, what I don't know was who was responsible for calling the shots."

"I..I have no idea what you're talking about. I had nothing to do with that. That was decades ago, way before I became a senator."

Brandt picked up a metal rod from the table and showed it to the senator. One end had been encased with a rubber insulator to protect the user from the electrical current that would discharge upon contact. A small connector extended from that part of the handle, as well. The other end had been wrapped with a cloth which would be dipped into water to allow the current to cover a larger area as it was held against flesh.

"I don't have time to play games with you, Senator. The most sensitive parts of the body are feet, testicles, hands, teeth and eardrums. I'm going to start with your feet and work my way up."

She dipped the cloth end into the bucket and attached the electrical connector. Sparks flew as the connection was made. Without hesitating, she touched the bottom of the senator's left foot. The muscles constricted, causing his body to arch upwards as Brooks bit down hard on the inside of his jaw, cutting clean through the tissue. Blood began to pour out of his mouth as he spit and swore at Brandt.

"Amperage is what kills a person, Senator, and I've hardly got yours up very high. I'm going to ask you again to tell me about the project and I hope you will answer me this time. If not, I will continue."

The senator was still heaving, trying to catch his breath. "I don't know anything, I swear to God!"

She increased the amperage and placed the end against the right foot, holding it to that foot longer this time. The senator's body began to jerk. She heard the vertebra of his spine begin to pop and removed the rod.

With his eyes wide open, the senator tried kicking at her even with his ankles bound, but she simply moved out of his reach. The action caused the cable to cut deeper into his wrists and he stopped. As his body swung from the cable, she reached out to steady him getting closer than she realized. A knee caught her under the chin sending her staggering backwards against the edge of the table and down onto the floor.

Infuriated more by the fact that she had allowed herself to be caught off guard, she stood, walking slowly towards the man who, in that instant, knew his fate. Picking up the drill, she tested it as she moved around behind the senator. "I will stop when you begin to answer me."

Driving the drill bit into the calf muscle, she drove it forward until it hit bone, pulling it slowly out as the senator screamed. Repeating the act on the other calf, she heard Brooks begging for her to stop. Ignoring the plea, she raised the drill higher, placing it against the thigh and pushed hard as she pulled the trigger. As she moved to the next leg, she heard the senator shouting "Alright. Oh my God, please, I'll tell you all of it. Just get me down."

Brandt returned to the table and placed the drill back on its hook. She would clean the flesh off of the bit later. Looking up at the senator, she could see the tears and blood running down his cheeks and neck, dripping at a steady pace onto the floor mixing with the blood droplets from the back of his legs.

Hitting a switch, Brandt began to lower him to the floor until he was flat against the concrete. Undoing the cable from around his hands, she pulled them behind his back and reattached a new plastic band as she had done before. Pushing a chair next him, she waited as he slowly crawled up into it. Once he settled, she attached a second plastic cable to his hands, running it through and around the inner framing of the chair.

When his breathing pattern resumed to normal, she decided she would ask the questions most important to her since she had most of them already answered by the information from the drive. "Who was responsible for overseeing the entire operation and who ran it?"

"My father, Senator James A. Brooks. He had strong ties to the military community and provided funding needed to run the project."

"Did you have any involvement in the project?"

"I was one of the instructors or handlers as they called us. We spent years with our assignments and made sure they were able to handle the vigorous daily routines physically and psychologically. It was not easy on any of us."

"What do you know about a woman named Stephanie Pierce?"

Brooks raised his head, looking directly at the interrogator. By this time, the inside of his cheek had swollen and he was using his tongue to try and stop the bleeding. "Why is she important to you?"

Brandt could tell by the look in his eyes, he knew all about her and was answering a question with a question, attempting to delay and think of an answer that might throw her off track. "Answer my question before I string you up and start using the drill again!"

"I know she was the top recruit and surpassed all of the tests we administered. She completed her training ahead of schedule, but we had to keep her progressing until the rest of the members caught up and finished. She was extremely intelligent even for this group."

"How did you keep her progressing?"

"She was given privileged information that only the top brass and President knew about. There was a lot of debate if that should be done, but in the end, the President gave the authority."

Brandt took a seat in front of the senator and leaned in forward. She was not concerned that the senator would try another attempt to hurt her, especially with the .45 she held down by her side. "Is that why she was hunted down and killed?"

"The death of Stephanie Pierce, and the rest of those that we could find, had nothing to do with the project. Is that what you think?"

"What other reason would there be if it didn't have anything to do with the project? There were leaks and the government hunted them down because the information was getting out."

The senator began to laugh then cough as the blood trickled into his throat. "There were no leaks. That was all a lie in order to protect me and my future. My father circulated those falsehoods in an attempt to bring everyone in. It would give him the chance to see who knew what I had done and silence them if they had any idea of his illegal activities, as well."

Brandt looked confused by this admission.

Brooks continued. "Except our government took it too far and executed those people as traitors. Once my father realized Pierce was dead, he put an end to the hunt so no one else would die. It was about the only moral thing he ever did. He figured since the rest of the people had not come forward by then, they didn't know anything and the skeletons would remain in the closet with her death."

"But not before my mother died you fucking bastard!" Brandt placed the gun against the senator's temple and pulled the hammer back .

Both D'Amore and West placed a finger on their own triggers and West saw both red dots light up on the back of her head. "Wait. Give her a minute!" said D'Amore. West held position trying to decide if he would have time to hit both the shooter and Brandt before either one would be able to fire at him.

"Who is your mother? Pierce was the only female killed!"

"Who do you think I'm talking about?" Brandt was screaming at the top of her lungs as she repositioned the gun to the front of his forehead, dead center between his eyes.

"That's not possible. We had a son! Stephanie Pierce had a boy that neither of us ever got to meet or hold. My father would not allow me to see my own son! He had him quickly processed through an adoption agency and shipped him out of the country. I searched for years, but the only information I could find was that he was adopted by an Italian family."

"Your father knew who adopted him though, right?"

"Yes, but he would not tell me. All he would say is that he was sending them checks to make sure 'it' was well taken care of."

West looked over and saw D'Amore staring straight at the man, tears beginning to roll down his cheeks. It had not only been Brandt who desperately wanted answers but D'Amore, as well. He turned back towards Brandt and the senator.

"You and my mother were romantically involved? She never mentioned your name! Why wouldn't she do that if you had a child together?"

"Why? Because I raped her! We were young and I misread her intentions. Hell, we had all been drinking that night after graduating and I mistook her kindness as a desire for me. She thought I was Dexter at first, it was dark. When she realized it was me, she tried to fight me off and I raped her. I was a God damn senator's son and no woman said 'no' to me!"

"My mother and those people died because you raped her and had a bastard son together? Your father tried to hide it by spreading lies and getting them hunted down like rabid dogs so he could protect you and himself?"

"No! He did it to protect himself more than me. That's all he cared about! What do you think would have happened to his career if his son is charged with rape? If anyone were to discover who the mother was, they would have investigated further and possibly uncovered the entire project. That could not happen at any cost. "

"The project was classified and the government could have easily covered it up without anyone learning the real truth."

"My father couldn't take the chance. Senator Brooks was not an honest man. He had been taking illegal bribes for years from large corporations to vote in their favor when it appeared they may lose a bid. There were a lot of underhanded deals. An investigation would have uncovered that. He would have been stripped of his office and humiliated. In those positions, you do what you have to do to hide your wrongdoing. Nothing has changed."

"I was told Dexter Morgan was my father. Is that possible?" Brandt stood and walked several steps away from Brooks. Her lips were quivering, trying to hold back her emotions.

"Dexter Morgan and Stephanie Pierce, your mother if that's true, were deeply in love. Given their differing positions, they were not allowed to display it in public or the classrooms. If you're their child, than you were born out of love, not the way Stephanie and I had our child." The senator began to cough and split blood again.

Tell me how a man so deeply in love, could kill a woman he loved as much as you're saying."

"We truly didn't believe that would happen. We thought Dexter could bring her in and we meant her no harm. If anyone could talk her into coming back to the facility, we knew it could only be Dexter. But she wouldn't and he knew what her fate would be. The team had been given orders to kill her and destroy any evidence if she did not cooperate."

"So where is Dexter Morgan now?"

The senator looked at her with a blank stare on his face. Brandt really did not have any idea that Morgan had taken his own life after killing Pierce. "He's dead. He shot himself after taking your mother's life and died next to her. Morgan loved her and the thought of what he had to do that he would not allow anyone else on the team to do, was insufferable."

Brandt eased the trigger back into place as her body began to shake uncontrollably. She had gotten her answers. After several minutes, she addressed Brooks again.

"What happened to her afterwards? Is she buried somewhere?"

"Yes, somewhere on the island, but her and Dexter's graves were never marked. No one knows where for sure."

"So all of this happened because of you? Innocent people died in order to protect a corrupt senator's reputation and his boy? You took my mother away from me! We were having a wonderful life together and you took it away!"

"I'm sorry. If I could change that one moment in my life I would, but I can't. I'm sorry."

Brandt could no longer hold back. She charged at Brooks, striking him with closed fists until the senator lost his balance and fell to the floor. She began kicking him in the ribs, kidneys and legs as D'Amore ran down the stairs, screaming at her to stop.

Halfway down the stairs, he lowered his rifle and continued screaming at her as he descended further. Survival instinct took hold as Brandt turned and fired in his direction, missing by only inches. West lowered the red dot and pulled the trigger.

D'Amore watched as his sister spun from the impact and fell across the senator. He could see where the bullet had struck, nicking a major artery, the blood pumping out in a stream with each heart beat.

Dropping to his knees beside her, he lifted her head as he placed a palm over the wound, hoping to apply enough pressure to minimize the bleeding. In between his fingers, the blood still flowed with a rhythmic beat.

Her eyes were still open as she took shallow breaths, knowing her life was draining away. She had taken the lives of many others and knew from experience there was little time left. Looking up at D'Amore, she gathered what little energy she had left, looking into his eyes that were as blue as hers. "I guess this is our fate. Separated in life, now by death. I'm so sor.."

D'Amore lowered her head as he reached for the weapon attached to his side. Standing, he looked at West.

"I was trying to stop her, you son of a bitch. She took a shot at me only because of she didn't know who I was. Another second and she would have seen my face and lowered her weapon."

West swung his rifle across his back and stood at the top of the railing. "You can believe that, but given the situation and my training, I say you're wrong. I couldn't second guess what she was going to do or not do. As a prior agent, my duty was to protect the senator and whether I like it or not, I still have to hold true to that obligation."

"Then you failed." D'Amore angled the weapon towards the senator's head and fired twice before West had time to swing the weapon off his shoulder and get off a round. Running under the staircase, D'Amore slammed through the door as West fired through the open slats of the metal floor. He heard D'Amore cry out, but not stop.

By the time he had reached the ground floor and passed through the door, D'Amore was gone. A blood trail ran to the side of one of buildings but disappeared. The brown gravel flung from a vehicle's spinning wheels, still hung in the air. The man was gone, disappearing completely behind a veil of dust.

Chapter 28

West sat quietly as the President signed the papers. The Oval Office had been cleared of all personnel and the tape recordings turned off. Streaks of sunlight stabbed through the windows, but slowly vanished as the summer clouds moved across the horizon. Just outside the entry door, two Secret Service men stood guard.

Through the windows, West could see the gardeners and landscape staff pruning and cutting everything to exact detail. He chuckled to himself as he watched a member of the Secret Service detail used for dog duty. Apparently the normal dog walker wasn't available at the moment. All of those years of education and training, just to be assigned to take the dog out for a crap, then have to scoop it up and dispose of its waste. He felt for the agent, knowing that if the man could, he would cap the dog and get away with it, he would. A new nickname for the agent was sure to follow.

When the President finished, he handed the papers over along with two folders marked "POTUS". It was the most classified of stamps and anyone caught in possession of the folder without authorization, was immediately arrested and imprisoned. No trial and no bail.

Two weeks had passed. There had been little mention of the senator's death in the papers other than he had been killed in a car wreck, suffering a heart attack while driving. It also advised that the car had exploded and his body burned beyond recognition after exiting the highway and striking a tree. A private ceremony had attended by the family, but no other guest where allowed.

The President rested his elbows on his desk, clasping his hands in front of him as he spoke. "Nick, I'm not ordering you to find those people listed on that document, but as a personal favor, I would appreciate it if you would handle it yourself. Those are dedicated

Americans who served their country to the highest degree and I want them honored. As a starting gesture, I've ordered their accounts reinstated with deposits back to the time they were originally shut off.

"You're right. That's a start."

"If they have passed on, then we will make arrangements for the deposits to be transferred to their living children. I want their children and grandchildren to know how proudly they served their country and will be honored as patriots by their government. That paper gives you the authority to use whatever means you or we have available to fulfill my request."

And if I do find them, then what?"

"I want you bring them here as I would like to meet them personally and have a small ceremony in their honor."

"What about these folders?"

"The files you have are as much information as I can release to you on the agents. Brandt was a genius that had the highest scores anyone in any of the agencies had ever seen. She excelled at every aspect of training we could put here through, especially at intel gathering. She never showed emotions, which made her very frightening to those she extracted information from. Unfortunately, no one ever put the connection between Stephanie Pierce and her together. She hid that very personal fact from all of us."

"How did she learn about the project and her mother's involvement? Even at her level, she wouldn't have access to that information." West sat the folders in his lap, picking up Brandt's first.

"When her grandmother died about six or seven years ago, she left Brandt several possessions, amongst them a diary her mother had written just for her daughter. In it, Pierce told her as much as she could without giving away names. There were no mention of any men in her life, but it did mention a lot about the project. We suspect her interest came from there."

West began to thumb through the file on Brandt. "So Brandt discovered the project's file and tried to find out more. Do we know how the file ever got released or who did it?"

"From what I have been told, Brandt did it herself. Once she discovered the location of the files, she began copying them into another location a few at a time so no one would be the wiser. Once she had them all, she merged and encrypted the documents into one file and tried sending it offsite to herself, but it got intercepted."

"What about the man who stole it from the hacker?"

"If it hadn't been for Lane, we would have never identified him. He used to be one of ours - actually he still is as no one ever declassified him because we thought he was dead."

"Declassified? What do you mean?" asked West.

"Meaning he's just like you, Nick." The President paused letting that fact sink in. "We can't touch him and neither can anyone else. And as far as skills - if you two were put in a cage to fight it out, I would not place a bet on the outcome."

"What about now?"

"He killed a senator and no matter how moral or immoral that man was, at the time D'Amore was protected. As of now though, he is not. I've signed an executive order terminating him from the agency. From now on, he will be on his own, so if you want to pursue it, that will be strictly your call."

The President stood indicating the meeting had come to an end. As he escorted West towards the door, he suddenly stopped. "Do you have any idea where D'Amore might have disappeared?"

To the surprise of the President, Nick responded. "Actually Mr. President, I do."

Chapter 29

The seaplane touched down and idled four hundred yards off the shoreline of Hanakapiai Beach. A man sat next to the pilot, pointing towards a small breach in the sand that led through the break towards a manmade canal. Ahead lay a rotting dock extending seventy five feet from the property line, dotted with seagulls and pelicans waiting for their next meal to swim underneath.

D'Amore watched as the seaplane crept closer. When he was able to recognize the passenger, he turned walking up the dune, over the crest, finally stopping at the unmarked grave. It had taken him five months to locate where the team had disposed of the bodies four decades earlier. He waited patiently for the other man to join him.

Ten minutes later, West stood next to D'Amore looking down at the remains of Pierce and Morgan. The call D'Amore had made three nights earlier requested that they agree to set aside their duty to country and meet on neutral ground. After understanding the reasons, West accepted.

West could not help but note how the bodies had been arranged in the singular grave. Like lovers, they faced each other inward, arms wrapped around the other on their eternal journey to the hereafter. He imagined that God had somehow shown special favor on these two and had welcomed their souls into heaven with open arms.

D'Amore finally broke the silence. "It looks like someone was aware of their secret and buried them appropriately."

"Yes, but who?" responded West.

"There are a lot of secrets to which we will never know the answers.. I want to thank you for seeing this through to the end." D'Amore extended his hand to West.

It was a handshake between two men that knew someday they would meet under different circumstances and on that day it would be their duty to take the other's life. But that was not today.

"I've made the arrangements as you requested. Pierce and Morgan will be buried in their current state alongside their daughter, Mary. They will all receive full honors. I was also able to make contact with the remaining members and they have all agreed to attend for Stephanie's sake."

"Thank you again. I knew that you would honor our agreement today and come unarmed. I've learned that my classification was terminated, so it would have been very easy for you end this all now."

"I am honoring the fact that I took your sister's life without you getting the chance to meet her. If I had any other option, I would have taken it, but your own life was at stake and I had to make a choice." West watched as D'Amore turned to him, tears beginning to form in his eyes.

As professionals, West decided he needed to advise D'Amore of a recent confirmed rumor he had heard. "When this task is complete, we will both return to our professions and continue with our lives. I've learned that a contract has been placed on you, someone willing to risk it all to see you dead."

"Do you plan to accept the contract?" asked D'Amore.

West thought about it for a moment. "No. I will let you handle it in your own way, but you killed a United States Senator and a CIA employee. For that, you have given me little choice. I will have to come after you at some point."

"And I will have no choice then but to protect myself and the ones I love. You will need to take precautions and do the same."

There was no misunderstanding of what D'Amore meant. West recalled what the President had said about not wanting to bet of the outcome should D'Amore and he meet. For the first time in his life, West found himself fearing another man.

End

About the Author

Jim Burkett is the author of 'Declaration of Surrender', 'American Sanction' and the popular children's series 'Read With Me, Pops'. In addition to writing, he is also a Senior Systems Analyst for a major corporation and Staff Photographer for a lifestyle magazine headquartered in Florida.

If you have any questions, comments or constructive criticism, contact the author at JWB@inknbeans.com. Please visit his website at www.jimburkettbooks.com

Jim Burkett's books are available at Amazon, Barnes & Noble, other fine booksellers and

Fresh Books Brewed Daily